"Such beauty, such courage," Jacques murmured, his deep sensual tone sending a disquieting ripple of awareness through Arielle. "A real aristocrat, aren't you, *ma chère*, but then, you are a Duplantier, and the Duplantiers bow to no man." His fathomless black eyes bored into her.

Arielle flinched. Her lower lip trembled slightly, but she refused to be the first to look away. Arms akimbo, she returned his fierce stare with one of her own.

Jacques' mouth twitched into a smile as he observed her with amusement. "Who are you, little one, to reach inside me?" he asked as he cupped her chin with one lean hand. Jacques searched her upturned face with a gaze that now contained the sensuous flame of desire. "I could crush you like a butterfly, but you are not frightened." His strong, bronzed fingers tightened on the fragile bones of her chin, but still her haughty stare never wavered.

Releasing her chin, he gently traced her full coral lips as he whispered, "Smile, *ma belle blonde*. Your mouth was made for kissing, not for anger."

Before she could protest, he swept her into his arms.

His voice was a hoarse rasp of desire. "Why did you come, *ma belle blonde*, if not for this?"

FIERY ROMANCE

CALIFORNIA CARESS (2771, $3.75)
by Rebecca Sinclair

Hope Bennett was determined to save her brother's life. And if that meant paying notorious gunslinger Drake Frazier to take his place in a fight, she'd barter her last gold nugget. But Hope soon discovered she'd have to give the handsome rattlesnake more than riches if she wanted his help. His improper demands infuriated her; even as she luxuriated in the tantalizing heat of his embrace, she refused to yield to her desires.

ARIZONA CAPTIVE (2718, $3.75)
by Laree Bryant

Logan Powers had always taken his role as a lady-killer very seriously and no woman was going to change that. Not even the breathtakingly beautiful Callie Nolan with her luxuriant black hair and startling blue eyes. Logan might have considered a lusty romp with her but it was apparent she was a lady, through and through. Hard as he tried, Logan couldn't resist wanting to take her warm slender body in his arms and hold her close to his heart forever.

DECEPTION'S EMBRACE (2720, $3.75)
by Jeanne Hansen

Terrified heiress Katrina Montgomery fled Memphis with what little she could carry and headed west, hiding in a freight car. By the time she reached Kansas City, she was feeling almost safe . . . until the handsomest man she'd ever seen entered the car and swept her into his embrace. She didn't know who he was or why he refused to let her go, but when she gazed into his eyes, she somehow knew she could trust him with her life . . . and her heart.

REVENGE SO SWEET

DIANE GATES ROBINSON

ZEBRA BOOKS
KENSINGTON PUBLISHING CORP.

For James, who never stopped believing in my dream

For Christopher, a journalist who understands the satisfaction in a story well told

And

For Susie, constant companion of the heart

ZEBRA BOOKS

are published by

Kensington Publishing Corp..
475 Park Avenue South
New York, NY 10016

First printing: February, 1991

Printed in the United States of America

Revenge, at first though sweet,
Bitter ere long back on itself recoils.
                              — John Milton: *Paradise Lost*

Prologue

Bayou Barataria, Louisiana
1798

"No! No! 'Tis not the fever! She can't have it." The harsh cries rent the silent, tropical night echoing through the gnarled branches of the giant live oaks. There was anger and despair in the voice that floated out the open door of the crude cabin. Wild creatures of the swamp, who came out to hunt at night, sensed the anguish and scurried off into the safety of the cypress woods.

Men, with shoulders slumped in fatigue, shook their heads as they passed the cottage that echoed with the *heartbroken* cries of grief. They would have to return, after burying the body they carried in its simple pine box, to claim still another. Sadly, they made the sign of the cross as they bore their burden toward the hastily dug grave at the edge of the swamp. The full ivory moon, hanging low in the indigo-black sky, shone its cool, opal light down on the men, casting their long, ghostly shadows against the walls of the cluster of rough shacks.

"Come, boy. We best bury your pa. Tante Marie will look after your ma," the young man sighed, rising to his feet. His thick red hair brushed the low ceiling of the cabin as he stretched to his full height.

"Leave me be. I am staying here." The voice was harsh and raw with emotion. The light from a single oil lamp fell across his heavy black hair as he sat bowed over the slim figure of a woman prostrate on a faded quilt stretched over a rough cot. He clutched her thin, wasted hand as if by force of will he could cure the fever that consumed her. She tossed back and forth on the crude pallet in the throes of delirium, but her fingers held tight to those of her son.

"Laddy, 'tis naught that you can do for her now that the yellow jack has struck. You need to get out of this foul cabin and get some fresh air," the tall Irishman pleaded, placing a beefy hand on the boy's broad shoulder. Sean Kelly knew the woman wouldn't last the night, but the lad didn't have to witness his mother's death, as he had his father's only hours before.

"I am staying, Sean, she needs me." Huge black eyes stared up at Sean, and the Irishman's heart broke at the pain, the torment, he saw reflected in that strangely adult gaze.

"Aye, Thane, you must do your duty as you see fit," Sean agreed, too exhausted to argue. "I will see to your pa."

Staring back at the proud boy, who was standing on the threshold of manhood, the Irishman thought with a sad shake of his head that Thane had never been allowed to be young and carefree. There was an intense, wary quality about him. *What a man he will be when he's grown,* Sean mused as he left the fetid cabin. *I sure wouldn't want to be his enemy,* he thought with a shudder.

"Help her, Tante Marie," Thane ordered harshly. Ebony eyes, that glowed like burning coals in his lean, golden-bronze face, watched his mother seem to lose strength, for suddenly she lay still.

"I give her tisane quick," the old Acadian woman

6

promised as she poured the contents of a bubbling pot into a dented tin cup. "Hold this to her lips."

Doing as the old healing woman instructed, Thane lifted his mother's slight body in his strong arms and forced a little of the liquid between her trembling lips. Her eyes fluttered open as she drank, and he could see she was lucid for the first time in days. Hope rose within him. Gently, he held the cup to her mouth once more.

"Enough," Thane's mother whispered, turning her head from the bitter liquid. "I must tell you . . ." She stopped for breath, then continued, "while I can."

"Rest, Mother, there will be time later to talk," her son insisted as he placed her back against the stained, thin pillow.

"Nay, Thane, I am dying. We must face that," she urged, giving him a gentle smile. "There is much I must tell you while I still can. I had intended to explain it all to you one day, but now I fear that time has come. Listen well, for 'tis your only legacy." Her voice wavered and she stopped until she could find the energy to continue.

"Mother, please, you are tiring."

"Look at me, Thane, and remember," his mother insisted, clutching his long, tapered fingers, her eyes burning into his with the urgency of her confession. "You are the grandson of a wealthy man, an English lord, my father. I was his only child. Soon you will be his only heir."

The young man looked up at the ancient Acadian crone with an incredulous expression in his black eyes. What fever fantasy was his mother spinning?

"Thane, pay attention!" his mother demanded with the last of her strength. "When I met your father he was our head groom, and Irish, but I fell in love with him. My father was furious. He had pledged my hand to another more suitable man. I, however, was willful and so much in love. There could be no other man in my life

7

but Patrick." The exhausted woman paused. Her eyes had a faraway look, as if she were seeing once more that impetuous girl and handsome young groom.

"Mother, you can tell me this later. Now you must rest," her son ordered, his voice firm and unyielding.

"Hand me the box on the mantel," she said, gesturing with a trembling hand toward the fireplace as if she hadn't heard him. With a resigned expression, he obeyed, bringing the familiar box to her. "Open it," she commanded.

"There is only an old leather bag," he muttered, picking it up in disgust. He knew his mother had guarded this box through all their travels, as the family fortune sunk lower and lower till they found themselves in a shack deep in the swamps of Louisiana.

"Inside is a symbol of your heritage," she whispered, her voice harsh and gasping for air.

Pouring the contents of the pouch onto the soiled sheet, Thane's dark eyes widened as he beheld a small, carved gold ring with a deep red stone in the center that glowed like a red-hot coal. It was a ruby, he realized. They had lived in conditions worse than slaves, and his mother had possessed this jewel worth hundreds, even thousands!

"Put on the ring," his mother ordered in a whisper. "It is the Ryder crest—the two leopards beside a shield of crossed swords." She smiled as she saw how it fit his little finger. "It was mine, and now yours, as the Ryder heir. You must write your grandfather at Penrydis Castle, Land's End, Cornwall. He does not know of your existence, for I ran off with your father when he refused to let us wed."

"But why did you not contact my grandfather?" Thane asked his mother, puzzled at the strange story.

"Pride, and your father," she answered softly. "Patrick didn't want your grandfather to know how low we had

8

fallen. You see, he had predicted life would be hard for me if I chose the man I loved."

So my charming wastrel of a father allowed his wife and son to suffer rather than offend his pride, thought Thane, bitterness filling him like a poison. Patrick Malone had gone from one job to another throughout Thane's childhood. His father's taste for the bottle had often resulted in his being laid off.

As their situation worsened in Ireland, they were forced in desperation to sail to Louisiana to seek their fortune. Patrick had painted glowing pictures as they crossed the ocean in the hideous hold of an overcrowded ship. Their dreams soon turned to nightmares as they found New Orleans a hot, humid hellhole where most of the jobs were held by slaves or free men of color. The wealthy plantation owners often hired Irish immigrants to clear away the swampy, fever-ridden land because their slaves were too valuable to risk at such dangerous work. Driven by hunger and despair, Patrick had taken such a job, and there he had contracted the yellow fever that killed him. His wife, worn out by the ordeals of her life, was now succumbing to the same deadly disease.

"Remember, my darling, you are a Ryder. I give you your heritage." His tired mother smiled up at him. Then she turned her eyes away from her son, and, staring straight ahead at something only she could see, whispered, "Patrick, I am coming," and was still.

"Mother!" The terrible cry of some wild, motherless creature filled the hot, oppressive bayou night.

Thane stumbled from the rough cypress shack, running he knew not where, trying only to assuage his grief. Across the long grass he staggered, his eyes blurred by tears of anger and sorrow. The long curtains of Spanish moss, hanging from the huge live oaks, were an impediment to be torn aside. All around him was the dark, decayed scent of the swamp, and he ran from the smell of

9

death. Breaking free at last, he raced forward till he stood on the high levee overlooking the great inland sea that was the Mississippi River.

The remote alabaster moon shone down on the river, causing it to glow silver and clean. Tearing the faded clothes from his body, Thane dove into the cool, swift water. Down, down he went till his lungs threatened to burst. When he could take no more, he shot to the surface gasping for air. He felt barely alive. It was as he shook the water from his hair that he saw the house, gleaming white and elegant as a Greek temple. The magnificent mansion was the jewel of Belle Rivière plantation, the home of Faustien Duplantier. As Thane stared at the symbol of the wealth of the man who had hired his father to clear his swamps because his slaves were too valuable for such work, a deadly anger grew within him. At that moment an obsession took root deep within in his heart allowing him to control his grief, giving him a reason to live.

Swimming strong, even strokes, Thane quickly reached the shore and climbed back up on the long grass of the levee. As the soft Louisiana night air swirled around him drying the river water from his slender body, he saw the little girl. Golden curls gleamed in the moonlight as she ran across the manicured lawn to hide behind an enormous live oak.

"She's here. I found her, Seraphine," cried a small boy, chasing after the girl, his hair equally golden.

A black woman, in the gingham dress of a house servant, came running. "André, you and your sister must come to bed. Your father will be furious if you two disturb the party he has planned for weeks."

"We will come," the little girl agreed with reluctance, taking the woman's hand. With a sigh, she allowed her to lead them back to the splendid mansion glistening in the moonglow.

Staring after them, Thane's stern visage hardened, hinting at the man he would become, as he made his vow to the hot, empty night. "Someday Belle Rivière Plantation will be mine. The Duplantiers will have nothing," he muttered aloud, his face a mask of loathing, his black eyes narrowed with contempt. "I shall ruin them as they destroyed my mother and father. They shall know, each and every one of them, the wrath of my revenge. I swear it on my parents' grave!"

His burning ebony gaze devoured the sight of the pristine, elegant mansion for several long minutes, comparing it in his mind with the loathsome shack in which his mother had just died. It was as if he were committing the sight to memory. Then he turned, the pain carved in merciless lines on his young features making him appear much older than his years, and walked back to the swamp to bury his mother.

Part One

Who ever loved that loved not at first sight?
—Christopher Marlowe: *Hero and Leander*

Chapter One

La Belle Rivière Plantation
Louisiana, 1812

"Come back, *ma petite!* It will solve nothing if you are harmed. There is a storm approaching. Feel its power in the air!" The woman's melodious voice called out from the shaded verandah, cutting across the foreboding stillness of the sweltering afternoon heat.

Air, sultry and oppressive, pressed down on the moss-green lawn surrounding the classical alabaster mansion where all was silent and somnolent. It was not a peaceful quiet, but the nerve-wracking lull before a storm. Lightning flashed across the horizon, where the sky met the Mississippi River, and left its sulfurous tang in the damp air. The low roar of thunder began to rise, then fall, never completely disappearing.

The steady drum of a horse's hoofs on the hard ground echoed across the velvet grass as a lone rider urged her mount down the avenue of giant live oaks ignoring the pleas of the woman who stood on the second-floor gallery. The chestnut gelding raced between the enormous oaks toward the river and the gathering storm. Bent low over the magnificent animal, the rider, with tears streaming down her pale cheeks, urged him faster and faster till her long honey-colored tresses streamed out to blend with the auburn mane of the horse.

Billowing storm clouds, black and blue as bruises, raced up the churning Mississippi from the Gulf of Mexico to quickly darken the sky in promise of the turbulent weather to come. The rider, oblivious to the danger of the threatening storm, seemed to rush out to meet it and embrace its fury.

Horse and rider raced on across the lawn and up onto the long grass of the levee. Restraining the spirited animal, the young woman stared down into the swirling ocher waters of the river below.

"Oh, André, how can it be?" she moaned, brushing the tears from her cheeks with an impatient gesture. Then, with a toss of her long, tangled hair, as if she had come to a conclusion, she gave the gelding a prod, and they were off racing along the levee, leaving the elegant mansion far behind.

The wind came in gusts as the storm gathered force, and it blew across the river, tearing at the rider's clothes, pushing her down till her face rested against the horse's satin neck. Woman and beast fought the driving storm, but as the sky began to weep, she urged the gelding down off the embankment into the shelter of the surrounding swamp. Unaware she was observed, the rider didn't slacken the animal's pace as they reached the dense forest of tangled oaks and trailing Spanish moss.

"What in hell is she doing?" the man muttered, flinging the cheroot from his lips. He was hidden in the shadows of the twisted cypress tree trying to control his own mount, nervous in the fury of the storm. He watched as the young woman drove the horse through a maze of twisted oak branches. His mouth thinned with a contemptuous smile as a low-hanging bough caught on her long tangled hair and pulled her roughly from the

16

gelding's back.

The slight feminine figure dangled for a moment in the air before crashing to the hard earth below. The frightened horse, free of its rider, ran crashing through the woods back toward the levee. The young woman lay still on the mossy ground.

"Come, Pegasus, we better see to the little fool," the observer murmured to his ebony stallion as he dismounted and tied the animal to the gnarled branch of an ancient cypress.

The fallen rider lay on her back, one arm outstretched as if she were asleep. Long honey-gold hair lay about her shoulders and curled over her ivory temples in the light misting rain. The man felt his breath catch in his throat as he stared down at the lovely, heart-shaped face with its delicate, high cheekbones and golden widow's peak. A smudge of dirt on the young woman's forehead and an ugly bruise on her left cheekbone did nothing to detract from her beauty, only made her appear more vulnerable. The retroussé nose above full coral lips gave her face a piquant air. Bending down beside her, he observed a tiny beauty mark near the left corner of that delicious, pouting mouth. How he would like to taste those provocative lips. It was a face that would tempt the passion of any man.

Gently, the man reached out and brushed away a bit of twig that was caught in her hair, but the young woman didn't move and her thick, sooty lashes stayed closed. Concerned, he leaned closer till he noticed her rounded breasts gently rising and falling with each breath. Relieved she was alive, he raised an eyebrow in amused contempt as he considered her clothing. She was dressed in breeches and a faded muslin boy's shirt. Her small feet were clad in boy's worn riding boots scuffed at the toes.

Feeling the wind gathering force and the rain beginning to come in torrents, the man gathered the unconscious young woman up in his arms. She was light as a child, although her rounded hips and full breasts pressed against him left no doubt in his mind she was a woman. The sweet, alluring scent of some exotic flower drifted from her warm body to his nostrils, and he felt his loins involuntarily tighten.

Shifting her against him so he could untie the stallion, his pulse quickened as the tiny nipples of her breasts, hardened by the pounding rain, brushed across his chest and burned through the lawn of his shirt into his skin. Mounting the horse, the man held the young woman tight to him, trying to shield her from the driving rain as he urged the impatient animal toward shelter.

The swamp appeared impenetrable, but the tall, dark, determined man knew his way through the hanging moss and twisted tree limbs. Gusting wind bent over the small saplings, and he cursed the storm, for he well knew the signs of a hurricane.

Peering through the mists, he at last saw the outline of a raised Acadian cottage. Forcing the powerful stallion to travel the last few yards, the man and the young woman found sanctuary. Few people knew of the cabin's existence, and that was the way he wanted it.

Once inside the two-room cottage, he carried the woman into the smaller chamber, which contained a larger tester bed made of pine and draped in voluminous mosquito netting. He placed her gently on the muslin counterpane before venturing out into the storm to see to the stallion. Leading the animal into a crude lean-to barn, he rubbed him down and ensured he was secure for the duration of the hurricane.

The man returned to the cottage and drew the bolt on the heavy cypress door, closing out the fury of the storm. Lighting several oil lamps, he took one in hand and strode into the bedchamber. He stood for a moment looking down at the lovely young woman, almost a girl, lying before him and felt the blood surge through his veins at the thought of what he must now do for her own good. She was soaking wet and would take a chill if not made warm and dry.

His muscles tensed as he gently removed her wet shirt, the satin of her skin sending tremors of pleasure through him. Removing the rest of her worn, wet clothes, his breath caught at the delicate perfection he uncovered. Petite and flower-like, she was a miniature Venus, with her firm, up-tilted breasts, slender waist that flared into softly rounded hips, and shapely thighs. Her skin was a velvet apricot-and-cream color that glowed like fine porcelain. What marvelous coloring she had, he mused in wonder as he stared down at her. He had known many women, beautiful women, but this one would delight the most discerning connoisseur. A real blonde by the look of her, for that rich honey hair, with its shadows of gold and highlights of silver, shone also from the vee of the woman's mound. He dried the damp ivory of her skin with a linen towel, and then, with some reluctance, slipped her between the muslin sheets. She needed to rest, and he could use a drink of the brandy he kept in the cupboard in the other room.

The wind hurled its fury at the raised cottage, rattling the windows, but the small structure had known many storms and held together. After changing into dry breeches and shirt, the man lit the fire, for the cottage had a damp chill about it. Pouring a large helping of brandy into a crystal glass, he sat before the fire listening to the force of the storm and wondering about the beauty the hurricane had thrown his way.

From her clothes, he decided the golden-haired stranger must be some wild Acadian girl raised in the swamps. Her mother could be dead, he mused, for the Acadian women were reared to be modest and retiring.

19

Without a mother's guidance she would have to fend for herself, which would explain the boy's attire.

His questions were to be answered, for soon he heard a low moan from the bedchamber. Rising in one fluid motion, he strode into the shadowy room carrying an oil hurricane lamp.

As she tossed from side to side on the feather pillow, the young woman moaned and cried out a single name, her eyes still closed but the lashes damp from her tears. "André! André!" she muttered, her voice tormented as a raw and primitive grief seem to overwhelm her.

"Hush, *chérie,* you are going to be all right," the man crooned, sitting beside her on the huge bed. His voice was firm, strong, and protective, as he soothed her with endearments. Her emotional pain smote his heart. He could be ruthless, cold, and relentless, but he had one vulnerable spot and that was for innocent, hurt creatures, whether animal or woman. Before him he saw a lovely young woman, almost a child, who was as defenseless as a kitten and suffering great sorrow. She touched something long buried in his soul.

Smoothing the tangled locks of her tawny-blond hair from her forehead, he caressed her cheek with one lean finger. Who was André? It was a common name among the Acadians. He envied the man who could mean so much to this beautiful creature. As he stared down at her intently, it was as if he willed those dark lashes, with their tips of gold, to open.

Huge gray-blue eyes with strange deep violet rims stared up at him in confusion as Arielle Duplantier gasped, "Who are you?"

Temples pounding, she stared up into intense black eyes that regarded her from an arrogant masculine visage. His hair was so black, the light from the oil lamp on the table beside the bed caught night-blue shadows in its luxuriant thickness. Skin bronzed from the sun told her

20

he was a man used to the outdoors, but his watchful stare gave her no other clue to his identity. Thick black eyebrows met in a wicked frown over piercing eyes that gave her no quarter; a proud, aquiline nose that bespoke aristocratic lineage jutted over full lips that appeared both sensual and cruel. Arielle became increasingly uneasy under his scrutiny as the silence between them lengthened. She experienced a shiver of unease at the base of her spine as she tried to met his unwavering stare with no sign of fear.

"Who are you?" she repeated.

"Someone who happened by when you were being very foolish, *chérie*," he suddenly replied in a deep and sensual voice as one corner of his stern mouth pulled into a slight smile.

Biting her lip, she looked away, then, shaking her head, turned the intensity of her violet-gray gaze back on his dark, handsome visage. There was strength and arrogance in that swarthy countenance. Ebony eyes seemed to bore into her while keeping their own closed, secret expression. His deep voice had reassured her — something that his face didn't quite do, for the scar that went from one sleek black brow to temple gave him a rather diabolic look. The man was handsome, Arielle had to admit, with his sun-bronzed skin, aristrocratic features, and black satin hair with its slight wave. She adored the cleft in his strong, square chin, but who in the world was he, and why was she with him in this bedchamber completely unclothed?

"You didn't answer my question, and, furthermore, where am I?" she demanded, rising a bit off the pillow only to fall back as the pounding in her temples intensified.

"Better lie still. You fell, or rather, were pulled off your horse by a low-hanging oak branch," the mysterious man told her with a hint of amusement in his deep-timbered voice that spoke an elegant French with a slight accent.

"You are not French, m'sieur, though you understood my words," Arielle mused aloud, "and speak it well."

"Louisiana now belongs to the United States, mademoiselle. One could say I am an American," he answered in cryptic tones that gave nothing away as to his origins.

"Pouf," she made a Gallic moue of her mouth, "and we are now involved in her war with England. The blockade is most inconvenient. If it weren't for Lafitte's smugglers, we would be without life's pleasantries." She looked up at him with annoyance. "You don't look or sound like a kintuck," she stated.

"Nor am I. Shall we say that I am recently returned from a stay abroad, and now make my home here." Amusement flickered in the black-smoke eyes meeting hers.

The man was a challenge, and Arielle always enjoyed a challenge. Glancing about the small, plain bedchamber with its rough whitewashed walls, she decided to change the subject. She would find out his secrets, all in good time, in her own way.

"Is this your home?" Arielle inquired sweetly, allowing her lashes to veil her eyes for a moment, then staring up at him with her most innocent yet provocative expression.

The little flirt was trying out her skills on him, he realized with cynical amusement. She must be quite the belle with her rustic Acadian swains. He would show the little kitten to play with him.

"I use this place when it's convenient," he murmured as his dark gaze caught and held hers. "It's completely isolated," he added in a lower, seductive tone.

"Really, m'sieur, how interesting," Arielle responded with a deliberate yawn behind a delicate hand, only low-

22

ering her eyes for a moment. "I don't believe I have ever run across this place, and I do know this part of Louisiana. It must be well hidden. Why would you want such an isolated cottage unless you have something to hide?" she added, with a slight smile of challenge of her own.

"We all have something to hide, mademoiselle," he answered with a bland half smile, his onyx eyes unreadable as they contemplated her with a cool detachment.

"I beg to differ, sir, for I have nothing to hide—but then I am not a smuggler," she responded, her violet-gray eyes sparkling with triumph. Two could play this game, Arielle thought with a growing excitement. She had him, for she suspected what he was hiding. He was one of Jean Lafitte's men, or *ma foi*, he could be Lafitte himself. The ruler of Grand Terre was said to be a handsome man, and this one certainly fit that description.

"Are you Jean Lafitte?" Arielle blurted out, unable to contain her suspicions any longer. There was a tinge of wonder to her voice as she struggled to once more sit up.

"No. I am sorry to disappoint you," the mystery man replied, his mouth twitching with amusement as he observed her dashed hopes. "It would be romantic to be marooned in a hurricane with none other than Lafitte, but, alas, *chérie*, you will have to make do with me."

"Well, who are you? We haven't been introduced," Arielle retorted, giving him what she hoped was a withering stare.

Bowing his head in an elegant gesture, he murmured, "Jacques. You may call me Jacques. A fine name for a smuggler, don't you think?" His firm lips twisted into a cynical smile as a mischievous gleam came into his ebony eyes.

Arielle glared back at him and countered in a icy tone. "Where are my clothes, Jacques? I would like to leave this isolated cottage when the storm abates. It will be soon, I should think."

23

"Your clothes were soaked. I removed them to save you a chill. They are drying in the other room, but I fear that the storm has still not vented its fury. This is no ordinary thunderstorm, but a hurricane. As you know, a hurricane can last for hours, perhaps for days. You must have experienced their force before, mademoiselle . . . and what should I call you?" Jacques inquired with quiet emphasis.

"Arielle, I believe, is enough for now. And I have not experienced a hurricane that I can remember. You see, I have been away . . . at school, in France. I just returned several months ago . . ." Her voice trailed off. She turned away, but not before he saw the tears well up in those lovely, unusual eyes. There was a look of tired sadness upon her delicate features as if a forgotten pain had just returned.

Recalling her anguished cry for André, the man called Jacques stroked his chin as he regarded her thoughtfully. This was no wild Acadian girl from the swamps if she had been schooled in France. The beautiful wench was a mystery, and he had to admit it added to her allure.

"Arielle, I don't want to add to your pain, but sometimes it helps to talk. A wound festers if it is not opened, cleansed, and allowed to heal," Jacques spoke in a low, gentle voice as if to a hurt child. He wanted to know just how much this man meant to her. "Before regaining consciousness you moaned the name André."

"He . . . he is dead. André is dead. How could I have forgotten for even a minute?" She shuddered at the thought, biting her lower lip to control the sobs that threatened to overwhelm her.

She had ridden away from the house on Sultan hoping in some way to leave behind the crushing grief. Seraphine had warned her of the coming storm, but it had not mattered. Nothing mattered, but that never again would she talk or laugh, or even argue with André.

"You must have loved him very much," Jacques said softly. "I know what it is to lose one you love. At first the pain of the loss in unendurable, but gradually, with time, it does become bearable. You never forget, but you learn to live with the loss. He was lucky to have had someone who loved him as much as you do."

The understanding words loosened the dam in Arielle, and she yielded to the compulsive sobs that shook her entire being. Gathering her into his arms, Jacques held her to his warm, muscular chest and gently rocked her back and forth as she let the hurt flow out of her.

"Let it out, *ma chère*," he whispered into her silky hair as he tried to stifle the hunger that surged through him at the touch and scent of her. Jacques wanted her with a primitive passion which was tempered by a need that puzzled and annoyed him. Somehow he wished to cherish this fragile, lovely young woman as well as ravish her.

"It is as if a part of me died," m'sieur," Arielle confessed against the strong chest, another shudder shaking her delicate frame. Grief and despair tore at her heart as the hot tears fell on his shirt soaking the fine lawn material. He held her with great tenderness, awed by the depth of her sorrow.

"He must have been a fine man to warrant such devotion," Jacques commented, trying to keep any hint of envy of the dead André from his voice. Had this man been her husband, or her lover? The question burned through him as his hands tightened against the slender waist and lovely curve of her back.

"André could be wild and thoughtless, m'sieur, but he was my twin — part of me. I shall always feel the rupture as if I am not quite whole," Arielle sighed, lifting her head from his chest.

25

Jacques' heart leapt at her words. Then a scorn followed that he should feel such relief that André had been her brother. He had no room in his life for a spoiled young Creole even if she was as beautiful as Arielle. She was a daughter of that wealthy, indulgent class he hated, he could see that now.

As his dark gaze caught hers, Arielle was startled by the smoldering flame she saw in those obsidian eyes. Her breath caught in her throat as his look of compelling desire captured and held her, allowing no retreat. The closeness of his masculine, powerful body was overwhelming. She wanted to pull away, but could not move, feeling frozen. She soon melted as her senses leapt to life, aware of his firm fingertips burning into her skin. Unable to ignore the strange aching in her limbs, she felt the magnetic pull between them, and could not, or would not, resist.

The lull in the storm had been only temporary. Gathering fury, the wind hit the cottage from the opposite direction causing the windows to rattle and the walls to shake. Arielle took little notice of the tempest outside. Her world was this small room within the circle of golden light from the oil lamp.

Blazing black coals searched the pale oval of her visage with an intense look that was halfway between pleasure and pain. Then, with a violence he was struggling to control, Jacques pulled her to him as she gasped her objection.

"No! That is not what I want . . ." Arielle began, only to have her protests muffled by his demanding lips that caressed her mouth with a hard, seeking hunger. She must fight him, she thought with a surge of fear and anger, but were those emotions directed at him or her own growing need?

Jacques's sinewy-muscled arms held her tight against him as the muslin sheet fell to her waist. The ivory mounds of her uncovered breasts pressed in sensuous contact to the heated warmth of his chest and beating heart. Shocked at her body's response to his urgent need, Arielle experienced the fire of desire racing through her as his tongue traced the soft fullness of her mouth.

Trembling, her lips opened, allowing him the entrance he sought with such persuasive mastery. She returned his kiss with reckless abandon, wantonly pressing her sensitive, throbbing breasts against the thin linen of his shirt, seeking the contact with his heated skin. It was as if his kiss were some strange drug that lulled all thought, all reason, from her mind.

How could she forget her self-control? a small voice echoed in the recesses of her mind. She tried not to think as the compelling force of his desire sent a delicious shudder of heat through her body, weakening all of her defenses. The small voice of reason was drowned in a passionate arousal that called forth an overwhelming need.

The violence of the hurricane pounded the small cottage, hurling a broken branch against one of the shuttered windows, but the two lovers were unaware as passion met passion, need met need. His firm yet sensitive, fingers, with their slightly calloused tips, caressed the silken skin of her back as he explored the planes and hollows with a sensual stroke.

Surrendering completely to his masterful seduction, hypnotized by his knowing touch, Arielle instinctively reached out for him. Her hands sought the hard muscle of his broad shoulders, stroking, learning the feel of his powerful, masculine strength.

The force of life, and all its sweet mystery, drove them toward fulfillment. Each sensed that here was the other half that would make them a complete whole. Until this moment, they had not realized how alone they had been, each in a separate life. Something deep within their hearts recognized each other, and they experienced the strange feeling that somehow they had come home.

There was a pounding rhythm in the room which was becoming louder and louder. In the dim recesses of her mind Arielle wondered how their hearts could cause such a clamor. The persistent rapping continued, till both reluctantly realized it was an intruder trying to attract their attention. They slowly pulled apart with the dazed expression of sleepers awakened from a wondrous dream.

"Someone is at the door. Poor devil out in that storm. I must answer it," Jacques's hoarse whisper was resigned, but full of regret as his ebony eyes devoured her for a brief moment before he rose to leave her.

"Mon Dieu," Arielle breathed, staring after him. How was so much emotion possible? Never had she known such intensity, and she shivered at the vivid recollection. *Non,* she didn't enjoy the knowledge that a man could awaken such a hunger within her. What power it would give him! She was furious at her own vulnerability. Arielle Duplantier, the belle who had always led the men a merry dance, had melted in this stranger's arms like a common whore. Her face burned with the shame of her surrender.

Vowing to impose an iron control over her emotions, Arielle pulled the sheet up to her neck with trembling hands. She must leave this place as soon as the storm ended. Aware of how isolated the cottage must be, she tried to gather her wits about her. Had she ever heard of such a place near the plantation? She knew this cabin could be any one of the many trappers' shacks that existed throughout the swamps around Duplantier land. She was entirely at the mercy of this strange man called Jacques . . . And what did he want with her?

28

Chapter Two

Hearing a male voice holler above the storm as Jacques opened the front door, Arielle slid gingerly off the high tester bed, trying not to ignore the throbbing in her head. Perhaps their visitor could give her some clue as to where she was — and with whom. She wrapped a quilt around her like a sarong and padded to the door.

"*Sacré bleu, mon ami,* but 'tis a night!" the visitor exclaimed, entering the cottage from the porch and shaking the water from his burly form.

He was a short but powerfully built man. His shoulders, twice as broad as those of an average man, gave him a strange resemblance to an ox. Swarthy, with piercing black eyes and a hawklike nose, the stranger gave a frightening appearance, as the left side of his face was covered with dark scars.

"I didn't think you would try and make it with this storm brewing," Jacques replied, handing the man a rough cloth with which to dry off his wet face and hair. *He knows him,* Arielle thought with fascination. She now realized her first suspicions had been correct. The man she had embraced so passionately was a smuggler, for the ferocious-appearing stranger was familiar to her. She had seen him once before in New Orleans. André had pointed him out to her at the French Market. He had told her the man, with the dark burn scars on his face was Dominique Youx, one of the famous smugglers of Barataria Bay.

Her father had dealings with the smugglers of Barataria and Lafitte. Most of New Orleans, and the surrounding plantations, did business with the infamous men of Grand Terre if they wanted their fine liquor and perfumes and didn't want to pay the high American tax on imported goods.

Arielle experienced a thrill of guilty excitement as she thought of her father's reaction to the knowledge that she had been in the passionate embrace of one of the notorious Barataria smugglers. He would be furious — maybe even enough to notice she existed, she thought bitterly. She was, after all, only a girl, and for her father, that meant she mattered very little. As long as she behaved, he paid her scant attention. Consequently she misbehaved frequently.

"This is a night for the devil himself," the rough-looking visitor commented, taking the tankard of rum Jacques offered, then sitting down on one of the rustic chairs with a sigh. "The *bos*, he wanted you to know that the *Tigre* will be leaving soon as the storm is over. If you wish to take out the *Leopard* with him, the *bos*, he will wait for your return. He always likes to sail with you, Jacques Temeraire, as do we all. Lafitte, he send you some of that fine cognac you two think so much of. Now me, I care only that it warm my belly," the gruff man chuckled, nodding his huge head in the direction of the burlap bag he had dropped in the corner.

"You must thank Jean for me. The cognac is much appreciated, Dominique. I think that for now, however, I will stay close to New Orleans. There is a business matter that concerns me, but I will return to Grand Terre in a month — say the first of October," Jacques replied. He took the bottles of fine French cognac from the

30

bag and placed them on the pine sideboard.

"The *bos* will be disappointed *mon ami*. He looks forward to some excitement with those British frigates. News of your business has traveled to Grand Terre. Lafitte will be relieved all is well in that department," Dominique told him in cryptic tones, draining the tankard before holding it out for a refill.

The implication of the man's words sent a wave of excitement through Arielle as she pressed against the wall. They were Lafitte's men, or at least Dominique was, Jacques seemed to have his own ship. Jacques Temeraire — Jacques the bold. The name suited him, Arielle decided as she tried to see through the small crack of the door. All of New Orleans knew that Jean Lafitte was called *Bos* by his men, but he seemed to consider Jacques as an equal. Pushing the door a little wider, she tried to stare unobtrusively at this intriguing man who had come to her aid.

"Mon Dieu, did I disturb you?" The visitor was quickly on his feet, his eyes fixed on the shadowy figure he saw lurking behind the slowly opening door.

Seeing the direction of his companion's gaze, Jacques' lips curved into a knowing grin. "Mademoiselle Arielle, would you do me the honor of joining us?" he requested, a hint of amusement in his deep voice.

Throwing back the tangled mane of honey-gold hair, Arielle entered the room with what she hoped was an aloof manner. "Gentlemen, forgive my appearance," she drawled, holding the faded quilt together with her left hand as Dominique Youx bowed low over the curved, outstretched fingers she extended.

What a little aristocrat she was with her fine airs, Jacques observed with cynical detachment. Arielle, though dressed in a worn cloth and her hair snarled, somehow managed to appear regal as a countess while a disreputable smuggler from Barataria Bay bowed over her hand. Life was full of small ironies, he mused, staring at her with a hard, cold-eyed smile of mockery. These Creoles thought they owned the earth, and homage was their due. Remembered old grievances struck through him like a knife.

"Mademoiselle, may I present Captain Dominique Youx of Grand Terre." Jacques' silky voice held a mocking tone as he made the introduction.

"*Enchanté,* beautiful lady," Dominque murmured, bowing even lower over her hand, his lips never touching her skin.

"Mademoiselle does not wish to tell us her surname. She wishes to be known only as Arielle," Jacques informed his companion as if she were some temperamental child.

The man could be insufferable. He had started the whole game by telling her his name was Jacques and refusing to tell her more. She was not ashamed of who she was, for her name was an old and proud one. Lifting her delicate chin high, Arielle met his mocking gaze boldly, her violet-gray eyes ablaze with pride.

"Mademoiselle Arielle Duplantier of La Belle Rivière Plantation," she announced in a cool tone full of hauteur and privilege. "*Enchanté,* Captain Youx."

Was it her imagination or had those ebony eyes flickered with shock? With pleasure she noted Jacques' set face, the muscle that twitched at his firm jawline. He was surprised, she was glad to see, but the other emotions in that closed face were not discernible.

It was only a moment before he returned her gaze with a twisted smile that didn't reach his ever-watchful eyes. "We are honored, indeed, Dominique, to have Faustien Duplantier's daughter here with us." Jacques spoke softly, but his tone was oddly menacing.

A chill ran up Arielle's spine as a tense silence enveloped the room. What had she done, announcing her complete name like a fool? Her father's wealth was well known throughout Louisiana. He would be able to pay a high ransom for her return. Lafitte's men were dangerous no matter their romantic reputation. They were really no better than pirates, seizing ships and taking the passengers hostage, even if they claimed letters of marque from Cartenga. Her stupid, arrogant pride had once more complicated her life. What would they do with her now that they knew she was a Duplantier?

Jacques' cynical smile and speculative stare caused Arielle a twinge of fear at the base of her spine. As violet eyes challenged his piercing onyx gaze, the tension stretched ever tighter between them. She knew that with her announcement their relationship had changed, and not for the better.

"Now that the formalities have been dispensed with, would you care to dine with us, *Mademoiselle Duplantier?* We can't forget our manners. Faustien Duplantier is famous for his hospitality," Jacques stated, breaking the tension with a mocking bow, each word edged with sarcasm as he gestured for Arielle to take his chair next to the fire.

With head held high, she swept past him to take her seat across from their visitor. Anger was visible in her rigid posture as her delicate face paled with the intensity of her wrath. Tossing back her honey-gold mane in a gesture of defiance, she deliberately turned her slender back to her host. Whatever the reason for his change in behavior toward her, she would not allow him to know how much it had disconcerted her. He was no better than the men she had known in her young life, her father and her brother, swift in his changes of mood and thus not to be trusted.

Captain Youx regarded Arielle with a troubled expression as she sat stiffly on the edge of the rough-hewn chair. She saw sympathy and concern in his mahogany-brown eyes, but she wasn't sure if it was for her or his friend Jacques.

"My condolences on your loss, Mademoiselle Duplantier. The news of your brother's *affaire d'honneur* has swept New Orleans," Dominique commented softly, lighting a clay pipe from the fire when she nodded it was all right with her if he smoked.

"Thank you," Arielle murmured, the tears welling up once more threatening to burst forth. Using every ounce of control, she forced her emotions back under restraint. She must show no weakness in front of these men. Regardless of Jacques' show of tenderness earlier, she really knew very little about them except that they were both privateers with Lafitte. Jacques appeared to be capable of taking any advantage when he saw the opportunity. His honeyed words were probably false, a facade to gain her confidence so he might use her as he wished.

"André will be avenged," she stated with desperate firmness, struggling hard against the tears she refused to let fall.

"Ah, mademoiselle and how is that to be?" Dominique Youx inquired, blowing rings of fragrant blue smoke in the air as he watched Jacques spread a blue and white checked cloth on the wooden trestle table.

"I shall find this M'sieur Ryder who killed my brother and seek justice for his murder," Arielle responded in sharp tones, as if there would be any question to her purpose. A silence seemed to fill the room as the two men stared first at her, then each other. A warning glance passed between them.

"The law does look the other way in these matters of the Code Duello. A man's death on the field of *honneur* is not considered murder, mademoiselle," Captain Youx reminded her.

Dueling was a common occurrence among the hot-blooded young Creoles, and as such tolerated in New Orleans. Many of the young men looked for an insult as an excuse to prove their prowess in an *affaire d'honneur*.

"It is said my brother's murderer challenged him after a game of chance at Maspero's Exchange, while buying him as many drinks as he could consume. André . . . André, unlike most of his friends, had no head for alcohol . . ." Arielle hesitated, fighting to keep her anger under restraint before continuing. "When my brother was quite drunk, this M'sieur Ryder taunted him, claiming André was cheating. Such an insult could not go unchallenged by any Creole of *honneur*. According to the rules of the Code Duello, M'sieur Ryder was allowed to pick the weapons. He chose the rapier, a deadly weapon with little margin for error when one has been drinking. When my foolish, drunken brother demanded immediate satisfaction in the garden of the cathedral, M'sieur Ryder agreed, even though he knew André was in no condition to defend himself. These are not the actions of a gentleman, but of a murderer." Arielle's lips thinned with rage as her huge eyes, purple-gray like thunderclouds, looked through him at some private pain.

"You know this man who fought your brother?" Jacques questioned, breaking the tense silence that had followed her words.

Arielle nodded woodenly. "I know his name — Thane Ryder. That's all I need to know. It may take some doing, but I will find him."

"Pray tell, then what will you do?" Dominique Youx queried, his voice troubled, his eyes compassionate.

"I shall seek my revenge," Arielle replied with quiet but desperate firmness.

"What does your father think of your plan?" Jacques asked. There was more than a hint of derision in his deep, cool, melodious voice.

35

"My father knows nothing," Arielle answered, looking at him with a deep sadness reflected on her exquisite face. "He is heartbroken at my brother's death. André was his only son, his heir. Our mother died at our birth. It is as if his will to live is gone. He came into the house after my brother was buried three days ago and locked himself in his room. I have not seen him since. Only his valet Jubal is allowed in to tend to his needs. His food tray comes back to the kitchen hardly touched. The doctor says time will heal his mind, but until then, m'sieurs, I must see to the family matters." Arielle struggled to maintain an even tone, but both men saw the delicate lips tremble as she forced a stiff smile of determination.

Jacques' hand tightened on the knife he was using to slice a long loaf of French bread. This spoiled young Creole had courage. Glancing back at her, he observed her — head up, spine rigid, she sat not touching the back of the chair. The nuns had taught her well. She held herself like a queen, allowing none of her despair to show in her posture, only in those remarkable violet-gray eyes.

"The doctor is right — your father will soon learn to live with his grief, mademoiselle. Faustien Duplantier is a hard, strong man," Jacques said quietly, but there was an undercurrent to his tone that caused Arielle to glance at him with surprise.

"You know my father?" she queried with interest. Perhaps this explained Jacques' abrupt change of attitude when he heard her family name. Her father had many enemies, and not without reason.

"Everyone in South Louisiana knows of Faustien Duplantier and La Belle Rivière Plantation. Is it not called the Versailles of the New World . . . ? Now shall we dine?" Jacques changed the subject smoothly, handing her a white crockery plate containing a slice of crusty bread, golden cheese, and a thin piece of smoked ham.

Merci. It looks delicious," Arielle replied with a faint

smile. She realized she was hungry for the first time in days. Holding her plate on her lap, she tried to eat without appearing ravenous.

Jacques exchanged a grin with Dominique as he handed his friend the other plate. The haughty young Creole was wolfing down her food like a famished child.

After several glasses of delicious dry white French wine, Arielle began to relax. Finishing her food, she curled up in the large rustic chair to listen to Dominique's entertaining tales of life with Lafitte. The storm swirled around them, lashing the cottage's small windows, but inside it was warm and dry. Arielle had not felt so at peace for days.

Dominique was good company, making her laugh with his droll humor, but strangely Jacques said little. Her rescuer sat on a bench he had brought from the bedchamber and placed against the wall. She could not see him without turning rudely away from Dominique, but her every nerve was conscious of Jacques' intense scrutiny.

As Arielle listened to Dominique, she tried to keep from her mind the feel of Jacques' firm, masculine lips burning on her mouth, the touch of his knowing hands, the sandalwood smell of his silky hair. She was amazed that such a man could intrigue her so, for she had met many handsome, wealthy men in the last few months.

Her father had pressured her to choose from her many suitors, but she had rebelled, wanting no placid Creole marriage. *Toujours coucher, toujours grosse, toujours accoucher,* always bedded, always pregnant, always bearing babies, while her husband amused himself in the gambling halls, brothels, and cafes of New Orleans. She would be expected to stay at home, a good Creole wife, never complaining. *Non,* she would never make such a marriage. There had to be more to life, and Jacques' swarthy handsome visage once more came to mind.

37

Although her host sat in the shadows, out of her range of vision, Arielle had felt those intense black eyes, as dark and impenetrable as Barataria Bayou, studying her. Jacques had spoken few words since their meal, but his tone when speaking of her father still rankled. What had caused the bitterness in his voice she wondered. She had witnessed his reaction of shock and dislike, almost hatred, on those arrogant features when she had spoken her last name.

The Duplantier family was respected in New Orleans society. Arielle's father had been the son of a French marquis. Seldom had she encountered Jacques' lack of respect, and it mystified her. Often she had heard fear in a person's voice when they spoke of her father, but always there was respect, for he was a powerful man in Louisiana.

"Mademoiselle, I fear I have tired you," Dominique Youx said in gentle tones, noticing her faraway expression.

"But no, m'sieur, your stories are fascinating. How I should like to visit Grand Terre someday," Arielle protested, to her embarrassment yawning behind a graceful hand. She gathered her makeshift garment together and rose to her feet. "I do find, however, I am fatigued and, with your permission, will retire till the morrow. I fear the storm has not abated, so I must intrude on your hospitality a while longer," she said, giving them a wan smile of regret.

"We are happy to have such beauty grace this humble cottage." The rich timber of Jacques' masculine voice startled Arielle, as he stood up and came to face her. With a cool, aloof stare he said, "You will find a shirt in the chest at the foot of the bed. Wear it if you like. Good night, mademoiselle. We will try not to disturb your slumber."

"Merci . . ." Arielle hesitated a moment, for he was so

38

formal, as if they had never touched. Ink-black eyes clashed with hers, and their look was impersonal, distant. She, too, could be remote, she decided, irked by his frigid, aloof manner. "You will not bother me, for I am a sound sleeper," she replied coolly. Her head held high, she walked, with rigid posture, to the bedchamber door. *"Bonne nuit, m'sieurs."*

After shutting the portal tightly behind her, and searching in vain for a lock, Arielle stepped to the pine chest at the foot of the bed. The scent of vetiver and tobacco, used to protect the contents from moth damage, wafted up as she opened the lid.

She rummaged through the pile of masculine clothing till she found a soft muslin shirt with long sleeves. Holding the cloth to her cheek, she inhaled the faint fragrance of sandalwood that reminded her of Jacques' silky black hair. Allowing the quilt to slide to the floor, Arielle slipped the shirt over her head. The garment engulfed her, falling to below her knees. Long, full sleeves hung down over her hands, but she relished the feel of the shirt Jacques had worn. It was as if his strong, sinewy arms were about her in an embrace. Shaking her head at her foolishness, she put her fantasy from her mind and rolled up the sleeves. After closing the chest and blowing out the lamp, she crawled under the quilt determined to sleep . . . but sleep would not come.

The memory of intense, probing ebony eyes lingered and made her restless. Her mouth burned with the remembrance of his kiss. Although the mattress, filled with Spanish moss, was comfortable, Arielle tossed and turned aware that on the other side of the door was Jacques Temeraire.

For the first time since André's death she had thought of something else other than her grief. She felt ashamed. How could she have put all memory of her brother from her mind because of a handsome rogue who was a smuggler, and maybe worse. Listening to the driving rain against the shuttered window, Arielle allowed her mind to drift back over the years, blotting out the darkly handsome face of Jacques Temeraire.

André the golden one, they had called him. How the young Creole ladies — and some not so young — had adored her brother. He had been self-centered and spoiled, but how she had loved him. Her twin had always looked after her, insisting the other boys allow her along when they had been on one of their adventures in the swamps. How proud she had been trailing after André, for his ideas, usually dangerous, had been so much more exciting than perfecting her sewing as Seraphine, her nurse, had ordered. What trouble he had often led them into in those halcyon days of childhood.

Sighing, Arielle wiped a tear from her cheek as the memories overwhelmed her. Never again would she hear that lazy drawl regaling her with slightly naughty stories of his carouses in New Orleans. Early in the afternoon, having just arisen from a late night, André would stroll out of one of the matching octagon-shaped *garçonnières* that flanked the big house. Calling for a cup of café au lait laced with brandy, he would proceed to tell her all the latest gossip. His mimicry of some society grand dame would reduce her to giggles. Now, all that laughter and high-strung temperament were no more.

Turning over in the large bed, Arielle pulled the quilt higher. There was a chill in the room. *"Grâce à Dieu,"* she muttered. She must push those heart-breaking memories down where they could not cause such pain.

The forceful wind of the hurricane as it buffeted the cottage was beginning to wear on her nerves. Wrapping her arms around her chest seeking some added warmth, Arielle inhaled the faint scent of sandalwood surrounding her. The muslin was soft against her cheek, like a caress. Her pulse raced as she pictured the shirt clinging to the lean, muscular torso of the mysterious man called Jacques. Was that his real name? She had heard that when a man joined with the corsairs of Grand Terre, he often assumed a false identity.

Who was he, and where had he come from? Arielle mused, staring out into the darkened bedchamber. Something in his bearing and speech told her he was a gentleman. Fine breeding showed in the aristocratic, bronzed features and lean, muscular form. Although his French was fluent, she could discern a slight accent that told her French was not his native language.

Whatever was the true identity of her handsome host, Arielle doubted she would ever know, for Jacques appeared to be a paradox. He was a smuggler, living by his wits and daring, who could be as coldly haughty as a prince.

As the netherrealms of slumber beckoned to her Arielle closed her eyes, welcoming the escape that sleep would bring. But to her dismay she could see in her mind's eye that intense black gaze flashing with anger, hear that deep voice tinged with ridicule as he spoke her father's name. To this man, who lived outside the law, the respected name of Duplantier meant only contempt. As sleep claimed her, she wondered why the man who had held her with such passion and tenderness now considered her with disdain. Was it because he knew she was a Duplantier? But why should that make such a difference?

Chapter Three

Golden streaks of sunlight slanted through the cracks
in the shuttered windows to stream across Arielle's face.
The warm, bright light gently awakened her, revealing
that the storm had vanished with the night.

Sitting up gingerly, the slight throbbing in her temples brought back the tumultuous events of the previous
day. Touching the soft sleeve of the too-large shirt that
served as her nightdress, Arielle whispered, "Jacques
Temeraire" with a husky catch in her voice. Remembering those broad, sinewy shoulders, those strong arms
that had held her close to his powerful chest, she was
filled with a strange inner excitement. Had it really happened, that intense surge of emotion she had experienced in his embrace? she wondered, not daring to
believe such depth of feeling was possible.

Staring at the closed bedchamber door, she wondered
if the two men were also awake. The cottage was quiet,
so quiet it was unnerving. There was no sound but her
own quickened breath as the thought occurred that she
might be completely alone. Had the men vanished with
the storm, leaving her to fend for herself? A flicker of

apprehension grew within her as she saw that her clothes, now dry, were folded on the chest at the foot of the bed.

Slowly, as if rising from a sickbed, Arielle placed first one unsteady bare foot and then the other on the cool wooden planks of the floor. The bed creaked, under its Spanish moss-stuffed mattress, as she stood for a moment swaying, clutching at one of the thick pine posts to get her balance. Taking several deep breaths, her dizziness soon passed, and she felt stable enough to walk across the room.

Pouring water from a blue-and-white pitcher into the matching basin that stood on a simple pine chest, Arielle splashed the sleep from her eyes. Making use of a bar of sandalwood soap and a linen cloth that lay beside the basin, she pondered on the idea of a man living in such a primitive dwelling deep in the swamps using fine, milled French soap. *Remember, he does have access to the best Lafitte's men can smuggle,* she told herself with a sigh.

She finished her hasty washing and donned her crumpled, small clothes with a grimace of distaste. Although dry, they were none too clean, and nor were André's faded breeches, shirt, and old scuffed riding boots. They were all spotted with dried mud from her fall.

Glancing in a small, silvered glass over the chest, she observed with dismay that her hair was a tangled mess. Jacques, however, had foreseen her needs and had placed a fine boar's-head brush next to her clothes. Gratefully, Arielle gave her long, honey tresses a brisk brushing. The humidity, seeping into the cottage from the surrounding swamp, caused her hair to wave and curl in an unruly manner in spite of her best efforts. While away from Louisiana all those years at school in Paris, she had forgotten the effect the climate could have on her hair. The more she brushed it, the more it seemed to take on a will of its own, till it fell about her

43

head and shoulders like a golden aureole. She had lost all her hairpins on her wild ride on Sultan. Arielle dismissed her hair with a shrug; it would have to do.

Taking a deep breath, she squared her shoulders as if for a battle, and strode to the door, firmly wrenching it open. She was ready to demand to be taken back to Belle Rivière immediately. A curious sense of disappointment surged through her as she found the other room empty. A deep frown creased her delicate features as she realized she was alone in the cottage.

Disconcerted, Arielle looked about the room for clues to how long it had been since the men had left. There was a coffeepot hanging on a hook over the low-burning fire in the stone fireplace. She decided her search could wait until she had a bracing cup of coffee and she looked for a cup. Finding a mug on the sideboard, she observed bread, cheese, and fruit laid out on the wooden trestle table as if for breakfast. They couldn't have been gone too long, she mused, helping herself to the coffee, for the food was still fresh and, though low, the fire burned steadily.

As she placed the coffeepot back on the hook, Arielle experienced a sudden heightened awareness, as if each sense was tuned to its peak. The fine hairs on the back of the neck rose as her pulse pounded in her veins. Rising to her feet, she quickly turned around, her breath caught in her throat. The door was open. There was someone watching her.

Standing in front of her, filling the doorway, was the tall figure of a man. Shielding her eyes with her hand from the glare of the morning sun she saw that it was Jacques. His silhouette against the golden light was one of great strength, but also of lithe grace. Arielle was reminded of the magnificent oaks that formed an avenue from Belle Rivière to the river.

"You have awakened, mademoiselle. Good," Jacques'

voice was clipped, cold. Onyx eyes flickered over her as if she were some tiresome problem he was eager to be rid of. He strode past her to the sideboard not looking once in her direction. "There is bread and cheese on the table if you want," he said tersely, his back to her as he took down a cup.

"How could I refuse such a gracious invitation," Arielle replied in a sarcastic tone, making no move toward the table even though she was famished.

Was this the same man she had found so irresistible the night before? She must have been mad. Good-looking he might be, but many handsome men had tried to win her. Arielle had enjoyed the flirtation, the chase, but had never found a man to penetrate the wall she had built around her heart. In her young life she had known only two kinds of men—charming wastrels like her twin brother André, or cold, rejecting men like her father, who considered all women idiot children. It appeared M'sieur Jacques Temeraire was one of the latter kind. His warmth, compassion, and understanding had vanished.

Stiffening, Arielle raised her chin, her amethyst eyes blazing. "I would like to leave now," she demanded.

Jacques turned to face her, a slight smile turning up the corners of his firm, sensual mouth, his dark eyes glittering for a moment with respect. "If you wish, Mademoiselle Duplantier . . . Then this is good-bye." He raised his empty cup to her in salute, then, as if she were already gone, walked past her to fill his cup from the pot.

Arielle bit her lower lip, managing to quell her anger, but her thoughts were racing furiously. The man was insufferable. He knew she had no idea how to return to Belle Rivière from this godforsaken place. He was taunting her. If he thought he could make a fool out of her, he was in for a surprise. Arielle Duplantier did not ever beg or lose her poise, she simply turned the game around to her rules. Trying to control the white-hot rage that threatened to engulf her, she forced a smile to her pale face. Laughing lightly to cover her annoyance, she replied in a silky voice, "You have had your little joke, m'sieur. I find myself at your mercy, for I know not where we are."

Rising to his feet in one fluid motion, Jacques towered over her as he lifted his cup to his lips. He regarded her over the rim as he lifted one dark brow in amused contempt. Lowering his cup after a long drink, his lips twisted into a cynical smile. "But, Mademoiselle Duplantier," he drawled, "I am known as a man without mercy."

Arielle's heart-shaped face flushed with anger, her eyes huge dark-purple thunderclouds, as she glared at him with loathing. "You do not frighten me, m'sieur," she countered icily, placing her cup on the mantel. Tossing her golden mane across her shoulders, she placed her hands on her slender hips, boldly meeting his cynical gaze.

"Such beauty, such courage," Jacques murmured, his deep, sensual tone sending a disquieting ripple of awareness through Arielle. "A real aristocrat aren't you, *chérie*, but then you are a Duplantier, and the Duplantiers bow to no man." Fathomless black eyes like burning coals bored into her as an expression of bitter mockery settled across his handsome features.

Arielle flinched before the contempt she saw in Jacques' unwavering dark gaze. He seemed to hate her. This was not the man who had held her in his tender yet exciting embrace. Instead, before her stood a remote stranger who seemed to resent her very presence.

She refused to be the first to look away, her lower lip trembling slightly and arms akimbo, her small feet in their scuffed boots planted firmly on the wooden planks

46

of the floor, she returned his fierce stare with one of her own.

Suddenly, she heard a deep chuckle that began as a dry, cynical sound, then grow into a low, husky laugh. Jacques' mouth lifted first into a smile, then into laughter as he regarded her stubborn refusal to be intimidated. A wry but indulgent glint appeared in those dark eyes as he observed her with amused wonder.

"Who are you little one, to reach inside me?" he murmured huskily as he cupped her chin with one lean hand. Jacques searched her upturned face with a gaze that now contained the sensuous flame of desire. "I could crush you like a butterfly, but you are not frightened." His strong, bronzed fingers tightened on the fragile bones of her chin, but still her haughty stare of contempt never wavered.

Arielle's reaction seemed to amuse him, but there was also admiration on those arrogant features as his smile widened in approval. Releasing her, he gently traced her full coral lips with one sensitive finger as he whispered, "Smile, *ma belle blonde*. Your mouth was made for kissing, not for anger."

Caught off guard by his abrupt change of mood, he swept her into his arms before she could protest. Held tight against his chest, she felt his mouth come down on hers, caressing her lips with a tantalizing persuasion. She wanted to resist, but as his tongue traced the outline of her burning mouth, shivers of desire and longing shattered all her defenses. Her soft curves were pressed against his lean hardness, and she could feel the heat of his body course down the entire length of hers. His rigid manhood pressed his arousal, making her weak with its implication.

"*Ma petite belle*, what a delight you are," Jacques sighed, pressing light, teasing kisses across her chin and up to the delightful beauty mark beside her heated lips.

She whimpered as his tongue, like a scarlet sword, flickered there for a brief moment before thrusting inside the waiting warmth of her mouth. Exploring that honeycomb of sweetness, he moaned as she meet his parry, and he swirled around the thrusting velvet of her.

Lifting her arms, not to push him away but to curl around his broad shoulders, she succumbed to the forceful domination of his passion. He was leading her to a place she had never known, where emotion and feeling ruled. The world, and their position in it, had no meaning in this enchanted cottage. There was only their overwhelming need and hunger for each other.

Feeling her arms clasping him to her, Jacques gave a moan of pleasure as his mouth moved down the hollow of her ivory throat. His hands stroked the planes of her back with a sensual touch that caused her breath to come in surrendering sighs of desire.

"Who are you, Jacques Temeraire, to make me forget all reason?" Arielle whispered against his shoulder. He raised his head, his burning, dark eyes capturing hers in a gaze that told of his amazement at what was between them.

The innocent wonder he saw shining in those wood-violet orbs smote his heart as no woman's look had ever done. This was no wanton to be taken for a brief satisfaction of the flesh, although what a revenge that would be on old Faustien Duplantier. He had high aspirations for her, Jacques was sure, and he was shocked at the stab of jealousy he felt at the thought of her in another man's arms. Take her now, and be done with it, his mind told him. Once he had possessed a woman, her allure for him was usually diminished. Have her, get her out of his blood, and leave damaged goods for her father to barter away to some rich old Creole.

Hearing his uneven breathing and seeing his eyes darken dangerously with an unreadable emotion,

Arielle gasped. Tears of emotion welled up in her violet-gray eyes, spilling over to her pale cheeks.

Her tears were Jacques' undoing. Pulling her arms from his shoulders, he held her hands so tightly, he hurt her, as he roughly thrust her from him.

"Non! Non! I take you home," he cried in a harsh, raw voice. She saw unspoken pain, alive and glowing, in his expressive black eyes.

Turning abruptly away from her, Jacques strode to the open portal. Standing in the doorway, he stared out to the swamp, his hands clenching the doorframe so hard his knuckles were white. Looking back over his shoulder, his face a frozen mask of resolve, he commanded, "Come, we will return you home to Belle Rivière." As she hesitated, her body stiffened in shock, her smoke-lilac gaze widened with astonishment. He repeated in softer tones, "Now, while I can still remember I am a gentleman."

Arielle struggled to hide her confusion as she followed Jacques out into the sunlight. Once more she had been surprised by this most unpredictable man.

"Are you a gentleman, Jacques Temeraire? Who are you really?" Her soft question hung in the warm morning air.

As he stood on the top step of the gallery and turned to face Arielle, she saw, for an instant, a wistfulness cross his stern countenance as he shook his head regretfully. "It is best that I remain Jacques Temeraire of Grand Terre, *ma belle blonde* — best for both of us." With a shrug of his broad shoulders, he turned and left the gallery to fetch his stallion from the lean-to.

Pondering the meaning behind his cryptic statement, Arielle stared across the clearing to the dense, dark forest of the swamp that surrounded the Acadian cottage. She felt a deep reluctance to leave this quiet, secluded place. If she were completely honest, she would admit her fear that once the world intruded upon them, she would never see Jacques again. It surprised her how much it mattered that he not walk out of her life never to return.

Annoyed at her own longing, she walked down the steps to the long marsh grass, trying to clear her head. A man had never before rejected her, for she had never let anyone close enough to have the opportunity. Her guard would come back up, she vowed.

It was this place, she decided. It had a bewitching quality. There was an unearthly beauty. The twisted oaks and cypress, hung with crawling vines — some as thick as a man's wrist — close about the cottage seemed a protective wall to keep out the uninvited or the unwanted. The sun, throwing a finger of light across the twisting fan of a palmetto, hardly penetrated the dark, mysterious swamp waiting only a few steps away to swallow up whomever ventured into its fecund depths. Men had gotten lost in the marsh-swamp and been driven mad. Arielle remembered the old legends told to her in childhood and gave a slight shiver of unease.

"Are you all right, *chérie?*" Jacques' sharp inquiry intruded on her melancholy reflections as he brought his black stallion up to where she stood.

"Of course," Arielle answered quickly. "I hope Sultan returned to the stables before the storm hit," she commented with a frown of concern, changing the subject as she stroked the ebony satin coat of the magnificent horse.

"He was headed in that direction back down the levee," Jacques said dryly, the hint of a grin about his mouth. "Come, we will both have to make do with Pegasus."

His strong hands lifted her up onto the saddle as if she were no more than a feather. Then he was behind her, so close she could feel his warm breath on her neck and the

50

heat of his body surrounding her like a sensual cloud. Arielle's heart hammered in her chest when Jacques' arms came loosely around her waist as he took the reins. His own masculine scent, mingled with the faint fragrance of sandalwood, caused her blood to surge through her heated body. Arielle held herself rigid, afraid the merest brush with his person would cause her to be lost. This strange magnetism between them was baffling. Arielle didn't know if she even liked him, yet the pull between them was strong, drawing them together beyond all reason.

On they rode through the primeval swamps. A humid somnolence hung over the trees and lagoons as Jacques' sure-footed stallion made his way through the overripe terrain. Ancient oaks touched branches overhead, making patterns of sunlight on twisted, gnarled trunks. Jacques seemed to know his way through the tangled labyrinth, Arielle realized, but nothing looked familiar to her. She had no idea how far they had come, or how long they had been riding.

The pungent smell of the swamp in the heat of early autumn was overpowering. Warm, humid air, close as an embrace, enveloped them as they rode on past a narrow bayou. The willows and oaks, meeting high over the olive water, dripped their gray curtains of Spanish moss into the murky stillness below.

"Bayou Barataria . . . Good. We will soon be on Duplantier land," Jacques told her in flat, impersonal tones that implied he was anxious to be rid of her.

Arielle stiffened at these first words he had spoken since they left the cottage. Was he that glad that their association was soon to be over? she wondered with an odd twinge of disappointment.

"My father will want to thank you. If you hadn't come along, I fear, with the storm, I may have suffered greatly," Arielle responded icily, staring straight ahead as she spoke. His rejection of her in the cottage had hurt more than she had thought possible. How could she have allowed her defenses to be lowered in front of this man? Her strongest resolve seemed to crumble when he took her in his embrace.

"I want nothing from Faustien Duplantier." Jacques ground out the cold, precise words, his tone low but holding an ominous quality.

Arielle flinched at the hatred she heard in his voice. Her father was a hard man. His only soft spot had been for his son André, and though he had many friends, he had many enemies as well. With more than a slight curiosity, she wondered once again what he had done to elicit such a response from Jacques. To her surprise, she felt a strange reluctance to inquire, for she was beginning to realize it would do little good to question him. This mysterious man had many secrets that he was unwilling to divulge.

"You are almost home," Jacques said softly, a trace of regret in his deep voice as the terrain began to change. The swamp gave way to cultivated fields of what once had been sugarcane.

The scene before her drove all other thoughts from Arielle's mind. Where there should have been tall, waving green plants, there was nothing but devastation. Arpent after arpent was nothing but flattened cane stalks, some even shredded into pieces. The sour smell of sugarcane rotting in the sun permeated the hot, humid air.

"Mon Dieu!" Arielle gasped, leaning forward in the saddle as shock flew through her. The much-needed cane crop was destroyed. Since her father's retreat, the overseer had come to her with the business of the plantation. He had told her they were deeply in debt, but that a good crop would do much to alleviate the situation. She had enjoyed learning about the plantation, for she had always taken more of an interest in it then her

charming but irresponsible brother. Time after time, Faustien Duplantier had tried to interest his son in his legacy, but André had turned a deaf ear, while to her father's displeasure, Arielle had listened eagerly. Girls, he thought, were not intelligent enough to know about business. Ah, she had often thought, if only she were a male, Belle Rivière would have been hers.

"The hurricane has done its work well," Jacques commented in wry tones. "I hope your father was not counting on this crop. It is ruined."

"We were," Arielle replied in a choked voice of dismay. "André . . ." She stopped, feeling disloyal, then continued with a Gallic shrug. "André accrued large debts—gambling debts. My father must pay them so as not to disgrace the family name." Without the cane crop how would they meet all the obligations? Arielle felt a wave of despair sweep over her as she stared at the devastated fields.

Strong fingers gently clasped her forearm, pulling her back from her frightened musings. *"Ma chérie,* are you sure the situation is that desperate?" Jacques asked. "Is there anything I can do?"

"Rid the world of M'sieur Thane Ryder," Arielle responded bitterly. "Since my brother met him, we have been cursed."

Jacques seemed to stiffen at her answer. "We usually bring our own bad luck on ourselves, mademoiselle." There was a sudden chill in his voice as he moved his hand away to grasp the reins once more.

Her mood veered sharply to anger at his words. Who was he to criticize? He didn't even know André. She knew she was being illogical, for Jacques was right, her brother had been his own worst enemy, but she didn't want to hear it from a stranger. Then, as she stared out across the cane fields, her anger dissolved, to be replaced by unease.

53

Turning around, she looked up at Jacques with a shadow of alarm in her pansy-violet eyes. "Please hurry," she begged. "There is something terribly wrong. There are no hands in the fields. Even with this disaster, there should be someone out here clearing the mess away."

There was a curious sense of disquiet in the air. Arielle felt it in her bones. Looking up, she saw an owl asleep in the branch of a live oak. Hastily she made the sign of the cross as she muttered, "A bad omen." A cold, hard knot formed in the pit of her stomach as she remembered Seraphine's warning about seeing owls in the daytime.

"What are you mumbling about?" Jacques queried in disbelief, urging Pegasus down the well-worn path beside the cane field.

"Over there, in the tree." Arielle pointed to the sleeping owl. "To see an owl in the daylight is an omen of tragedy. Something terrible will happen," she assured him, giving a shiver.

"Now where did you hear such nonsense?" he retorted, teasing her.

"Do not jest about such things," Arielle warned, glancing uneasily over her shoulder. "It means bad luck. Seraphine told me so."

"Ah, and who, pray tell, is Seraphine?" he inquired with amused interest.

"Seraphine reared me from the day I was born when my mother died. She was mother's maid from girlhood coming with her from Santo Domingo. There isn't anything she does not know about such things," Arielle recounted, as she stared out at the empty fields. "I learned to read the portents from her."

"Stuff and nonsense," Jacques snorted in disgust, urging the black stallion on under the white-hot sun burning down on them and the decaying stalks of sugar cane.

"Something is very wrong," Arielle muttered, glaring

54

back at him with worried, reproachful eyes. "I can feel it." Her voice faded into the hushed, hot stillness that hovered over the ruined fields of Belle Rivière Plantation.

Chapter Four

Soaring above the emerald lawn, La Belle Rivière Plantation stood majestic in the slanting, burnished shafts of late-afternoon sun. It had been undamaged by the hurricane. The focal point of an alley of twenty-six giant live oaks, the structure built like a Greek temple was a breathtaking sight. A few broken branches lay on the ground, the only testament that the storm had passed this way.

There should have been a sense of calm and tranquility about the grounds, but instead a strange feeling of unease hung in the hot, humid air like an unseen presence. The disquieting atmosphere was quickly communicated to the two riders as the black stallion made his restive way through the vaulted green tunnel of overhanging oak branches draped in garlands of Spanish moss toward the shadowed, cream stucco mansion.

"It is too quiet," Arielle commented softly, narrowing her eyes against the sun, as she glanced about the manicured grounds. "Where is everyone? Moses' staff should be tending to the gardens."

The sultry air was heavy with the perfume from the four hundred rosebushes growing behind the hedge of waxy yuccas that enclosed the garden to the left of the house. Every sense alert, Arielle leaned forward in the

56

saddle looking toward the right to the maze garden, but even there she could see not one slave. She gasped in horror as she lifted her eyes to the second-floor gallery of the graceful house with its enormous columns. Draped across the railing was the traditional Creole black bunting of mourning announcing to all who passed that there had been a recent death at the plantation. The dark muslin blew back and forth in the light breeze from the river like the Spanish moss swaying from the live oaks. Arielle remembered that the Indians had considered the moss a sign of bereavement.

As Jacques urged the horse closer, the silence that loomed like a heavy mist over Belle Rivière was broken by a high, mournful cry that pierced the quiet afternoon. The unearthly sound gained momentum and was joined by others from the direction of the slave quarters behind the big house.

"What the hell is that?" Jacques demanded, grasping the reins tighter and forcing Arielle against his chest as Pegasus, frightened by the noise, reared.

"That is the sound of the slaves mourning. There has been another death at Belle Rivière," Arielle answered, aghast, making the sign of the cross once more with a trembling hand.

From out of the huge, double cypress doors of the house came a graceful, mature mulatto woman dressed in the blue-and-white checked gingham dress of a house servant, a snowy white turban, tied in stiff points, known as a *tignon* on her proud head. As she hurried across the wide gallery, she exclaimed in delight, *"Chérie, you are alive!"*

Alighting from the calmed stallion, Jacques tied the horse to an iron hitching post, then helped Arielle down. She slid from his arms to be clasped in the emotional embrace of the excited woman.

"Seraphine, I am all right," Arielle reassured her, then

57

lifting her golden head, asked quietly, "What has happened? The mourning cloths for André's funeral had been removed. Why is the bunting back on the gallery?"

Sighing, Seraphine wiped the tears from her high-boned cheeks with the corner of her apron. "We were so worried when you didn't return yesterday. The storm was *très dangereux*." The woman shook her head, biting her lip in agitation, for she did not want to answer her mistress's question but knew there was no alternative. She placed her graceful hand on Arielle's shoulder as she gazed at the young woman with melancholy black-velvet eyes and told her, *"Ma petite,* you must be strong. Your father . . . your father is dead."

Arielle heard Jacques' sharp intake of breath as her body stiffened in shock. *"Mon perè est mort,"* she repeated in a low voice in French, stunned by the woman's words. She swayed for a moment, recovering as she felt Jacques' strong arm steady her. His strength flowed into her and, like an anchor in a world gone mad, she clung to him.

"How did this happen?" she managed to whisper through trembling lips.

"The master has not been himself lately as you well know," Seraphine replied softly, her observant eyes noticing the bond between her Arielle and this handsome stranger. "The storm found your father locked in his room, but it seemed strangely to rouse him from his lethargy. Early this morning, when the wind and rain had abated, he rode out with the overseer to check the crop. When they returned an hour later, Miche Faustien went straight to your brother's bedchamber. He locked himself inside . . ." Seraphine paused, taking a deep breath she reached out and, grasping Arielle's hand in hers, said quietly, "He took his life, *ma petite,* with Miche André's dueling pistol."

Arielle shuddered at Seraphine's words. Shocked and sickened by what her father had done, she felt fingers of ice seep into every pore as she stood trembling in the hot afternoon sun. The swell of pain within her was beyond tears, for she understood that her father had given, as usual, no thought to her. He had cared only that he had lost his only son. Faustien Duplantier had left his daughter alone to cope with the mess he and André had made of her life.

Jacques had gone rigid with astonishment as he listened to Seraphine's explanation. *"Mon Dieu,"* he muttered. "The old bastard."

"Come in the house, *chérie,* and bring the m'sieur. There is much to be decided," Seraphine instructed the grief-stricken Arielle guiding her toward the double doors with Jacques following, his expression one of brooding disbelief.

Seated in the elegantly furnished drawing room, with its gilded furniture upholstered in gold damask and marble-topped tables, Arielle introduced Jacques to Seraphine, relating how he had rescued her from the storm. The attractive mulatto woman gazed at him with thoughtful eyes, taking his measure as she heard the story.

"Thank you, m'sieur, for returning *ma petite* to me," Seraphine told him gravely. Looking first at Arielle, then back to the tall, commanding man, who leaned against the marble fireplace as if the delicate room made him uncomfortable, the older woman smiled in something like relief. "Ah, it is good you two have met. It is destined, I can see that quite clear."

Jacques stared at Seraphine, an arched black brow indicating his surprise at her words. "You think it was destined that Mademoiselle Duplantier and I meet at this time?" he asked in a light, mocking tone.

"Oui, m'sieur. Ma petite mam'zelle needs a strong man now that she is alone. The fates have been kind to direct you here now when you are needed, but then, as I have

59

said, you both have been destined for each other. I have the gift to know these things," Seraphine replied with complete confidence, holding her elegant head as proud as a queen.

"Then the fates must have a strange sense of humor," Jacques told both women, shrugging his massive shoulders as his mouth twisted into a wry smile.

"What do you mean, m'sieur?" Seraphine asked, her handsome features puzzled.

"Hush, Seraphine. Captain Temeraire does not believe in fate. Such nonsense," Arielle cried, jumping to her feet, her eyes flashing in anger at both of them as a blush, like a rose shadow, crept over her delicate face. "I need no one. I am certainly capable of taking care of both myself and Belle Rivière."

"She is very courageous, Seraphine, and very stubborn." Jacques spoke to the older woman as if Arielle were not in the room. Although his voice was grave, there was a twinkle of amusement in his ebony-black eyes.

Smiling up at him with comprehension and deep appreciation, Seraphine nodded her *tignon*-clad head. "This is so, Captain Temeraire," she stated. "And that is why she needs a man like yourself to watch over her."

"Have any arrangements been made?" Arielle asked, changing the subject. She was mistress of the house now, and of her life. There was to be no doubt on that subject.

"The men are making the coffin in the quarters, *chérie*," Seraphine said softly, covering Arielle's tightly clenched hands with her own warm touch. "Jubal has gone to New Orleans to fetch M'sieur Boudreaux and post the funeral notices. The other surrounding plantations are being notified at this moment, *ma petite*. Dr. Murat has come and gone. He will take care of the death certificate. Because of the heat, he has suggested the funeral take place on the morrow. Does this meet with your approval?" Seraphine paused, noticing with concern the young woman's pale face and trembling mouth. At Arielle's nod of agreement she continued. "M'sieur Boudreaux will attend to the matters of the funeral service as soon as he arrives."

Arielle nodded once more in comprehension, for funerals in the Creole culture were the concern of men. Women were considered too delicate to view the burial or entombment of a loved one. According to custom, she would attend the mass, but must retire to her bedchamber while her father's friends escorted his body to the family tomb on the other side of the rose garden.

"You have done well, Seraphine. See that the kitchen staff prepares refreshments for the morrow," Arielle told the mulatto housekeeper in cool tones. "We could use some brandy, I think," she continued, flinching as she heard the sound of the hands bringing an awkward object through the back door. She realized with a heavy heart that it was her father's coffin.

Seraphine rose quickly and crossed to the sliding doors that closed off the parlor from the huge central hall. Turning to Jacques, she instructed, "See that she stays here. I will return quickly with the brandy." Her eyes met his with perfect understanding before she closed the heavy doors behind her.

"It seems you will not have to suffer my father's appreciation after all," Arielle said in a choked voice, not meeting his eyes, staring at her hands clenched in her lap.

"*Ma petite belle,* don't do this," Jacques protested, moving to join her on the fragile settee. His tall, muscular form overpowered the spindly piece of furniture and, in spite of her anguish, a smile trembled on Arielle's lips. Leaning toward her, he brushed a tendril of hair from her cheek, his dark eyes gentle and understanding. He covered her hands with his warm protective fingers as

61

his gaze searched her face, reaching into her grief-stricken thoughts. *"Chérie,* life has dealt you a double blow," he told her. "Maybe I can be of some service to you."

"There is nothing, nothing anyone can do," Arielle answered in a flat voice devoid of any emotion but a great weariness. The events of the past few days threatened to overwhelm her. She was fighting with all her willpower to stay out of the deep void of despair that beckoned. Jacques' warmth and ready sympathy were too tempting. The strength that emanated from him was a lure that called out to her in her need. If she gave in to her longing for his comfort, she was afraid she would crawl into those strong waiting arms and never want to leave.

"My godfather, M'sieur Boudreaux, will see to all the funeral details. He was my father's good friend as well as his lawyer. Uncle Jules, as I call him, is competent to see to the family affairs," Arielle said stiffly, her voice cool and aloof as she fought for control. "I am sure he will be most grateful for your kindness to me."

"Jules Boudreaux will arrive soon," Jacques mused, his mouth a taut line, his eyes narrowed, as if he were trying to decide on something.

"Oui, by this evening if he rides from New Orleans, sooner if he catches a boat heading this way," Arielle replied, looking at him through lowered lashes, but he was staring past her, deep in thought. Why did she feel Jacques was not anxious to meet her godfather? His manner had changed from warm sympathy to a wary circumspection, as if he regretted his offer of assistance.

As the silence grew between them, Arielle struggled to hide her confusion. It was as it had always been for her — she had only herself to depend upon. Squaring her shoulders and lifting her delicate chin as if for battle, she moved away from him slightly, her bearing stiff and proud. She needed no one. She would find her own strength from deep within to face whatever fate had in store.

Her withdrawal stirred Jacques from his introspection. "What will you do?" he asked tersely, his brilliantly dark gaze intent on her exquisite profile. "Return to France?"

"Return to France!" Arielle exclaimed, turning her golden, tawny head, her violet eyes meeting his with astonishment. "Why should I go back to France? Belle Rivière is my home. I shall live here and run the plantation."

"*Ma chérie,* you can't run a plantation. While I admire your spirit, it simply wouldn't work. It is no job for a woman," he said softly, a mocking tone in his deep voice. He regarded her with a patronizing expression on his handsome, arrogant visage. "Sell the place. It should fetch a good price, enough to keep you in style till you find a husband." He was shocked to find out how much the thought of Arielle married to another man bothered him. Why did he care what happened to this spoiled little beauty?

"Sell Belle Rivière? Never!" Arielle glared at him with burning reproachful eyes as she spat out the words with contempt. "This house, this land, is mine. I shall work and care for each arpent as long as I have breath left in my body. *Tiens!* There will be no time for the encumbrance of a husband."

Jacques stared at her, a glint of humor sparkling in the depths of his ink-black eyes. Shrugging his shoulders in mock resignation, he sighed. "I see you are a woman with her mind made up. With such determination, how can you fail?" He rose to his feet and gazed down at her, his mouth twisted into a cynical smile. Lifting her limp fingers to his lips, he bowed over her hand. "I leave you, fair lady, with no fear for your future," he murmured.

Arielle jumped to her feet, surprise written across her

heart-shaped face. "You're leaving?"

Dark eyebrows arched mischievously as he gave her a bemused grin. "Does this mean you will miss me?"

"*Non,* of course not," Arielle spat out like an angry kitten. "Leave if you want, it is nothing to me." She waved her hand in dismissal, turning her slender back to him so he could not see the sudden tears that welled up in her eyes.

Strong, warm fingers grasped her shoulders, whirling her around to face him, then pulling her to his chest. Sinewy arms clasped her to him, molding her soft curves to his lean, muscular contours. Holding her tightly against him, his mouth descended to her lips with a demanding urgency. Caressing her moist, waiting mouth with a burning need that he could not deny, Arielle succumbed to the forceful domination of his desire. She wrapped her arms around the corded muscles of his broad back as she relaxed, sinking into the cushioning warmth of his embrace. Abandoning all restraint to the refuge Jacques' embrace offered, Arielle opened the flower of her mouth to his insistent, thrusting probe. As the rose velvet of their tongues touched, she became aflame with the wondrous sensations she had felt only with him. Her blood coursing through her veins like an awakened river drove all sense of time and place from her mind. There were only the two of them and this overwhelming, inextinguishable need. They could no more resist each other than they could turn away from food when hungry or drink when dying of thirst. But, oh, she must try to fight this attraction — she dared not call it love — for to acknowledge such a truth would leave her vulnerable to him. But how, even when she knew she must, could she turn away?

As his hand caressed the hollow of her spine, she felt the hardness of his manhood press against her soft thigh. Now, her mind thundered, she must stop now, before it was impossible to stop the fiery river of desire and need that flowed between them. Terrified of her own hunger for this man who was a stranger in every way but of the heart, Arielle found the strength to tear her lips from his, but not to leave his arms. Burying her face in the curve of his shoulder, she trembled like a trapped wild animal.

"*Non,* please help me. This is not right. Not now, not at this time." Her muffled whisper stabbed through him and smote his heart. With most women he would have continued his skilled seduction, having realized she was ripe for him. A few more kisses, the right caresses, and this innocent girl would be his next conquest. Taking her would be the final revenge on a man he despised over all others. Even now that his enemy lay dead in this house, the hate was strong. Was that why his feelings for this golden beauty struck him as all the more remarkable? She was *his* daughter, a Duplantier.

In the waters of the Caribbean he was known as a man without mercy, cold and ruthless. But with this slight girl in his arms, his heart had softened, as well as his brain, he thought with chagrin. Holding her to his chest, his lips in her hair, he tried to master the strange, conflicting emotions she invoked within him.

The deep thudding of his heart echoed through Arielle as she felt the tension in his lean body. He was fighting for control, as was she, over the all-consuming passion that threatened to overpower them. Then, as constraint won, his chest rose in a deep, shattering breath and his hold loosened.

Suddenly the warmth surrounding her was gone, and Jacques was thrusting her from him. He stared at her, his face a mask of stone. Only his burning coal-black eyes showed the passion that raged beneath the controlled facade.

"If you should ever need help from me, place a red

flag on the post at the landing on the river. Lafitte's men check from time to time. They will contact me. If you are in New Orleans, leave word at Lafitte's house on Rue Bourbon that you need me." Jacques' voice was rough with emotion as his fathomless gaze captured hers and bore into her soul. *"Adieu, ma belle blonde.* We shall meet again."

With a few lithe strides he was out the French doors and gone from her. Arielle, her legs trembling, sank to the settee. She felt as if she were awakening from some strange dream. A sense of desolation swept over her as she sat alone in the room, awash now with the burnished light of the setting sun.

What lay ahead for her? Arielle's pale face clouded with pain as she thought of the uncertainty of her future. She was alone, completely alone, responsible for her own life. The idea was both frightening and somehow exhilarating. Would Jacques be part of her destiny? She had to admit unwillingly that she wanted to see him again. When she was with him she felt every nerve tuned to its highest peak. The very blood in her veins pulsated with a passion she didn't know she was capable of experiencing. It was terrifying, it was wonderful . . .

Shaking her head at her foolishness, she rose to her feet and crossed to the long French doors that opened out to the gallery. Jacques Temeraire was a smuggler, a pirate. Their lives didn't revolve in the same circles. It was unlikely that they would ever meet again, and that was for the best. She had spoken the truth when she said there would be little time for a man in her life. Looking out across the verdant lawn as the dying rays of the sun fell in long streaks of gold through the emerald leaves of the gnarled branches of the stalwart oaks, Arielle knew that here was her destiny — Belle Rivière. Whatever she had to do, whatever she had to give up, she would, for this was her land and she meant to keep it.

Life for her was now a solitary road. The realization that she was completely alone, an orphan, without parent or kin, washed over her in a tidal wave of grief and desolation. She had to admit some of her sorrow at her father's death was a poignant regret for the love that might have existed between her and her father but never had — and now never would.

Swallowing the sob that rose in her throat, she stared out through eyes filled with tears at the giant oaks that stood so strong and unyielding. Their roots went deep in the soil of Belle Rivière, as did her own. Like the enduring oaks she would find her subsistence, her reason for living, in the beloved land of her plantation. The land was all she needed. It would be enough, she told herself as she fought hard against the tears she refused to let fall.

She could live without love, without a man. They all proved false in the end. *Trust only in yourself,* she resolved with bitter determination, but try as she might to banish them from her mind, Jacques' parting words echoed through every fiber of her being. They would meet again, he had said. Though hating her weakness, Arielle couldn't stop her heart from hoping he foretold the future.

Chapter Five

The soft night air, heavy with the fragrance of sweet olive, blew through the open French door of the library. Seraphine moved with quiet grace through the chamber, lighting the tall ivory tapers on the rosewood tables.

"That will be all for now, Seraphine," Arielle told the dignified woman as she entered the room, "You may go." Her black handkerchief-linen gown, clasped high under full breasts with a back ribbon, lent a sober note to the luxurious chamber decorated in shades of rose and gold.

"Are you sure I should not stay, Mam'zelle Arielle?" the maid inquired, obviously reluctant to leave.

"Quite. Please see that Uncle Jules' bedchamber is in order," Arielle answered firmly, a trace of a smile on her wan, tired visage. "Bébé and Samantha can stay in here with me. Leave them be, Seraphine. She gestured for the huge dog of indeterminate origin and the tiny, agile black cat to come sit at her feet. The dignified maid sighed as the two animals scurried to their mistress's side. With an expressive shrug of her shoulders, she glided from the room, but left the door slightly ajar.

"These two are new, are they not, *ma chère?*" inquired the distinguished-looking older man who had accompanied her from the dining room. His dark coloring, pale skin, and black, lustrous eyes showed him to be a true Creole, those descendants of the first Spanish and French founders of Louisiana. Full of the delicious dinner he had just eaten, he sank down gratefully across from his hostess on one of the two matching rose silk settees.

"I brought them home with me from France," she said, "but Father would not allow them in the house. They are not pure-bred animals, you see, so of course he would have nothing to do with them. Now . . . now that he is gone and I am mistress of Belle Rivière, they can be with me all the time," Arielle's voice became firm and defiant as she stroked the dog's shaggy head. The tiny cat quickly settled down on her lap and the sound of her contented purring filled the quiet room.

"Oui, of course, if that is what you wish." Jules nodded, suddenly lost for words, a condition he didn't usually find himself in. "They seem quite fine animals. Ladies do like their pets," he beamed, happy he had found an explanation for Arielle's rather rebellious statement. She always had been a rather strange girl, far too independent for a proper Creole lady. It really wasn't her fault, he mused, for her father had never taken an interest in her. André had been the only child that mattered to Faustien. It had been an obsession with him and he had completely ruined the boy. Look what a tragedy it had all come to, Jules thought with a sad shake of his head.

"Would you care for a brandy, Uncle Jules?" Arielle asked with a wry smile as the butler, Jubal, entered the library carrying a silver tray with a decanter and one glass. Creole ladies would never drink strong brandy if they were ladies, and Jubal had not even considered she would care for a brandy.

"You have held up amazingly well under trying circumstances, *ma chère.* Faustien would have been proud, most proud indeed," her guest complimented her as he accepted a pear-shaped crystal goblet containing the rich amber liquid from Jubal.

"My father disliked displays of excessive emotion, especially from women," Arielle commented dryly as she waved Jubal away. "I would like to thank you, Uncle Jules, for arranging that the true facts of my . . . my father's death did not become public knowledge. His friends all seemed to accept the story that his gun misfired while he was cleaning it. Your quick thinking allowed my father to have a priest bury him with the full rights of the church as he would have wanted. I am in your debt," she continued softly, her voice catching on the words several times.

The last few days had been a great strain, but now that the funeral was over and the guests departed, Arielle was determined to discuss Belle Rivière's future with her godfather. Jules Boudreaux had been her father's friend as well as his lawyer. He knew what condition her father's finances had been in and where she would stand now that he was gone. If André had been alive he would have inherited the plantation, but now it was hers as Faustien Duplantier's only heir. Uncle Jules would object to her plan of running it, as had Jacques. She would just have to convince him of her seriousness, for she would not be deterred.

"It was nothing, *ma petite.* I am only glad I could help my old friend and his daughter. You are very dear to your aunt Lala and me." Her godfather sighed, then took a long drink of his brandy.

Arielle had known this kindly man all her life and realized something more than her father's death was weighing heavily on his mind. "Fevers can be so dangerous at this time of year. Is Tante Lala better?" Arielle inquired, thinking it was concern for his wife, who was recuperating in New Orleans, that caused the furrow in

70

his brow and the heavy sighs.

"She is better, quite on the mend, though still weak as a kitten. Lala was devastated not to be able to accompany me. To us, you are the daughter we never had." Jules' eyes held great sadness. The devoted couple, to their great disappointment, were childless. Then, as if a weight had been lifted, he straightened his shoulders. The frown gone. Why had he not thought of it before? It was the perfect solution. *"Ma petite,* she wants you to come live with us now that my dear friend Faustien is gone. Ah, how happy Lala will be to have you to fuss over." The man spoke with obvious relief as he gazed expectantly at his godchild.

So this was what was troubling him, what to do with her. *"Mais non, cher* Uncle Jules. Thank you, but I plan to stay here at Belle Rivière. Later, when I come to New Orleans for the *saisons des vistes,* Tante Lala and I can have a long talk and do some shopping."

Sighing deeply once more, Jules Boudreaux drained the last of the brandy from his glass, then placed it on the graceful table between them. Reaching across the polished wood, he took Arielle's small hand in his own. *"Pauvre petite,* how else can I tell you but quick to the point. You cannot stay at Belle Rivière, for it must be sold, along with everything your father owned, to meet, God rest his soul, your brother's debts." His voice was low and filled with pain as he observed Arielle's violet-gray eyes widen with astonishment and disbelief. "André signed many letters of intent to cover his gambling losses. Your father, as a point of honor in André's name, agreed to pay each and every one. I am sad to say Faustien had to mortgage Belle Rivière. He was counting on a bountiful harvest to help him make the payments on the plantation. But *ma chère,* as you know, the cane crop has been destroyed. There is no money left, everything including the house, land, and furnishings

71

must be sold to pay the loans that will now be called in upon his death."

"Surely there is some other way?" Arielle asked with a cry of despair. She couldn't lose Belle Rivière. It was hers, each beloved inch. When she had been in France, the memory of every verdant arpent, the elegant perfection of the house, the view of the river from the gallery had been an escape from the cold, Spartan life of the convent school. Louisiana had seemed a warm, luxuriant paradise always beckoning to her to return. On those long winter nights in France, Belle Rivière had become the living embodiment of lush, fertile Louisiana to Arielle.

"Ah, *ma petite,* if only there was some other answer." Jules shook his head in despair, his black eyes pools of regret. "The knowledge of what lay ahead was what drove your poor father over the brink, *ma chère.* He could not bear to see his life's work given to a stranger, a man he detested."

"A stranger? You mean one individual holds my father's mortgage? I thought he borrowed the money to pay André's notes from a bank," Arielle stated in amazement, shaken by this twist.

"Oui. M'sieur Thane Ryder holds the mortgage on Belle Rivière. Most of André's gambling notes were also to this man, who, in the end, killed him on the field of honor. Your father could not raise the money from a bank, *ma chère,* for he had run out of credit months before. M'sieur Ryder was not the first man André owed money to, for your father had been paying off his gambling debts for several years. It was like a sickness with your brother."

"But did my father never try to stop him? If he had refused to pay his vouchers, André would have had to quit. Everyone in New Orleans would know he was not good for the notes, so no one would have allowed him in their game," Arielle protested, feeling a helpless anger at her father grow within her. How could he have let this go on? The man who had been so strict with her had indulged her brother beyond belief.

"Your father had a blind spot when it came to his son. He always believed André when he said he would stop if he just helped him this one last time. The concept of honor was everything to Faustien. He could not have allowed his son to be considered a man without honor by New Orleans society."

"I cannot allow the man who killed André to have Belle Rivière," Arielle sputtered, glaring at Jules with burning, reproachful eyes. "What manner of man is this Thane Ryder to take the home of the father of the man he killed?"

"A strange, reclusive man, I think. He is not well known in New Orleans, for he does not frequent society, although he could afford to. It is said he is quite wealthy and is seen at many of the coffee houses and gambling halls, though always alone. He has invited speculation and rumors since he arrived in New Orleans about a year ago. Some say he is a compatriot of Lafitte and sails with that infamous bunch when so inclined, others that he is a British lord, in New Orleans to spy for his country. Ah, who knows what is true about such a man?" Jules gave a Gallic shrug.

"You have met this M'sieur Ryder, Uncle Jules?"

"Only the one time, *ma chère*. It was at night in a private room at Maspero's Exchange. He insisted that your father and I come there to sign the notes of mortgage instead of my office as I had suggested. Never have I met a colder, more arrogant man. He seemed to enjoy your father's discomfort and humiliation. I really don't think you could call him a gentleman," Jules explained, trying to stifle a yawn.

"Then the papers are legal? There is no loophole anywhere that we could use?" Arielle asked, her eyes narrowed in concentration. Somehow she would defeat this man who had ruined her life.

"*Non*, I wish there was something I could do, but your father signed them against my advice. They were drawn up by another lawyer, *ma chère*. M'sieur Ryder did not trust me to prepare them," Jules said with a sniff of dislike. "It was all quite legal and binding, I assure you. I have gone over them several times looking for just such an avenue of escape. Unfortunately none exists. But you must put this from your mind, *ma petite*. I will handle all the distressing details; you needn't think of it again. Think of your future in New Orleans with Lala and me. She will be so happy to see you. How she will plot and plan helping you find a husband. You'll see, 't will all work out." Jules' voice became soothing, as if he spoke to a child, as he squeezed her hand.

"Who would marry me without a dowry, Uncle Jules?" Arielle answered bitterly. Marriages between Creoles were arranged by families to further their fortunes. There was no objection to a young man marrying for money; in fact, it was expected. Love between the couple was to come later, after several years of marriage and children. Few penniless girls made good matches. The dowry was everything. Perhaps an old widower would consider her as a mother to his children, but that was the best she could hope for.

"You are not entirely without funds, *petite* Arielle. There is your mother's former shop on Rue Royal. Your father kept it in her name out of sentiment. It was not part of the deal with M'sieur Ryder. The shop now belongs to you, although the income from the rent is not large. A quadroon runs it as a millinery shop, but she wishes to join her son who is living in France. She will vacate at the end of the month and we could sell it outright. The money will provide you with a small dowry.

You will not go to your husband without a *sou*," Jules reassured her with a smile.

"My mother had a shop? I knew nothing of its existence," Arielle said quietly as her mind raced with the new possibilities.

"When your dear mother came to New Orleans from Santo Domingo after her family was killed in a slave uprising, she was alone except for Seraphine, her maid. With a small amount of money—all she had—she bought a small building on Rue Royal. She opened a perfume shop in the front and lived in the rear with Seraphine. It was in that shop that Faustien first saw Celeste Laronde and fell in love with her. After their marriage, your father wanted to sell the building, but your mother always refused. It meant a great deal to her, for it was all she had, she said, that was her own. I always thought that an odd thing to say when you consider she was mistress of one of the largest plantations in Louisiana. But we must be thankful for the little charming quirks you women have, for now it is yours as a dowry."

"Oh, *maman*, how I understand you," Arielle whispered, wiping a tear from her cheek. "Uncle Jules, I agree with my mother. The shop is not to be sold," she stated firmly as ideas began to take shape. This was an answer to her predicament.

"But, *ma chère*, why not? What could you want with such a shop? The rent, as I told you, is not that much. If you will forgive my observation, the profits would hardly keep you in dress money."

"It is not the rent money I want, Uncle Jules. It is the building. I shall turn it into the finest perfume shop in New Orleans," Arielle announced to her uncle's shocked dismay, with steely determination.

"If you will forgive the obvious, *ma petite*, you know nothing about running any type of shop," her godfather admonished her, a look of weary disbelief on his distinguished features. What had this child thought of now? he wondered, feeling an overwhelming fatigue. It would be good when they returned to New Orleans and Lala could take care of this stubborn young woman.

"I shall help her, Miche Boudreaux, for I do know much about running a shop and creating original perfumes. As I assisted Madame Celeste, so shall I now instruct her daughter," Seraphine interrupted from the doorway where she stood holding a tray of iced petit fours. Gliding into the room with her grace, she placed the ornate silver tray on the table between them. "As you know, *m'sieur,* I am a *femme de couleur libre* and have been such since birth. Nothing holds me to Belle Rivière. I shall take care of *ma chère* Arielle as I promised her *maman* on her deathbed." The mulatto woman's voice was haughty, firm, and allowed no argument.

Drat the woman! Jules thought with surprise and dislike. Did she know everything that happened on the plantation? He was almost inclined to believe the stories about her being a priestess of the Voodoo cult. She seemed aware of anything that pertained to her "child" even before it happened. The woman was as protective of Arielle as she had been of Celeste. Faustien had claimed the mulatto maid had never liked him, but Celeste had adored her, and on her death, Seraphine had taken care of the twins with such devotion that he had allowed her, though with some reluctance, to stay.

"Seraphine, thank you!" Arielle exclaimed, with fervor, her eyes bright with hope for the first time.

"Your devotion is admirable, Seraphine, but there is a blockade. How do you expect to order any merchandise with which to stock this shop?" Jules inquired dryly, with something like triumph in his gaze as he reclined back against the settee, his arms crossed in front of him.

"Like the rest of New Orleans, Uncle Jules, we will deal with Lafitte," Arielle replied in vexation, a gleam of stubborn intent in her wood-violet eyes. Suddenly she had been given a way to be independent. She was determined to take it. All of South Louisiana knew that for a price, one could obtain almost anything from the smugglers of Grand Terre.

"What we cannot obtain from Lafitte, we can create. Miche Ryder may own the plants of Belle Rivière, but I shall harvest the blossoms and herbs tomorrow. From this harvest I shall create the perfumes and sachets the ladies of New Orleans shall purchase from us." Seraphine flashed the contemptuous man a look of disdain.

"*Oui*, Seraphine, you are right. Even in France, the girls at my school wanted to know what scent I used. They all wanted a bottle. They could not believe you created it for me here in Louisiana."

"Even if you are determined to go through with this mad idea, you must still come live with your aunt Lala and me. The quarters above, and in the rear of the shop, may be in bad condition. They are certainly not what you are used to. The Duplantier townhouse, I am sorry to say, has been pledged to M'sieur Ryder as well. I believe he plans on selling it. You needn't fear—our home is your home." Jules Boudreaux spoke with an indulgent tone that implied, when Arielle came to her senses and gave up her foolishness, she would still have a place to live.

Arielle could see behind her uncle's honeyed words of concern. He didn't believe she would succeed. Once she gave up and was living with them, she could be persuaded into a marriage, mayhap with an old widower so hungry for young flesh he would overlook her small dowry. Never, never, would she submit to such an arrangement. Her father had taken his own life with little regard to the mess he had left behind for her to deal with. Men! She was through being at the mercy of their whims. Control of her own destiny was within her reach, and she was going to grasp the opportunity. Neither her father, André, Uncle Jules, nor Thane Ryder was going to destroy her or bend her to their will!

"We will take your kind offer of a visit, Uncle Jules, until Seraphine and I can make the quarters livable. We will not intrude on your hospitality any longer than necessary." Arielle's voice was uncompromising as she gave him a stiff, cool smile.

"If you are determined to be one of the *chacas,* I shall save my breath. It will be difficult, *ma chère* Arielle. Have you thought of the reaction of the friends of your family?" Jules questioned, playing what he considered his last card.

A wry smile crossed Arielle's delicate mouth as she listened to his warning. She knew that the Creoles of New Orleans looked down upon those of their kind who were forced into trade and called them *chacas,* a derisive term.

"Oui, Uncle, I have given thought to the reaction of my 'friends.' How they will flock to see my downfall. The chance to see me in such a position should bring in many wealthy customers," Arielle replied with a bitter cynicism, meeting Jules' startled gaze with a look in her violet-gray eyes that was old beyond her years.

"Do not let life make you cold, *ma chère.* That is an unbecoming trait in a young woman," he cautioned, rising to his feet. "Now, I would like another brandy and then a walk before retiring. You have given me much to mull over, but I promise to help you in whatever way I can." Crossing to stand beside her, he gently patted her delicate shoulder. "You have your mother's strength and courage, Arielle. Oh that your brother had inherited her fine qualities as well. Celeste would be proud of you . . ." His voice broke on the name of the woman he had loved from the moment Faustien Duplantier had introduced her as his fiancée. He had been happy with Lala, but there had never been the great love between them that he had felt for the beautiful Celeste.

Watching Jules Boudreaux lurch out the front door to the veranda with a double brandy in his glass, Arielle experienced a momentary panic. Was she doing the right thing? She knew nothing about running a shop. Biting her lip, she looked out over the immaculate lawn where the silvery moonlight, streaming through cracks in the canopy of the giant oaks, cast long shadows across the grass.

How could she relinquish Belle Rivière and its people? It was as if she considered leaving a part of her own body or soul behind. She didn't have any other choice, she reminded herself, but to depart. The land, the house, the slaves — all belonged to her enemy Thane Ryder. She could only hope he would be a fair master to the people of Belle Rivière, some of whom had been born on the plantation. Their faces, young and old, passed before her, and tears filled her eyes. It was not the first time that she had questioned the concept of slavery, but she had learned to keep such thoughts to herself in Louisiana. To cast any doubt on an institution that was vital to the Creole economy would be to invite strong censure — or worse. Her father had laughed at her protest that not all masters were benevolent after she had heard stories of whippings and unbelievably cruel treatment of slaves on a neighboring plantation.

"Such a female concern you have, my daughter," Faustien Duplantier had joshed her with mild derision. "Do not worry about such things. It is for the men in your family to handle such matters."

Remembering her father's words, she walked to the open French door, breathing deeply of the mingled scents of rose and sweet olive, Bébé at her side, Samantha close behind. She experienced an anger growing strong and indomitable deep within her being. Because

79

of her father and her brother, she was to lose her heritage to a man she had never met.

As the warm, soft night swirled around Arielle, the anger that threatened to overwhelm her focused on one faceless man. All her bitterness and despair fused in a hatred that took root in her very soul. What he had done to her family became a personal sense of injustice. He must be made to pay, she vowed. Both the loathing for this man she had yet to meet and her need for revenge would become her strength. Somehow she would survive in New Orleans on her own and find a way to avenge the Duplantier name.

Jacques' words, promising her help if she should need him, came back to her like a whisper on the breeze from the river. She could almost hear his deep, reassuring voice. She would leave word at Lafitte's blacksmith shop that she wished to contact him. With his help, she could obtain supplies from the privateer's storehouses on Grand Terre. Once her shop was a reality, she would find a way to seek her revenge on the enemy of the Duplantier family. Somehow she would destroy M'sieur Thane Ryder.

Chapter Six

"Look, mam'zelle, Nouvelles Orléans!" Seraphine's husky, melodious voice rose above the sharp flapping of the sails. Her mouth curving in a slight smile, she pointed to the spires of Saint Louis Cathedral that rose above the rooftops of the city as their schooner rounded a bend in the ocher-brown waters of the Mississippi River.

"It is quite a sight," Arielle agreed. She leaned against the rail of the sleek boat that Jules Boudreaux had arranged for, to take them from Belle Rivière, before he left for New Orleans. Looking down from the deck as the schooner edged closer to the dock, she saw the riverfront teeming with idle sailors, ships at anchor, unemployed roustabouts, all stranded by the British blockade of the gulf. The late-afternoon sun turned the spires of the cathedral gold as they slipped into one of the few vacant moorings at the wharf.

Staring down at the busy scene below, Arielle's heart pounded as she spied the dark, familiar figure of a tall and powerful man. Her eyes froze on that long, lean form that moved with a lithe grace as he strode down the wharf with a commanding, arrogant air. Unable to see the man's face, she still knew without a doubt that it was Jacques. She could never forget those broad shoulders, that firm strength that radiated from his sinewy form. Even from this distance and in a crowd of other men, his presence was compelling. Try as she might, she couldn't stop the warm glow that flowed through her at the knowledge that Jacques Temeraire was not far away. Maybe they would meet by accident on one of the busy streets, at the French market, or in one of the numerous shops in the city. Arielle's mouth unthinkingly curved into a smile as she indulged in her daydreams while watching the tall, masculine figure vanish into the crowd.

"Come, mam'zelle, Miche Boudreaux is signaling for us to join him." Seraphine took Arielle's arm, steering her to where Jules stood waiting impatiently at the bottom of the gangplank.

Arielle's godfather, unable to wait, hurried up to meet them. "The bags will be brought later. We best hurry, for Lala will be waiting with her special cakes and some good strong coffee." The older man urged Arielle down the uneven plank with Seraphine close behind leading a huge, ungainly black-and-white dog by a leash.

"Watch Bébé, Seraphine — all the noise may frighten her," Arielle called over her shoulder as she tried to keep her footing.

"Really, *ma chère*, calling that monster dog Bébé is ridiculous. That animal would certainly be happier in the country than in New Orleans," Jules grumbled.

"M'sieur Ryder may have Belle Rivière and her people, my townhouse, my furniture, even my horses, but he will *not* have my dog or my cat," Arielle stated with vehemence as a loud meow issued from the covered basket she carried. "Bébé and Samantha came with me from France, and they will stay with me."

Jules shook his head in resignation. He hadn't realized how headstrong Arielle was, or how determined. Lala would have to take over, for he had little experience dealing with stubborn young women.

Somehow, all of them, including cat and dog, were ensconced in the roomy Boudreaux carriage. Once all were inside, Jules give one rap on the ceiling with his silver-headed cane to signal the coachman, and they were off.

Arielle leaned forward on the seat of the roomy barouche. She didn't want to miss any of the sights of the languorous city that lay sprawled in the mud between river, swamp, and lake. Breathing deeply of the warm, damp air, fragrant with the aroma of roasting coffee and pungent spices so beloved in Creole cooking, she thought no other city was quite so unique as New Orleans, not even Paris.

The carriage rambled on through the narrow lanes that oozed mud from an afternoon's shower. They passed a stately woman, the color of coffee with cream, on one of the second-floor galleries of an elegant townhouse. She carried a wooden bucket, her head swathed in the white *tignon* that each woman of color, whether slave or free, was required by law to wear. In several swift motions, she doused the wooden floor, washing away the dirt from the street. The sound of her voice, singing a lilting French tune, floated down to Arielle.

Turning a corner onto Rue Chartes, they pulled through a porte cochere, the tunnel-like corridor so often used in New Orleans dwellings, that led to a secluded courtyard barely glimpsed from the street. Arielle heard squeals of delight and the clatter of footsteps as Lala Boudreaux hurried across the flagstones.

Flinging open the door before the coachman could disembark from the box, Lala greeted her husband as he stepped from the carriage. "She's here, my pet, safe and sound," he reassured the short, plump woman, patting her rounded shoulder before helping Arielle to the ground.

"*Oui*, Tante Lala, 'tis I," Arielle smiled as the emotional woman broke into tears of joy. Arielle was smothered with kisses and hugs, and then led into the fragrant serenity of the Boudreaux courtyard with Seraphine and Bébé bringing up the rear.

"*Mon enfante*, you are now at your new home with your Aunt Lala. We have our daughter with us as you promised, Jules." The little woman's eyes were filled once again with tears of joy as she clung to Arielle's arm with the same tenacity as the jasmine vine that entwined the iron filigree of the gallery. "How can I tell you of my sadness upon hearing of *cher* Faustien's death. What a burden *le bon Dieu* has sent you, *ma pauvre petite*. But now you are here with me, and I shall take such good care of you till the day you go to your husband's house. What fun it will be to plan your wedding, *ma chère* Arielle." Lala chattered on, as she led her goddaughter into the cool, luxurious townhouse.

Managing a slight smile tinged with exasperation, Arielle allowed Lala Boudreaux to guide her into an overdecorated *petite salon* crowded with elaborately gilded furniture, tables draped in layers of silk and lace, and walls crowded with portraits of dead members of the Boudreaux family. She loved Tante Lala, but already Arielle was beginning to feel suffocated by the woman's cloying manner and overembellished home.

"Put the tray here," Lala Boudreaux commanded to an elderly butler. He carried in a heavy silver tray containing an ornate coffee service with tiered plates, also of silver, laden with numerous cakes, pastries, and pralines, those beloved pecan candies of New Orleans.

"Café blanc ou noir?" she questioned — coffee white or black — as she poured the hot, fragrant liquid into egg-shell-thin cups.

"White, tante," Arielle replied, leaning back against the too-soft cushions. While she was staying at the Boudreaux townhouse, she would have to yield to La-la's smothering concern, but she was now all the more determined her stay would be brief. Although a good, caring person, her godmother would never allow her to live her life the way she wanted. Lala Boudreaux was a pillar of Creole society and deeply believed in all its tenets.

"I am so distressed to tell you that we will not be dining *en famille* this evening, *chérie.* We accepted an invitation weeks ago to dinner with the Claibornes," Lala fluttered, a frown creasing her round, lily-white forehead. "Sophronie is such a dear friend, and her husband, the governor, is in a most distressing position with this accursed American war. I feel she does need my support. It isn't easy for her, being a Creole married to an American, even if he *is* the governor of Louisiana. Sophronie, of course, would be delighted to have you come along, but I know since you are in first mourning, it would not be quite right," the plump little woman concluded, her gray ringlets dancing about her face as she pondered Arielle's situation from behind a second cup of highly sugared coffee.

"Oui, tante, it would not be correct for me to attend even a small dinner party so soon," Arielle agreed in solemn tones, inwardly sighing in relief at her chance for an evening of peace.

What will she think when she discovers this oh so proper Creole lady will be opening a business while still in first mourning? Arielle wondered with a tinge of rebellious glee. Her uncle must not have informed his wife of their

85

goddaughter's plans or he was sure Arielle would change her mind. They would both be surprised at how determined she was to lead her own life.

"Claiborne is kept quite busy with this Lafitte business." Jules interrupted her musings, sipping a glass of absinthe with relish. "The fellow brought it on himself, offering a five-hundred-dollar reward for the capture of the Bos of Barataria. While the man may be a pirate and a smuggler, he has such style that much of New Orleans admires his daring. Lafitte made Claiborne look like a fool issuing his own proclamation offering fifteen hundred dollars in gold to the first man to deliver the governor to Grand Terre." Jules chuckled over the dashing exploits of the pirate boss who was patronized by persons of every rank and protected by wealthy businessmen, lawyers, and legislators. Without the Baratarians, the flood of "black ivory"—smuggled slaves—would stop, as well as the many luxury items desired by indulged Creole wives and mistresses.

"Sophronie told me the governor is worried Lafitte's men will join with the British," Lala confided helping herself to another chocolate eclair.

"Ah well, that would be a problem for the Americans," Jules agreed with a Gallic shrug, as if the war didn't affect the Creoles of New Orleans at all.

Listening to the words of her host and hostess, Arielle thought of Jacques Temeraire. He had not really been out of her mind since the day he walked out of her life. His handsome, arrogant face would float before her at the oddest times, and she would wonder where he was and what he was doing. Remembering the man she had seen on the wharf, she wondered if her eyes had been playing tricks on her. Or was it her heart? Had it really been the mysterious stranger from the swamps or only a figment of her imagination? His

86

last words to her were burned into her mind and had become part of her plan for her survival in New Orleans. She would leave word at Lafitte's house on Rue Bourbon that she wished to contact the man known as Captain Jacques Temeraire about buying goods for a shop. His name would be the password she needed to make contact with the smugglers.

Arielle's mind was racing as she realized she would be alone in the house tonight except for the servants, and that this might be the only opportunity for days to leave word at Lafitte's house. Once Lala was not occupied with social obligations, the full force of her attention would be centered on Arielle. It had to be tonight.

"Ma petite, you will never guess who has been asking after you?" Lala waited expectantly for Arielle's reaction.

"Who would that be, tante?" Arielle replied, a playful smile curving her generous mouth.

"M'sieur Carlos de Galvez," her godmother announced, setting her cup down on the delicate table with a clatter. "Such a handsome older man, Arielle — and so wealthy," she enthused. "He saw you at your debut at the opera house and was much impressed with your beauty. A widower for several years, I do believe he is looking for a wife. What a good catch he would be."

A wave of revulsion swept over Arielle at Lala's words and her broad hints at a match between herself and the man known throughout Louisiana for his evil disposition. It was rumored his wife had committed suicide because of his cruelty. André had told her all about Carlos de Galvez. Her godmother, while known to have a good heart, was naive and often believed what she wanted, instead of what was true. The sooner she moved to Rue Royal, the better, Arielle decided, feeling once more an overwhelming sense of suffocation as she put down her cup only half drunk. Her appetite was suddenly gone.

She could never be independent in this house, for her tante Lala would fight her every step of the way. The weak and clinging could be tyrants when they wanted their own way, Arielle had observed, and she knew Lala Boudreaux was of this ilk.

"Tante Lala, please excuse me. I fear I am weary from the trip and the events of the last week," Arielle sighed, trying her best to look overcome with fatigue.

"Mai oui, ma chère, you must rest. Paulette will show you to your chamber." Lala was all solicitation as she rang for her maid. "A good sleep, a tray in your room, and you will feel much refreshed."

"A quiet night is just what I need," Arielle murmured, giving a polite yawn behind her hand. Her heart was pounding as she thought of her real intent for the evening.

The moon was a silver crescent low in the night velvet sky when the sound of the voices of Arielle's godparents drifted up to her from the courtyard as they prepared to leave for their dinner party. Time was passing as she sat wool-gathering over her dinner tray. Giving a slight shake of her honey-gold tresses, she rose to her feet, realizing she, too, should be leaving soon. She didn't want to be out on the New Orleans streets late at night, and wasn't sure how long her errand would take, as she would be walking.

"Come, Seraphine, I must dress. Something plain and inconspicuous, I think, with a light cloak and hood," Arielle called to her maid who was turning down the counterpane.

"You are not accompanying the Boudreaux, Mam'zelle Arielle? They are just leaving," Seraphine murmured in surprise.

"*Non,* of course not. This may be my only chance till we move to contact Lafitte, and I intend to use it. There is merchandise we need, Seraphine, if we want to open in time for the *saison des visites.* I shall go to his house on Rue Bourbon tonight and leave word that I wish to do business with him. Captain Temeraire informed me that is how it is done by the merchants of New Orleans."

"*Bien.* I will accompany you; I can tell your mind is made up." Seraphine's tone was firm, and the expression on her haughty features was implacable.

"Not tonight. I need you to stay here in my room and allow no one in. Tante Lala would be horrified if she knew of my sojourn. If anyone comes to the door, you must tell them I am asleep and must not be disturbed."

"It is not seemly for a young woman of quality to be alone on the streets of New Orleans at night. I will not hear of it, for it is *très dangereux* as you well know. *Non,* I shall deliver the message, mam'zelle," Seraphine replied, folding her arms across her chest, her black eyes intent and determined as she stood in front of the armoire, not lifting a finger to help Arielle dress.

"Seraphine . . ." Arielle sighed in frustration, "even if I write you a pass, it is more dangerous for a person of color to be out on the street after curfew."

"You forget, *ma petite,* that I am a *femme de couleur libre*—a free woman. The curfew does not apply to me, only to slaves."

"*Oui,* I understand." Arielle nodded in exasperation. "But you do not have your papers with you. They are in the deposit box at the bank with the rest of father's legal documents. Women of color are often not believed by men who wish to take advantage of someone who has little redress. *Non*, Seraphine, I must go alone."

"Do not be foolish. You need some sort of escort or you, too, could be taken for a woman of the streets," her maid protested, moving to stand in front of the French door as if to physically detain her if need be.

Frustrated, Arielle bit her lower lip, for she knew that look of Seraphine's. She had seen it enough as a child! Suddenly her gaze fell upon Bébé enjoying a ham bone she had been given as part of her dinner. "I will take Bébé on her leash. No one would bother me with a large dog in tow, for women of the town do not solicit business in such a manner. It will appear I am only a rather foolish young lady walking her dog."

"She is not exactly what I had in mind as an escort, mam'zelle, but she *is* some protection," Seraphine conceded, her mouth forming a ghost of a smile as she regarded the large shaggy dog that was almost the size of a small pony.

"*Bien*, then it is decided," Arielle rushed on before Seraphine could change her mind. "Help me dress."

Once she donned a black muslin mourning gown, severely styled with a high waist, Seraphine dressed her honey-gold tresses in a chignon high at the back of her head. In the humidity, wisps of hair soon pulled loose from the severe style to curl about her face and neck. Leaving off all jewelry except for simple black pearl studs in her ears, Arielle slipped on flat-heeled black boots and a mantle of dull black silk with a hood that came down low over her face.

Fastening the leash about Bébé's neck, Arielle waited in the shadows of the gallery as Seraphine checked to make sure the courtyard was empty. At her maid's signal that it was clear, she started quietly for the stairs.

"Go with God, *ma petite*. I shall be waiting," Seraphine whispered as Arielle urged Bébé down the curved iron staircase that led to the patio.

Reaching the courtyard, Arielle's breath seem to solidify in her throat as she heard voices coming from the lower gallery. Darting into the shadow of a huge sweet olive bush, she prayed Bébé would keep quiet. Placing her hand on the dog's muzzle, she watched as the Boudreaux butler and Paulette crossed the courtyard in front of her. They were walking toward the slave quarters located in a building in the rear of the garden over the kitchen house. Waiting a few minutes till all was silent, Arielle led Bébé quickly across the flagstones, through the shadowy porte cochere, opened the latch on the filigreed iron gate, and slipped out onto Rue Chartes.

The wooden banquette, consisting of simple planks, was rough under her boots but deserted of people, for which she was thankful. Although the street was dark, she could make out a pool of dim light coming from one of the oil lamps that hung from chains at each corner in the city. Arielle was grateful for the slight protection the small island of light gave her, but the blocks seemed long and dark between corners. Every sense seemed to vibrate as she hurried down Rue Chartes, keeping close to the buildings that lined the narrow street.

With a sigh of relief, she quickly reached the heart of the city, the Place d'Armes. The large square faced the river and was bordered on two sides by fashionable shops. Majestic Saint Louis Cathedral stood flanked by the Cabildo, the seat of government, and the Presbyter, on the right, was to the back. In the center of the square was a park where lovers often strolled among

91

the jasmine bushes and blooming orange trees.

Here, in front of the cathedral, Arielle found more people hurrying toward their engagements for the evening. As she approached the square she pulled her hood even lower, keeping close to the walls of the shops that lined the streets. As the bell in the church tower rang out the hour of nine, the cannon boomed on the levee signaling the curfew hour when all slaves had to be off the street unless they had a permit.

Bébé growled low in her throat at the din of noise, and Arielle stopped to stroke the dog, reassuring her. Aware of attracting the attention of a man who stood lighting a thin cheroot under the glow of a lamp by the cathedral, she quickly straightened and urged the animal on down the street.

Crossing Royal Street, she hurried on, keeping to the shadows toward Rue Bourbon and Lafitte's house. Passing one of the numerous coffee houses that the Creoles of New Orleans loved, she heard singing and masculine laughter. These cafés were where the young blades congregated in the afternoon and evening to imbibe drinks much stronger than coffee. Gambling was a favorite pastime in the so-called "coffee" houses, and Arielle wondered if this had been one of André's haunts. Shuddering slightly as she passed by, she wasn't aware of a man striding into the raucous café until she crashed into him. Spinning around, her mantle caught in Bébé's leash, she would have fallen if strong hands hadn't gripped her arms, holding her up.

"Forgive me, mademoiselle." A deep familiar voice broke through the confusion that over came her. "Please reassure that animal—" He spoke with a tinge of humor which turned to disbelief as her hood fell back to her shoulders revealing the delicate oval of her face in the light from the café. *Ma belle blonde!*

"Jacques! *Grace à Dieu* but I am thankful it is you," Arielle breathed in relief, leaning against him for a moment as she tried to steady her erratic pulse. The remembered faint scent of sandalwood and tobacco clung to his black-waisted tailcoat and immaculate white waistcoat.

In his elegant evening dress he was even more handsome than she had remembered. A slender ebony sword cane was held in one powerful hand, the long, tapered fingers gripping the silver knob with a careless grace. Here was another side of this mysterious man, for he looked as comfortable in the costume of an aristocratic gentleman as he had as a man of the swamps.

"Why are you in New Orleans?" Arielle murmured, as she tried to gather the tattered remnants of her composure about her once more. His mere presence was disturbing, for his intense gaze seemed to reach out and touch something deep within her. The emotion he invoked frightened her. She wanted to look away from those burning ebony eyes that glowed in the light from the streetlamp, but she was unable. He seemed to hold her to him by invisible bonds that she couldn't break.

"I might ask you the same question, mademoiselle. Have you tired of plantation life so soon?" he questioned as one black brow, dark as a raven's wing, rose a fraction. As the light from the suddenly opened door of the café streamed across his arrogant features, it highlighted the unusual scar that arched from one heavy brow to bronzed temple, giving him a diabolical look.

"*Non, m'sieur,* I have no choice but to be in New Orleans. Belle Rivière has been taken from me," Arielle countered in icy tones, drawing back from the protection of his arm, for his words had nettled her sorely. "Everything is gone." She heard the bitterness in her voice.

"Surely not everything, Mademoiselle Duplantier?" he asked with a tone of mocking disbelief, but she noticed he didn't seemed surprised by her words.

"Non, not *everything.* That devil didn't steal everything of mine," Arielle confirmed tersely, her eyes flashing, her chin lifted high as each lush curve of her body spoke defiance. Leaning toward him, she implored, "But I need your help, or Lafitte's—"

A burst of harsh, drunken laughter came from the café as several well-dressed but drunken young Creole dandies swayed out the door to stand arguing on the banquette. Turning her back to the boisterous young blades, Arielle drew the deep hood of her mantle back over her honey-gold tresses and down lower so that it obscured her identity.

"Come, this is not a place where you should be seen, and that animal is hardly inconspicuous," Jacques stated sharply, taking her arm. Half pulling her, Bébé in tow, he started down the wooden planks toward Rue Bourbon. His long fingers dug into her arm as he strode along with lithe grace, his long legs moving easily over the rough banquette. Arielle, however, had difficulty keeping up with him, and even Bébé seemed to sense the urgency in the tall man walking beside her mistress.

"Where are you taking me?" Arielle inquired with irritation as she tried to pull her arm from his grip while holding on to the dog's leash tightly. Jacques Temeraire was as domineering as she remembered, and anger surged through her veins at his treatment. He acted as if she were some half-wit child unable to be responsible for her own actions. Such had been her father's attitude toward her. How could she have thought she was attracted to this overbearing, tyrannical man?

"To an establishment I keep for my infrequent visits

94

to New Orleans," he replied in a voice that boded no dissension, not slacking his stride.

"I have changed my mind, m'sieur," Arielle told him, her teeth clenched as she spat out the words. "Lafitte is the man I feel I should deal with in my situation. Please release me so I may continue on my way."

"Pray spare me your demands you little fool. Do you think Lafitte or his brothers would be in New Orleans now that Claiborne has put a price on their heads? If you desire help from the men of Barataria, then it will have to be me you deal with, mademoiselle," Jacques responded, not looking at her, but continuing his pace as he half dragged her past Rue Bourbon and on through the dark, silent streets of the city.

Arielle lost track of the streets as they turned several corners, and she could not even read the signs in the dark. She knew that they had left the shops and cafés behind as the shuttered windows and locked gates of private townhouses lined either side of the quiet, narrow road they traversed. Their boots echoed on the wooden banquette, the only sound in the still night.

Fatigue came over Arielle as they continued on, the pace not slacking. She thought she would drop. It became like a nightmare, this silent walk on and on through the darkened city. The heat was oppressive, her layers of clothing adding to her discomfort. Feeling the dampness of her skin under her dress, she knew that she could not walk much farther without danger of collapsing.

"Please . . . I must stop," she implored, stumbling on the uneven planks. He caught her from falling as Bébé whirled around, entangling them in her leash.

"We are almost there," Jacques said softly, loosening his grip. "There, boy, it's all right," he murmured to Bébé, straightening the leash and reassuring the animal.

"He is a she," Arielle replied wearily.

"With all that hair I really couldn't tell." There was dry humor in his voice as Jacques regarded Bébé looking up at him with trusting eyes from under a shaggy mop of fur. "If you ladies are rested, maybe we could continue. Our destination is only a few steps away."

True to his word, they walked a short way and then turned into a shadowy porte cochere lit by a flickering oil lantern high on the brick wall. The building was dark, with the same shuttered air as the houses they had passed. Taking a key from his pocket, Jacques slipped it into the lock of the ornate iron gate. The barrier, higher than a man's head, creaked open, and they stepped into a moonlit courtyard filled with the heavy perfume of the sweet olive bush so common to New Orleans.

"Where is this place?" Arielle inquired of the man who stood so close to her. "Why are you in New Orleans if it is dangerous for the men of Grand Terre?"

"So many questions, mademoiselle. If you will follow me, you might find some answers." He moved away from her, motioning her to follow him up a spiral iron staircase that led to a second-floor gallery.

After Jacques unlocked a French door, he led Arielle and Bébé into a darkened room that, as he lit an ornate oil lamp, turned out to be lavishly furnished. Before she could get more than a quick glance at the gilded furniture and the fine paintings on the walls of the high-ceilinged chamber, strong hands closed around her forearms, pulling her hard against a lean, masculine body.

A soft gasp escaped her as she twisted in his arms, arching her body trying to get free of the embrace she had thought of all those long nights she had tossed and

96

turned in her lonely bed. Memories of those dark eyes, those burning lips, the pleasure his strong, caressing hands could elicit had almost driven her mad in her solitude, but she had fought her desire then and she would fight it now. He was a weakness for her, a weakness such as some people had for wine, and just as dangerous. If she did not guard against him, it would be too easy to drown in his passion till she had no will left.

Feeling her struggle almost drove Jacques to lose all control and take this woman, who had become an obsession haunting him day and night, here on the floor like a wild animal claiming its mate. The touch of her, the scent of her perfume, filled him with a hunger he had never known.

He had come to New Orleans to try to rout her from his mind, but it had not worked. Every golden-haired woman had reminded him of her; even the heavy scent of the sweet olive that filled the courtyards of the city had recalled her perfume. Cursing himself for a fool, he had gone out tonight to attend to some unfinished business and then to drink in one of the gambling halls until the early-morning light in the vain hope that her image would dim a bit in his mind. He had tried his usual remedy — Maura's, the finest brothel in New Orleans, but the girls had all seemed suddenly vulgar and coarse. To Maura's amusement, he had spent the evening in her office discussing the success of her business and playing cards to the wee hours. He had not, however, been able to forget that beautiful, aristocratic face, those smoke-violet eyes that a man could drown in, that peach-ivory body that was made for a man's touch. Fate had stepped in and played another trick upon him. She had been thrust into his arms once more, and, by God, this time he wasn't walking away until he had his fill of her!

He tightened his hold on her deliberately, pinning her arms behind her back as she struggled more frantically. It was as if she sensed his thoughts. Her cloak had fallen back in the struggle so that only the muslin of her gown and sheer chemise underneath separated her soft body from his hard, sinewy one. Slowly he pressed her against the long length of him, feeling the nipples of her ivory breasts taut with her growing arousal. In a sensuous movement, almost as if he were leading her in a dance to some unheard music, he swayed her back and forth against his body. Skin burned against skin through the fabric of their clothing as smoldering ebony eyes stared down into violet, startled gaze, holding her with an effect that was total and devastating.

Arielle drew a long, shuddering breath as she reveled in the feel of that hard, strong, masculine form, teasing her until she was a flame. She hungered for him, for all of him, in a way she barely understood. Was this what the girls at school had giggled and guessed at? They had not known about the glory, the joy of the wanting between a woman and a man that was almost pain. They had not known that the need for joining one with the other could be so strong, so overwhelming that nothing else mattered. Swaying with him in complete harmony, Arielle knew that she should resist, but her will was ebbing away as the vast pull of his passion kindled her own deep hunger for the complete knowledge of fulfillment.

"This is not why I came," she whispered, her mouth trembling as she stared up at those fathomless black eyes that seemed to see into her soul.

Jacques' voice was a hoarse rasp of desire. "Why did you come, *ma belle blonde,* if not for this?"

Chapter Seven

There was a waiting stillness all about them in the empty house. Arielle would find no one to come to her aid no matter how much she protested. They were alone with only the sound of their quicken breath and beating hearts to break the silence.

"This is madness. I know nothing about you," Arielle murmured, unable to tear herself from his arms as she knew she should.

"What do we need to know about each other but that there is this between us, *chèrie,*" he whispered, his voice deep and full of sensual promise as his lips brushed hers, at first teasing, then insistent. His strong arms wrapped around her, caressing each sensitive nerve of her spine with knowing fingertips.

Close . . . he was holding her so close. She was surrounded by the scent of sandalwood, tobacco, and his masculine aura that she had come to associate with only Jacques. Arielle felt mesmerized by his presence and his touch, unable to deny him as his mouth brought a throbbing heat to her own. Shyly, she returned his kiss, savoring the taste of him, the glorious gentle assault he made teasing apart her trembling lips to explore her sweet, moist inner surface. She felt those strong arms encircling her, his hands stroking her spine

99

until each nerve sang with the pleasure of his caress. Weakness flowed down her legs, which were locked against his muscular thighs. Emotions warred within Arielle as she clenched her fists tightly at her sides. *Don't touch him,* she willed herself as every instinct cried out for her to cling to his warmth, to explore that lean, sinewy masculine form.

As his tongue slowly circled hers, coaxing with infinite patience the response he sought, her body betrayed her resolve. She swayed closer to him, no longer fighting the overwhelming need. Her hands reached up, tentatively at first, to stroke the rich material of his evening coat, seeking the heat of his body underneath.

"Ah, yes," he breathed in excitement, lifting his lips for a moment, only to return with light, butterfly kisses that feather-touched her temples, the curve of her cheek, the corner of her mouth, with a teasing persuasion that drove her mad with desire. Fire flowed through her veins. The anticipation of an ecstasy she could only guess at grew in the hidden woman's core at the apex of her thighs. Flowing outward through her being, the urgency of her hunger was both shocking and frightening.

"You . . . shouldn't do this. I . . . should stop you," Arielle sighed as her hands touched the dark satin of his hair that curled at the strong column of his neck. The feel was pure sensual delight as his hands moved down her spine to caress the rounded fullness of her bottom pressing her against his aroused manhood.

"And this, *chérie*, should I stop this?" he questioned, her moans of desire filling his heart with the sweetest music. His tongue traced the shell-like contour of her ear, darting inside and out with a tantalizing persistence as his hips moved against hers in a dance as old as time.

In the dim recesses of her mind, she knew he was

playing her, evoking responses from her body with the mastery of an accomplished artist, but somehow it didn't matter. There was a beguiling lassitude seeping through her limbs, making the mere act of standing up a monumental effort.

"No . . . don't stop," she gasped. Fire seemed to consume her, causing her to spread the palms of her hands over his shoulders, kneading, caressing, the sinewy muscles. Wanton, she was acting the wanton, she thought as she realized she wanted to touch his bare, heated skin and to feel his unclothed length against her own.

The hunger, the need, was all consuming as she pressed so close, her hips now moving in an uncontrollable, primitive frenzy she had never known she was capable of. Filled with the molten flow of desire, a wild cry was torn from her throat as she approached the pinnacle of passion.

Suddenly they were torn apart by the force of a large object trying to push between them as, with a low growl, Bébé came to the aid of what she perceived was her mistress in distress. The cry of ecstasy had sounded like a cry of pain to the dog, and with all the loyalty of her species, she tried to stand between her mistress and danger.

As the full force of the large dog struck Jacques, he lifted his head, his hair gleaming like ebony satin in the wavering light of the oil lamp. Black-smoke eyes glittered for a moment as the shadow of a smile touched the mouth that had caused her lips to burn like fire. "It seems you are well guarded, Mademoiselle Duplantier. Did you train her to do that?" he asked, an arched brow indicating his humorous surprise. Releasing her, he reached down to reassure Bébé with a pat to the head that he would not harm her mistress.

"It seems my dog has more sense than I do," Arielle

said in a choked voice, stepping back from Jacques and fighting to control the swirling emotions that raged within her. Bébé quickly moved between her mistress and the man she sensed to be dangerous. "A business matter is all I wish to discuss. You must understand there will be nothing else. I should leave now if you do not agree."

"Business it is. Does this canine chaperon bite?" Jacques questioned, his mouth twitching with amusement as, completely unruffled, he strode to an ornate sideboard. "I could use a drink. Would you care for a brandy?" He held up a fine crystal decanter filled with amber liquid.

Struggling to regain her composure, Arielle inclined her head in the affirmative. "Bébé only bites those she thinks are trying to hurt me."

"Bébé! That animal is named Baby?" Jacques shook his head in amused disbelief, the deep, rich sound of his laughter filling the room.

"She has a very affectionate nature," Arielle said stiffly, flashing him a look of disdain.

"I can see that," he replied, his voice solemn, but there was a twinkle in the depths of his dark eyes as he handed her a delicate, crystal globe.

"Merci," she muttered, and even to her ears, her tone sounded ungracious. How could he act like nothing had happened when her world had been turned upside down by his touch, his kiss? It was good Bébé had intervened, she told herself, knowing down deep within, she still hungered for the completion of their lovemaking. She felt shame at her need, and was determined Jacques would not know how she felt. With a pang of humiliation, she realized he probably treated every woman he had even the mildest interest in with the same practiced lovemaking. It was a game to many men, she thought with a growing sense of anger and

despair. Hadn't her own brother André been a skilled player of the sport?

"My pleasure," he replied formally to her, but the words suddenly had a second mocking meaning. Bending down to gently rub behind Bébé's shaggy ears, he asked, "What can I do for you, girl?" Arielle watched in amazement as the dog rolled over on her back, allowing Jacques to stroke her belly until the animal was lolling in ecstasy.

"I find this hard to believe," she said slowly, shaking her honey-gold tresses. "Bébé usually doesn't like strangers, especially men. I found her on the street in Paris, starving and frightened. She had been abused. I have never seen her react that way with anyone. She seems to have decided to trust you."

"If only her mistress were as easily convinced," Jacques told her in a gentle tone, his handsome visage displaying an uncanny awareness of what her thoughts and feelings were toward him.

"I trust no man, m'sieur," Arielle said softly, looking beyond him into the shadowy room. "Men have not shown me that they are to be trusted."

"Please sit down. I am being a poor host. You must be tired," he told her not without kindness, but strangely distant, as if they had just met. Taking his glass from the table where he had placed it, he sat down on a settee facing her. "Surely there has been some man you have trusted in your young life, *chérie?*"

His intense gaze fastened on the delicate heart-shaped face, searching for the key to this unusual woman who drew him to her like a magnet. This woman who somehow managed to touch his heart in spite of his best intentions that it be otherwise. He found he wanted to know all about her—what made her happy, what made her sad. It amazed him, for he had never cared what any of his woman thought about.

Once the lust was satisfied, they were forgotten. With this Creole beauty, daughter of a man he despised, he felt a strange contradiction. He wanted more than one brief night of satisfaction of the flesh. He realized, with shock and dismay, that he wanted her to desire him with all the intensity he sensed she was capable of feeling. *Fool,* he thought bitterly. *You are a fool.*

"*Non,*" she whispered, staring down at her glass.

"Your father, your twin brother André, certainly you trusted them?" he insisted, his hand clenching the delicate glass of brandy so tightly, his knuckles turned white.

"Especially not those two," Arielle replied in a choked, bitter voice, continuing to stare into the amber brandy. "I loved them, but . . . they let me down."

Recognition flashed across Jacques' firm yet expressive features. For a brief moment, he experienced an urge to pull her onto his lap and cradle her in his arms like a forlorn, hurting child. *Remember, she is Faustien Duplantier's daughter,* he reminded himself with caution. *The Duplantier blood flows in her veins, and their arrogance as well. Her fortune may be gone, but she will never lose that aristocratic pride.* Against his will he felt a grudging respect for the slender, beautiful woman who sat across from him. What it must be costing her to come to him for help of any kind.

"You did say you wanted my help." His words were cool, indicating only a polite interest as he seemed to withdraw further from her, back into a remote stranger.

Arielle nodded, slipping the hot, suffocating mantle from her shoulders. His intense gaze never wavering from her face was disconcerting, and to her annoyance she felt a moisture on her upper lip. He was making her nervous with his cool, aloof manner that seemed to judge her, and find her wanting. A spark of anger grew within her, and she debated for a moment whether or not to leave. The reality of her situation, however, forced her to throttle her fury, her humiliation, and stay. She needed goods for her shop, and he was her only link to Lafitte's storehouses on Grand Terre.

"Although, upon my father's death, my home, my legacy, was stolen from me by my brother's murderer, I was not left completely penniless." Her voice was low, controlled, but the anger was there just beneath the surface. "I still have a small inheritance from my mother, a shop that M'sieur Ryder cannot touch. It is located on Rue Royal and is now a millinery. When the current occupant leaves, Seraphine and I intend to open a perfume shop. We can make some of the fragrances ourselves, but there will always be ladies who want only perfumes from Paris. The other merchandise will have to be imported as well, and the only way I can do this with the British blockade is through Lafitte. Everyone in New Orleans knows it is possible to obtain 'imported goods,' shall we say, through the Baratarians."

That dark, unfathomable gaze did not waver as he said with a tinge of disbelief in his deep voice, "You plan to open a shop?"

"*Oui*. You sound like my godfather, Uncle Jules. I intend, m'sieur, to make it a success. I want no arranged marriage to an elderly widower who is, if you will excuse my being so bold, so hungry for young flesh he will overlook the meager dowry." Arielle's amethyst eyes flashed with a pride that showed she would bow to no man.

How much he admired her at this moment. She had nothing — only an old building and her determination to build a future — but she would not beg. Jacques realized that the only Duplantier with courage was this beautiful, fragile-appearing woman who he found he

105

desired above all else.

His hands ached to touch her once more, to pull that seductive figure, not even hidden in the plain black dress of mourning, to his own body, which was throbbing with a hunger he had never known in such intensity. Jacques had not been able to forget her, though he had tried. That delicate face haunted his days and nights. Here she sat before him, alone, totally alone, but not beaten. Admiration warred within him with his need to keep her from his mind, his heart, his life. He would take her now, no matter her protests, if he thought it would satisfy him once and for all. But a strange, dawning realization told him it would not be the end of her fascination for him, but rather an obsessive beginning that would never leave him free of her.

"There will be an auction at the Temple in one month. If you are serious, I will arrange for you to attend. Do you have the capital for such purchases? We do not sell on credit, *ma belle blonde*." His tone was challenging, mocking, as his ebony eyes consumed her.

Bemused, Arielle lowered her gaze in confusion, momentarily chagrined by his question. How stupid! She chastised herself for forgetting such an obvious point of business. There was little cash in her meager bank account, but there was her mother's amethyst-and-diamond necklace with its matching earrings. Uncle Jules had bought them from her father's estate, and had graciously presented them to her. Her father had promised them to her on her wedding day, she remembered with a bitter sorrow.

"I have the money. Not a great deal, but enough. If I must go to the Temple to bid on merchandise, then I shall indeed wish to attend the auction." Her voice was firm. She lifted her violet-smoke eyes, blazing with determination, to boldly meet his gaze, which was fastened on her with something like respect.

106

"You are not frightened of the journey to the Temple? It is only a mound in the swamps and quite a trip from New Orleans," Jacques cautioned, as if testing her.

"M'sieur, you forget I was born at Belle Rivière and am quite familiar with the terrain around the plantation. Everyone on the river, in this part of Louisiana, knows of the Temple. My father frequented it often. He was fond of his French brandy, but disliked paying the American tax," Arielle replied dryly, rising to her feet with fluid grace. "There is no time to be frightened, for I have no other choice, do I?"

"It would appear you do not," he agreed, his mouth curved in a half smile that raised her ire once more. The man was infuriating! He seemed to derive amusement from her predicament.

"When and where shall we meet?" she asked, keeping her voice as cold as possible. This pirate might find her situation humorous, but he would pay for this humiliation. If he thought she would allow him any more liberties, he was wrong. It was galling enough to have to ask for his help. He had derived such pleasure from seeing how far this seduction would take him. Arielle felt a shudder of shame, for she knew if Bébé hadn't interfered, bringing her to her senses, she would have been lost, and he would have been the victor in his game of love. She had acted like a foolish, schoolgirl, but never, she vowed, never would he catch her so innocent and trusting again. When they had first met, she had taken him for a gentleman, although she knew he was a privateer, a compatriot of Jean Lafitte. She would not make that mistake again, for he was clearly a rogue who fancied himself a ladies' man, Arielle reflected with scorn and bitterness.

"A message will be delivered to you giving instructions on where to meet our contact. There will be little warning. You must be ready at a moment's notice," Jacques instructed her tersely. "No one must know where you are going. Claiborne's men are on the alert, as are the British."

"You can depend on my discretion, m'sieur. I shall await your message. Although I am currently staying at the Boudreaux townhouse, I plan to move as soon as possible to my property on Rue Royal."

"Do not concern yourself. We will find you when the need arises," Jacques assured Arielle, his manner firm and confident. "There is little that goes on in New Orleans that we do not know about."

"That is true, I am sure, m'sieur," Arielle answered with pained tolerance. The idea of being spied upon was disconcerting at best.

"Pray, call me Jacques. M'sieur sounds so formal. We do, I believe, know one another well enough to dispense with such terms." His voice was warm and intimate and the smile in his eyes contained a sensuous flame that reached out to touch her everywhere. He, however, did not step closer, for he would not force his attentions on her again, no matter how deep his need for their next encounter, she would come to him willingly, wanting him with a hunger as deep as his own. He would bide his time, gain her trust till she came to him of her own volition. Only then, on those terms, would his victory be complete.

"The time is late . . . Jacques," Arielle whispered, a wistful smile upon her face, delicate as a budding rose. Eyes, dewy as wood violets after a storm, reached across the room and clung to him a brief moment, before thick, black lashes lowered to conceal the need she couldn't vanquish. "I must return before my godparents."

"If you insist."

"*Oui*, I do," she replied, her voice soft but firm, giving a sharp tug on Bébé's leash to awaken the animal from her sleep. The dog awoke with great reluctance after several more proddings from her mistress.

"That's quite a watchdog you have there," Jacques commented dryly, rising to his feet. Amusement flickered once more across his handsome, arrogant visage. "Allow me to accompany you to the Boudreaux house. I will awaken the groom and have him see to the carriage. The streets really are not safe at this hour. Look who you ran into! The next man might not let you go as easily." His laugh was low and throaty as she flashed him a look of disdain.

Jacques Temeraire was an infuriating man, but an exciting one, Arielle admitted reluctantly as he disappeared out the French doors to summon the groom. Bébé whimpered, looking up at her mistress as their host left the room. Did the man have this effect on all females, or just foolish ones like Bébé and her mistress? Arielle wondered.

She soothed the animal, stroking her pet's rough fur. "Hush, we don't have room for a man like him in our life, Bébé. Jacques Temeraire is a wanderer, a privateer, and, *mon Dieu,* who knows what else. He does not fit into our plan. We will forget him after he has served his purpose." Her voice was hard, determined, but she wondered, in a moment of honesty if it was Bébé she was trying to convince or her own heart?

Chapter Eight

"*Romonez la cheminée,*" sang the chimney sweep as he carried his sooty broom, his melodious song drifting up on the still-warm November air through Arielle's bed-chamber window. The sounds of a New Orleans morning gently awakened her from the netherworld of slumber. Slowly she sat up in the bed, with its lavender silk canopy, and yawned, brushing the honey-gold tresses from her face.

Crossing the Oriental carpet of muted rose, violet, and gray to an enormous armoire, she smiled with contentment. Since moving to the apartment over her shop, the days had been full, filled with the excitement of realizing her plans for her new life.

Opening the heavy doors of the armoire, she took down a rose-and-white-striped hat box from the top shelf. Checking to make sure the silver-mesh reticule was still under the plumed and flower-trimmed bonnet, she breathed a sigh of relief. This had become a ritual each morning, for inside the dainty reticule were gold pieces, gold intended for Lafitte's auction at the Temple.

Arielle's face clouded with concern as, biting her lower lip, she placed the hatbox back on the shelf. Turning to the many gowns hanging on satin hangers, she selected a simple dark-blue linen dress in the Empire style waist, long giglot sleeves trimmed in crocheted ivory lace, and a lace ruffle around the high neck. Worry continued to nag in the corners of her mind as she realized it had been almost a month to the day since she had seen Jacques on that strange night. There had been no message, no sign, that she would be taken to the Temple, although rumors of an auction were circulating throughout New Orleans.

"Mam'zelle Arielle, are you determined to leave off mourning?" Seraphine's disapproving tones caused Arielle to turn from her worried musings.

"Don't speak of this Seraphine. We have been over it before. I will wear only somber colors of half mourning, but the total black of deep mourning would be totally wrong for waiting on customers. It would give the wrong atmosphere. André . . . Papa," there was a catch in her throat, "did not like me to wear black. André said it reminded him of an old crow. He said I was sunshine and light, like spring, and that is how I think he would want me to dress. He had such an eye for fashion. No matter what the occasion, all of New Orleans waited to see his entrance and his costume. The next day the tailors would be bombarded with requests for a coat, or caveat, like André Duplantier wore the night before."

"La, that one cared only for his person. If he had used more common sense, we would not be in such circumstances as this, *ma petite.*" Seraphine sniffed, for she had seen André without the blinders of love.

"*Tiens!* You try my patience this morning, Seraphine. I wish to hear no more about my choice of dress."

"*Oui,* but you will become a scandal. People in this town can count, and they know you should still be in

111

first mourning," the older woman stated, getting in the last word as she set the breakfast tray she was carrying down on a small, gilded rosewood table.

"I already am, Seraphine," Arielle sighed in frustration. "Think of all the customers my scandalous demeanor will bring into the shop," she added with a mischievous grin. "Everyone will want to see and disapprove with their own eyes. Once they are here we must intrigue them with our merchandise so they will return. In some cases we will only get one chance, so I have been trying to think of something unusual, exotic, we could supply besides perfume. What do you think of this?" Arielle opened a drawer in an ornate bombé chest and pulled out several wispy, sheer chemises dripping lace.

"What are they, mam'zelle? I wondered when I unpacked them from your trunk when you came home from Paris."

"They are chemises, the latest fashion from Paris," Arielle answered with triumph, observing her maid's shocked expression.

"But they are so sheer, one could see right through them," Seraphine protested.

"Exactly. Why, in Paris, Seraphine, fashionable women wear only a sheer chemise under a silk gown. Their maid wets the chemise down in a manner called sprinkles so the material of their gowns cling to every curve. It is all the rage."

"Creole ladies would never wear such a fashion," Seraphine sniffed in distaste. "And all their lingerie is sewn in the convent by the nuns."

"Think how fashionable they would feel if they wore one of these wispy chemises under their proper dresses. They would feel so Parisian, but still remain oh so correct. And their husbands, they would look at their

112

wives with new interest," Arielle enthused, her eyes sparkling as she sat down before the breakfast tray. "The husbands may even stay home nights instead of seeking company at the Quadroon balls."

"You should not know of such things," Seraphine continued, disapproval in every word. "The only customers you will have for such garments will be the *femmes de joie,* and a shadow wife or two."

Arielle smiled as she buttered a croissant. She knew Seraphine was referring to the Quadroon women known as *placées* who were kept by white men in small houses on Rue Rampart. These ladies were often known as shadow wives, for their lovers often had a legitimate white family as well. "I will welcome anyone's business, Seraphine."

"Sacrebleu! but you are stubborn. How will you order these garments from Paris? The British blockade of the gulf is said to be complete," Seraphine countered as she laid Arielle's lingerie and stockings on the counterpane of the bed.

"I will buy the material from Lafitte and we will make them up. We can hire a seamstress or two later. The perfume, sachets, and gloves will bring them in the first time, but the lingerie will bring them back."

"If only your brother had had such a head for business, and your father your courage," she said almost in a whisper, smiling at her mistress with respect and love.

"We need those materials, Seraphine. I wish I would hear from Captain Temeraire. The rumors tell of an auction to be held within the week."

Staring down at Arielle as she finished her breakfast, Seraphine warned, "It is said to be *très dangereux* to deal with Lafitte at this time. Governor Claiborne's men are watching all roads out of New Orleans. He is afraid the

113

boss of Barataria is working for the British."

"*Pouf!*" Arielle shook her heavy honey-gold tresses in dismissal. "I am not some old, skittish Creole lady who is afraid of her own shadow. When you lose everything, there is little left to fear. Come, we have no time for old ladies' gossip."

Seraphine gave an elegant shrug of defeat. She knew it did no good to try to stop Arielle once her mind was made up. The daughter was so like her mother. How often she and her dear Celeste had plotted, and planned in this very bedchamber when they first had arrived from Santo Domingo. Celeste Laronde had made a success of her small shop, and Seraphine sensed her daughter would do the same.

With Arielle dressed, the two women made their way down the outside, winding iron staircase to the inner courtyard, Bébé trailing at their heels. Like many of the dwellings in New Orleans, the front rooms of the first floor were used as a shop. These rooms opened onto a private walled patio. Above were living quarters for the family, and to the rear, smaller chambers with wooden galleries at right angles to the main ones. It was above here that Seraphine had her room, and below was her studio as well as the kitchen house. It was in the brick-walled studio that she and Arielle created the colognes, perfumed bath oils, sachets, potpourri, and herb infusions that they would sell in the small shop in front.

"It is good that Josephine Hilaire cared for flowers; she left the garden in excellent condition. Some of your mother's roses and sweet olive bushes are blooming profusely. I harvest a few of the blooms each morning," Seraphine commented to Arielle as the two women paused to admire the small garden around the edge of the flagstone patio. The air was filled with the pervasive perfume of jasmine from the tangled vines creeping over the brick walls. Fragrant flowers, and more herbs, edged the walls and small, meticulous flowerbeds. Every use had been made of the confined space to create a beautiful and useful garden.

A soft meow startled Arielle as she followed Seraphine to the studio at the rear of the courtyard. "Samantha, is that you?" she called, as a small, black, triangular face peered from behind a clump of lavender. Blue almond-shaped eyes blinked back at her.

"That one is finally settling in," Seraphine chuckled. "The garden has become her home. She would never leave her basket at the Boudreaux house."

"Samantha knows when she has found her home," Arielle murmured, stroking the small, graceful cat's ebony silk fur.

"To have a sleek black cat in the house signifies that you have warded off bad luck. She will bring good fortune," Seraphine prophesied, permitting a small smile at the graceful feline's antics as she chased a tiny bug across the flagstones.

"Pray that it is so, Seraphine," Arielle muttered, as she entered the fragrant studio.

The walls of the room, from floor to ceiling, were lined with shelves crowded with glass bottles. Some of the jars were large and full of dried flower blossoms and herbs, while others were small and empty waiting to be filled with the perfumes and oils created by Seraphine and Arielle. Tightly stoppered jars of oil stood next to baskets of harvested herbs tied in bouquets from Belle Rivière.

Arielle breathed deeply of the mingled scents, for they brought back happy memories of her childhood when she had helped Seraphine in the still room at the plantation. "Did you leave any flowers for M'sieur Ryder?" she queried with a grin.

"The plants are still there. They will bloom again," Seraphine answered with a shrug, taking down her mortar and pestle of white marble. Pouring harvested blooms of tiny yellow jasmine flowers into the marble bowl, she crushed them with the pestle. Her slender, golden-brown hands worked with a sure, strong grace.

"Indeed they will," Arielle agreed, her violet-smoke eyes sparkling. She thought of the faceless man she considered her enemy viewing his gardens stripped of every single blossom. Pulling a long white apron over her dress, she put M'sieur Ryder from her mind. She had work to do and should not let any distractions interfere.

They had given names to all their creations. Each scent could be purchased in the form of cologne, perfume, sachets, oil for the bath, and soap. There was Celeste's own, for Arielle had named her shop in honor of her mother. The perfume created for Arielle, by Seraphine, was not used, for she wished to keep it hers alone. They had, however, altered the formula, and this had been named Belle Rivière. They had made up lines of pure one-flower scents such as rose and gardenia as well.

"Seraphine, what if we advertise that we would create a one-of-a-kind perfume, and a complete fragrance wardrobe for any lady who desired such a service. It would cost a great deal, thus assuring the customers it was quite the fashion." Arielle's voice lifted with excitement. "Would such an undertaking be possible?"

"*Oui,* but we would have to caution it would take time, and if it did not please them, the formula would be destroyed. We would have to keep accurate records of each creation so we could duplicate it when needed."

"What a draw to the shop it would be. La, we would

become quite the fashion. Shall we make our first personal perfume for Tante Lala? It would be a lovely surprise for her, and she will tell all her friends." Excitement and determination spurred Arielle on as she reached for herbs and jars of dried flower blossoms. What did Lala's personality bring to mind, she mused? Pulling her mother's worn herbal book down from the shelf, she ran her finger down the faded French words listing the meaning behind each flower and herb.

The sun was high overhead when Arielle suggested they stop for luncheon. With only the two of them to see to all the work, they kept a pot of gumbo bubbling on the hearth in the huge fireplace for their noon and evening meal. Jules Boudreaux had insisted upon depositing a small amount of money in Arielle's bank account to cover household expenses till they opened for business. Wanting to draw on the money as little as possible, they ate simple foods to keep their expenses down.

"It will be hot as Hades in the kitchen house. Let us dine in the courtyard," Arielle told Seraphine as she left the studio.

The patio was cool and shaded as Arielle walked across the smooth flagstones. Hearing the mail bell on the door of the shop, she went to answer it, not wanting to call Seraphine from the kitchen house.

A small black boy of about ten stood holding an envelope sealed with red wax. "Mam'zelle Duplantier?" he asked.

"*Oui*, it is I."

"Here," he told her, thrusting the envelope into her hand and then disappearing down the banquette before she could pull a few pennies out of the pocket of her voluminous apron.

Closing the door, Arielle walked slowly back through

117

the shop, its selves only half filled with merchandise. Staring down at the thick parchment, she noticed the seal embedded in the wax. It was a coat of arms. There were two leopards holding up a shield of crossed swords with an impression of some type of stone in the middle.

Her luncheon cooled as Arielle sat at the iron filigree table reading the brief note. In a bold hand of black ink were scrawled the words:

The *Flying Gull* sails at midnight. Be aboard by sunset.

J.

Arielle's pulse pounded with excitement, for she knew this was the message she had been awaiting the last few days. Touching the large letters with the tip of her index finger she gave a slight smile. How like the man was his writing, bold, the letters taller than normal, with a firm forward slant. It was the scrawl of a strong, confident man who was used to authority and instant obedience. This time it was to her advantage to follow his terse instructions.

"Mam'zelle, bad news?" Seraphine's melodious voice inquired as she poured Arielle's coffee.

"Non, it is the message I have been awaiting. Please pack me a small valise with sturdy clothes, a riding habit, boots, small clothes for a day or two." Then, as she saw Jacques' handsome face drift across her mind, she added, "And some of my perfume."

"Captain Temeraire, he sent you word," the older woman affirmed. "I will not worry if you are with him. He is a good, strong man. While you are gone, I will finish the perfumes."

Would Jacques be aboard the *Flying Gull?* Arielle wondered as she studied the letter as if it could answer her question. Turning the parchment over, she stared at the seal. What was a smuggler doing sealing his letters with what appeared to be an ancient coat of arms as if he were a titled aristocrat? Such impertinence, she thought with scorn. He probably stole the seal from some lord aboard one of the ships he had plundered!

Putting the letter aside, Arielle pondered the character of the man she might be meeting that evening. The seal had reminded her Jacques was a thief, and a scoundrel, no matter how romantic was the reputations of the two men of Grand Terre. He was not to be trusted, not even an inch. His manner might be charming, his face handsome, but a man who led a life on the constant edge of danger had to be ruthless to survive. Remembering their meeting on her first night in New Orleans, her pulse quickened. He was used to taking a woman when he wanted her. They probably threw themselves into his arms, Arielle mused in disgust, thinking of how she, too, had almost surrendered to his practiced passion. Her guard must be kept up. She must not forget Jacques Temeraire was a man used to having whatever he desired. What price would he demand for his assistance, and what would she be willing to pay?

Chapter Nine

Sailors of many nations strolled the wharves of New Orleans, their voices rising and falling in a myriad of different tongues. The sound created an exotic babel as Arielle's hired landau rolled slowly past the numerous ships tied at the docks. She searched the name of each tall mast ship, each sleek schooner, and even the rough flatboats with whiskey bottles high on poles to announce that their contents of grain, hides, and pork were for sale. The *Flying Gull* had not been among them. Arielle nervously bit her lower lip as she waved the driver on down the wharf.

The neighborhood was becoming rougher and more run-down as they made their way along the wharf. Her carriage was attracting an unwanted attention from the idle, milling men. She turned a deaf ear to the numerous lewd proposals that were shouted in her direction. The British blockade had stranded many ships and their crews. Men use to the discipline of the sea were now at loose ends creating havoc all along the docks.

As frustration threatened to overwhelm her, Arielle suddenly caught sight of a small, sleek schooner gleaming cobalt-blue in the setting sun. The name the *Flying Gull* shone gold in flowing script across the side.

"Stop here," Arielle called out to the driver. She paid

him, took her satchel from his outstretched hand, and made her way across the crowded, uneven wharf. Rough masculine fists reached out to grab her arm, as leering, sometimes drunken faces twisted their mouths to call out obscene questions.

Hurrying, she tried to ignore the grimy, grasping hands and indecent calls, fixing her gaze on the graceful and what appeared to be a deserted, schooner. Reaching the gangplank, Arielle hesitated, for she saw no crew, only the gleaming ship with its sails flapping gently in the breeze from the river.

"Come aboard, *ma belle blonde,* you are expected," a deep, familiar voice summoned from the deck above her. Shielding her eyes from the glare of the sun, Arielle observed the tall, masculine figure that had appeared at the teak rail. Unable to discern his face in the blinding light, she recognized the broad shoulders and arrogant stance of the rapier-lean form. Awaiting her at the top of the sloping gangplank stood Jacques Temeraire.

To her dismay, her heart pounded as she struggled up the uneven planks tripping on her skirt. *"Sacrebleu,"* she muttered through clenched teeth. The man could have come down and helped her. Instead, he stood watching her as if she were one of his crew come back from a day's leave, she thought with indignation. When she reached the deck, Jacques' strong, bronzed fingers took her arm with a gentle authority as he guided her onto the schooner.

"I see you left your guard dog at home," his deep-timbred voice quipped. Ebony eyes smiled down, caressing her with an intimate gaze that set each nerve in her body atingle.

"You might have come down and offered assistance," Arielle retorted, using anger to mask the fiery effect he

121

was having on her. Placing the satchel on the deck, she noticed the hem of her dress had been torn.

"You have always struck me as such a self-sufficient young woman, as well as a beautiful one, that I didn't dare risk offending you. Yours is such an irresistable combination of beauty and spirit." There was a seductive tone to his voice and a flame in his eye that Arielle chose to ignore.

"Where, pray tell, is everyone?" She changed the subject, avoiding that too-knowing gaze by looking about the deserted deck. They appeared to be alone on the *Flying Gull*.

"The crew will arrive later before we sail. I thought you might enjoy a light dinner with me in my cabin. We can discuss the coming auction and what supplies you might need in the future. You do not fear to dine alone with me?" Jacques inquired in mock surprise, lifting one black brow. White teeth flashed against his bronzed skin as he grinned down at her.

"Non." She spat the word at him with contempt, reacting to the challenge in his voice. *He does resemble a swarthy pirate,* Arielle observed, trying to hold on to her temper. "It will be strictly a business dinner, I am sure. What would I have, m'sieur, to fear from a gentleman such as you?" Arielle cast her eyes downward in mock ladylike innocence. *Two can play this game,* she decided, determined this time she would not permit herself to fall under his seductive spell.

"Indeed, mademoiselle, I shall be the soul of discretion. I pray you will not be disappointed, or bored," he protested, teasing laughter shining in his ebony eyes.

"Talk of business matters never bores me even with the most inarticulate of companions," Arielle responded, managing a cool, indifferent air she was far from feeling. "Mayhap you could tell me when this auction is to take place, and how long I shall be aboard this vessel?"

"Touché, *ma belle blonde*," Jacques' tone was tender, a husky murmur as his smile widened with approval. "We shall reach the Temple on the morrow in plenty of time for the auction. Come, I will show you to your cabin. You must not stay on deck while we are docked; you might be recognized. It would not do to tarnish your reputation." He motioned toward the door leading toward the quarters.

"*Merci* for your concern, but I fear that when I moved to Rue Royal, and my shop, I took the first step toward making myself a scandal," Arielle replied with candor. Allowing Jacques to direct her down a short corridor, she missed his look of respect mingled with a sad regret.

"Your cabin," he announced, stopping before a low portal. Throwing it open, he revealed a tiny, cramped room containing a single small window, a bunk built into the wall, and a chair next to a narrow chest containing a pitcher of water and a basin.

"This will be adequate," Arielle stated coolly, as he placed her satchel on the narrow bunk.

"I am glad it meets with your approval," he answered smoothly. Arielle glared up at him, not failing to catch the laughter in his voice. The room was awful, hot and cramped. "When you have freshened up," Jacques continued, "please join me across the hall." The door closed softly behind him.

Arielle's hands trembled as she untied the wide brown silk ribbons of her mocha silk bonnet with its pink roses that framed her face. She did not know if it was from nervousness or anger, but why did that man always undermine her poise? Jacques Temeraire made her feel like a very gauche, very young girl. Determined he would not best her again, Arielle placed her bonnet on the narrow bunk, then smoothed her heavy honey-gold tresses dressed in a fashionable apollo knot. In the humid heat, ringlets had already sprung loose to curl around her face and neck. She straightened the skirt of her chocolate silk taffeta gown with shaking fingers. It was very chic, with its high waist set off by an ornate buckle that clasped the coffee-brown velvet ribbon high under her breasts. Looking down, however, she saw the effect was spoiled by the sagging hem where her bronze kid slipper had trod, tearing out the fine stitches. Well, it would have to do, she decided with a delicate shrug, for she had neither thread nor needle. After all, what did one wear when dining with a smuggler and privateer?

The tiny cabin was unbearably stuffy with the heavy New Orleans air coming through the one small window. Arielle felt she could reach out and wring the moisture from the air with a few quick twists. She would have to go on deck till the coolness of evening descended.

Clutching her reticule with its gold pieces in one hand, she opened the small portal just as the entrance to the cabin across the corridor was flung wide.

"Ah, Mademoiselle Arielle, you have read my mind. Come join me for our repast," Jacques invited, standing aside so she might enter the more spacious captain's cabin.

"It *is* rather warm down below," Arielle protested, crossing the threshold to find his spacious quarters much cooler with its large wide-open windows and higher ceiling. He had given her a cubbyhole — without a doubt the most uncomfortable cabin on the schooner, she thought, her temper flaring. "However, it is a bit cooler in here," she retorted with a nonchalant air,

124

holding a firm grip on her temper. She would not react although she was sure he had planned for her to dislike her accommodations, thus forcing her to spend time in his quarters if she was not to faint from heat exhaustion.

"Pray be seated." Jacques closed the portal behind them as he gestured toward a trestle table set for two by the open window. He lived well even on board ship, Arielle mused, observing the fine linen tablecloth, delicate china, and gleaming crystal and silver.

"The *Flying Gull* is your ship?" Arielle inquired in polite tones as she sat in the chair he held for her in front of the window. The breeze from the river blew a welcome coolness across her face, flushed from anger and the heat.

"*One* of my ships," Jacques replied, his deep, confident voice a husky murmur. He stood so near, she caught a whiff of the scent of sandalwood she remembered with a sharp pang from the cottage in the swamp. "The *Leopard* is the largest, my favorite, but it would be too conspicuous in port with Claiborne's men about, and the Temple is located on a narrow bayou. It is docked at Grand Terre."

"I should like someday to see Grand Terre," Arielle confided wistfully as Jacques sat down across the table from her. "One hears such exciting stories about the place."

Ebony-black eyes glowed like burning coals for a moment as he replied quietly, "Aye, mayhap one day you will."

Meeting his intense gaze, her heart turned in response to the double meaning of his words. The smoldering flame she saw in his eyes brought back memories of what it was like to be held in his strong yet tender embrace, with those oh so sensuous lips pressed

125

on hers. His lean, handsome visage was so compelling she could not drop her eyes from those arrogant features. They were so symmetrical, so classic, that the strange scar that arched up across his brow kept him from being too beautiful for a mere, mortal man. His looks were those of the Greek sculptures of the ideal masculine face and form. His soft linen shirt worn unbuttoned at the throat, his collar held casually in place by a cloth of pearl-gray silk, was fashionable and elegant, drawing her attention to the broad shoulders beneath.

"Some wine?" Jacques asked, lifting a long, slender dark-green bottle from a silver bucket filled with that precious commodity in New Orleans — ice.

Arielle nodded, unable to speak for his nearness. The husky, caressing sound of his voice struck some deep cord within her. As the last golden, dying light of the sun shone through the leaded window, it caused his blue-black hair to gleam like the wing of a raven. She wanted to reach out with her hand and brush the heavy silken lock that fell across his forehead. Her fingers burned with the need to touch him, a need she found hard to subdue.

"Champagne!" Arielle exclaimed as he poured the sparkling pale-golden wine into a fluted crystal goblet.

"Aye, this is a special occasion having you here alone with me," Jacques' voice was a seductive challenge. "You like champagne then?" He held out the glass, his warm fingers brushing hers as she accepted the goblet of dancing golden bubbles.

"*Oui,* it has been so long since I have tasted champagne. With the British blockade, it has become very dear in New Orleans, and with my budget . . ." Arielle stopped, giving an expressive Gallic shrug, her eyes meeting his over the rim of her glass.

126

Pouring another glass, he lifted it in her direction. As he touched the rim of her goblet briefly, he declared, "To a beautiful lady who should drink nothing but champagne."

A smile trembled over Arielle's lips, and one enchanting dimple appeared in a flushed cheek. *"Merci, m'sieur,* you are too kind."

Her breathtaking beauty quickened his very soul as he watched the mellow rays of the setting sun turn her honey tresses to spun gold streaked with silver. She was a prize beyond compare that any man would want to possess. A pink-and-gold rosebud begging to be picked and brought into full bloom.

"Come, drink; tell me what you think of the vintage," Jacques urged, his extraordinary eyes blazing with an emotion Arielle could discern.

Lifting the goblet to her lips, she slowly sipped the champagne. It was cool, dry, and sparkling, tingling her delicate nose as she savored it on her tongue. "Quite remarkable," she murmured at last, holding the goblet by its slender stem, watching the bubbles dance in the light of the tapers Jacques had just lit. The sun had set, and it was *l'heure bleu,* the blue hour, that special time between light and dark.

"You savor your pleasures I am glad to see. I, too, like to prolong that stimulation of the senses till I find complete satisfaction. It is such a waste to hurry through the delights of life. Do you not agree, *ma belle blonde?"* Midnight-black eyes pierced the distance between them, and there was no mistaking the invitation in those smoldering depths.

A tumble of confused thoughts and overwhelming feelings assailed Arielle as she fought to control her swirling emotions. Under that fiery scrutiny she found it hard to think, for she felt she was drowning in those

127

eyes, in the raw hunger she saw reflected there. Forcing her gaze toward the darkened window, she dug deep within her reservoir of determination to strengthen her crumbling defenses. "I have no idea of what you speak," she whispered into the soft wind from the river.

"Do you not, Arielle? How I should like to instruct you. You would enjoy the learning, *ma petite innocente*. Pray allow me to be your teacher." His deep, velvet voice reached out and caressed each nerve of her spine and she could not control the tremor that swept over her.

Seconds lengthened into minutes as privateer and mademoiselle stared across a ringing silence, neither speaking. Two strong wills battled as they fought each other and their own strong desires. Ebony-black eyes clashed with violet-smoke orbs as thoughts were exchanged without a sound. One sought total surrender, the other refused to capitulate.

Rich, warm, deep laughter floated up from the bronzed column of Jacques' throat, clearing the tension from the cabin as he shrugged broad shoulders and said, "Shall we call it a draw, *ma belle blonde?*"

Nodding, she gave a slow, tentative smile that she understood. It was impossible not to return his disarming grin even though he could act the very devil, Arielle thought. He seemed to enjoy playing a game with her, the rules of which only he knew. She would have to watch herself, for she sensed there would be many twists and turns before her host was finished with his gambit.

"You must be famished so I shall detain no longer," Jacques commented with mock concern. With a flourish, he whisked the silver cover off an ornate platter to reveal oysters on the half shell nestled on a bed of ice. "Try the sauce; it is superb. The meal was prepared in the kitchen of a friend of mine."

"They are delicious; your friend is to be congratulated," Arielle replied coolly.

Jacques was a correct and entertaining host throughout the meal as if his earlier conduct had not occurred. His changes of mood were disconcerting, but Arielle realized this was exactly what he intended. As long as she didn't know what to expect next from him, he remained in control. He might explain the rules of the auction at the Temple and tell her about life on Grand Terre, but he volunteered no information about himself or his past life. Jacques remained a mystery, and she knew he intended to stay that way. She was all the more determined to discover the truth about him.

As they sipped the last of the champagne and nibbled a remarkable chocolate pecan pie, Arielle began to experience a hazy sense of well-being that she surmised was due to the intoxication of the wine. She did not have a good head when it came to champagne and vowed to be more careful. The thought slid away as quickly as it had come, for her head had begun to feel so light. "Carefree" was the word, she thought with a grin. *I feel so carefree.*

Night had descended, and the tapers flickered in the cool evening air. The cabin was dark, full of shadows, but the small circle of light on the table held the two of them in its golden embrace.

"And how, pray tell, is your shop progressing?" Jacques inquired with interest, playing the correct host.

Forcing her concentration from the hypnotic light of the tapers, Arielle sat up straighter as she said, "We will open as soon as I return. We need French goods on our shelves to bring the customers in for the first time. We hope they will return after they discover our own

129

perfumes. Do you know what will be for sale at the auction?"

"There will be French perfume, although if your scent is any indication, I think your own products will be most successful." He gave her a warm smile that sent her pulse racing once again. The scent of her had lingered in his mind, giving him many a restless night. "I believe there will also be wine, brandy, gloves, cigars, various bolts of lace, silk, satin, cotton, muslins, and wool. A few household items, boots, and a saddle or two. Claiborne has promised to interrupt the proceedings. The American merchants, as you know, usually do not deal with Lafitte; thus their merchandise is much higher than the Creoles. He is being pressured to put an end to the auctions," Jacques mused. His expression sobered as he leaned across the table to cover Arielle's hand with his own lean, strong fingers. "You must stay close to me at the Temple tomorrow. If Claiborne's men succeed in disrupting the auction, we must make our escape quickly. It could be dangerous; you must be aware of everything that is going on around you."

"I understand," Arielle said in a voice shakier than she would have like, for his fingers were warm and firm as he interlaced them with her smaller ones. The touch of his skin on hers was upsetting her resolve to remain cool and aloof.

"You have become important to me, *ma belle blonde*," Jacques told her in low, husky tones that simmered with a barely checked passion, sending a shiver of awareness through Arielle.

She had a sudden premonition that danger lay ahead, but it was not a trap set by Claiborne at the Temple that worried her. The threat was here within her own heart. It was her deep and overwhelming attraction to the privateer called Jacques Temeraire.

Once again he was silent, watching her, his intense gaze seeming to memorize each delicate feature of her visage as he tried to gauge her reaction to his words. The golden glow of the flickering tapers reflected on her high cheekbones, the amethyst jewels that were her eyes, giving her an unearthly beauty that sent a fire racing through his veins to stir a potent desire in his loins. With ruthless control, he tried to suppress his growing hunger for this ethereal child-woman who sat so self-assured across from him. Arielle must never become aware of the power she had over him by her mere presence.

"I . . . I have no room in my life for entanglements," Arielle replied after a long silence in a voice choked with repressed emotion. Thick sable lashes lowered over violet-smoke eyes filled with sadness and regret.

"Not even a small corner," he mocked her, gently caressing her palm with the calloused tips of his warm, sensitive fingers.

Giving a slow, deliberate shake of her head, she murmured, "No, not till I accomplish what must be done."

"And, pray tell, what is that?" Jacques' ebony eyes seemed to reach out and forced her to return his gaze as he probed deep within her being.

"To destroy the man who destroyed my family," Arielle's voice was flat, unemotional, filled with the determination that came of a mind set on a unwavering goal. It was only in the eyes, those windows to the soul, that Jacques saw the pain, the uncertainty.

Something uncoiled in him at her words. Dropping her hand, Jacques rose to his feet, his face a mask of rage and despair. A soft gasp escaped her, but before she could speak, he was behind her, his strong arms sweeping her out of her chair.

Long fingers of iron dug into the soft flesh of her arms as he pulled her roughly, even violently, to him. Arielle twisted in those unyielding arms, glaring up at him with furious, reproachful eyes as she arched her body seeking to break free.

"Fool, little fool," he muttered, pinning her arms behind her, crushing her to his chest. Hot, demanding lips were pressed to hers in a fiery act of possession. His mouth, hard and searching, shattered her control with such a savage intensity it took her breath away.

There was no room for anger, or need for revenge, in her heart, only the spell-binding magnetism Arielle found in the golden circle of Jacques' embrace. The world and its troubles had slipped away under the delicious sensation of his lips trailing down her cheek to savor the delicious taste of the hollow of her throat. His mouth seared a path with soft kisses that ached with a tenderness that she found even more exciting.

"You drive me beyond sanity." Jacques breathed each word harshly between kisses.

Tremor after tremor raced up and down Arielle's spine at his husky declaration. As his hungry mouth once more sought hers, she returned his kiss with reckless abandon, for she had an aching need, a burning desire, for more of his caresses. The sweet wildfire surging through her veins had stunned any resistance, and her soft, moist lips parted under his fierce yet tender assault. Her pliant feminine form melted against his remembered rapier-lean, hard body as he demolished the last of her defenses with the warm honey of his mouth. A small voice of reason warned her that once more she was yielding to his passionate spell. The delicious sensation, however, of being caressed, stroked, enfolded, by this strong, overwhelming, virile man was more important than anything. Arielle needed his touch as a starving woman needed food. She, who had been alone so long, had found refuge and comfort from the storm of her life in the anchor of his arms.

As Jacques' insistent tongue thrust into her waiting coral mouth, Arielle heard her involuntary moan of pure, welcoming desire. Her own tongue met his and they touched, tasted, and caressed like two entwined scarlet ribbons. She clung to him with every fiber of her being, her fingers clutching the warm flesh of his back, radiating heat through the thin linen of his shirt. His tongue teased her now with a subtle expertise that ignited the fire in her blood as he exerted complete control over her senses.

Jacques' hands moved over her, caressing, exploring with a gentle but insistent mastery. Knowing masculine fingers pulled the pins from her hair, then slid through the silken, golden tresses, freeing them to cascade down her back like rich honey. With one dexterous movement his hands were under that river of tawny-gold and were unfastening each button from its tiny loop.

She must protest, pull away, Arielle thought hazily as her gown opened and the soft humid air touched the skin of her back. Unable to speak, for his mouth covered hers in deep, drugging kisses that drove her mad with a wild, sweet yearning she had known only with him, her protest was stilled.

Slowly, he drew her gown from her body till it lay in a silken puddle at her feet. The cool night air touched her with a light caress as his mouth sought the hollow of her throat. "Ah, that is better," he murmured against her fragrant skin. "Such beauty should be displayed, not covered up."

"We should not do this," Arielle moaned, Jacques'

133

fingers stroking the length of her spine through the thin material of her chemise. She could offer no more resistance than that one feeble sentence, for she was beyond such any other gestures. Molten-hot desire was centered in the depths of her womanhood, and she arched against him seeking his exploring hands.

Jacques' mouth was at the valley between her breasts as he bent her back, as pliant to his will as a willow to the wind. Arielle rejoiced as firm hands pulled her chemise down from her shoulders, exposing her ivory mounds to his expert touch. Her rosy peaks hardened into throbbing points of wanton desire as his tongue circled first one and then the other. Taking the awakening bud of one pear-shaped breast into his mouth, he caressed, then licked the delicious morsel, lightly sucking its sweet nectar. Her breath came in ragged gasps of pure pleasure as she became an instrument, tuned to the highest sensitivity, for him to play with consummate skill.

Reckless longing surged through Arielle as her slender hips felt the hard surge of his manhood through the thin silk of her chemise. Did every woman experience such fiery passion in her lover's embrace or was her nature truly wanton?

Strong masculine arms swept her up against him, and in a few swift strides he had carried her to the wide bed with its gleaming brass posts. Gently Jacques lowered her onto the burgundy silk counterpane.

A moan of pure sensuous pleasure escaped her parted lips as he peeled the chemise from her slender, trembling form. The cool silk of the counterpane caressed the length of her nude back, her rounded bottom, and shapely legs. Towering above Arielle, his blazing, ebony-black eyes stared down, impaling, consuming her, as his hands, with slow, sure strokes,

134

learned the contours of her quivering body. Her arms, with a will of their own, reached up toward him. Feminine hands clutched his sinewy forearms, her oval fingernails digging into his flesh, so great was her need, her all-consuming hunger elicited by his knowing touch.

Jacques knelt beside her on the enveloping bed, his tongue tasting once more each rosebud nipple, then on down the silken ivory skin of her rib cage to the satin pillow of her abdomen. His hands stroking, tracing the indentation of her small waist and on to the gentle curve of her hips. Breathing in ragged gasps of desire he could no longer control, his mouth found the golden fleece of her Venus mound.

Arielle's fingers were kneading the sinewy muscular strength of his shoulders, then rose higher up to entwine in the midnight silk of his hair. Her breath was suspended as she felt those knowing masculine hands slip to her thighs. A gasp tore through her as one tapered finger thrust into that most secret cavern, gently opening the petals of her woman's rose. Molten fire surged through her at this new passionate invasion. Modesty fled as he stroked her, fanning the flames of her desire till her body cried out its wild overwhelming need to be completely consumed by fulfillment.

"A moment, *ma chère,*" Jacques whispered, his voice raw with his need as he withdrew his wonderful touch, his burning mouth, from her. Arielle's cry of protest shocked her, and she pressed her fingers to her trembling lips.

As he swiftly shed his garments, his dark, depthless eyes burned down into hers, holding her with the intensity of his ardor. "On Grand Terre when we take a special woman for our own, *ma belle blonde,* we make a vow before everyone to be true to each other for as long

135

as we both desire the bond to last. We declare that we are one forsaking all others. Although we are alone here on the *Flying Gull*, I want us to make this vow now, between the two of us."

Her violet-smoke eyes widened at his words. What was she thinking? a part of her mind protested. She, Arielle Duplantier, to become a privateer woman! She must be mad. But as he stood before her, his male beauty awe-inspiring, his bronzed muscular form that of a Greek sculpture, her breath caught in her throat. Those wide shoulders, sinewy chest with its sable mat of curly hair that led in a V down the taut, narrow hips to the thicker, darker nest surrounding the proud thrust of his manhood, caused her reason to flee before the force of her yearning. The only mar to his perfection was a long scar that ran from one shoulder through the luxuriant sable fur of his chest to the opposite slender hip. She felt an overwhelming desire to trace its length with her mouth.

This might be her only chance, in all her life, to learn the sweet mystery of life with a tender, loving man whose appearance resembled that of a Greek god. Her plans for revenge could wait a few bittersweet days. She would know passionate love, if for only a brief interlude, and the memory would have to last her for all time.

"Do you take me, my sweet, elusive Arielle, as your own lover and protector, forsaking all others?" His voice was a silken compelling question, as his fathomless dark eyes challenged, willed her answer.

"Oui," she answered in a barely audible whisper, her eyes liquid violet pools that shone with a sweet, wild happiness that knew no yesterday, no tomorrow.

"And I take thee, Arielle Duplantier, as my woman, my lover, to protect and cherish," Jacques vowed, his deep baritone edged with passion and triumph as he slipped a signet ring from his little finger. Taking her left hand, he first placed the ring on her ring finger, but when it was too large, moved it to her middle finger, finding it a perfect fit there. He lifted her hand to his lips with reverence. "You are mine, *ma belle blonde.*"

Arielle was startled at the unreadable emotion in Jacques' ebony eyes, but then he was beside her on the bed, pulling her into his arms, molding her soft curves to his lean form. His fingers, warm and slightly calloused, once more stroked the length of her spine, his mouth on hers in a tender soul-reaching message that banished all thought. Her heart swelled with emotion as the heat of his body flowed up to meet hers, and she felt the hardness of his masculine hunger against the softness of her hips. Excitement swept over her as she realized that soon she would know complete fulfillment as a woman.

Jacques' touch became more insistent as he stroked her full, aching breasts and their rosy peaks, down, down, across her hips to caress the silken oh so sensitive skin of her inner thighs. His heart beat against hers, and she felt his rigid control. He was wooing her, preparing her for that supreme moment, submerging his own need that she might be completely ready for him.

Needing him, wanting him to be part of her, and in a rapture of love for his consideration Arielle opened her slender ivory thighs crying out, "Now, *mon coeur,* my heart!"

Jacques rose above her, his hand seeking that most intimate part of her being. Gently, he opened the petals of her woman's rose. With careful, knowing fingers he tenderly caressed the tiny inner rosebud of ecstasy. Arielle was suffused with a high series of golden shuddering waves of passion, soaring higher, higher as she clung to his strong arms. Unable to think or reason, she was pure sensation as she arched her slender body up seeking that final pinnacle.

Slowly he entered her. Fighting for control, he hesitated for a brief moment as he encountered her maidenhead. When she moaned for him not to stop, he was lost, and thrust forward with his passion. She stiffened at the pain from his thrust for only a heart-stopping second, but it was soon banished in a swell of rapture as he held her in his arms, moving in a dance of love that made them one.

Arielle began to move with him, following his lead as her pleasure now grew with each thrust. The ecstasy he gave her caused her to want him deeper, and deeper still. She welcomed each of Jacques' powerful sorties into her waiting, throbbing body, rising to meet his effortless, seemingly endless strength.

Together they rode on in a frenzy of hunger and desperate longing. Learning each other's rhythm till their bodies were in exquisite harmony with each other, they moved as one. Together they soared higher and higher until their crest was reached.

"Jacques!" Arielle cried out his name, arching upward against him in an explosion of fiery release.

With a harsh cry, he joined her with a wrenching plunge into the enchanted magic of release. Shaking with the depth of his fulfillment, he eased from Arielle. Lying beside her, he gathered her to his chest as he tried to quiet his breathing.

Arielle lay her cheek on the soft fur of his chest unable to stop the tears of love, joy, and sadness that it was over. They flowed onto his skin as she lay too tired to control the ragged gasps of her breathing.

Finding his control, Jacques lifted Arielle's delicate

face with a gentle hand. Tenderly, he kissed the tears from her cheeks whispering, "It will be all right, *ma chère*. 'Tis only the *petite morte*, little death. It occurs between lovers when they find ecstasy in each other and become one. The separation after such intense joining brings a sadness that they are no longer together."

Held tight in Jacques' arms, his hands stroking her hair, the tears stopped and Arielle slept. Her legs were entwined about his long, powerful limbs, her arms clasped about his chest.

Jacques, however, did not find slumber so easily. Inhaling the sweet fragrance of her hair, he experienced a stab of regret. Arielle was no privateer's woman, no Baratarian drab. He began to question his plan for her, ashamed of his ruthless seduction of her innocence.

Looking down at the petite, beautiful woman, he cursed his stupidity. How had he let this little one into his heart? Jacques had never allowed himself to care for a woman before, and now look at the one he picked! Or had he? He did not seem to have much control over his attraction to his brave, lovely Arielle. Fate seemed destined to make fools out of the most determined of men. He smiled in derision at his own behavior. Where had all his carefully laid plans gone to? He well knew the answer to this question — they had gone up in smoke in the arms of this strong-willed yet delicate girl. God, he was the world's biggest fool. Perhaps, in time, he would weary of her as he had of most women. If not, he was lost. The Duplantiers must not be allowed to win once again, he vowed as he slipped quietly from the bed, covering her with the counterpane.

Chapter Ten

Morning's bright sunlight was flooding the cabin when next Arielle's eyelids fluttered open. As she slipped from the bed, she stretched, and the warm moist air of the swamps touched her bare skin like a caress. Glancing out the window, Arielle realized they had left the Mississippi and were sailing down one of the many hidden bayous leading to that strip of Indian ground called the Temple.

The particular fecund smell of the swamps was in the humid, close air. A red-wing blackbird balancing on a reed derided the heat with his curious singsong note that was like a young boy's voice breaking. Although November, in the marsh it was as warm as deep summer.

Turning from the passing scene at the window Arielle spied, with pleased surprise, a small tin hip bath. There were two, tall brass containers full of water, once probably hot, now tepid. It would feel delicious in the humid heat to have a long soak, she thought as she filled the tub to the brim.

Slipping into the water, her hair coiled in a knot on top of her head fastened with a hairpin she found on the floor, she gave a shiver of delight as it cooled her sticky skin. A bar of sandalwood soap lay on a large linen towel spread across a chair beside the tub. Arielle held it to her nostrils, for a brief moment before she began her bath remembering Jacques. As she soaped her slender limbs, she wondered when the tub had been delivered to the cabin. She could not believe she had slept so soundly not to have heard it, but then it had been a night like no other she had ever known. Her violet-gray eyes grew thoughtful as she remembered the ecstasy of Jacques' lovemaking.

What had she gotten herself into? she mused staring down at the curious ring on her middle finger. It was a bit loose and slid around her knuckle in the soapy water. The ring, of two gold leopards holding up a shield of crossed swords with a brilliant ruby in the center, glittered up at her from the water. It was the same seal she had noticed on the red sealing wax of the letter delivered to the shop. The crest appeared to be that of some noble family. Could it really belong to Jacques? Was this the Temeraire shield? She did not know if that was even his real name. Many of the Baratarians took new names when they joined with Lafitte, leaving old lives and old names behind. The ring was undoubtedly stolen, part of a pirate's loot, as false as the masquerade they were playing. There was no room in either of their lives to allow their love to blossom. They had other commitments, other responsibilities, but for a brief magical time, mayhap they could love like there was no tomorrow.

Submerging her hand in the water to rinse off the soap, she knew that the events of the previous night could not be erased so easily. Forever she would be marked by what she had done, for in Jacques' arms she had become a woman. She, Arielle Duplantier, was now a buccaneer's woman. A thrill of excitement surged through her. For a few brief days she would enjoy all that life could offer, but she knew sadly it would not be forever. Buccaneers were known to take women they fancied when they found them, and then just as quickly leave, never to return. Shocked at how much it hurt to think that to Jacques she was only a passionate interlude, she rationalized that was all he could be to her as well. Her life was planned, and that plan did not include a lover, a husband. A rose blush stained her cheeks as she realized she was thinking of Jacques in terms of marriage. She must be mad. The whole situation she found herself in was mad. A few more days and it would be over. She would never, must never, think of him again. *Oui*, she thought, and it must start today. There would be no more repeats of last night, she vowed. It was only a matter of will, and she could be very strong-willed.

Hearing the creak of the door opening, she slipped further down into the water. Someone was coming into the cabin, and it was too late to get out of the bath and cover herself.

"Could you use some help with your back? I always find it the very devil to reach around in that minuscule bath," a familiar deep voice drawled as she looked over her shoulder, crossing her arms over her pale breasts half submerged in the soapy water.

Jacques stood, his sinewy form filling the doorway, his black eyes burning into her soul as they swept over her startled visage and alabaster shoulders in a hungering gaze. The sensual mouth she so well remembered curved into a unconscious smile that became as intimate as a kiss when he beheld the delicious sight of her creamy peach mounds peeking from the water of her bath. Coral, rosebud nipples flashed into view as she gasped, turning away from him in confusion, dropping the bar of soap into the tub.

"Here let me fetch that," Jacques insisted, crossing in a lithe stride to where she sat vulnerable and blushing

142

in the hip bath. Slipping his lean hand into the water, his bronzed fingers grazed her thigh as he searched for the vanished bar.

A shudder passed through her at his touch. Arielle bit her lower lip to stifle the moan of delight that threatened to burst forth as, finding the soap, he slowly caressed her back with the fragrant suds. Sensitive, knowing fingers stroked her shoulders and down the delicate bones of her spine, kneading muscles, nerves, with an expert touch.

Mesmerized by Jacques' hands, and the nearness of him, Arielle relaxed, allowing her ivory rose-peaked breasts to ride high and full in the water. She heard the sharp intake of his breath as he devoured their perfection with his smoldering gaze. Warm, wet, gentle hands slid over her shoulders and down, down, to cup those perfect mounds. Sensations swept over Arielle in pulsating waves as masculine fingers stroked erect nipples till they throbbed with longing.

Leaning back, she arched up into that expert, all-consuming touch. His lips caressed the hollow of her neck with butterfly kisses that sent a spiral of wanton desire through her to center in her throbbing loins. Arielle could not control the tremors of arousal that surged through her, turning her body to liquid, warm honey. She was pliant clay under his searching hands, his burning mouth. All resistance fled, for she was raw sensation responding to a master as he played her, eliciting a response that was pure ecstasy.

As Jacques' right hand descended into the warm water, sliding over the slight rounding of her abdomen, down to part the velvet of her sleek thighs, he sought and stroked that soft inner wetness that was hers alone. Carried to a height of passion she had known only with him, she heard her moans of pleasure, and surrender as she arched and twisted under his insistent, tender

143

touch. His tongue traced the outline of her shell-like ear as his left hand caressed one perfect breast, and his right the ultimate core of her womanhood. Sighing, Arielle yielded once more to his masterful seduction of touch and kiss.

The exquisite sensuality of his lovemaking carried her higher, higher, till she was beyond thought, beyond speech. Her breath came in long, surrendering moans. As if sensing she was reaching the pinnacle of her ecstasy, Jacques withdrew for only a brief moment to disrobe, but the cabin was filled with her gasp of protest.

"A moment, *ma belle blonde*," he breathed, quickly shedding his clothes.

A deep laugh of pleasure rippled through Arielle as he lifted her up, then slid into the tub behind her, his long legs wrapping around her slender limbs. Water sloshed onto the floor as he pulled her against him.

"Ah, it is better this way, *chérie*," Jacques sighed as her wet, rounded bottom pressed against his lean, taut abdomen the warm water surrounding them in a liquid embrace. He gently took one pear-shaped breast in his hand with those oh so knowing fingers causing her to arch up in a wanton gesture that shocked her. She found herself capable of a passion she had never known existed as her body reacted with an intense hunger. As the hard sword of his manhood slid between her thighs, she leaned back into his chest as his fingers separated her woman's petals.

"*Oui*, oh, yes! Now!" Arielle urged.

With a swift motion, he lifted her onto his erect, throbbing shaft. Tapered masculine fingers played their magic as he moved within her, leading her in circles of desire. His lips trailed kisses of fire down her slender neck, his quickened breath a song of passion in her ear.

Shuddering waves of white-hot ecstasy broke over

her, lifting her higher, higher, as her body vibrated with a liquid fire. His need, his hunger, drove him on till they reached the summit of their overwhelming passion. Crashing over the precipice together, Arielle and Jacques found complete union, exquisite fulfillment, in that most intimate joining of body and soul.

Exhausted, she leaned against his chest, his lips in her hair, his arms holding her as they savored the golden glow of completion. Hearts beat together as one as they savored the memory of the magical, soaring rapture that had occurred between them. Each realized that what they had experienced was more then most people were ever allowed to know, and they were awed by that knowledge.

"Shall I ever get enough of you, *ma belle blonde?*" Jacques sighed, wonder in his voice.

"You make me a wanton with no will of her own," Arielle replied with a sigh of her own, resting her head against his broad chest. "It is frightening, this feeling between us. I do not like to surrender my control." Her voice was a troubled whisper.

"I, too, feel the strangeness of the bond between us. It will not be denied, *chérie.*"

"I shall try and fight it," Arielle said, her voice quivering as she looked across the cabin at the morning sun streaming into the room.

"It will be for naught, little one, but I am sure you will try," Jacques murmured against her ear, and she heard the teasing laughter in his husky voice. Relaxed with such complete contentment, and enveloped by the peace that surrounded them, Arielle had not the energy to argue.

A gentle rap on the door elicited no response from the sated couple till it grew more insistent. Rousing himself, Jacques called out, "Leave it."

"What was that?" Arielle asked, daydreaming

against the soft fur of his chest.

"Breakfast, *ma chère*. Come, our idyll seems to have ended. It will soon be time to disembark at the Temple."

Reluctantly, they rose from their bath to dry each other tenderly, playfully, as Arielle dissolved in giggles trying to reach all of Jacques' broad back. The top of her head barely reached his wide, sinewy shoulders.

"Your clothing, mademoiselle," he announced, handing her the tapestry satchel that one of the crew had brought from the cubbyhole of a cabin across the hall. "Although you are absolutely beautiful *au naturel,* please don a gown so I may concentrate on my breakfast," Jacques mockingly pleaded, pulling on a open-necked linen shirt and tight, dark-blue breeches he had taken from a chest.

Arielle teased him slowly, slipping on a translucent ivory silk chemise trimmed with delicate ecru lace that didn't conceal the rosy nipples of her full breasts. Lacing up the long, slender stays covered in a dark-blue lace over French nude she watched his dark eyes glow with desire as the garment pushed her ivory breasts full and high.

" 'Tis a naughty garment, more revealing than concealing," Jacques murmured, lifting an arched black brow as his gaze swept over her graceful figure. He was enjoying the wanton game she was playing with him. This lovely child-woman was a delightful combination of innocence and natural seductiveness.

"It was made to entice, and I hope copies of it will do just that to the customers at my shop. Seraphine and I plan to carry a whole line of these garments to tempt the ladies of New Orleans. They are all the rage in Paris," Arielle replied with a mischievous smile. She slowly donned a simple, dark-blue linen gown with a high waist and a high collar of ivory lace.

146

"The gentlemen of New Orleans will be eternally grateful, *ma chère*," Jacques told her as he carefully buttoned up the many tiny buttons on the back of her gown.

He does that with nimble fingers, as if he has assisted many women, Arielle thought with a pang. A women's garment held no mystery for him. She stiffened holding herself slightly away from his knowing hands.

"Ah, now, I understand why you were concerned that there would be silk for sale at the Temple," he commented, finishing the last of the buttons.

"Silk is very dear in New Orleans if one could even find it a bolt, and I will need as many bolts as I can afford," Arielle replied in cool tones, moving away from him to sit formally on one of the heavy, carved chairs at the table. "You said there was breakfast?"

"Right outside the door on a tray. I could use some hot coffee," Jacques assured her, giving a weary yawn as he crossed to the closed door with his lithe stride.

He had slept very little, Arielle realized with a start. While she had been fast asleep in the comfortable brass bed, he had been on deck guiding the sloop down the twisting Mississippi River.

"It's still hot," Jacques sighed with thanks, pouring a cup of rich black coffee from an ornate silver pot he had carried in on a large, heavy silver tray.

Arielle marveled once more at the luxury with which the sloop was furnished. This mysterious, intriguing man to whom she had given her heart might be a rogue, a smuggler, a privateer, but he lived like a lord.

As they ate their fill of the delicious breakfast, Jacques made light conversation, touching on many different topics, none of which were personal. He seemed familiar with Europe, especially France and England. When their meal was over, Arielle realized she still knew little more about his life than she had before.

"We shall soon be at the point where Bayou Pierrot and Barataria empty into Little Lake Barataria. It is here, where the *chenière,* the mound, called the Temple, rises up from the marsh. We are expecting quite a crowd," Jacques informed her, rising to his feet. "Have you something to wear that will disguise your appearance. A cloak perhaps? There may be someone from New Orleans or the surrounding plantations who would recognize you, a Duplantier, in the company of a notorious smuggler." He spoke with a light bitterness.

"I have brought a dark mantle and a riding mask that covers my face completely," Arielle answered quietly, for she understood that the world would now intrude. Here, asail on the *Flying Gull,* they were in a magical enchanted limbo where the pull of their other, public, lives could be forgotten for a few brief golden hours. All that would change when they docked at the Temple, and reality would return. A pang of regret surged through Arielle as she pulled the dark-blue linen cloak with its tasseled hood from her roomy satchel, along with the white silk mask with its slanted eye holes. She was glad she had remembered at the last minute to have Seraphine include them. Under no circumstances did she want anyone from New Orleans to recognize her as she arrived at the auction on Jacques' sloop.

As if sensing her thoughts, Jacques came to stand behind her and spoke with cool authority. "If there is any trouble, we must leave as quickly as possible. I shall be near, but if we are separated, return to the ship as fast as you can. Put on your cloak and mask. We will go on deck. The first sight of the Temple is quite an experience." Then with a brief touch of her silky hair, he seemed to withdraw into himself as he waited while she donned her enveloping cloak and tied on her mask.

"I am ready," Arielle stated quietly, turning to face him.

"Good. I, too, shall don my mask. I will be allowed more freedom on the streets of New Orleans if I am not recognized by the good citizens at the auction as one of the corsairs of Grand Terre," he confided wryly. He took a black loo mask from his pocket. Placing the half-mask over his eyes and acquiline nose, he quickly tied it over the black satin cap of his hair.

Holding out his arm, he commanded, "Come, we go on deck. Speak little, signal with your hand for your bid. Remember, Claiborne's spies could be anywhere, as well as the British. It will be dangerous *ma belle blonde*. Be aware every minute."

The clear beautiful song of an elusive bird in the shadowy green of the forested bank pierced and lightened the steamy heaviness of the Delta morning as they stood on deck at the rail. Arielle smiled beneath the silk riding mask wishing she might fling the stifling cloak and hood from her heated body. How good it would be to cool herself in the shade of the gnarled branches of the live oaks trailing Spanish moss like gray lace over the olive-green water.

"Another bend and we shall be at the Temple," Jacques informed her in terse tones, his intense gaze scanning the dense jungle of first the starboard, and then the port bank.

Standing beside her, Arielle sensed the wariness within the tall, proud man. He was like some great, predatory wild animal, every nerve alert, every muscle tensed. She followed the direction of his dark gaze, but saw only a water snake asleep on a dead cypress branch, several wakeful turtles watching them as they passed by and a armadillo scuffing through dead leaves.

"Capitaine, excusé-moi . . . mademoiselle, we have sighted the flag," a leathery-visaged sailor announced, intruding on their musings as he lifted his battered cap to Arielle.

"Well done, Pierre." Jacques nodded to the burly man, their eyes exchanging a signal only they understood. Turning to Arielle, he stated, "The flag is up, the auction is about to begin. Best pull your hood lower over those golden curls, for we will soon be docking."

Nodding her understanding, Arielle adjusted the voluminous hood so it covered her tresses, completely obscuring her identity. It was suffocating in the confining garment and mask, but she knew Jacques was correct about the necessity that she not be recognized. In New Orleans she had caused enough of a scandal opening a shop; if it were known she was a privateer's woman, she would be beyond the pale of society. None of the aristocratic Creole ladies would patronize the establishment of a notorious white woman. The discarded quadroon mistresses might served many of the finest families as hairdressers and dressmakers, but then they were of color and did not have to conform to the same standards of Creole behavior.

As the sleek schooner rounded a twisted bend of the bayou, the strange sight of the Temple came into view. Clutching Jacques' arm in wonder, Arielle gasped, "Oh you were right!"

Three or four feet higher than the surrounding marshland rose a vast mound of milk-gray shells that glared a hot chalk-white in the blinding light of the intense noonday sun.

"It is said the Indians built it long before the white man came to Louisiana. It was believed they used the sight for some religious ceremony, thus the name the Temple," Jacques related as they prepared to tie up at one of several rickety wooden docks along the bank. There were many pirogues — those narrow canoes hollowed from a single tree trunk, beloved by the Acadians and other men of the swamp — pulled up on the alabaster shells. Two other long, low sloops were at dock. Arielle wondered if one belonged to the Lafitte brothers.

The vast mound of shells teamed with people, many dressed in fine clothes, their sleek horses tethered to low branches of the live oaks or their skiffs pulled up on shore. Arielle was thankful for her concealing disguise. Some of those people were either from surrounding plantations or New Orleans, and would be sure to know her. Included among the customers were ladies dressed in fashionable riding habits, but they, too, wore riding masks. Although considered a daring lark to come to an auction at the Temple with the proper escorts, the women did not want their identity brazenly displayed.

"Come, we best join the crowd. The auction is about to begin through the trees beyond," Jacques advised, offering his arm.

Placing her hand on his sleeve, she felt the hard muscle under the material of his coat. Whatever adventure lay ahead, she had this strong, self-contained man at her side. Eagerly, she strode along beside him down the swaying gangplank.

White-hot heat rose to greet them from the glaring surface of the shells as they joined the milling throng awaiting the start of the auction. Curious masculine glances followed Arielle as Jacques escorted her across the barren rocky stretch to the luxuriant, dense foliage at the edge of the swamp.

Under the spreading branches of an enormous live oak, Arielle recognized the privateer called Dominique Youx from that night at the cottage. He stood, without

151

mask, behind open chests spilling out their contents of silk, satin, fine muslin, and lace. Casks of brandy and fine wines stood beside him. Delicate crystal bottles of scent lay atop the brilliant bolts of material.

"It is quite like a store," she giggled to Jacques.

"Oui, 'tis true," he agreed.

"Attention! Attention! Mesdames, m'sieurs, we will begin!" Dominique Youx cried out, drawing the crowd to where he stood.

Arielle drew closer to Jacques as the throng jostled one another to get a better view of the merchandise. It was a rowdy but good-natured gathering.

It was as Dominique Youx sold the case of fine French brandy to the highest bidder that disaster struck. There was a loud crashing from the dense thicket far to the right as men dressed in American uniforms surged onto the chalk-white shells. The humid air was filled with the sound of feminine screams as the crowd realized they were caught.

Jacques reacted instantly, ordering Arielle in a harsh voice to follow him immediately. Strong fingers clasped her hand in a grip of iron. Wordlessly she nodded her understanding. He strode quickly away from the startled crowd of bidders, dragging her with him.

From the corner of her eye, Arielle realized that Claiborne's men were between them and the *Flying Gull.* There was to be no escape to the trim schooner. As the sound of a single shot rent the hot, hazy air, she and Jacques reached the concealing sanctuary of the dense swamp.

Stumbling on her long cloak, Arielle almost fell, but sinewy arms caught her. Half holding her in a firm grip about the waist, Jacques dragged her into the impenetrable, verdant jungle.

"I cannot breathe," she gasped against his chest as he carried her on through the dense forest, her silk mask

152

choking her.

Giving a sigh of impatience, Jacques leaned her against the trunk of a massive live oak, and, pulling the hood from her head, tore the suffocating mask from her face. Untying his own loo mask, he stuck it in the deep pocket of his coat.

Breathing deeply of the humid air, that seemed like nectar after the confines of the silk mask, Arielle rested her honey-gold head on the rough bark of the oak. "Those were Claiborne's men?"

"*Oui*, the man's a fool if he thinks arresting a few Baratarians will stop Lafitte. The good citizens of New Orleans will not take too kindly to being deprived of their luxuries," Jacques answered with a knowing cynicism. "What a hornet's nest he has opened back there."

"What shall we do?" Arielle asked with a tremulous whisper, for she knew Jacques faced arrest if he went back to the Temple, and she faced certain disgrace when her identity became known.

Studying her thoughtfully for a moment, one dark brow arched mischievously as he told her, "We are going to Grand Terre, *ma belle blonde*."

"Grand Terre! How?"

Holding out his arm, Jacques bowed formally and murmured, "First we walk."

"You must be mad!" Arielle exclaimed, bristling with indignation. She was suddenly filled with self-doubts. What had she been thinking of joining up with this rogue of a privateer. *She* was the mad one. What had seemed like a little adventure was rapidly turning into disaster.

"The Temple is behind you. If you care to, you may return — but alone, Mademoiselle Duplantier." Jacques' voice hardened ruthlessly as the amusement left his ebony eyes.

"I . . . I cannot do that," Arielle stammered, her

153

gray-violet orbs flashing in anger. He knew that if she returned, everyone in New Orleans would know she had traveled to the Temple with one of the men of Grand Terre. They had made quite an entrance on the *Flying Gull.*

"I grow weary, mademoiselle. We have quite a journey ahead of us. If you care to accompany me . . . If not . . ." Jacques' cool impersonal tone broke the stillness of the forbidding swamps as he gave an elegant shrug.

Disbelief, followed by anger, surged through Arielle. He acted as if it mattered to him not at all if she stayed or returned to the Temple and Claiborne's men.

Slipping the cloak from her shoulders and folding it over her arm, Arielle shot him a defiant look. "I am ready."

"Good. It will be hard going. When we reach Small Lake Barataria, I know where there is a piroque hidden. Come," Jacques ordered, striding away from the massive oak into the long marsh grass. "Follow close behind!" he commanded over his shoulder.

"Oui, mon capitaine," Arielle muttered as she tripped after him holding up the hem of her gown.

Whatever dangers lay ahead, she was ready to face them, even the most threatening concern of all—her growing love for the reckless man who was leading her into the wild swamps on foot with complete assurance. Lifting her chin in a gesture of bravado, she followed him to meet her fate.

Chapter Eleven

The flaring vegetation of near-tropic Louisiana surrounded the two of them as heat rose in shimmering breaths. They struggled on through a dank, oppressive tunnel of foliage gone wild.

Arielle picked her way carefully over vines thick as a man's wrist. Recoiling, she pushed away webs that spiders had woven from tree to massive tree. Thankful she had worn low, stout-heeled boots, she groaned as the firm ground turned into the soft vegetable mold that was the swamp. Shuddering, she tried not to think of what repulsive creatures made this spongy earth their home.

Determined to ask no quarter from Jacques, Arielle plodded on, her gaze fixed on the tall, broad-shouldered figure walking ahead of her. He rarely turned around to check that she was all right, and his lack of consideration aroused her ire. Mounting rage gave energy to her step, and she kept up with the pace he was setting. Deep in the forest primeval, they had left the Temple far behind. There was nothing but the silence of the humid oppressive swamp surrounding them.

We could slow down, she thought through clenched teeth, but she would not give him the satisfaction of knowing she was tiring. If only she had dressed in her boy's breeches — for her skirt was damp and heavy against her legs from the muck they continued to wade through on their endless trek.

All that long afternoon they plodded on through the endless swamp. After what seemed an eternity to Arielle, as the sun began to grow low in the sky, they suddenly broke through the dense junglelike wood to stand on the shore of a large, tranquil body of olive-green water. It looks so cool, so inviting, she wanted to peel the hot, damp clothes from her mosquito-bitten body and dive into those still waters.

"Lake Barataria," Jacques announced with satisfaction. "We will spend the night here."

"Here? Where?" Arielle was incredulous. She had thought they would find the pirogue, and by nightfall be at Grand Terre. "But surely it is not far from Lafitte's? How I should enjoy a bath and a feather bed."

"It would be dark before we were even halfway. You say you know the swamps but your sense of direction is quite off, *ma chère*." His voice carried the meaning of "what else could he expect from a woman."

"You arrogant oaf," Arielle sputtered. "We have walked far enough to have reached China. How do you expect us to spend the night in this . . . this place?"

"What a temper you have, *ma belle blonde*. I find I am constantly learning new facets to your character. You have wounded me deeply by your lack of faith," Jacques chided, mocking Arielle gently. He smiled down at her as if she were a small child. "A privateer, even an arrogant oaf of a privateer, always has several routes of escape and suitable places of concealment. Come, there is shelter, if of a rather rough nature."

"A bit of food would be wonderful, but I suppose that is too much to hope for," Arielle muttered as his hand, massive and warm, clasped hers.

"Perhaps something could be arranged," Jacques said softly. Turning toward her, he brushed a damp lock of hair from her cheek with his other hand.

"Then you are a conjurer," Arielle replied with a catch in her voice, for the effect of his touch, and the warm ebony gaze that reached deep within her, smote her heart. Anger fled, to be replaced with the exciting knowledge that they were alone here deep in the swamp. She was filled with a wild yearning thinking of the coming night.

Hand and hand they followed the lakeshore till they came to a small clearing overhung with gray veils of Spanish moss, trailing from the enormous branches of live oaks and carpeted with a velvet dark-green moss. A small, rough shack of weathered cypress with a high, pitched roof stood near the water's edge.

"It is not the *Flying Gull*, nor the cottage near Belle Rivière, but it will have to do for tonight," Jacques stated, opening the heavy door to reveal a dim musty-smelling room.

Walking inside, Arielle noticed a simple cupboard to one side of the stone fireplace, while firewood stacked to the low ceiling flanked the other side. Two rough benches and a heavy trestle table were the only furnishings. One small window with heavy shutters let in little light, but after hours of uncertainty in the dense jungle of the swamp, it seemed a sanctuary.

Dropping her cloak on the table, Arielle sank in exhausted relief to the rough wooden bench. Her gown was torn and caked about the hem with the rotting vegetation of the marsh swamp. Resting her head on the table on folded arms she let the weariness roll over her tired mind and body.

"It will soon be dark. I shall start a fire and see what there is in the cupboard." Jacques began to place kindling and logs in the large stone fireplace.

Lifting the dirt-streaked oval of her pale face, Arielle moaned, "Not more heat."

157

"It is necessary if we are to eat," Jacques replied, his words hard and terse, implying she was a fool to complain. His broad back was to her, but she saw the derision in the rigid posture of those muscular shoulders and proud head.

Something broke inside her at the thought of the leaping flames adding more heat to her fevered body. Remembering the cool green waters of the lake, Arielle staggered to her feet as the kindling caught fire from the Lucifer stick Jacques had taken from a box on the cypress mantel. Turning her back to the crackling fire, she stumbled from the cabin. The earthy fragrance of the fertile swamp surrounded her as she pulled her gown from her body. Next came her long, narrow stays with its front busk, then her chemise following in one swift gesture. Stopping only to pull her boots from her aching feet, she peeled her torn silk stockings and garters from her slender legs.

Free now of her hot, sodden clothing, Arielle stood for a moment savoring the feel of the soft air on her heated skin. How delicious the water would feel, she thought, her mood rising as she tread with bare feet across the mossy velvet of the bank. Pulling the pins from her hair as she ran, the long tresses fell about her ivory shoulders, and back, in a glorious, honey mane. She was a forest sprite of moonstone and gold as she waded into the cool olive-green water.

The lake surged around her, cradling her tired body, soothing her fevered skin, calming the numerous mosquito bites. Floating on her back, her golden hair streaming out around her, Arielle experienced a total pleasure that was almost as sensual as Jacques' caresses. The water stroked her exhausted limbs and up over the concave of her belly to the alabaster mounds of her breasts, causing the coral peaks to harden in enjoyment.

Staring up at the rose-lavender sky of the setting sun,

Arielle felt at peace content to float forever in this tranquil water far from the cares of reality. The peeper-frogs played their symphony to the dying day as she lay suspended from all care. How long she floated in the still water she did not know, but it was the irritating sound of Jacques' shouting that broke the peace of her idyllic swim. Arielle turned over, diving down into the refreshing cool, opaque green water seeking escape from anything that pulled her back to the world. Lungs bursting, she broke through the dark stillness to the surface and the urgency of Jacques' harsh refrain.

"Get out! Get out! Gator! Gator! Hurry!" The frantic cries carried out across the lake to where Arielle paddled in a slow, lazy arc. Following his pointing arm, she saw the long, low, shadowy outline of the huge reptile on the far bank. The dying light caught the yellow gleam of the alligator's eyes as they stared intently above the broad snout.

A cold stab of fear struck through her, twisting in her stomach like a knife. How foolish she had been not to have remained more alert. André had cautioned her over and over, on those lazy afternoons of childhood when they swam in the Bayou, to look out for gators and water moccasins. Now she had done neither.

"The little fool," Jacques muttered, clutching the curved hunting knife he always kept in his left boot. Arielle's ivory body and golden hair gleamed in the murky water like some exotic silver fish.

As the wind changed, Jacques caught the scent of the musky odor of gator given off by the glands in the reptile's head. Watching, waiting, the ancient lizardlike creature suddenly made its move. Thrashing the giant tail that could break a man in half, it slid into the lake as it gave the soul-shattering bellow of the bull alligator.

The unmistakable cry echoed across the lake sending creatures of the swamp into a frenzy of alarm. Birds on their night perches came awake with cries of warning. From somewhere high above, an owl screeched an eerie signal of danger.

The gator was heading with deadly intent toward the flashing silver figure nearing the shore. His heart pounding, Jacques plunged into the water, standing between the reptile and Arielle as she reached the shore.

"Run to the cabin!" he shouted, never taking his eyes from the long, deadly shape closing in on him in the murky water. The creature was determined to have his prey.

Jacques knew he had only one chance. A gator could be brought down by a bullet, or an axe between the eyes. He had neither, only a heavy blade knife. It would have to be enough.

As the gray-green reptile circled, Jacques lunged, trying to avoid the enormous thrashing tail. Clutching the tough, slimy hide, with both arms and legs, he rolled with the enraged creature under the murky olive waters of the lake. Determined not to swallow water, he clung to the gator, working his way up slowly to shut those powerful snapping jaws. Heart pounding, muscles crying out with the strain, Jacques held on as, together, man and beast surfaced. He gasped for air, working blindly, the water from the dive clinging to his eyelashes and sealing them shut.

Slowly, with an immense act of will and strength, he pushed those menacing steellike jaws shut as his body protested the strain, the veins in his forehead stretched to bursting. Holding the reptilian jaw shut with one iron arm and the force of his entire body, Jacques wiped the water from his eyes with a quick gesture. His vision clear, he lifted the knife high in an arc with his free hand before plunging it with bone-breaking force between those furious, glaring, yellow gator eyes.

The creature roared and threw Jacques upward, but

160

he clung for a moment till he saw the crimson cloud of blood seeping out into the lake as the bull alligator rolled over, sinking beneath the surface of the darkened waters.

Stumbling backward out of the shallow end of the lake, Jacques stood panting on the mossy bank. Flinging his sodden hair from his face, he heard a low moan and, turning, saw Arielle.

Standing completely naked, her perfect alabaster form glowing against the dark-green of the thickly forested trees, she held a butcher knife from the cabin raised high in her tiny hand. Her pale face was frozen in shock, violet eyes wide, staring but unseen, her honey-gold hair hanging in watery ribbons down her back.

"Non, ma chère, The creature is dead," Jacques murmured softly, prying the weapon from her clenched hand. What a woman this fragile-appearing female was, he thought with deep admiration for her courage. She had disregarded her own fear to come to his aid, to save his life she would have fought that devil.

Sliding the knife into his dripping belt, he picked up the trembling Arielle in his arms and carried her across the moss-covered ground into the security of the cabin. Shutting the door behind him with his foot, he closed out the primeval dangers of the coming night. Within the cabin, bright with the light from the fireplace, they were a man and a woman alone, safe from predators to celebrate the joy of being alive.

Arielle whimpered as he placed her on the soft black fur of the bearskin he had taken from the cupboard earlier and spread on the floor before the fire. Her hands clutched his forearms, for she was frightened to let him out of her reach.

"Hush, there is nothing to fear," Jacques soothed, pulling the wet clothes from his body. His masculine form, glowing bronze in the firelight, stood above her for one glorious moment before he lay down beside her and pulled her frozen, trembling body to him. "Come, *ma belle blonde*, let me warm you," he whispered against her damp golden curls. She sought his strength and warmth, nestling into the silky fur of his chest like a frightened kitten.

Arielle clung to the strong, solid warmth that was Jacques. He was her anchor in this strange foreign world that threatened her with terrors she could not bear to remember. The heat of his muscular, lean body burned into the length of her, melting the frozen shock that had turned her into a block of ice. Insistent yet gentle hands stroked the long curve of her back, the voluptuous swell of her bottom, her trembling thighs.

"Arielle, my sweet Arielle, how brave you are. Such courage in such a beautiful woman," Jacques breathed, his lips against the tangled honey masses of her hair. "You are safe, my love, here within my arms," he crooned. His hands soothed her as if she were a frightened wild creature he had caught and decided to tame.

Her ivory breasts, soft against his chest, the rose peaks taut now with her growing need, instead of the cold, were a hot brand fueling the fire that surged through his veins. Slender, silken thighs opened to his questing touch, and the cabin was filled with the sound of her soft, trembling moans of pleasure. Gently pushing her back onto the dense, luxuriant fur of the rug, his mouth devoured the moist honey of her lips, then traced lower to those proud alabaster mounds quivering with her desire. Arielle was all intense sensation, every nerve singing with the joy that only Jacques could command.

"My love! My love!" she cried out, filled with the exquisite sensual enjoyment that was almost pain.

His mouth traced slow circles down across the satin of her hips to the sensitive inner surface of her trembling thighs. He was gentle, with a slow, insistent tenderness

162

that drove all thought but desire from her mind.

She should be embarrassed at the wanton motion of her hips in response to his moist, circling tongue, but she could not. It seemed so right, he made it so natural, so perfect. She was woman, he was man. This ecstasy they gave to each other was what they were intended to share from the beginning of time.

"Now! I must have you inside me, *mon coeur!*" Arielle gasped, twisting and arching her slender form, seeking the fulfillment of her searing need.

Jacques rose above her, his bronzed body magnificent in the firelight, his ebony eyes glowing coals of urgent passion demanding fulfillment. With a harsh cry of need and capitulation, he was a flame within her, searing her soul as they rose together in one bright, consuming fire of passion. Hoarse words of love in two languages were ripped from his throat as he surged within her in wave after wave of almost unendurable pleasure. The small pearl ovals of her fingernails cut into the sinewy muscles of his back as they crested the peak of shimmering rapture together. Their celebration of life was complete.

Exhausted, they lay content in front of the dancing flames of the fire. Loosely entwined, Arielle's honey-gold head on the soft, dark fur of Jacques' chest, they slept.

Food, hot and fragrant, performed its magic, and Arielle was reluctantly awakened by her own pangs of hunger as the delicious aroma filled the cabin. Lifting lids still heavy with slumber, she opened violet-smoke eyes to stare into a fire where a cooking pot bubbled away. For a moment she knew only confusion, unable to think where she was, but as the events of the day rose to her mind, she shivered even though the room was warm. Feeling the panic rise within her, she looked about the room with a frantic gaze, seeking the reassuring form of Jacques.

"Ah, good. You are awake," the deep familiar voice stated, coming from behind her.

Sitting up, she clutched at another fur rug that had covered part of her. Trying to maintain a semblance of dignity as she covered her nude body she whispered, "I am hungry."

"*Oui*, I should think," Jacques answered softly, kneeling beside her. "You are all right, *ma chère?*"

"*Oui*, but it was so awful . . ." Arielle halted, unable to continue as she remembered the long, dark figure of the gator swimming toward her in the still waters of the lake.

"It is past. Think no more of it." Sable-dark eyes studied her intently as he brushed a lock of dried matted hair from her cheek. There was a strange look on his face halfway between pleasure and pain. Arielle wanted to reach out and smooth the pain away, but something kept her from the gesture.

"The food smells delicious. I think I could eat the whole pot myself," Arielle joked, changing the subject, for she suddenly felt shy remembering the intensity of their union. They had been like a primitive man and woman seeking shelter from the dangers of the night in each other's arms.

"There is a kind of stew I made of what I could find, and a bottle of wine. The supplies were meager. Someone has been here before us . . . Here, this shirt was in the cupboard. The breeches will be too long, but you can roll them up. Your gown is quite beyond repair."

Arielle took the muslin shirt and soft doeskin breeches from him. As he turned his back to take wooden bowls and spoons from the cupboard, she quickly slipped on the garments. Placing the utensils on the trestle table, he looked up to stare at her for a moment. Laughter, deep and warm, floated up from his throat. "You resemble a half-drowned kitten, *chérie*. Roll up those sleeves and tie up the pants." Still chuckling, he handed her a length of twine he took from a drawer.

Arielle's nerves were still raw, and she was stung by his laughter. A deep frown on her lovely visage, she tried to make the awkward clothing fit as well as she could. "I must have been mad to allow you to involve me in this escapade," she spat out, vexed sorely by his remark.

"Eat!" he ordered, filling a bowl from the pot and placing it on the table. All laughter had vanished from his expressive face to be replaced by a dark, brooding expression.

Her words cut him deeply, for the same thoughts had been troubling him. It had been foolish from the start to become involved with this beautiful aristocrat, for even penniless, her breeding was obvious in her bearing and manner. At first it had amused him, the irony of his relationship with old Faustien Duplantier's daughter. How the old bastard would have hated the idea of a member of his illustrious family involved with the likes of him. Jacques could almost hear his sneering voice addressing him with contempt. Somehow his feelings for Arielle had become much more than an act of revenge. He was becoming obsessed with this delicate beauty who possessed such courage.

Turning away from the irresistible sight of her in those ridiculous clothes, he strode to the cupboard. Taking one of the dusty bottles from the shelf, he poured golden wine into a pewter tankard. "Would you care for some wine?" he inquired, glancing over his shoulder.

"Oui, I am parched."

Placing the tankard on the table in front of her, Jacques sat across from her on the other crude bench. Even with her hair a tangled, matted mess, she had a strange appeal for him. There had been many women in his life, beautiful, seductive women, but this waif, a mere girl, has captured his heart like none before her.

"Will I be able to purchase any materials or perfumes on Grand Terre?" Huge violet-dove eyes stared up at him as she finished the contents of the bowl like a famished child.

"Pray tell, do you ever think of anything but business?" he asked with a mocking sigh of exasperation.

"Not often. You did not answer my question," Arielle persisted, sipping the rather bitter wine.

"Lafitte has several warehouses on Grand Terre. You will find, I am sure, many items to your liking."

"How long will it take us to reach the island?"

"If we leave at first light, we should arrive by sundown. Using the pirogue, we should make good time," Jacques replied, finishing his bowl of stew.

Sighing with relief, Arielle took a long drink of her wine, and then said lightly, "*Grace à Dieu*, at least we will not be walking."

The corner of his sensuous mouth curved in the trace of a smile. "You may rest your delectable little bottom, *ma chère*. There is water all the way." Jacques rose to his feet, then crossed to the door with the lithe grace of the outdoors man. "I should check the pirogue. The events of the evening have left me negligent."

"Where are you going?" Arielle questioned, a note of panic in her voice at the thought of being left alone.

"Outside where the pirogue is stored," Jacques replied, a pleased glint of understanding in his dark gaze. "I will be all right. The gator is gone, *ma belle blonde*. In fact, he is bubbling away in yon pot."

"What!" Arielle's face paled as she jumped to her feet staring in horror, first at her empty bowl and then up to meet the laughter in Jacques' eyes.

"It is good for you, gator. It gives you energy which you will need on the morrow." With that parting statement, Jacques exited into the black of the swamp night.

Nausea rose in Arielle's throat as she tried not to think of what else she had eaten besides the red beans, various herbs, sausage, and rice that had made up their meal. Hearing stories about how the Acadians often ate alligator was one thing but actually eating the repugnant reptile was another. She had to wash away the taste of the food she had eaten.

Crossing to the cupboard, she took the wine bottle and lifted it to her lips. Perhaps if she drank enough of the raw liquor, she could keep the meal down.

After several long swallows from the long-necked green bottle, Arielle felt a lovely numb warmth flow through her, and the thought of eating gator was not so repellent. Stumbling, she walked on unsteady feet to the bear rug and sank down to its soft surface. Staring into the banked fire, she lifted the bottle to her lips several more times.

"By my faith, little one, but I fear I have driven you to drink." Jacques' voice, with more than a trace of laughter in it, floated to her on the cool, damp air from the opened door.

"Washing down the gator," Arielle mumbled, then unable to suppress them, broke into giggles.

"Good Lord!" He shook his dark head in exasperation taking the empty bottle from her hand. "You are going to have quite a head on the morrow."

"Non, I feel wonderful," she giggled, violet eyes sparkling up at him as she hiccupped. Blushing a rosy pink, she held a tiny hand to her lips.

"I am sure you do," Jacques answered dryly. "But we both need to rest. First light will be here in a few hours. Lie down like a good girl."

"Alone?" Arielle inquired with a naughty gleam in her eye.

His lips twitching, Jacques tapped her retroussé nose with one bronzed finger. "You have had quite enough

167

for one night. Now behave, *ma belle blonde*. You try my gentlemanly resolve. Rest is what we both need," he admonished her, trying to keep his voice firm as he gently pressed her down on the bearskin.

"Oui, sleep," Arielle replied as the soft fur surrounded her. Slumber beckoned as the wine lulled her tired body and mind into the realms of Orpheus. Thick lashes fluttered against her ivory cheek as she slipped into a deep sleep.

Pulling the other fur up about her shoulders, Jacques' eyes darkened with conflicting emotions. Fatigue threatened to overwhelm his body. Every nerve, every muscle, cried out for rest. His mind would not, however, allow him peace.

Desire for the lovely Arielle flooded his veins. He wanted her as he had never wanted another woman, even more, to his amazement, after he had made love to her. She was like an elusive melody that he heard over and over in his mind and was unable to stop.

It was impossible, this obsession that threatened to rule his life. Clenching his fists to keep from touching her, he rose to his feet. They were too different. The past lay between them. There were so many reasons it was wrong, wrong to continue. After Grand Terre, yes, after Grand Terre, he would end it. "If I can, God help me, if I can," Jacques whispered, his voice hoarse with emotion. He turned away from the woman who drew him to her with an allure he could not resist. She was his obsession, his torture, his heart's delight.

Chapter Twelve

Whatever Arielle had fantasized Grand Terre to be in the recesses of her rich imagination, the reality did not disappoint. The busy wharves were an exotic sight of all manner of vessel from fully equipped brigantines, graceful clippers, several stately Spanish galleons that were spoils of the privateers, sleek schooners, and long, low sloops, to all manner of swamp boat.

"Jacques, *mon ami*," the hearty welcome of Dominique Youx greeted the couple as they disembarked. His visage gave the appearance of the most cruel and dangerous pirate imaginable, Arielle thought, but when he broke into a grin at the sight of her costume, his black eyes twinkling, she had to grin back.

"You escaped, my friend," Jacques observed with approval. He patted the much shorter man on his broad shoulders with an affectionate enthusiasm.

"*Oui*, that fool Claiborne will have to work much faster to trap this old fox. Come, Jean waits you."

Slipping his arm around Arielle's slim waist, Jacques escorted her away from the wharf up a narrow path of white, crushed shells as rough, dangerous-appearing men stopped their work to watch. Feeling their hot stares like a burning brand, she moved closer to Jacques' powerful, reassuring masculine form.

As they passed palmetto-thatched cottages, built among oaks dwarfed and twisted by the constant wind from the gulf, their leaves scalded by salt thrown up from the sea, she sensed they were not alone. Slowly, women with knowing, fiery eyes and buxom figures, emerged to cast lewd, measuring glances at Arielle. She was a new, unknown rival, and they studied her like fierce jungle cats sizing up their prey.

Out of one cottage, larger than the others, with oleanders clustered around to protect it from the constant gulf wind, appeared a tall, statuesque woman with coppery-gold skin and a mane of midnight waves reaching to her voluptuous hips. Black almond-shaped eyes glared above high, broad cheekbones. Her fiery gaze pierced the distance between them to impale the golden-haired interloper. Arms akimbo, the women held herself like a queen. Her full breasts strained against the low-cut, flame-red satin blouse, while a skirt of many vivid hues swirled about her slender, high-arched bare feet.

Warning spasms of alarm surged through Arielle. This woman was different from the other drabs. There was a wild, magnificent pride about her. This one was trouble, thought Arielle with a deep sense of foreboding, for the strumpet exuded malevolence like a fragrance.

With a few lithe strides, the wild-eyed woman was in front of them blocking their way. Shaking back her lush ebony mane, causing her large, gold hoop earrings to jingle, she demanded with well-fired indignation in a husky, deep voice, "And who is this creature, Jacques?"

"May I present Mademoiselle Arielle Duplantier," Jacques stated formally, but his mouth twitched with humor as he felt Arielle stiffen. "Señorita Yolanda Torres."

Giving a snort of disgust, Yolanda's dark gaze narrowed as it traveled from Arielle's dirty boots to her tangled, matted hair. "Where did you find this one? Fish

170

her out of the gulf?" Then, without waiting for a reply, she motioned toward Jacques with a creamy shoulder, and not taking her cold, savage eyes from Arielle's pale visage, she inquired in harsh tones, "Are you his woman?"

"Leave us, girl. The boss is waiting." Dominique brushed the statuesque woman aside, allowing Arielle and Jacques to precede him.

With the quick, deadly motion of a predatory cat, Yolanda lunged, a flashing knife in her hand. Arielle felt the cold metal of the weapon against her throat as the woman's musky perfume filled her nostrils.

"Leave!" the exotic Yolanda hissed, a wild, mad look to her onyx-black eyes. "You do not belong here!"

Strong, masculine hands pulled the knife from Yolanda's hand, jerking her head back with a snap of her long hair. She hung for a moment, her ebony tresses twisted in Jacques' sinewy hand before he threw her to the ground.

"You tempt my patience, jade. Never, never try that again, or I will break your pretty neck. Now be off with you!"

Hissing curses in Spanish, French, and some other language Arielle did not recognize, the woman rose to her feet. Spitting in Jacques' face, she turned her back to them and strode back into the cottage set apart from the others.

"That one grows more impossible. Come, my brother will be growing impatient. There is much he wants to discuss with you," Dominique told Jacques, gesturing for them to follow him.

Shaken, Arielle allowed Jacques to take her arm as they followed Dominique Youx through a forest of oaks, past a lush orange grove, to arrive in front of a graceful two-story house of stone and brick painted white. Built in the style of the West Indies, wide galleries graced both the first and second story. It was as elegant as many of the plantation homes on the Mississippi, thought Arielle with surprise.

Entering the wide double hall that bisected the first floor, Arielle received an impression of gleaming floors of wood and delicately patterned wallpaper. Lofty ceilings soared high above, making the dwelling a cool, shaded sanctuary from the heat of the island.

"Mon ami, we eagerly awaited your arrival and that of your lovely lady," the deep, suave voice of a handsome man, tall but not as tall as Jacques, greeted them as their host strode gracefully down the breathtaking spiral staircase.

Bowing in the correct formal manner over Arielle's hand, Jean Lafitte regarded her with admiring interest. Staring up into those warm brown eyes, into that lean good-looking face with its silky mustache and trim beard like an exclamation point on his chin, she was suddenly conscious of her disheveled appearance. The man standing before her dressed in conservative black evening clothes was a gentleman, impeccably groomed.

"Enchanté, mademoiselle. A room has been made ready for you. Please ask, if there is anything you might wish. I hope you enjoy your stay with us," Lafitte said smoothly, bowing over her hand.

"Merci, m'sieur, I am sure I shall," Arielle murmured in as gracious a manner as she could muster in her rough clothes and unkempt hair. Although he had treated her like a lady, she feared he must think her no better then the doxies she had seen at the wharf.

"I am honored to have a member of such an illustrious family visit on Grand Terre. Your father was well known to me, mademoiselle. My condolences on his passing."

Inclining her head in acknowledgment, Arielle could not help but stare in astonishment, for Jean Lafitte seemed to know all about her. Had he learned his information from Jacques, or was it true the boss of Barataria had his spies everywhere, and knew everything that occurred in South Louisiana.

"But forgive me, Mademoiselle Duplantier, you must be tired. Odette will see you to your room. We will dine at eight," her host told her, giving her a charming smile. Turning to Jacques, who had been strangely silent, he said, "You, I think, could use a drink. There is some fine cognac I want you to try.

The two men stood aside as a large African woman, dressed in the red-and-white-checked gingham of a house servant, with a bright red *tignon* tied in several points on her head, appeared from a room in the back. With a clucking sound, she motioned to Arielle. "Follow me, mam'zelle. You must be plumb tired out. Odette will fix you up real fine."

Giving a shrug, and a wan smile, to the two men, Arielle followed Odette up the curving staircase, aware of her muddy boots on the elegant Aubusson runner. She hoped the capable Odette could find her something clean and decent to wear, as well as a hairbrush. Oh, *mon Dieu,* Arielle pleaded silently of fate, a hairbrush.

The bedchamber was lovely and cool, painted a pale shade of blue trimmed in white. A graceful white-and-gold-painted French tester bed, with blue silk hangings and counterpane, stood against one wall. Draped in fine blue mosquito netting, it appeared to be floating in a cloud. There was a white marble fireplace standing between two French doors that led to the gallery where the blue-green waters of the gulf could be seen. At Arielle's feet glowed another lovely Aubusson carpet. A chaise longue upholstered in blue satin looked inviting, but what delighted her the most was a bathtub shaped like a swan and made of gleaming silver.

Catching sight of her dirty, bedraggled appearance in a long ornate pier glass that stood by the open French doors, Arielle cried, "Odette, I must have a bath immediately."

"*Oui,* the water has been brought, mam'zelle, and your satchel from the *Flying Gull,* too. I have bath salts from Paris so fragrant. Soon you shall be good as new, Odette promises."

As Arielle stripped the breeches and shirt from her body, she extracted the mesh reticule from the pocket of the breeches. Holding it her hand, she breathed a sigh of relief. The gold was still there. She would be able to buy from Lafitte's storehouses after all.

Slipping into the scented warm water that Odette had poured from brass containers, Arielle luxuriated in the bath salts that turned the water a pale violet. She felt docile as a child under the black woman's expert hands as the maid washed and rinsed her hair till it shone. Finished with the shampoo Odette walked to the armoire and took out a peach silk *robe de chambre* trimmed in heavy ecru lace.

"There was not much in your satchel, mam'zelle, so I took the liberty of retrieving some garments from the warehouse. I hope you find some of them to your liking."

"*Merci,* Odette, I am sure I shall," Arielle replied with a grateful smile, admiring the lovely garment. Stolen clothes from some fine lady whose ship had been captured would be her attire on Grand Terre. With a thrill of abandonment she realized it did not matter where they came from. She was having an adventure, and for the moment that was all that mattered.

"Mam'zelle, if I may make a suggestion on your gown for dinner . . ." Odette paused in her brushing dry of Arielle's long honey-gold tresses.

"*Oui,* Odette, and what would you choose?"

"This mam'zelle," Odette replied, putting down the brush and crossing to the armoire. She pulled out a magnificent gown of gold silk. Simple, without trim, its beauty came from the luster and drape of the cloth.

"From Paris, mam'zelle. There they would wear it without a chemise so the fabric clings to the body in the way it was intended by the designer," the black woman told her, a naughty gleam in her black eyes.

"Then so shall I, Odette," Arielle stated with a slight smile of defiance. Tonight she would be bold, daring, and without shame.

Wearing only delicate gold lace stockings, held up by gold satin garters with silver rosettes, under the lovely gown, Arielle felt deliciously wicked. Staring into the oval pier glass, she was a little shocked at her image. Odette had dressed her hair high on her head, allowing several long, honey-gold ringlets to tumble down her bare ivory shoulders. The high-waisted gown in the Grecian manner was cut so low, both front and back, that there was little bodice. Her breasts rose full and proud, the rosy peaks barely concealed. Small puffed sleeves left her own arms bare, but Odette had appeared with long, fingerless gloves of gold lace. Although clothed, the effect of the clinging gown to her bare body and see-through lace gloves made her appear nude and gilded in gold. The black woman had dusted the light tan Arielle had received in the swamp with gold powder. She touched her lips with Spanish paper and outlined her eyes with kohl.

"You will dazzle them, mam'zelle," Odette assured her, winding a vine of white, fragrant honeysuckle in Arielle's hair, having clipped the blooms from the vine that wound around the gallery outside.

"Have you known M'sieur Lafitte and Captain Temeraire long?" Arielle asked with seeming nonchalance. She was curious about these men whose demeanor was that of courtiers, but whose kingdom was an island, and swamp, inhabited by all manner of desperate men.

"Long enough, mam'zelle. I come from Saint-

Dominque with Miche Jean and his brothers. Capt'n Jacques I have known for only three years."

"Pray tell, where does Captain Temeraire come from? He speaks French fluently, but there is more than a hint that he is an Englishman."

"I am sure I would not know, mam'zelle. When a man comes to Grand Terre he leaves his past behind. That is why most all take another name." Odette's jovial expression had turned to one of cool, closed reserve. If she knew anything of Jacques' past, she was not, Arielle realized, about to relate it to her.

"Who is Yolanda Torres?" Arielle inquired, taking another tact. She stalled for time by opening her satchel and applying her special perfume from the small vial Seraphine had packed.

"Sacrebleu!" Odette made a face of disgust. "That one is bad, bad through and through. Her *père* was a crazy Spaniard, and her *mère* was Indian, Choctaw, and all wild. They both died of the fever five years ago. Miche Jean, he felt responsible for Yolanda, for her *père* had saved his life one time at sea. The boss wanted to send her to the Ursline Sisters convent in New Orleans, but Yolanda would have none of it. Said she would run away so he let her stay in her parents' cottage. She done be trouble ever since."

"Was she ever Captain Temeraire's mistress?" Arielle asked as if she were only making conversation, but her mouth was dry, and her pulse was pounding as she awaited an answer.

"Oui, for a while I think they have had some kind of liaison. But there is something crazy about Yolanda . . . she would not be satisfied unless she had a man's soul. Capt'n Jacques he not be owned by any woman. It was all over within a few weeks, but Yolanda would not accept that it had ended. She kept hanging around him, demanding his attention. Then one night they had a big

176

fight. Yolanda yelled that he would be sorry, that she would make him pay, then she flounces off with the first man she could find. She lives like that now, going from man to man, playing with them, putting them against each other, making fools out of them. But never does Capt'n Jacques look her way. It makes her mighty mad. You best be careful, mam'zelle, that Yolanda gal, she'll go after you now that she knows you're Capt'n Temeraire's woman."

A shiver of apprehension flowed through Arielle at Odette's words as she remembered the feel of the cold steel against her throat. *"Oui*, the woman is mad. She tried to attack me with a knife on our way up from the dock," Arielle confided ruefully.

"Mon Dieu!" Odette exclaimed, making the sign of the cross. "I bring you gris-gris, mam'zelle. There is a powerful conjure woman on Grand Terre. She will have something to protect you."

"Merci, Odette," Arielle flashed her a wan smile. She knew that none of the Voodoo black arts would stop Yolanda Torres if she was determined to get rid of the woman she saw as her rival. A chill went through her even though the night was warm. What kind of danger had she gotten herself involved in by accompanying Jacques to Grand Terre?

Chapter Thirteen

Sweeping down the curving staircase in the now-darkened wide hall, Arielle experienced a growing sense of unease. It was impossible to tell what lurked in the shadowy corners of the mansion.

A shaft of golden light streamed out into the gloom of the foyer from the room on her left. Reaching the half-open door, Arielle paused to adjust her gown and heard Jean Lafitte's deep voice talking to someone inside the chamber.

"You walk a tightrope with this plan of yours, *mon ami*. There are people in New Orleans who would delight in bringing Thane Ryder low, as you well know. 'Tis madness to continue such an enterprise. We will talk of this later. My beautiful house guest will be coming down for dinner."

Arielle's heart caught in her throat, for she could not believe her ears. Thane Ryder here on Grand Terre and obviously on good terms with Lafitte. The rumors in New Orleans had been true — her brother's murderer did consort with the men of Barataria. Too stunned to move, she stood in the dark hall, her mind racing. At last she would confront the man who had destroyed her whole life.

Feeling as if her chest would explode from controlled

anger and the anticipation of at last telling M'sieur Thane Ryder of her contempt, Arielle flung wide the door. Standing frozen on the threshold, her violet-gray eyes dark as bruises in her ivory-pale visage, she searched the elegant drawing room for her enemy. The room was empty except for her host. An open French door allowing a cool draft from the gulf to ruffle the lace curtains told of Thane Ryder's departure.

"Ah, Mademoiselle Duplantier, you are *ravissante!*" Jean Lafitte exclaimed, striding across the lovely room to bow over her trembling hand with lithe grace. If he noticed her expression of frustration, he did not mention it, inquiring instead if she would care for a glass of champagne. "Jacques has gone to his ship, the *Leopard,* to change into more appropriate attire. I shall enjoy having you to myself."

"The man to whom you were speaking before I came in, will he join us for dinner?" Arielle inquired, trying to keep her voice polite but disinterested.

"You were eavesdropping, mademoiselle?" Lafitte raised an eyebrow, his swarthy face paling slightly.

"I heard only your last words. You see it is very important I meet M'sieur Ryder." She could not contain the desperation from her plea.

"And why is that, pray tell?" Lafitte questioned, his voice wary.

"We have unfinished business between us."

"Permit me, mademoiselle, to say that I know of your business with Thane Ryder. Anger, the need for revenge—these are strong emotions. Often they destroy the holder."

"I cannot forget, nor forgive, what he has done to me and my family, M'sieur Lafitte," Arielle responded sharply, staring at him with haughty rebuke in every line of her body. "André was my twin brother, and there is a special bond between twins. I can feel that his soul will

179

never rest till I avenge his murder."

"Please call me Jean," her host urged, his dark eyes sad as he regarded her with what she realized was pity. "Here, have a glass of champagne. I did not wish to upset you. What a poor host you must think me. We shall speak of happier topics. M'sieur Ryder has left the island by now, and we shall not mention him again."

"And you must call me Arielle," Arielle replied taking the slender crystal flute of sparkling golden wine from Lafitte. Sighing, she realized that to her host the subject was closed. Gentleman he might be, but she sensed under the manners and obvious education, he could be very tough, very ruthless.

"Excuse my manners, *m'sieur* . . . Jean . . . I have not thanked you for the charming room and this lovely gown." Arielle forced a smile to her lips and lowered her thick lashes in a flirtatious gesture.

If she wanted information about Thane Ryder she would have to be more circumspect. The two men were obviously associates in business, or even friends. Lafitte would not betray such a relationship, but mayhap, whilst on Grand Terre she could discover what was the true nature of their business. Her heart beat faster at the thought that she could find something to use against Thane Ryder.

If her enemy was dealing with Lafitte he must be involved in illegal activities of some sort. Governor Claiborne would be very interested in such information, for he had a price on the heads of the men of Barataria. She would give a lot to know the details of the plan about which Lafitte had warned Thane Ryder.

Her charming host interrupted her musings as they sipped the excellent champagne. "I am delighted you were pleased. Jacques tells me you are interested in making some purchases for the new shop you are opening in New Orleans."

"Oui, that is why I was attending the auction at the Temple . . . Jean," Arielle replied with a smile, lowering her thick lashes shyly for a brief moment before glancing up at him in her best flirtatious belle manner. "Would it be possible to conduct my business here on Grand Terre? I need so many items, and you are my last hope," she drawled, giving him her most wistful lady-in-distress look. How she hated to play these games, but if her survival depended upon it, she would use every weapon in her feminine arsenal.

"I would be honored to help such a *belle femme,* but somehow I do not believe you are as helpless as you appear. In fact, you must be *très formidable* to have captured the heart of Captain Jacques Temeraire.

"Captured his heart?" Arielle questioned, raising a delicate, arched brow. "You give me too much credit. I do not believe there is a woman alive who could mastermind such a theft. Captain Temeraire's heart is entirely too well guarded."

"Ah, you have wit as well as beauty, mademoiselle. It is an irresistible combination to a man," Lafitte replied, raising his glass in salute to her.

"It is indeed," a familiar deep, velvet-edged voice agreed from the direction of the gallery.

Arielle, startled, whirled around to face the French doors. Jacques stood there, filling the open doorway with his broad shoulders and tall, lean body. Ebony eyes, glittering like black diamonds in the stream of moonlight that crossed his bronzed visage, reached across the room to meet her violet-smoke orbs, and she became ensnared as if held by invisible bonds.

A quiver of excitement, and almost fear, surged through Arielle as she saw the naked hunger in Jacques' stunning gaze. He was sending her a private message of passionate, wanton desire. Sweeping his magnificent eyes over her figure, sensually displayed in the clinging gown of gold, he inclined his sleek head in a gesture of homage to her beauty.

He, too, was dressed for dinner in an immaculate dove-gray tailcoat that displayed his broad shoulders to advantage. A black satin cravat tied elegantly about his strong neck was the perfect background for a magnificent glowing pearl stick pin. His waistcoat was of silver brocade, and his sleek gray breeches, showing the muscular perfection of his sinewy thighs and long legs, were tucked into high, polished boots.

"We shall dine," Lafitte announced, holding out his arm to Arielle. Leading her across the wide hall, he escorted her into another beautiful chamber containing an enormous, highly polished table in the design of Chippendale, with matching chairs to seat twenty.

Placing her on his right, Lafitte sat at the head of the long table while Jacques sat across from Arielle. Fathomless sable eyes devoured the sight of her as a young black man served them a delicious light soup in dishes of delicate Sèvres ware in the color known as rose pompadour trimmed in gold. As she lifted the heavy silver spoon to her lips, Arielle wondered for whom all this elegance had been originally intended. It was all stolen spoils of privateers, but she had to admit Lafitte and Jacques lived very well.

"I am afraid our beautiful mademoiselle was distressed this evening when she discovered that I had another guest, if only for a brief time," Jean Lafitte interjected.

"Really, and to whom are you referring?" Jacques inquired coolly, but Arielle noticed a flash of concern in those expressive eyes, and his firm jaw seemed to tighten slightly.

"M'sieur Thane Ryder was here although . . . Jean is being quite secretive about his visit," Arielle responded before her host could speak.

Lafitte gave a rueful smile and an infinitesimal Gallic shrug. "There are many men here on Grand Terre who have secrets that beautiful young women are better off not knowing."

A long look of complete understanding was exchanged between the two men before Jacques replied, "Thane Ryder is a dangerous man, Arielle. It is best you stay away from him."

"But you deal with him?" Arielle persisted, aware of undercurrents that she did not understand.

A brooding, warning cloud came over the hard, bronzed planes of his visage. His voice hardened ruthlessly as he told her, "We deal with all manner of men in our business. It is nothing a woman need concern herself about. Stay away from Thane Ryder for your own good."

"And, pray tell, what if I do not?" Arielle questioned through clenched teeth. She threw the words at him like stones, glaring across the table with burning eyes conveying the anger she felt.

"You will most certainly regret it," Jacques replied, each word cold and exact.

"Ah, the duck," Lafitte announced with relief, watching the sparks fly between his two guests. "You must taste what my cook does with wild duck, Mademoiselle Arielle. 'Tis quite superb."

Trying to calm the fury she felt at Jacques' treatment, Arielle turned her attention to the golden-brown breasts of fowl resting on a bed of wild rice put before her. He had acted as if she were a child with only a childish grudge against a man who had in reality done her a grievous wrong. Then as a startling thought streaked across her mind, the delicious food turned to sawdust in her mouth. Was the man who held her heart, to whom she had given body and soul, friend or comrade of Thane Ryder?

183

"My compliments to your chef. The duck is delicious. I do not believe I have ever eaten it cooked quite this way," Arielle told her host, trying to stop the racing of her thoughts.

"*Ma belle blonde* has been introduced to various new culinary treats since we left New Orleans." Jacques regarded her with an irresistible, devastating grin.

Arielle's heart fluttered wildly in her chest at the intimate caressing look in those dark eyes. Remembering their time together in the cabin by the lake, she tried to throttle the dizzying current that was racing through her. Her body wanted him, to feel his touch, to taste his lips, to know that rapture once more that came only with him. How could he have this hold over her? One minute he so raised her ire she could have killed him, the next moment she could have melted in his arms.

"I find the duck much more to my liking than the gator," she responded as Lafitte laughed at her words.

"So, *mon ami*, you fed her gator. I shall make sure you only dine on the finest cuisine, Mademoiselle Arielle, whilst you are my guest," Lafitte assured her. "Tomorrow we shall tour the warehouses and you may pick what you need. But I beg you not to hurry back to New Orleans. Jacques, I am sure, concurs."

"Maybe I shall never let her go," Jacques answered with an intensity in his voice and gaze that reached deep within Arielle, touching a responsive cord. She realized with a spine-tingling shock that she did not want to leave this mercurial man. There was a bond between them that was beyond any simple understanding, for when she was with him nothing else seemed to matter.

"I shall stay for. . . . for a while. Would it be possible to send a message to Seraphine at the shop? She will worry if I do not return tomorrow," Arielle questioned the two men.

"*Oui,* I have men going in and out of New Orleans all

184

the time. Claiborne would be most interested, would he not?" Lafitte shook his handsome head and gave a deep laugh.

The young black slave took the empty dinner plates from the table and returned with a rich dessert of flaming bananas in a sauce of brandy and spices and rich, hot coffee. Lafitte was the perfect host regaling Arielle with tales of the life of a privateer on the high seas of the Spanish Main.

"If you would care to see another side of Grand Terre, you must come to the fête tonight," Jean Lafitte told her. "There is to be a wedding at midnight. I, of course, must attend, but I would be delighted to have you and Jacques accompany me. It will be quite a sight."

Arielle looked across the table to meet Jacques' dark gaze. He nodded his agreement. Here in this elegant chamber he gave the appearance of the handsome aristocrat to the manner born. Where had a buccaneer acquired such a polished veneer? she mused, nodding with a smile to Lafitte's invitation.

Jacques caught her staring and gave her a smile that was a promise of intimacies yet to come on this magical night. His eyes glowed with an insolent fire. Were they to share her room? She felt a flush of shame at her wanton speculation. She was wishing they could dismiss Lafitte's invitation and be alone. What had she become since she had met the man they called Jacques the bold? She, Arielle Duplantier, had agreed to be his woman, and in the process had known an excitement, a sensual fulfillment, that she had not known was possible. Glancing at her hand, as she lifted the delicate porcelain cup, the ruby captured in the ring on her finger glowed like a fire in Jacques' eyes.

This was all a dream, a respite from the painful reality of the last few months. It was a romantic adventure, but how she would hate to awaken. Shaking her golden head, she decided to put it all to the back of her mind. Tonight she would celebrate life in the here and now. There would be time to mull and worry over the future later, for now she would be free as the wind.

"Shall we leave then, *mes amis*. The hour is late and the wedding party awaits." Jean Lafitte rose to his feet. "You are in for a rare spectacle, Mademoiselle Arielle, a Grand Terre wedding is like no other."

"That I can believe, for I have discovered Grand Terre is like nothing I have ever experienced. It is a fantasy isle, indeed."

As Arielle took Jacques' arm, she sensed the barely controlled power that was coiled within his body, and his words echoed in her mind. "Maybe I shall never let her go."

The soft air of the tropical night caressed the three as they strolled out of the luxurious house known as the mansion. A full alabaster moon hung low in the navy-blue velvet sky lighting the path for Arielle and Jacques to follow Lafitte's lithe form down the crushed shell path. The heavy fragrance of honeysuckle, late-blooming roses, and sweet olive, drugged her senses already tingling from champagne and the closeness of Jacques' masculine body.

Reaching a clearing of twisted cypress trees, near the thundering surf of the gulf, Arielle saw to her surprise a small chapel of weathered cypress. The narrow steeple was a graceful black silhouette against the moonlit sky.

"It is half past midnight. The wedding will begin now, in the early hour of the morning, so they may start their marriage with the beginning of the new day," Lafitte explained softly.

"And who are the bride and groom?" Arielle asked breathlessly.

"A young Spanish girl called Bianca. She was a ladies' maid to a rather disagreeable woman, a grandee's wife.

186

Bianca was happy to be rescued by a young lieutenant of mine called Pierre when we attacked their ship. Grand Terre appeared a welcome alternative to a future of servitude in the Spanish Colonies. Theirs does seem a true love, however, for they wish to marry and this is unusual on the island. Come, the ceremony begins." Lafitte gestured toward the chapel.

Tall flickering tapers shone down on the people of Grand Terre who packed the tiny church. The air was heavy with the scent of orange blossoms and greenery that festooned the walls. Arielle sensed the deference of the men and women, who sat waiting on the wooden benches, as Jacques and Lafitte escorted her down the narrow aisle to the first row.

Bittersweet sounds of a lone guitar soared on the soft night air through the open windows. A fierce-looking man standing in the corner of the chapel strummed the strings of the instrument, creating a sweet song that sent a thrill of longing through Arielle. As an elderly priest and a young handsome man with golden hair entered the sanctuary from a side door, all turned to watch a lovely young woman with midnight tresses glide down the aisle. Dressed in a simple white muslin gown, her face glowed with joy as she spotted her beloved waiting for her at the altar.

A sob caught in Arielle's throat as she observed the young bride radiant in her love for the man she was about to marry. As if he could read her thoughts, Jacques' warm, strong hand clasped hers as they shared a tender smile. Tears formed in her eyes as the young woman reached her groom and turned to him with all the love in her heart reflected on her delicate face.

Bending his sleek head close to Arielle's, his lips brushed her cheek as Jacques whispered, "Shall we be next, *ma belle blonde?*"

Intense surprise touched her pale visage as her luminous violet-gray eyes widened in astonishment. Had he just asked her to be his wife?

A few months ago the idea of she, a Duplantier, considering the suit of a privateer, a man with a price on his head, would have been ridiculous. But since she had met Jacques, how her life had changed. She had a freedom now that she could not have comprehended when family and position were everything. Now she was free to decide her own destiny without asking the permission, or approval, of anyone. Adventure and danger beckoned, for she knew as Jacques' wife life would never be dull or confining.

Feeling a warm glow of happiness flow through her, Arielle raised a dazzling face to his. Her smoke-violet eyes shining with excitement and determination she whispered, *"Oui, mon coeur."*

For the first time since he had met her, Jacques felt something akin to shame. What had caused him to make such a rash suggestion? Arielle could never live on Grand Terre. She was not a ladies' maid with no other options. Sitting beside him in her golden gown she looked like a princess. Grand Terre was a community of lawless men and the women who were willing to share such a life. It would be the ultimate revenge on that bastard Faustien Duplantier to make his daughter a buccaneer bride. Jacques' expression clouded with anger as he thought of the man he hated above all others. How Duplantier had strutted like a peacock when he had come to deal with Lafitte. Even now, knowing he was dead, Jacques was consumed with loathing for what Duplantier had been, and for what he had done.

A slight pressure on his hand from the small feminine one he held brought Jacques back from the memories that consumed him. Looking down at the pale flower of Arielle's face, he mused on her reaction if she knew the real story of his life. Would those sooty-lilac eyes fill with

188

hate and disgust? Then with an abrupt lift of his arrogant head he looked away, a closed secret expression coming over his proud visage like a mask. What did it matter what this slip of a girl thought of him? When she was his wife his revenge on the Duplantier name would be complete. And as an added bonus he would possess that lovely body and beautiful aristocratic face for all time. No man would ever touch her but him. The thought of possessing her completely filled him with desire and resolve. Arielle would be his bride. It would be the culmination of all his plans.

As the couple were declared man and wife, Jacques turned to Arielle and gave her a triumphant smile as if it were they who had been joined together. There was something in his eyes, however, that caused her happiness to flounder as she looked away in confusion. His gaze had been cold, remote, unfathomable. Arielle had not seen love reflected in those onyx orbs, only a strange detachment that almost frightened her.

"Come, the fête begins," Lafitte whispered to his guests, watching the bridal couple walk triumphantly back down the aisle arm in arm.

Arielle told herself she had imagined the strange look she had seen in Jacques' eyes, for he was all attentive concern as he led her out of the church after the bride and groom. Joining the others in pelting the happy pair with rice as they ran toward the beach, Arielle brushed aside her uneasy reservations.

Red-gold flames shot high toward the indigo sky as the myriad stacks of wood ready for bonfires were set ablaze for the marriage celebration of Bianca and Pierre. Champagne flowed from Lafitte's warehouses as the radiant bride danced with her groom to the music of guitar, flute, and fiddle.

"Are you enjoying your first Grand Terre fête?" her host inquired, signaling for another glass of champagne for her.

"It is remarkable," Arielle replied, her eyes sparkling at the scene whirling before her. She was pleasantly light-headed with fatigue and wine. The isle was enchanted, and time and care were suspended. It all seemed somewhat unreal, like a masquerade ball where all would return to their mundane lives when the night was over.

"Would you do me the honor of giving me this dance?" Lafitte took the empty crystal flute from her hand, giving it to a servant as she nodded yes.

Her host was a graceful dancer as he whirled her over the cypress boards nailed together to make a floor placed on the hard-packed sand. Arielle searched the crowd of onlookers for Jacques, but soon all was a blur as the Boss of Barataria led her faster and faster in the intricate steps of the fandango. The pounding of the surf seemed a counterpoint to the pulsating music as she felt her heart race with the excitement of the night. Although she was enjoying every moment, she wished it was Jacques' hand who held hers, and his dark gaze that stared down at her with fiery intensity. Where had he gone?

"Have you known Jacques for a long time?" Arielle managed to ask as the steps of the dance brought her close to Lafitte.

"Does anyone really know Jacques, *ma chère* Arielle?" her partner answered with a cryptic smile as the dance came to an end. Bowing to her graceful curtsy, he escorted her off the floor as Jacques emerged from the dense wood.

"Thank you, Jean, for looking after Arielle, but now I believe this is our dance. Is it not, *ma belle blonde?*" Jacques' arm was firm about her waist as he led her back to the dance floor. "You have been so in demand that I have had to wait entirely too long for our first dance," he murmured, swirling across the polished boards to join the other couples.

Arielle's heart swelled with the sound of the sensual music and the feel of Jacques' hand at her waist. How could it make such a difference that one man's touch could set her aflame while the other's did nothing. Whirling, turning, her feet flying, they moved as one. Strong hands clasped her waist as he lifted her in a high turn that caused her blood to race and her pulse to pound. She was a feather soaring into the tropical night. As the sweet, sensuous song came to an end, Jacques lifted her high above once more, then caught her to his all-encompassing embrace. Her head against his chest, she could feel his uneven breathing as he held her close. Marveling that such a tall, muscular man could move with such fluid grace, she allowed him to lead her away from the dance floor.

"Where are we going?" she asked in a tremulous whisper as they walked along the shore near the thundering waves of the Gulf of Mexico, the moon casting an ivory beacon on the blue-black water.

"The priest is waiting," he told her, as if the answer were obvious. His arm was a band of steel around her waist allowing her no retreat.

As her heart pounded an erratic beat, she heard his words with a sense of disbelief. "You mean we are to be wed, now, tonight?" Arielle's voice was breathless, her senses spinning so she could not think clearly.

"*Oui*, before you fly away, my little bird," Jacques answered in a husky murmur against her golden head.

Arielle, as if in a dream, followed his lead to the chapel on the point. The thick ivory tapers had burned low as they entered the empty church. Luminous shafts of moonlight streamed from the high, arched windows, casting an unearthly glow across the rough benches.

For a brief heart-stopping moment Arielle hesitated as Jacques started down the shadowy aisle, her hand

191

clasped tightly in his firm, warm fingers. What madness was this? She was going to become the bride of a man she knew nothing about, a privateer, one of the lawless men of Grand Terre.

"Are you frightened, *ma chère?*" Jacques' deep voice, velvet-edged and strong, held a challenge as his arm tightened about her waist.

Arielle raised her eyes, huge in the pale oval of her face, to find him watching her intently with an enigmatic stare. As the moon moved across the sky, she lost his classic, handsome features in the half darkness of the chapel and felt a tremor of fear. She should turn and run from here, and from him, but she was powerless to move. He held her to him, not just with the physical force of his strength, but by more nebulous bonds of a sensual and spiritual magnetism that was too overwhelming for her to fight.

"Come, *mes enfants,* my children, the night is waning and I fear I am weary." The aged voice of the old priest drifted to them on the heavy tropical air from the sanctuary.

Half pulling, half carrying Arielle, Jacques moved toward the altar and the waiting priest. His mind made up, he was determined to do this thing, to make her his before morning came and, with it, a clearer head. It was as if an obsession had taken hold of him, an obsession named Arielle. Maybe if she was his wife, he could think again, be in control once more of his own life.

The heavy incense and scent of wilting flowers made Arielle feel faint. She had to cling to Jacques to remain upright. Her strength of will had vanished, and she could not resist those dark, fathomless eyes that pulled her forward drawing her into his world. Was it the wine that caused her head to spin or her own emotions? Memories of what it was like to be in Jacques' embrace, to feel his strength, his tenderness, to know that ecstasy

192

once more flowed over and through her. Arielle did not care if it was madness, for suddenly she knew it was what she desired above all else, to be Jacques Temeraire's bride.

The beautiful poetry of the marriage ceremony coursed over her like the warm waves of the sea that pounded against the shore a few steps from the chapel. As the priest asked for the ring, Jacques slipped the signet with its glowing ruby from her finger, then replaced it in a symbolical gesture, his ebony eyes blazing in the wavering light of the flickering tapers. For a moment Arielle's heart plummeted, for she had no ring for him. Then her gaze fell on the ring she wore on her right hand. The twisted gold band with her birth stone, a small aquamarine, had belonged to her mother. With a question in her eyes she pulled it from her finger and, as Jacques nodded, she pushed it on the little finger on his left hand. Although a tight fit, the ring slipped in place, and Arielle's face lit up with a radiant smile.

When the priest pronounced them man and wife, Jacques swept her into his arms. His sable eyes shone down with some indefinable emotion in the pale light of the moon as he murmured, "You are mine, *ma belle blonde*. I shall never let you go." Reclaiming her soft, yielding mouth, he crushed her to him in a kiss that quieted all doubt within her.

Lost in each other, they were startled from their reverie of love when the front double doors of the chapel were flung wide, extinguishing several of the flickering tapers. Staring into the darkened church, Arielle felt her nerves tense as a shaft of moonlight illuminated a familiar figure. Jacques' arm muscles tightened under her hand as he too recognized Yolanda Torres.

"Leave us!" Jacques' voice was harsh, demanding instant compliance.

"Par Dieu, I curse both of you!" Yolanda's words were

full of menace and hate, reverberating through the small chapel as the old priest made the sign of the cross in horror. "May you never know the happiness you seek!" As suddenly as she had come, she disappeared into the dark heat of the tropical night.

"My love, pay her no mind," Jacques cautioned. "She is a madwoman."

Trembling, Arielle leaned against the powerful chest of her husband. His strong, sinewy arms reassured her as they clasped her protectively to him.

The moon had disappeared, and the night air seemed to grow more oppressive as they stood transfixed staring at the opened door. Faint rumblings of thunder were heard in the distance, echoing the pounding of Arielle's heart. Some sixth sense seemed to tell her that Yolanda's prophecy would come true, as warning spasms of alarm erupted within her. She had been swept away by a man's touch, his kiss, and now she was afraid she would have to pay for allowing her heart to rule her head.

Chapter Fourteen

A jagged streak of lightning rent the stormy sky as Jacques escorted Arielle from the chapel. Pausing on the crushed shell path, they turned their gaze upward as the first drops of rain fell large and wet on their faces. The wind seem to come from several directions at once, so strong and gusty it whipped their clothes and bent the gnarled branches of the live oaks to the ground.

"Follow me. It is not far to Lafitte's mansion," Jacques shouted above the roar of the sudden tropical storm. Clasping hands, they ran down the path through the orange grove.

The fierce wind and torrential rain made their going difficult. Arielle clung to Jacques' hand, his tall body shielding her as they ran. Reaching the wide gallery of the house, she found she was drenched. Motioning she had to catch her breath, Arielle leaned against one of the huge pillars and gasped, "I must look a mess. Look at my gown." Brushing her wet tresses from her eyes, she stared down in dismay at her sodden garment.

"You are beautiful, Madame Temeraire," Jacques told her, huskily pushing a damp tendril from her cheek.

Her heart fluttered wildly in her chest as she raised her gaze to the hard, bronzed planes of his visage. The timbre of his voice had been low, seductive, reaching deep within her to strike a vital cord. Suddenly, she was aware of how deserted the house seemed. Maybe everyone was asleep, she thought with a catch in her throat. They were alone on this their wedding night.

"This night is ours, what is left of it," Jacques murmured, his voice again deep, sensual, sending a ripple of fire through her veins. Sweeping her, as if she were weightless, up into his arms, he strode with fluid, purposeful strides across the foyer and up the curving staircase to Arielle's bedchamber.

"It is beautiful, but who, when?" Arielle gasped in surprise as Jacques carried her across the threshold.

Tall ivory tapers burned in silver holders. Deep-red, snow-white, and pink roses were massed in crystal vases, their heavy damask perfume scenting the air. Even the surface of the satin counterpane on the tester bed was scattered with crimson and white rose petals.

Placing Arielle on her feet, Jacques' mouth curved into a slight smile as he noticed the petals on the counterpane. "Odette has a romantic nature, I see."

"You had her do all this?"

"*Oui,* she exceeded even my instructions," he replied, picking up a translucent nightrail of delicate silver lace.

"*Tiens!* You were confident. What if I had refused your hand in marriage?" Arielle retorted.

"I would have taken you to the chapel against your will, and made you my bride regardless. Here on Grand Terre I am a lawless privateer. I may do want I want. Is that not what a buccaneer does when he must have a woman for his own?" Jacques stared down at her with a grin of amusement, but his liquid ebony eyes burned black coals of determined desire.

"My answer should have been no," Arielle whispered, alternately thrilled and frightened by his words. She felt uncomfortable with the fact that he had spoken the

196

truth, even if half in jest. He could do as he wished with her on Grand Terre, for he and Lafitte's word were law. Pulling her gaze from his knowing one, she walked quickly to the open French doors and stared out at the rain.

Her head was clearing of the champagne, and cold reality was intruding on the enchanted night. A dozen questions flooded her mind that strangely had not occurred before. Did Jacques love her? She remembered suddenly, with a pang, he had never spoken of his love, only of his desire. She had been so swept away by his overwhelming, magnetic allure that she had not even questioned what she was doing. The rest of her life was to be spent with this man and, as her misgivings increased with every minute, she realized she still knew very little about him.

"Why did you want me as your wife? It is important that I know," Arielle inquired, turning away from the rain to face him. Her voice was cool, controlled, her composure a fragile shell around her as, for an instant, his gaze sharpened.

With a few lithe strides he was in front of her, his strong hands clasping her shoulders, pulling her roughly, violently, to him. His voice hardened ruthlessly as he answered her. "You are mine, my sweet Arielle, all mine. It is enough that I want you."

His hands slid from her shoulders to the back of her gown. With deliberation, he unfastened each of the many buttons, and with one quick gesture stripped the material from her body. Dark eyes devoured the sight of her naked body glowing ivory in the light from the tapers. Only her gold stockings, with their fancy garters, and her lace gloves remained to bring a sensual smile to Jacques' handsome visage.

"Incredible!" he breathed. "You are more beautiful each time I see you. No! Do not cover yourself from me.

197

Let me admire such loveliness," Jacques' voice was hoarse with passion as he pulled her hands from her body, holding them out so he could feast his eyes on the alabaster perfection of her slender figure.

Arielle felt his hot gaze travel over her breasts as his knowing hands caressed, teased, each sensitive peak. Stunned, she realized, regardless of her mind's questions, that her body was betraying her as each rosebud nipple became erect with desire. Waves of heat were surging downward, ever downward, to center with an aching need in the throbbing petals of her intimate woman's rose.

Arielle's breath caught in her throat as Jacques slowly pealed one lace glove from her arm, and bending his head, he pressed his warm lips to the soft tender skin in the bend of her arm. His tongue flicked across the hollow, evoking a sensation so exquisite it was almost painful.

"You taste delicious," he whispered, lifting his dark head to pull off the other glove. He allowed his gaze to travel down over her full, throbbing breasts to her tiny waist, and then lower still over her slightly rounded abdomen, while one bronzed finger traced the path of his vision with a knowing, sensuous touch.

Arielle was trapped by invisible bonds of passionate need and hunger elicited from her trembling body by a master. As his gentle caressing hand reached the soft golden fur of her Venus mound, she heard, as if from a distance, her own shuddering moans begging for fulfillment.

Drowning in those bottomless midnight-black eyes that held hers as his touch caressed, controlled, ensnared, her will, Arielle writhed in his embrace. She was caught in the surge of her own physical response, a part of her mind wishing she could resist but finding she was powerless to pull away. She needed, craved, the ecstasy only he could give her. If she was hunger, he was food, if she was thirst, he was life-giving water. Her hands, with a will of their own, grasped his firm, muscular arms, strong as the oaks of Louisiana, as she bent to his fiery domination of her body.

"You are mine, my Arielle. You belong to me," he murmured, his voice simmering with barely checked desire. "Say it, *ma belle blonde*. Say you belong to me."

"No one . . . owns me . . . not even you," Arielle gasped, her nails digging into his arms as the ecstasy of his touch drove her mad with passion. But she would not say the words he demanded, even though she knew that she desired him with a depth of emotion she herself could not believe. He could control the reactions of her body, but some portion of her spirit remained inviolate. She would not capitulate. He did not own her, nor would he ever succeed in eliciting such a response from her.

As if sensing her rebellion, Jacques claimed her mouth with a savage intensity as he crushed her to him. Returning his kiss with an equal hunger, she met his tongue with a parry and thrust as they dueled with a fiery passion.

Lifting his mouth from hers, he breathed raggedly, his eyes blazing, "Mine, all mine. Say it. You belong to me, every beautiful inch of you."

"Non, you have only a part of me, only this part of me," Arielle gasped in victory, her eyes like huge, bruised purple pansies, her mouth swollen. Triumph and passionate desire mingled in her delicate visage as her slim, ivory arms wrapped around his shoulders pulling him back to her burning lips.

Sweeping Arielle up into his arms, Jacques' mouth still demanded, answered her challenge, as he carried her to the rose-strewn bed. Ivory tapers burned low as the sound of the storm outside filled the room.

It is like a flower garden, Arielle thought as the velvet rose petals caressed her naked back, hips, and legs. As her body crushed the petals, their rich fragrance surrounded her. Closing her eyes, she inhaled the damask perfume.

"Open your eyes, *ma belle blonde.*" Jacques' voice was a harsh rasp of passionate hunger as he stripped off his wet clothes and joined her on the flower-strewn marriage bed. His lean, sinewy form imprisoned Arielle beneath him. Pulling her arms away from her body, he held her slender wrists against the rose-strewn silk counterpane, and smiled down into her smoky-violet eyes. "Look at your husband, my beautiful wife. I am yours, and you are mine. Whatever life may bring us, we will have the memory of this night, when we are one."

Arielle gave a shudder as his words reached deep within her, binding her to him as their eyes locked, their breathing in perfect unison. Then he released her wrists and gathered her close to him. Jacques' warm lips sought her mouth in a kiss that was devouring, fierce with passion, yet tender. She responded with a like urgency, arching up against his masculine strength as if she could melt into him, become a part of him. Arielle was all sensation as his mouth traced lower to her quivering breasts, thrusting upward in hungry anticipation. He was ravenous, she was trembling sustenance. Silken thighs opened to his insistent hand, and the room was filled with her soft moans of joy. Feeling his bold, throbbing manhood against the satin of her skin, she rose up to meet him as he entered her like a flame. Filled with his warm, hard shaft she gasped in ecstasy as he moved with exquisite slowness. Taking delight in her quivering moist heat, he teased her, kindling her hot desire for the fulfillment only he could give.

Feminine fingers stroked taut male buttocks as he glided in and out, showing her the rhythm of his passion.

His tongue teased her mouth as she moaned against his lips, "Oh, yes! So good, so good!"

She was molten fire as he consumed her, seared her with his passion. Her slender hips moved against him, faster now as her hunger became all-consuming. Sensing her approach to that most sublime summit, his body increased its rhythm, leading her to that pinnacle she sought. Faster, faster, they thrust and parried in the exquisite duel of love between male and female, till together their crescendo was reached. Their voices joined in that final note of perfect harmony as Jacques thrust hard into her waiting velvet depths, and they found complete release in that climactic moment when two become one.

The rain beat against the French doors as the thunder shook the glass and lightning streaked the sky. Inside the chamber, on the bed of roses, Arielle lay at peace within the circle of Jacques' embrace. Their limbs entwined, her cheek resting on the soft fur of his chest, she listened to the beat of his heart as she luxuriated in the sense that all was right with the world. His hand caressed her golden tresses as he allowed his ragged breathing to quiet. Her fingers traced circles in the dark whorls of ebony hair on his bronzed chest. Gently, tenderly, she kissed where the long scar began at his shoulder. Shaken by the depth of emotion revealed in their lovemaking, neither spoke, not wanting to break the spell. They lay for a long time, only the sound of their breathing to break the silence, as each thought of what their passion had revealed about the other, and their own hearts.

Then, as the light from the flickering tapers burned down to mere stubs, Jacques lifted Arielle's hand, from where it lay on his chest, to his lips. The ruby in his ring on her finger glowed blood-red in the candlelight. Pulling her tight against him with his other arm, she sensed a change in his mood.

"You are indeed mine now, *ma belle blonde*. Mine and mine alone," he murmured possessively. The total male arrogance in his voice peaked her ire, and a swift shadow of rage swept across her delicate, heart-shaped visage.

"I may be your wife, Jacques Temeriere, but I am not your possession." Arielle lifted her proud head to stare into his sable eyes, her gray-violet orbs darkened like angry thunderclouds. "Remember, no one owns me."

The rich sound of his laughter filled the room as he cupped her defiant chin in one gentle hand. Smiling down at her, he shook his head in delight as he said, "What a life we shall have, my proud one. Will I ever tame you?" Her answer was lost as his mouth came down on hers.

"Madame, do you wish your *petit déjeuner?*"

The melodious voice awakened Arielle from her dreamless sleep. Opening her eyes, she saw Odette standing over her carrying a large tray. As she turned her head, she saw the place beside her in the bed was empty. The linen pillowcase still carried the indentation of the former occupant. It had not been a dream. She had married Jacques Temeraire last night, or rather early this morning. Where had he gone?

Looking away from the empty place beside her, she nodded, *"Oui*, Odette." Sitting up, she quickly pulled the sheet and counterpane up to cover her nude body. Rose petals spilled onto the Aubusson carpet with her gesture.

"Miche Jean, he will meet you downstairs in his office when you are dressed. I have placed some day dresses in the armoire, madame. If you wish, I will pick one for you." Odette continued to show a lack of curiosity about Jacques, but Arielle realized she knew of their marriage, for she had addressed her as madame instead of mademoiselle.

"That would be fine, Odette," Arielle agreed, sipping the hot café au lait from a delicate cup.

"Capt'n Temeraire was called away. Miche Jean will explain," the maid told her over her shoulder, taking a white, Indian muslin day dress from the armoire. It was a lovely creation printed in a flowing floral pattern of pink, blue, green, and mauve trimmed with delicate lace at the tiny puffed sleeves and low neckline. Odette took pink silk stockings, a wisp of a chemise in pale pink, and pink satin heelless slippers, called straights, from the bombé chest. Returning once more to the armoire, she retrieved a pink silk, pagoda-shaped parasol fringed in green with an ivory handle.

"The storm has blown out to sea, madame, and the sun is bright. You must carry the parasol if you do not want to burn and cause a scandal when you return to New Orleans."

"*Oui,* Odette, I will be careful." Arielle gave a wan smile, for the woman's words reminded her of all the decisions she must make now that she had become Jacques' wife. Would he even want her to return to New Orleans and the shop? They could not live with Lafitte forever, and they could hardly make their home aboard the *Leopard,* a ship she had yet to see.

Once dressed in the lovely gown, her hair brushed high on her head in a Grecian chignon of tawny curls tied with a pink silk ribbon, she clutched the parasol in one hand, her mesh reticule in the other, and descended the curving stairs to Lafitte's office.

"Ah, Madame Temeraire, you are a vision," Jean exclaimed as Arielle walked into the cluttered room at the back of the house that served as his office. "Your husband is a lucky man, as I told him this morning at our breakfast. He, alas, has been called away for a few days.

A British brigantine has been spotted a bit too close. You know, *ma chère* Arielle, how your husband hates the British. Rather an obsession I would say."

"*Non,* Jean, I did not know of this obsession, as you call it, but then I am afraid I have much to learn about Jacques," Arielle replied, a frown creasing her lovely visage. "He is not to return for several days? I find this most odd since, as you must know, we only married in the early hours of this morning."

"Ah, *oui,* this must seem troubling to you, but Jacques is a man to whom duty always comes first. Such an admirable trait."

"I fear I do not find it so. Surely there were others who could have gone to sea to check on this British ship?" Arielle's voice was cold. She bit her lower lip trying to quell her anger.

"But Jacques does so have to be in control, and as I said, he has a real hatred of the British. Pray do not be disturbed. I shall endeavor to entertain you. What would you care to do today? I am at your beck and call now that my paperwork is done." Her host gave a most engaging smile as he seated her in a chair across from his desk.

"I would like to visit your warehouses, and if you are willing, make the purchases I originally intended. As you see I have the necessary funds," Arielle replied, realizing that she would get nowhere with Lafitte in trying to find out more about her husband. When Jacques returned there would be much to settle, she thought with grim determination.

"But of course. Put your money away, my dear. As Jacques' wife you shall not pay for goods your husband, shall we say, helped acquire," Lafitte assured her, sitting across from her at his large mahogany desk. "He was most adamant that you have anything you thought you could use in the shop. The ladies of New Orleans will

204

flock to your establishment when they see what you have to offer from my warehouses. If you will allow me to seal this letter we can be off. Such a lovely day for a walk."

Her host escorted her out of the mansion and down another crushed-shell path that led in the opposite direction from the one they had taken to the chapel. The sun was hot overhead, and Arielle opened the sunshade, holding it so it shielded her complexion. Moist, warm air, heavy with the salt spray with the gulf only yards away, surrounded them like a caress.

They strolled under the twisted oaks, and Lafitte told her the names of the many tropical plants she had never seen before. Wild exotic birds, in brilliant colors, flew through the trees as they passed by, but they saw no people. It was as if the island were deserted.

"Many of the flora and fauna I brought with me from Saint-Dominque and Saint Christopher," he explained to Arielle, taking her arm so she would not fall over the huge cypress knots that pushed up through the sandy ground.

"You came from Saint-Dominque, then? So did my mother. She was Celeste Laronde. Maybe you knew her family? They are all dead now, but were well known at one time on the island. She spoke often of how lovely it was there. I believe she missed living close to the sea after coming to New Orleans."

"*Oui*, the Laronde family was an old and noble one. My dear wife also missed the sea after we fled Santo Domingo. Grand Terre was to have been our sanctuary, our Eden, but she died giving birth to our daughter and never saw it." There was a sadness in Lafitte's voice that Arielle had never heard before from him.

"I am surprised to hear you were married. I did not know you had a wife and children," Arielle said softly, looking at her host with new eyes.

"My sister Yvonne took Denise Jeannette when

205

Christina died in childbirth. Pierre's wife Françoise took the two boys, but now Denis has gone to live with Françoise as well. Maybe you are familiar with Françoise Sel, daughter of Babiste l'Etang Sel. She has a certain fame as a portrait and miniature painter in New Orleans."

"*Oui,* of course, but I did not know she was Pierre's wife. I thought her a widow," Arielle gasped in surprise. Francoise Sel was in great demand, for Creole husbands and fathers preferred their wives and daughters painted by a woman, rather than another male who would, in the nature of his work, spend a great deal of time alone with them. Françoise was known to be very talented.

"It is better, safer, for her if she is thought a widow than known as Pierre's wife, at least for now. Claiborne's men would give her no peace if the relationship was known."

Arielle nodded her understanding, but felt a stab of pain smite her heart. Was this the life she and Jacques would be forced to live? A life of pretense. Lost in thought, she allowed Lafitte to guide her toward the wharves where the storehouses were located.

Once inside the long warehouse, she put her husband to the back of her mind. Here spread before her was a treasure of goods the women of New Orleans would kill to have. Remembering Jean's words, she chose everything she could think of to bring in customers — silks, lace, delicate stockings, gloves, perfumes by the dozen, crystal bottles to hold the colognes she and Seraphine would create. A surly-appearing man walked behind them, noting her selections in a book.

At last she turned to Lafitte, flashing a grateful smile. "*Merci,*" she told him. "There is enough here to make my shop a sensation. You were right. How the ladies will flock when they find what a complete stock I have."

"For myself, I am glad you are pleased. Such a lovely

206

smile. Come, it is time for luncheon. We shall return to the mansion and one of Cook's special dishes."

As they walked out of the shadowy building into the bright sunshine, a striking figure darted out from the dense trees to saunter down the hard-packed sand toward them. A cold knot formed in Arielle's stomach as she recognized the sultry Yolanda approaching them.

Flashing black eyes with their hint of madness flickered over Arielle with contempt. "Alone, I see," she spat with triumph in her voice.

"And what am I?" Lafitte inquired with weary impatience.

"You are not her husband," Yolanda said softly, her mouth twisting into an ugly smile. "Jacques has gone to sea, and so soon after his wedding. 'Tis not an action of a happy bridegroom. Will he return to his bride, I wonder?" Yolanda tossed back her heavy midnight tresses, and laughed in their faces, before turning away to stalk down the beach. Head held high, hips undulating, she walked like some wild jungle cat looking for prey.

"Pray do not let her upset you, for that is what she wants," Lafitte cautioned Arielle, taking her arm in his, and directing her toward the mansion. "I fear her high-strung spirit verges on madness. Like a child she does not understand that she can not always have her way."

"She does frighten me, Jean, for she acts like she has some foreknowledge of the future, and that it will be all bad for Jacques and myself," Arielle sighed.

"Nonsense, it is only an act that Yolanda uses to impress the others on Grand Terre. It gives her a sense of power to watch the woman, and even some of the men, tremble to think she has special sight to see into the future. Come, we will forget such unpleasantness and enjoy our luncheon."

True to his word, Lafitte entertained Arielle as if she were the most welcome of guests. For the next three days they toured the island, seeing the orange groves, the wharves, the warehouses, and she came to realize that Grand Terre was like a small kingdom. In the evenings, after a delicious repast, they engaged in a game of chess, danced to a large intricate music box that played many different melodies, or stood out on the upper gallery and look at the stars through Lafitte's telescope. Her host was a learned, well-read man.

As they sat down at the huge dining table the fourth evening, Arielle knew that her nerves were beginning to wear thin. Although Jean was a delightful host and interesting dinner companion, this was her honeymoon. Where was her husband? She missed him, and with a blush, she knew she missed his warm virile body beside her in the bed upstairs in her chamber. Her shop, and Seraphine, awaited her in New Orleans. There were plans to be made. She could not wait here indefinitely for Jacques. Mayhap, she thought, it was time she returned to Rue Royal and her life there. It would serve her husband right to know that she would not always be waiting to do his biding.

"I must return to New Orleans, Jean," Arielle said with quiet firmness as they enjoyed oysters cooked in the half shell with a piquant sauce. "It seems Jacques will be gone for an extended period, and I am anxious to stock the shop with all the new supplies. He can reach me there when he returns."

"If you wish, Arielle, but I shall miss your company," Lafitte replied gallantly, but his dark eyes glowed with a complete understanding. "Often these trips take much longer than we anticipate. Such is life." He gave a slight shrug, then signaled for more wine.

"Really," Arielle responded in dry tones, trying to control the impotent rage she felt whenever she thought of her husband's abrupt exit.

"We can have my men escort you as far as the boundary of the city. Once there, friends of ours will escort you to your shop. When would you care to depart?"

"Tomorrow at first light, if that is possible. I have enjoyed my stay with you, but I am anxious to get started with my business."

"If that is what you wish, then it will be arranged," Lafitte agreed.

As they finished their meal and lingered over the hot coffee, the wind seemed to rise outside. Suddenly one of the French doors began to slam back and forth startling both of them. A gust of air blew across the table extinguishing several of the tall tapers. As Lafitte rose to see to the door, a burly figure appeared from the gallery. As he moved into the room Arielle saw the scarred visage of Dominique Youx.

"Boss, I have to speak with you. There is trouble, bad trouble . . ." Dominique Youx hesitated, his eyes dwelling on Arielle.

Ice seemed to grip Arielle's heart as a certain knowledge tore through her. "Dominique, it is about Jacques." Her voice was flat, unquestioning.

Twisting his hat in his hand, the huge man nodded. Turning toward Lafitte, he sputtered, "Someone told the British. Someone from Grand Terre. They were waiting, hiding in one of the bayous. *Sacrebleu!* What disaster!"

"Jacques? What about Jacques?" Arielle's voice quivered, the color draining from her face. Rising to her feet, she took a few steps toward Dominique, her hand outstretched as if in supplication.

"Gone. Run through by a British sword and tossed over to the fish. We . . . we could not find the *capitaine,* madame. It is a great sorrow to say that he has returned to the sea, and shall not return."

Arielle heard his words as if from a great distance. Jacques could not be dead. This must be a dream, a dreadful dream, and she would awake. Shaking her head slightly, she took a faltering step. *Wake up,* she told herself. She must wake up. It was her last thought as she slid to the floor into the welcome black void that blotted out all pain.

Part Two

Sweet is revenge — especially to women.
                              — Lord Bryon: *Don Juan*

The more violent the love, the more violent the anger.
                              — Burmese Proverb

Chapter Fifteen

New Orleans
July 1814

The sultry July sun slanted golden shafts of light through the sparkling windows of the shop making prisms out of the crystal perfume bottles on the shelves. A sleek black cat dozed in the mellow warmth that fell across the gleaming wood floor, ignoring the many female customers who debated over the delightful merchandise spread before them.

"Mademoiselle Duplantier, I really cannot decide between the rose or the ivory kid gloves," a fashionably dressed young woman mused, her rosebud mouth arranged in a pout.

"What color is your gown for tonight's ball, Mademoiselle Miro?" Arielle inquired in patient tones of the lovely raven-haired customer who was taking her time making up her mind while other ladies waited. Seraphine was busy at the perfume counter, and cast a knowing look in Arielle's direction. Delphine Miro was a very good customer who, along with her mother, spent a great deal of money at Celeste's, but she could try one's temper in the process.

"Ivory with rose accents," Mademoiselle Miro con-

213

fided, holding first one pair of long gloves, then the other, against her slender white arms.

"The rose would be most striking," Arielle replied with a professional smile. "See how the color sets off the alabaster of your skin. It will be most chic."

"Oui, oui, you are right as always, Mademoiselle Duplantier," the young woman trilled happily. "The ball is going to be so exciting. I understand you are attending with your godparents. The governor so seldom entertains, but I heard he hopes to raise the morale of the city with all these dreadful rumors circulating about of the British planning an invasion. For myself, I really could not care less if the British held New Orleans. British, or American, they are all the same; neither are French," Delphine prattled on.

"There are some in New Orleans who would agree with you, mademoiselle," Arielle replied stiffly, placing the gloves in a violet-and-white-striped box. The rumors had been flying that there were British spies in New Orleans making contact with those who had never given allegiance in their hearts to the Americans. There were some Creoles who felt they would benefit by living under the British, having been promised high positions when New Orleans was in the hands of the enemy.

"Has Seraphine finished my personal scent?" Delphine asked, her mind concerned only with her own desires.

"I shall see," Arielle responded, glad to leave the vapid Delphine Miro. Her hands were trembling as she thought of the promise she had made Governor Claiborne the evening before at her godparents' dinner. Walking back to the studio where Seraphine kept the private lines she created for customers, Arielle remembered his words. Aware that she had developed an intense hatred of the British, he had asked if she would listen for gossip among her customers that might indicate those families who were leaning toward a British victory. She

214

had agreed with enthusiasm, and inquired if there was anything else she could do.

Stroking his sandy whiskers, Claiborne had viewed her with speculation in his blue eyes before nodding. "You are a lovely young woman, my dear. Please attend the ball my wife and I are giving, and while there, circulate among the young men. Find out if you can those who maybe waver in their support."

Arielle had agreed. If there was any way she could help the American cause — *her* cause as she now saw it — she would do it. Clenching her fists, she bit her lower lip as she tried to still the tears that threatened to fall, even now after almost two years, when she thought of Jacques' death.

Closing the door behind her, she stood in the quiet studio fragrant with the scent of the ingredients used in her creations. She and Jacques had had three days together before being parted forever. That was all she would have to last her a lifetime. Despair flooded her, and Arielle felt that acute sense of loss that would come when she least expected it. The torment would overwhelm her in waves of grief and anguish that seared her heart.

Returning from Grand Terre two years before, she had told Seraphine everything, sobbing out her heart in the woman's comforting arms. She was the only one who knew Arielle had ever been married. As far as New Orleans was concerned, Arielle Duplantier was approaching the age when a young Creole woman who had not yet married could be considered a spinster.

At first she had been numb, almost unable to perform even the most mundane tasks, but with time she had made a quiet life for herself. The first of many supplies from Grand Terre arrived soon after her return, and she threw her energies into making the shop a success while trying to blot out her broken heart. The hard work and fine merchandise from Lafitte's warehouses had made

Celeste's a triumph, but the emptiness inside Arielle was never filled. Hours would go by when Arielle forgot her grief, lost in some business to do with the shop. She still had, however, periods such as at this moment when her sense of loss and pain threatened to overwhelm her.

There had been no other man in her life these long two years to take Jacques' place in her heart. She had turned aside all invitations to balls and parties the first year. It had only been in the last month that she had started to attend dinner parties at the Boudreaux when others were invited, thus announcing her gradual return to society. The Claiborne ball would be the first she had attended in two years, and she was going only at the governor's request. She had no wish to meet other men, for all seemed to pale in comparison with her precious memories of the man who had been, for what seemed a brief, shining moment, her husband. A sob rose in her throat as she bit her lower lip hard fighting for control. She had learned if she allowed herself the luxury of tears, she would be unable to stop their flow for a long, long time.

Taking a deep breath, she willed her mind to think of tonight and what she could accomplish. The British had killed her beloved Jacques and she would do anything to bring about their defeat. It had been a British spy who had alerted them to the *Leopard*'s destination. Every spy she unmasked was a blow against the one who had betrayed her husband.

Girding herself with resolve, she wiped the tears from her cheeks, and locating Delphine's perfume, and bath oil returned to the shop. The crowd had thinned a bit as the sun sank lower in the sky. Every woman was in a hurry to return home and prepare her toilette for the evening's ball.

"La, but today was busy," Seraphine commented as the last of the Creole ladies departed. "Shall we close up for the day?"

216

"What a good idea," Arielle agreed, giving a yawn. "A long, hot soak in a bath would be a delight. Uncle Jules and Tante Lala will call for me at eight."

As Seraphine walked to the door to lock it and place the closed sign in the window, a woman hurried inside from Royal Street. Although attractive, with red-gold hair and bright-blue eyes, the afternoon sun highlighted the beginning of age lines about her eyes and around her mouth. Her trim figure and quick step could not disguise the fact she was approaching middle age.

"I waited till those Creole ladies left," the customer announced with a charming Irish lilt to her voice. "Reckon they would not have known me, but I sure know half their husbands. Some are my regulars." She smiled with a mischievous glint in her cornflower-blue eyes.

"It is good to see you, Maura O'Connell," Arielle greeted the madame of the most famous and expensive brothel in New Orleans. She had first met the notorious Maura on a cold, wet day in January when the store was empty of other customers. At first Arielle had been unaware of her occupation, liking the friendly woman on sight. Seraphine had stiffened immediately upon hearing her name, a fact Maura sensed.

"I guess your woman knows who I am. Would you prefer I leave?" Maura had asked, her face a cold mask, but Arielle had seen the hurt in those blue eyes.

"*Non,* you chose the sapphire lace chemise, I believe," Arielle had continued, flashing Maura a smile.

"Aye, the blue one and, now that I think of it, the rose one as well," Maura O'Connell had replied. From that day on, she had been a constant customer, but always when the shop was empty, usually right before closing.

Seraphine had been shocked that Arielle would continue to serve Maura after being informed of who she was and what she did for a living. Arielle had merely shaken her head at her protestations. "We are both only trying to

217

survive, Seraphine, in our own way," she had explained.

"What may I show you today?" Arielle inquired. Seraphine, with an audible sniff, began to straighten merchandise in the windows.

"Your best French perfume," Maura replied, looking over the many crystal bottles displayed on the shelf behind Arielle. "It is for a special occasion. An old friend will be dropping by tonight after that governor's ball. Thane has been gone a long time. Want everything to be extra special, you know."

Arielle's hand tightened on the bottle she was taking from the shelf. It was an unusual name; there could not be two men in New Orleans named Thane. Upon returning from Grand Terre after Jacques' death, she had heard that her old enemy had left Louisiana. There had been rumors he had left for England. Now it seemed he was back and would be, at least for a time, at the governor's ball. Her pulse quickened a beat at the thought she might see the man she still hated with all her heart in only a few hours. But she must make sure he was the same man.

"Would your gentleman be M'sieur Thane Ryder?" Arielle questioned, keeping her voice polite, as if she were only making small talk. Lifting the stopper from the bottle, she placed a few drops of perfume on Maura's wrist.

"Aye, I guess most of New Orleans has heard of Thane. Missed him I have these years. He has been away a long time, thought I might never lay eyes on the man again. Then out of the blue I receive this letter from him that he has returned and will see me after the ball. Tonight, over a late supper, I shall hear all of his news. Now this is real nice, Miss Duplantier. I would like a bottle, and that black lace chemise I saw in the window," Maura decided, pointing to a wisp of lingerie that had drawn shocked comment all over the city, but which had brought in many new customers.

"An excellent choice," Arielle agreed, then turning toward Seraphine, ordered, "Please fetch the chemise for Madame O'Connell. Like most Frenchwomen, Arielle politely referred to all women of a certain age as Madame, regardless of their marital state.

Her mind awhirl, Arielle wrapped up the purchases in the shop's distinctive violet-and-white-striped paper. Tonight she would face the man who had become an obsession of hate. Remembering he had visited Grand Terre the night she had married, only to become, in a few short days, widowed, she felt a shiver run down her spine. It seemed he was always near when fate struck her a cruel blow. She had many scores to settle with M'sieur Thane Ryder. Tonight she would take her first step. Tonight she would meet him face to face for the first time.

"I hope you enjoy everything," Arielle told her customer with a polite smile.

"I shall. Ta, ta," Maura O'Connell sang out as she left the shop, packages in hand.

"Lock the door, Seraphine, before anyone else comes in. I need time to bathe and dress before Uncle Jules and Tante Lala arrive."

As Arielle lay in the warm, fragrant bath listening to the sounds coming through the open window of Royal Street below, she mused over her plans for the evening. Governor Claiborne had been most specific on what he wanted her to listen for from her dance partners. Tante Lala had been horrified at the thought of her goddaughter playing at being a spy, but the governor had assured the lady that Arielle would be in no danger.

"Seraphine, do you know anything about this man called Thane Ryder. Who is he?" Arielle asked her maid as Seraphine took her gown from the armoire. She knew that like most of the people of color in New Orleans, Seraphine was part of that secret grapevine that was aware of everything that happened in the city as soon as it occurred.

219

"It is said he has been in Europe and England these many months, but then, as an English lord, that would be understandable. He claims to take no side in the war, but there are rumors that he is a British spy. Although immensely rich, he is rather a recluse. I am surprised he is attending the governor's ball, but it is said he does enjoy gambling, and there is sure to be a high stakes game in the Claiborne library. He has turned the running of Belle Rivière over to M'sieur Tureaud, the overseer, and has only been there once."

"Is there anything you do not know, Seraphine?" Arielle shook her head in amazement over the depth of the slave grapevine in the city and countryside.

"Many things, mam'zelle."

"Come, I best dress for this fête," Arielle sighed rising from the cooling water. She wanted to look her best, seductive and eye-catching. Tonight she must make an impression on M'sieur Thane Ryder. A plan was slowing forming in her mind, a plan to finally achieve the revenge she had sought so long.

Standing in front of the pier glass as Seraphine slipped the heliotrope silk gown with its extremely low-cut neckline over her body, Arielle vowed to settle the score between herself and the man who destroyed her every chance at happiness. Tonight she must put all emotion deep within her and plan her every move with cold manipulation. The gown was perfect, and against Seraphine's protestations, she had donned no chemise. Silk clung to every curve as she walked. The low neckline and high waist showed off her high, full breasts to perfection, for her nipples were barely covered. Around her long neck she wore only a violet satin ribbon with a white fragrant rose pinned to it. Honey-gold tresses were piled high on the back of her head, but she had Seraphine allow several long golden curls to dangle provocatively down her back and over her shoulder.

Staring at her image in the mirror, Arielle snapped open a lavender lace fan trimmed in black and held it beneath her eyes in a seductive gesture. Tonight she would be a scandal when the other ladies saw her gown, but what did it matter? The men would flock to her like bees to nectar, and maybe one would be M'sieur Thane Ryder.

"You look *très chic, ma chère*," enthused Lala Boudreaux as Arielle entered their carriage. "That Kashmir shawl is quite the thing. How did you ever match the deep heliotrope of your gown?"

"*Merci*, Tante Lala," Arielle replied, knowing her godmother would be less pleased when she removed her shawl to reveal the extreme décolletage of her garment. She had chosen the enveloping shawl for a reason. It was important that her entrance be spectacular if she was to catch everyone's eye. Tonight Arielle had to be a belle sought after by the men if she was to be of service to Governor Claiborne.

Reaching the entrance of the Claiborne mansion, the carriage door was opened by the governor's majordomo, a tall African from the Ashanti tribe, known for their regal bearing. Dressed in the house livery of green and gold, he cut quite a figure. He handed each lady graciously down to the sturdy cypress boards laid across the muddy banquette.

Entering the wide hall of the house, with its floor of black-and-white marble, Arielle and her godparents were greeted by Governor Claiborne and his Creole wife, Sophronie.

William Claiborne, born into an old Virginia family, spoke only English and depended on his sprightly wife to converse with many of the old New Orleans families who refused to speak the tongue of their new country. Pleasant-faced with regular features, the governor lacked the dramatic flare of the Creoles. His short hair always seemed slightly disarrayed above his high forehead. There was a hint of a growing plumpness under his chin, making him look a trifle uncomfortable in his tight collar. Cool gray-blue eyes, however, revealed a certain candor and more than a hint of fixed purpose.

"How lovely you look, *ma chère* Arielle," dainty Sophronie Claiborne trilled, kissing her on both cheeks. "The men will flock around you like a honey pot."

"*Merci.* And you look *très charmante,* Sophronie. *Pêche* is your color," Arielle replied, smiling at the petite lovely woman in the peach silk gown who looked more like a delightful child. She and Sophronie had played together as children whenever the Basque family had visited their townhouse. Knowing the special mission her friend was on for her husband, the lovely Creole woman had expressed regrets she, too, could not play at this game of espionage. As the governor's wife, no one would feel free to reveal their true thoughts about the British so she must allow her friend Arielle to carry on alone.

"*Bonne chance,*" Sophronie had whispered to Arielle before turning to greet her next guest.

Walking into the ladies' parlor, Arielle handed her shawl to one of the Claibornes' maids. Checking her reflection in a low pier glass, she heard Tante Lala's gasp as she saw her goddaughter in the revealing gown of shimmering heliotrope.

"*Ma chère,* are you sure? It is beautiful, but rather scandalous," Lala whispered. The other women in the room stared at Arielle with envious eyes. "You will be talked about."

"I am sure, tante. What can they say that they have not already about the fast Mademoiselle Duplantier?"

Crossing the wide hall, Arielle swept into the white-and-gold ballroom with its many mirrors. Holding her fan in her hand, clad in its violet silk long glove, she stood, her head held high, coolly surveying the scene of elegantly dressed guests. An orchestra played up on a dais in one corner, while in another men sat at several tables playing *écarté*, a favorite card game in New Orleans.

As her eyes traveled across the room, Arielle gave a slight smile of recognition here and there. Gently, she waved her fan in a gesture of indolent grace, keeping herself aloof, alone from the crowd. Glancing toward the card players, she felt a slight chill that grew as it traveled up her spine. A man's profile stood out in relief against the ivory damask panel on the wall. The fan came to an abrupt stop as her heart jumped in her chest. Could it be? It was not possible. Then as the man turned, a shaft of golden light from the glittering chandelier above dashed her hopes to ashes. It was not Jacques. The light showed cruelly this was not her handsome privateer, her beloved husband, but instead a malevolent figure that seemed to cast a pall across the shimmering room. She must be losing her mind, she thought with despair. Having resisted going about in society for so long, she now fantasized that every strange man was her dead husband returned to her. Giving slight shudder, she tried to gather her cool, aloof pose about her once more.

Unable, however, to resist, she stared at the figure dressed in sober black clothes that, while plain, were of an expensive cut and material. Unfashionably long hair streaked with gray hung to the strange man's shoulders. A full black beard and mustache concealed his face, as did a rather frightening black eye patch. Only one burning black eye met hers, but it was enough to capture and hold her, impaled by the intensity of his will.

"Would you do me the honor of this dance, mademoiselle." A deep masculine voice broke through the fog that surrounded her, cutting the invisible bond that held her to the man in black.

"I should be delighted," Arielle agreed with a smile,

turning her attention to the handsome young man in front of her. Placing her hand in his, she followed him out onto the dance floor. "Would you happen to know who is that strange looking man seated at the *écarté* table?"

"But of course, mademoiselle, 'tis M'sieur Thane Ryder."

The room whirled about Arielle as her partner led her through the figures of the quadrille. That malevolent figure was the man who had destroyed her family. Somehow, she had pictured him differently — younger, more the dandy. The man in black so casually playing cards had an aura of mystery, of danger, that was so strong she could almost reach out and touch it. With a sinking heart, she wondered how could she reach such an individual. He was no callow aristocrat out to savor a new experience. The man she saw watching her from across the room was hard, knowing, and rather frightening. Did he know who she was, or was he only attracted by her face and form like the others?

As the night went on, it became apparent to everyone that Arielle was the belle of the evening, much to the dismay of several of the other young woman, including Delphine Miro. The young blades, and several of the older men, flocked around Arielle as Sophronie had foretold. When the orchestra took their break, and the midnight supper was announced, she found herself with one of André's old friends, Hugh Chauvin.

"What are you doing these days, Hugh?" she asked as he escorted her to the long banquet table, which was laden with numerous delicious-appearing dishes.

"Drilling with my company on the Place d'Armes. I belong to the *Carabiniers d'Orléans*. We will be ready for the British, have no fear, Mademoiselle Arielle," he replied, helping her select several tempting dishes.

"That is most reassuring. I wish more men felt as you do. I fear there are some who would welcome a British victory."

"That is true, I fear. The fools think the British will give them the Americans' land when they win the war, but what is to stop the British from taking everyone's property for themselves? They are idiots, that group of conspirators, but they continue their secret meetings where they plot and plan," the chestnut-haired Hugh confided to Arielle as they strolled out into the courtyard, around which were scattered tables draped with immaculate white cloths.

"Who are the members of this group of which you speak?" Arielle inquired as her escort seated her at a private table for two by a large magnolia in the corner of the walled patio.

"Well, it is only a rumor, but that mysterious-looking man by the name of Thane Ryder is said to belong, as well as several of the old Spanish families. No one really knows for sure, for they confide only in those they trust, and I, as a member of the militia, am not privy to their confidences."

The trilling artificial laugh of a woman interrupted their conversation, and they were joined by Delphine Miro and her enigmatic escort Thane Ryder. The couple passed by Arielle and Hugh to sit at a table not far from them.

Arielle noticed, as he held the chair for the vapid Delphine, that M'sieur Ryder walked with a decided limp, leaning rather heavily on an ebony cane with an ornate silver handle. His manner still was that of one use to command, even with the halting walk. His tall, broad-shouldered form seemed to dominate the courtyard, as he had the ballroom. Seating himself across from Delphine, his probing glance, from that one cold black eye fastened on Arielle and sent a shiver through her. This was the man she hated, the man who had figured in a hundred different fantasies of revenge, sitting a few feet

225

away and regarding her with a great deal of interest.

"Are you all right, Mademoiselle Arielle?" Hugh asked, startled by the expression of some intense emotion on her pale visage.

"*Oui*, the chicken is rather spicy. Could you please fetch me some more wine; my glass is empty," Arielle answered.

"But of course. These servants seem rather lax tonight," Hugh assured her, looking about the courtyard for one of the Claiborne slaves. Finding none, he rose to fetch her more wine from the dining room.

As her escort left the table, Arielle knew she had only a few minutes to intrigue M'sieur Ryder, for she realized that with his bad leg, he did not dance. Once they returned to the ballroom he would become involved once more with the gentlemen at cards.

Picking up her fan from the table, she opened it, gently waving it as if she were a trifle warm. Slowly, she allowed her gaze to wander about the patio till she was looking in the direction of the next table. Delphine was rattling on to her companion, but his interest was fixed on Arielle. There was a look of sardonic amusement about that closed bearded face.

With heart pounding, Arielle held the lavender lace fan beneath her eyes for a moment in a seductive gesture of flirtation. With a graceful gesture, he acknowledged her with a slight, knowing bow of his head before she looked away. Her mind in a whirl, she tried to think of how else she could make contact with him without appearing too brazen. Before she could act, Hugh was back with her wine, and she had to content herself with hearing all about his training with the Carabiniers d'Orléans.

As they were finishing the rich *gâteau chocolat*, Arielle's hopes were finally realized when a dark, looming, masculine figure appeared at their table. Her pulse racing, Arielle felt both fear and elation as she saw it was Thane

Ryder who regarded her with intense interest.

"Who is this lovely lady, Chauvin?" his deep, harsh voice demanded in English with a pronounced British accent.

"May I present, Mademoiselle Arielle Duplantier," Hugh answered stiffly, also in English, rising to his feet. "M'sieur Thane Ryder."

"Enchanté, M'sieur Ryder," Arielle replied in French with a slight smile, looking up at him from under lowered lids as she extended her hand.

"How do you do, Mademoiselle Duplantier? I do not speak French, alas, but dare I hope you speak English?" he inquired, bowing over her hand, barely touching it with his long, slender fingers. White teeth flashed against the dark fur of his beard and mustache. She noticed how he resembled a swarthy pirate with that wicked black satin eye patch covering one eye. The ebony gaze from his good eye stared down at her challenging, mocking, consuming her, for he knew now who she was — a Duplantier.

"Yes, I speak English, M'sieur," Arielle answered softly, meeting his stare with unwavering wood-violet eyes. She would show him she could not be intimidated, but she tempered it with a slight smile showing a deep dimple. Never could she forget her real purpose with this man.

"But then, perhaps you would not wish to speak with me, mademoiselle. I have surely grieved you, although that was not my intent, lovely lady."

Fighting an impulse to reply with all the hatred she felt toward this man, she managed to control her emotions. "The past is past, m'sieur, I look only toward the future. My brother's doings, and my father's, are not of my concern," Arielle answered sweetly, although the words stuck in her throat. Hugh looked down at her in amazement.

"How very wise of you," Thane Ryder murmured, but there was a question in his gaze. "If you should ever want

227

to visit Belle Rivière, it would be my pleasure to arrange it."

"Thank you, M'sieur Ryder, you are too kind," Arielle managed to reply. "I would like to inquire after a horse, a gelding named Sultan," she said, surprised at herself as the words came tumbling out. But the horse had been hers, and she had missed him since having to give him up when she left the plantation.

"He is fine, mademoiselle. In fact, he is stabled here in New Orleans at my townhouse on Rue Esplanade. I would be honored if you would be my guest at dinner on Thursday. I am having a small party, and this would give you a chance to see him for yourself."

Stunned it was happening so easily, she at first could only nod, then, gathering her wits, she answered, "I would be delighted, m'sieur." Hugh stared down at her with a shocked expression.

"Good. I shall send my carriage for you at your shop at seven. Until then, mademoiselle . . . Chauvin." Thane Ryder bowed his head formally and returned to the waiting Delphine.

"I do not believe you told that man you would attend his dinner party. You hate what he has done to your family. What exactly are you planning, Mademoiselle Arielle?"

"Seeking revenge, Hugh. But you must promise to keep what I have told you a secret. Swear now on the memory of your friendship with André," Arielle demanded, her delicate features serious.

Looking very uncomfortable, her companion nodded yes, but then, leaning across the small table, cautioned, "Thane Ryder is a dangerous man. I do not know what you are planning, but be careful. It would make no difference to him that you are a woman if he guessed what you are up to. He is completely ruthless, that one. If you need help, Mademoiselle Arielle, I would be honored if you would call on me."

"Pray do not worry. I shall be very careful in my dealings with M'sieur Thane Ryder," Arielle assured Hugh Chauvin. "We have a score to settle he and I, but I plan on winning. He has defeated the last Duplantier."

"I should call him out," Hugh said grimly, his hand tightening on the fragile stem of the wineglass, "but with his lame leg, it would be against the code of the *duello*. I wonder how it happened, that accident that maimed him. He is much changed since his return to New Orleans, a limp and missing one eye, but I fear as dangerous as ever."

"Perhaps he pushed someone too far. Whatever happened I am sure it was well deserved," Arielle replied, her voice taut with the anger she felt toward this forbidding man.

Watching the tall figure escort Delphine from the patio, his limp pronounced, she mused on the strange feeling she felt toward Thane Ryder. It was ridiculous, but somehow she experienced the oddest sensation when speaking with him, as if she had known him before. When that slender, masculine hand, with the aristocratic, tapered fingers, had touched hers, it had not seemed the touch of a stranger, nor was the gaze from that fierce black eye unknown. Shivering slightly, even though the evening was warm, Arielle tried to laugh at her foolish fancies. How could she feel drawn to her brother's murderer? The whole notion was appalling. But she feared that deep within her she was attracted to some aspect of the malevolent Thane Ryder. There was something about him that reached out to touch some cord deep within her being. She would have to be very careful when next they met, very careful indeed.

Chapter Sixteen

"The carriage is here," Seraphine's disapproving voice announced as she swept into Arielle's bedchamber. "Miche Ryder's man is waiting in the shop."

Merci. And you are right as usual about the gown," Arielle smiled over her shoulder at her maid as she checked her appearance in the long pier glass.

The gown was a new one Seraphine had finished that afternoon, and it was exquisite. The primrose-yellow silk gauze evening gown had full puffed sleeves trimmed in heavy blond lace that reached to her elbow, leaving her ivory shoulders bare. The neckline was so low that there was little material in the bodice before the high waist was caught up under the full, rounded mounds of her breasts with a wide golden sash. Decorated from hem to knee with lace panels edged in gold satin, it was a stunning creation that could have adorned the court of France.

Seraphine had dressed Arielle's honey-gold tresses high on the back of her head in elaborate curls, allowing tendrils to wisp loosely around the oval of her face and at the nape of her long neck. A gold ribbon band, with ivy-green leaves embossed upon it, was woven in and out of her curls, giving a classical air. She wore no jewelry but a pair of green shell earrings with delicate alabaster cameos and Jacques' ring.

"What do you think, Bébé?" Arielle questioned the large dog that lay at her feet. Giving a deep sigh, the animal rolled on its side and went to sleep. "I hope M'sieur Ryder is more impressed than that, Bébé," she chuckled, turning for a last check of her gown in the looking glass.

Satisfied with her appearance, Arielle touched the wand of her perfume bottle to pulse points and down the deep cleavage of her gown. Her yellow silk slippers were noiseless on the polished wood floor as she threw on the shawl, and with her gold mesh reticule on her wrist, she vanished down the curving staircase.

Sinking back against the soft gray velvet cushions of Thane Ryder's carriage, Arielle took a deep breath as they swayed down the muddy ruts of Royal Street. The evening she had both anticipated and feared was beginning.

Long purple shadows fell from Saint Louis Cathedral across the garden that lay to the back, where numerous duels had been fought. It was here André had been killed by the sword thrust of Thane Ryder, Arielle thought sadly as they rode past. Biting her lip, she looked away. She could not lose control of her emotions this night, for she would need all her wits about her when she met her adversary.

Arielle stirred uneasily on the velvet bench as they stopped so another carriage could pass. Inside she could see the beautiful woman of color dressed in the latest fashion, and her white male protector beside her off to an intimate rendez-vous. New Orleans offered every refinement of pleasure — and every refinement of vice.

How easy, Arielle mused, was it going to be to keep Thane Ryder at a distance. He did not seem like a man who would be content for long with a mild flirtation. Used to taking what he wanted when he wanted it, M'sieur Ryder could prove difficult to handle. Somehow, she took a perverse pleasure in the challenge of keeping this arrogant man at bay, dancing to her tune, as she led him on, but always withholding her surrender.

As the carriage turned onto that spacious avenue called Esplanade, where several wealthy Creoles were building homes, Arielle smoothed her gown with trembling hands. Pulling into a porte cochere, she leaned forward to see a tall, masculine figure awaiting them in the deepening shadows of the night.

"Welcome Mademoiselle Duplantier, to my home," the peculiar, hoarse voice of Thane Ryder floated on the soft night air to Arielle. He opened the door of the carriage and held out a hand to help her alight.

"Thank you," she placed her hand in his and replied in English, remembering he said he spoke no French. Warm, firm fingers clapsed hers and seemed to pull her out to him. Finding she was standing entirely too close to him, she took a step back, but her hand was still caught tightly in his.

"How beautiful you are," he said simply, staring down at her with a burning, intense gaze that made her uncomfortable.

There was something hard about his bearded visage, hinting at the hard and unyielding man inside. His appearance in the shadowy courtyard was arresting, causing Arielle to lower her eyes in confusion as she tried to conquer her involuntary reaction to his forbidding presence. Sensing his promise of danger if crossed, a cold knot formed in her stomach as her nerves tensed. Gently, she disengaged her hand from his tight grasp.

"If you will allow me, mademoiselle, I should like to show you something I think you will be most interested to see," her host stated in his rasping, deep voice. Although leaning heavily on an ornate silver-handled cane, he extended his arm to her with a certain grace.

Placing her hand on the rich broadcloth of his sleeve, she wondered idly if he always wore black. Injured he

232

might be, but she felt the hard, sinewy muscle of his arm under the expensive material as they walked slowly across the flagstone patio.

Lanterns on filigreed iron posts lit the large courtyard with soft pools of golden light as night fell across the city. Through an open door Arielle could see black women in gingham household livery busy preparing food in the brick kitchen house at the end of the patio. It appeared, except for the servants, they were alone as they walked slowly toward a building that appeared to be a stable. She wondered if she was the first guest to arrive.

As Thane Ryder dropped her arm to open the double door of the stable, all thought fled Arielle's mind. She gave a cry of delight as she spied her magnificent Sultan in the first stall. His coat shone like chestnut satin in the light from an oil lamp hung above his stall. Standing on tiptoe, she embraced the powerful neck of the gelding. The horse, catching her scent, nuzzled her golden head as he neighed his pleasure at being with her once more.

"Ah, he remembers you," Thane Ryder said softly, enjoying the lovely picture of Arielle and Sultan so happy in their reunion. "I think he will relish being with you once again. It seems he received little exercise at Belle Rivière. That is not good for such a fine animal, but I am sure you will remedy that now that he is yours once again. You do have a stable behind your shop, do you not?"

"Mine! You are giving Sultan back to me!" Arielle exclaimed, embracing the beautiful animal once more as he nudged her with his big, velvet-soft nose.

"If you want him," her host replied with a hint of amusement in his odd, deep, rasping voice. He stood in the doorway of the stable, leaning on a cane, his large form seeming to loom over her in the wavering light of the lantern.

"Of course I want him," Arielle answered emphatically, stroking Sultan's satin neck. "I guess I should thank you

233

for returning my own property." She could not help the stiffness that came into her voice.

"What a gracious acknowledgment," he said dryly.

Her host's sarcasm didn't go unnoticed by Arielle. She could not afford to anger this man, at least not until she found out the information she was seeking. There would be time for harsh rejoiners, fitting revenge, when she could prove he was a British spy. How she would enjoy seeing him hung in the center of the Place d'Armes. Until then she must be the sweet, empty-headed belle who was incapable of holding any kind of grudge, even against the man who had killed her brother and ruined her father.

"Pray forgive me. I am so overwhelmed at the thought of having my beloved Sultan back with me once more I fear I was quite unladylike." Arielle gave a sigh, looking down at the straw-covered floor with what she hoped was an expression of embarrassed regret.

"Indeed, mademoiselle. I shall send the animal over tomorrow with my man Hercules. He can help you ready your stable since you have not kept horses there in a long time. If you can tear yourself away from that noble beast, perhaps we can dine." He stood aside, holding out his arm to escort her to the house.

Managing as pretty a smile as she could with her teeth clenched in anger, Arielle allowed him to lead her across the courtyard and through French doors into a spacious high-ceilinged salon. Elegantly furnished in shades of blue, with gleaming pieces of the Queen Anne period, it could have been a room in an English manor house. From the center of the ceiling hung an enormous crystal chandelier that dangled from an ornate rosette of carved plaster. Looking across the tasteful chamber, Arielle saw another twin salon just like it, only in tones of rose. Massive sliding doors separated the two rooms and could be pulled shut if desired.

"It is quite lovely," Arielle commented to her host with

appreciation. "I see I am your first guest to arrive," she observed, seating herself in the blue damask wing chair he had gestured her to. "How many others are coming?"

"You mademoiselle, are my only guest. I thought a dinner *à deux* so much more relaxing. These large dinner parties New Orleans are so fond of, I find become rather tedious," her host answered. Walking over to a large, mahogany cabinet that opened to reveal crystal decanters and rows of delicate glasses, he asked, "Would you care for a glass of sherry?"

"Your only guest," Arielle repeated, stunned, realizing he had never suggested there would be others. She had simply taken it for granted. Violet-gray eyes stared across the room at him in astonishment as she nodded wordlessly that she desired a glass of the amber liquid. Trying to gather her wits about her, she slipped the concealing shawl from her shoulders and handed it to the young maid servant who had appeared in the room. Arielle felt Thane Ryder's intense gaze upon her revealed décolletage.

"Such beauty should not be concealed," he murmured as he handed her a crystal flute of deep amber sherry. "But the mystery first withheld, then revealed, is so much more exciting."

Arielle gave him a tight smile, lifting the glass to her trembling lips. Her host seated himself across from her in front of the marble fireplace that held only a huge basket of crimson roses at this time of year. How far with her flirtation would this strange man demand she go? With a cold chill in her veins she knew he would demand complete surrender and nothing less.

Feeling the smooth, warm liquid slide down her throat and into the hard knot of her stomach, she raised her eyes to that forbidding dark visage that seemed like a mask so little was revealed of his features. He seemed a rather intimidating figure with his unfashionable shoulder-

235

length, rather wild hair with its streaks of silver. His thick beard and mustache were black as a raven's wing, completely concealing his face. The black satin patch over one eye only added to his fierce, masklike appearance.

"Do you find me so forbidding, Mademoiselle Duplantier, or is it the sherry? I hate to see even the slightest frown mar such a lovely face. My appearance does cause concern among some of our more delicate belles. I am afraid even my money can not quiet their fears." There was amusement in his raspy voice as he stared at her with a mocking challenge in every word.

Lifting her chin, she met his gaze boldly. "You do not frighten me, M'sieur Ryder. I was only wondering what you are hiding under all that hair. Perhaps you are a handsome man—one cannot tell—and as for your money . . ." Arielle gave a Gallic shrug, "some of it is mine so I could hardly be impressed."

The sound of his deep laughter filled the room as he regarded her from his chair. "Touché! You must, however, call me Thane. May I be so bold to inquire if I may call you by your Christian name?"

"Yes," she answered coolly, concealing her delight at how her host seemed to be responding to her. She could sense he was interested. She was, however, aware of what a dangerous game she was playing and with a very worthy opponent.

"I surmise it would take a lot to impress you, Mademoiselle Arielle. It will be a challénge trying. Now, I see Doucette is signaling dinner is served. Perhaps my table will impress you, my dear," he told her with amusement in his odd, raspy voice as he rose to his feet having emptied his glass. He held out his arm.

The meal was superb, served in a dining room of monumental proportions with a table that could have sat twenty-two people. Arielle seated on Thane's right felt intimidated by the large room with its shadows and soaring ceiling. The open French doors that led to the courtyard allowed a warm breeze to flow into the room, but still she experienced a chill. Her host spoke little except to ask if each dish was to her liking. If she was to find out anything about his activities with the British sympathizers she would have to somehow broach the subject.

As dessert was served, a rich créme caramel and hot coffee with liquor, Arielle cast about in her mind for the right opening to start the conversation on the subject she desired. Once more her host caught her off guard before she could speak.

"That is an unusual ring you are wearing." His deep husky whisper startled her, so intent was she on her own thoughts.

Looking down at Jacques' ring she still wore, Arielle felt a stab of pain. "It was given to me by someone very dear," she said quietly, staring down at the crest.

"A lover?"

"I really do not think that is any of your business, m'sieur . . . Thane," Arielle answered, raising her head, her eyes violet fire as she glared her anger across the table.

"But, my dear Arielle, I do believe it is my business to know everything about the woman I wish to take as my wife."

The room was so silent all that could be heard was the sharp intake of Arielle's breath. She stared at him as if he were mad. "What did you say?" she asked, her voice breaking, and fighting the desire to laugh wildly, or scream.

"I am asking you to become my wife. Women, I understand, do like men to ask them on bended knee, but that, with my bad leg, is impossible. You do not have to give me an answer tonight, just think about it. Consider all the advantages you would have, my dear, as Mrs. Thane Ryder. Once more Belle Rivière would be yours. You would have a great deal of money, position once more in society.

Our children would have everything they could ever want."

"Children!" Arielle gasped out the word with a strangled cry.

"Of course children, heirs. That is the whole purpose of marriage, my dear. Certainly a woman such as yourself who has been educated in Europe does not believe in this American idea of marrying only for love," Thane chided her, leaning back in his chair. "Why, I thought all Creole marriages were arranged. I want to settle here in New Orleans. The climate is right for a man with vision. I wish, shall we say, to put down roots, so of course the perfect wife is a necessity. You fulfill all my requirements. If I may say so, you are beautiful, intelligent, spirited, and your success with your shop shows me your determination. Yes, you are everything I seek, but as I said, do not answer now; give yourself time to consider my proposal. It is really the best offer you will receive with only your shop as a dowry."

Shock had siphoned the color from Arielle's face. She stared at him blankly for a moment. The complete audacity of his words had left her dazed. Shaking her golden head slowly, she stated in a low voice, "M'sieur I have no wish to marry — ever."

They sat for a moment in a frozen tableau as Thane regarded her silently. She stared into the flickering light of the tall tapers in the silver candelabra in front of her. The rustle of the wind through the green leathery leaves of the magnolia outside the chamber was the only sound, till the lengthening silence between them was broken by Doucette.

"There is someone to see you, Miche Ryder." She spoke to her master in soft tones. "I have put him in the library."

"Thank you, Doucette," Thane told her in dismissal, rising to his feet. Leaning heavily on his cane, he bent down and took Arielle's hand from the table and lifted it to his lips. "I shall return as soon as I take care of this tiresome business. We can continue this discussion then. You are only surprised. Let it become a possibility, my dear, and you will see how right such a marriage would be for you."

Bowing once more over her hand, he left the room. Arielle shuddered as she caught the scent of sandalwood on the night air when he tuned to leave. Jacques! The name cried out in her heart as she watched the tall figure limp away — so different from the lithe stride of the man she had loved. It was absurd. She was surely going mad if the scent of sandalwood on a man could make her think he was her husband long dead. Many men must use that scent, but it had stabbed her to the marrow of her bones regardless.

Rising from her chair, Arielle walked to the open French door to stare out into the night. What was she to do? Her tidy plan was falling apart. What she had planned as a slight flirtation had turned into a proposal of marriage from a man she despised. Would it be possible to keep him dangling till she found the information she sought? As his fiancée she would be more privy to his affairs. Could she manage to insist on a long engagement, using the excuse she needed time to get used to the idea? she wondered with growing excitement. *Oui*, it would be the ideal excuse to spend more time with him, time she could use to find the evidence she needed to have him convicted and hung as a spy.

Clenching her hands together, Arielle tried to stop the spasmodic trembling within her. She would have to be so careful, for Thane Ryder was the worthiest of adversaries. Would she be able to defeat him? She would have to make the most of every opportunity in order to succeed. Only time would tell the victor, and she feared time for her was running out.

239

Chapter Seventeen

Warm, soft air, heavy with the promise of rain, blew up from the gulf, following the river to New Orleans where it caressed and teased the crescent city with anticipation. The heat of the day had not lessened with the coming of the night. A moist, suffocating blanket seemed to be covering the streets and hidden courtyards, straining nerves to the breaking point.

Arielle touched a scrap of lace she took from her reticule to her dewy face. It was stifling, she thought as she wandered out to the patio seeking relief from the muggy heat of the dining room. Turning her face up to the gentle breeze that blew through the giant leaves of the banana plant and waved the branches of the fragrant magnolia, she inhaled the faint scent of rain. The moon had disappeared under cover of indigo clouds — an omen of the storm to come.

As Arielle stood enjoying the cooling sensation of the wind against her skin, sweeping her gown out till it ballooned about her, she heard the sound of masculine voices raised in anger. Turning, she saw a light coming from another set of open French doors farther down the courtyard. The room must be the library, and the voices had to belong to Thane Ryder and his unexpected guest, Arielle surmised standing as still as a statue.

She moved across the flagstones, quietly, her canary-yellow silk slides silent as she traversed the patio. As she neared the open doorway, she realized the two men were speaking Spanish. Thankful she could understand the language, she stood against the plastered brick wall of the house listening intently to their conversation.

"The British grow weary of his cat-and-mouse game, señor. They want concrete plans of each bayou, each faint Indian trail into the city. I do not have to tell you of their plans to assemble a fleet in Jamaica Harbor. They demand a list of names of those here in Louisiana who stand ready to act on their orders when the time comes for that fleet to sail up the Mississippi," her host berated his guest in harsh, imperious tones.

"That may prove difficult to achieve, as you well know," the stranger answered coldly. "Our friends here in New Orleans want certain guarantees before they cooperate. As to those outside the city, I cannot speak for them. I believe you know more about that than I. How does Lafitte stand? Which side does he favor, or rather which side does he feel favors his own interest?"

"You know, Jean . . . first one way, then the other — never really committing his intention. I plan to visit Belle Rivière in a few days. I shall send word to Grand Terre that I wish a meeting," Thane Ryder said thoughtfully. "The Alliance Louisiane is another matter. Although I have some names, it is a short list at the moment. Many do not want to commit in writing to the British, for if the Americans should win, they want no evidence around to prove their guilt. We shall have to convince them otherwise. I must have a complete list."

"*Sí*, but it will not be easy, *mi amigo*," Thane's visitor sighed. "They are all a suspicious lot, and Claiborne's spies are everywhere. When you return from your plantation, I shall endeavor to have convinced them at least to another meeting here, to discuss what the British require from the Alliance. You may find your list growing longer if we can give them some firm pledges in writing from the English."

"*Bueno!* I shall contact you upon my return. Now, if you will excuse me, I have a lovely young woman awaiting me."

Arielle heard the scrape of a chair as Thane rose to his feet. With heart beating rapidly, she hurried from her hiding place across the patio till she stood in front of the open doors of the dining room. Trying to catch her breath, she mulled over what she had heard.

The Alliance Louisiane did exist, and it seemed Thane Ryder was a member, but even more important, he was in contact with the British command. If only she could get her hands on the list of names they were to compile for the British. It would be the proof she needed. Her face clouded with unease as she remembered her host's words about Lafitte. The British were trying to convince the men of Barataria to join with them. Claiborne was so stubborn and short-sighted about Lafitte. If he did not make his peace with them, they might decide to fall in on the side of the British with catastrophic results for the American cause.

Staring out into the darkened courtyard, Arielle chewed on her lower lip, suddenly feeling ill-equipped to undertake the task she had volunteered to perform for the governor. If she could only hear what offer Thane would make to Lafitte at Belle Rivière there could be a chance she could convince Claiborne of the seriousness of disregarding the men of Grand Terre. Then, as she clenched her hands together and felt Jacques' ring, it came to her how she could manage to be at Belle Rivière when Lafitte was meeting with Thane. A sense of strength and determination flowed through her, banishing the doubt, the frustration. With a pulse-pounding certainty, she knew how she was going to trap Thane Ryder and the Alliance Louisiane.

"My dear, I am sorry to have kept you waiting for so long. My business took longer than I thought." The harsh rasp of her host's voice startled Arielle, but she quickly recovered her poise.

"Pray do not concern yourself. I have been enjoying the cool breeze. It does look like rain," Arielle replied with a charming smile, turning to face him.

Standing across the room, he seemed even more sinister than she had remembered. He appeared like some harbinger of evil in his black evening clothes and fierce patch. Was that a handsome face or an ugly one under the mask of hair? she wondered with a shudder.

"I . . . I have had time to think as you advised, and I find I must agree with you." She trilled a high, artificial, shallow laugh. "A marriage between us could be quite advantageous for me. Poverty is not really what I am used to, and, I fear, it will not become an acquired taste," Arielle continued in what she hoped was the manner of a spoiled, unprincipled belle.

"As I thought, you are an intelligent woman," Thane replied evenly, but to her surprise, Arielle glanced a brief flicker of disappointment in that one intense black eye, the other so carefully hidden. "If you will accompany me back to the salon, I have something to give you to commemorate this moment." He held out his arm, his stern visage once more a frozen mask.

Placing her trembling hand on his firm, muscular forearm, Arielle allowed him to guide her back across the wide hall to the twin parlors. Thane led her into the rose salon to stand in front of the marble fireplace that was identical to the one in the blue parlor. Looking up, she noticed a large portrait hanging above the mantel of a lovely young woman with soft dark eyes and hair of a rich auburn, dressed in the wide-skirted fashion of many years earlier. Although the artist had painted the subject smiling, there seemed a sadness in the eyes that reached out to Arielle's heart. There was also something strangely familiar about those patrician features.

"It is a portrait of my mother, Rosemund," her host explained in a gruff whisper before releasing her hand. Moving closer to the painting, Thane ran bronzed, tapered fingers along the gilt frame till, to Arielle's amazement, the picture swung away from the wall to reveal the door of a small safe. Giving the dial a few quick twists, the door yielded to his ministrations. Reaching inside, he lifted out a worn blue velvet box and placed it on an elegant rosewood table.

"These belonged to my mother. They were her birthright, although she gave them up when she ran off with my father," Thane revealed in bitter tones. He lifted the lid of the box to reveal a magnificent necklace of brilliant sapphires and diamonds. On the white satin lining there was also displayed a pair of earrings, twin bracelets, and a breathtaking ring with an enormous blue sapphire surrounded by diamonds. "As my intended wife, the ring is yours. The rest I will give to you on our wedding day."

"La, but they are incredible, really the finest I have ever seen," Arielle breathed in awe, for she realized they were worth a fortune. She felt a surprising stab of pity for this strange, aloof man who appeared to have deeply loved his mother. Thane Ryder had looked upon her portrait with a deep sadness, and she wondered what terrible memories it must invoke to cause such bitterness in his voice.

"I am glad you are pleased . . . May I?" he questioned coolly, reaching for her hand, his intense gaze boring into her.

"Oui," she whispered. He took her hand in his, the palm firm, and, to her surprise, slightly calloused. When he reached to slip off Jacques' ring from the ring finger of her left hand, she stopped him. "Wait, I will move it to the other hand," Arielle muttered, trying not to see Jacques' handsome face pass before her as she quickly slipped the ring on her right hand.

"Really, you must tell me the story behind that keepsake, my dear. If I were a jealous man I fear I would be upset at the expression on your face as you took that signet from your hand. You were much moved, and filled, I think, with the memory of an old love, perhaps an old pain." Thane's voice was cold, almost mocking, as he placed the heavy sapphire ring on her finger.

Annoyed by transparency of her feelings, her lips thinned with irritation, but she forced them into a semblance of a smile. "As you said, we are people of the world, aware of what marriage entails. Only the Americans, I believe you pointed out, are foolish enough to marry for love," Arielle responded in a brittle voice heavy with sarcasm.

"But we are not that foolish, that naive, are we, my dear?" Thane's stare drilled into her and she felt a sudden chill.

What did this man want from her? Suddenly the reasons he gave for asking her to marry him seemed to be quite incomplete. Arielle had the frightening premonition that Thane Ryder had a hidden plan for their marriage, one she knew nothing about.

"Non, we understand each other perfectly," she replied, keeping her features deceptively composed as she endured his scrutiny. The ring, a perfect fit, felt like a weight on her hand, tying her to him if only in a figurative sense. She would never be his wife, she knew that

with every fiber of her being, but for now it was necessary to play the charade till she had the proof to unmask him.

"Aye, perhaps we do," Thane agreed with the strange sound of regret in his hoarse whisper. Lifting her hand to his lips, he stared at the glittering sapphire for a moment before turning her hand over and pressing the palm to his warm mouth.

Arielle went rigid at the effect the intimacy his mouth wrought on her. As his tongue lightly licked the soft mound of her hand, she heard with shock the moan that issued from deep within her being. How could she feel anything with this man whom she hated beyond reason? As his lips moved to the underside of her wrist with a slow, deliberate attempt at seduction, she felt something intense flare deep within her as he entranced her with his bold, unabashed pursuit of her senses.

There was a heat in the room surrounding them. It emanated from where his tongue traced circles of desire on her soft, fragrant skin. He breathed deeply of her scent and relished the taste of her on his tongue. What matter that he reviled everything she stood for, there was a primitive lure about her that he could not resist. He could take her now, force her to submit to his passion, his need, but he wanted more than that. She would have to know that she belonged to him, that she was his and his alone. It would take more than one rough tumble on the Aubusson carpet to satisfy him. There must be time to savor each inch of that haughty, beautiful flesh, to drink his fill of that moist, trembling mouth. He wanted those golden tresses flowing and loose where he could feel their silky texture against his bare skin.

"You tempt me, my dear," Thane murmured. He regretfully raised his head from her arm as she stood mesmerized by his skilled actions. "I fear our engagement must not be a long one, for I am impatient by nature."

"I must have some time to accustom myself to the idea. This is all so . . . new." Arielle stumbled over the words, intent that he should give her time. "It will not be easy to assemble a trousseau and plan an elegant wedding in a short time. There is so much to be done," she protested with a flirtatious pout, looking up at him with a playful glance, hating the need to continue the masquerade of a shallow, willful belle.

"And, of course, it is important to you that we have a large society wedding in the cathedral." Thane regarded her with a serious air, but each word had carried a mocking emphasis that cut into her. How she wanted to cry, *I shall never marry you in the cathedral, or anywhere else.*

"*Oui,* it will be fun to see all their envious eyes as I walk down the aisle to become Madame Ryder. I shall be richer by far than most of them. How the old cats will hate me." Arielle trilled a vain, mercenary laugh.

"You are brutally frank, my dear. I know you are not marrying me for my handsome appearance, but could you pretend a slight interest in something other than my money," Thane stated dryly, shaking his shaggy, gray-streaked head. "But you are right, we shall wait till the cool weather of October when everyone has returned to the city. With this heat, most will be leaving for the country, as I shall in a few days. It is time I become better acquainted with your Belle Rivière."

Her heart skipped a beat, for here was the opportunity she had been awaiting. Pulling her scrap of lace handkerchief from her reticule, she daintily dabbed at her temples giving a pretty sigh. "How I envy you leaving this heat for the plantation. It is always cooler there than in New Orleans. You must stand on the levee in the late evening; there is a slight breeze that comes from the river and it can be quite refreshing. Belle Rivière is so

247

lovely this time of year. I quite miss it." Arielle sighed once more, having little trouble squeezing out a tear as she glanced up at Thane from under fluttering, thick lashes.

"My dear, I would enjoy your company if you would care to travel with me to the plantation. Knowing, however, that society would frown on you visiting me unchaperoned, I will understand your refusal," Thane replied in bland tones, watching her as if to see what would be her next move in this elaborate game they played.

"*Pouf!* What do I care what those old cats think. They already talk about me because I opened the shop. I do not care what is said. I shall do what I want. *Merci, m'sieur* . . . er . . . Thane, I accept your invitation."

"Good! I admire a woman of spirit. We shall suit one another very well, my dear, very well indeed," he said smoothly, stroking his luxuriant mustache, one piercing ebony eye gleaming with some unreadable emotion. "Once I finish my business here we shall leave. Word will be sent to you concerning the exact day of departure."

"I shall wait with great anticipation," Arielle replied with a smile. She felt a great fatigue wash over her. The effort of maintaining her pose had exhausted her. She wanted only to leave this elaborate house with its many secrets and strange, magnetic master. "You must excuse me, but I fear that all this excitement has quite undone me. If you would be so kind, I would like to return to my home." She sank to a convenient chair in a slight swoon, giving him a wan smile. It was not hard to pretend, for her legs suddenly felt as weak as a kitten's.

"Aye, I shall. You do look a bit pale, my dear. This heat is beastly. A few days at Belle Rivière will do you good, and will give us a good chance to get better acquainted. You can show me all about the place," Thane

248

responded, limping to the long, embroidered bell pull next to the marble fireplace.

"How delightful it will be," Arielle managed to murmur from between clenched teeth. There was a pounding in her temples that told her a tremendous headache was imminent. The effort to control her swirling emotions was beginning to extract its toll. If she did not leave this house soon she thought she would begin to scream.

After what seemed like an eternity, the large, quiet black man, dressed in burgundy-and-gray livery, brought the carriage from the stable. As Thane helped her up the step into the welcome solitary interior of the barouche, she stumbled for a moment and leaned against him as he caught her. The scent of sandalwood once more drifted to her, and she closed her eyes thinking of Jacques. If only it was his strong chest she leaned against, his sinewy arm that held her for a brief moment, but it was not to be, could never be again. A stab of pain smote through her for an instant till she could not breathe.

"Are you all right, my dear?" The harsh voice of Thane Ryder shook her from her memories. She pulled away, climbing quickly into the carriage.

"I am fine," Arielle assured him from the window of the coach. "It is just a bit close. The storm is coming, I think." Her words were lost in the loud clap of thunder that exploded over the courtyard. A jagged flash of lightning had turned the night momentarily to day, and in that second she thought, with heart-stopping certainty, that the man called Thane Ryder, standing beside the carriage, was Jacques.

"Jacques!" she cried out the window as the barouche pulled out into the street carrying her away from him. A sudden lunge of the carriage threw her back against the seat jolting her back to reality.

Hot tears choked her as she yielded to the wrenching sobs that tore her apart. Burying her face against the soft velvet of the cushions, she gave vent to the frustration of the night. Her mind told her that Jacques was dead; it had only been a trick of the light that had made her think the malevolent figure of Thane Ryder was her beloved dead husband. Her heart had revolted at the thought of replacing the man she had loved with the man she hated. It was the intense pain of her betrayal that had made her think for one brief, mad moment that they were one and the same.

Taking deep breaths, slowly, one after the other, she was able to quiet her terrible grief as they rode on through the night-darkened streets. A sensation of intense fear and desolation swept over her as she realized she could not lose such control when at Belle Rivière. One false step and her intelligent, wary fiancé would be alerted to her game. Was she capable of doing what must be done if she was to exact her revenge?

The future lay before her an untraveled road full of hidden dangers. Tonight she had taken the first step upon the journey toward her goal of destroying Thane Ryder. She couldn't look back, but never had she felt so alone.

Chapter Eighteen

The soft light of the early-morning sun slanted down through the tangled branches of the giant oaks and twisted cypress as the three riders, followed by a small wagon, made their way along the narrow path through the dense forest. The day was already warm with the promise of the fierce heat of a summer's day in Louisiana.

Arielle brushed a gray-green wisp of Spanish moss from her face as they passed under a low, gnarled branch of an enormous live oak. They had been riding for several hours toward Belle Rivière Plantation. The day she had both feared and looked forward to had arrived. Today she had begun her first step in her plan of revenge against the man who rode with such arrogant unconcern in front of her on his ebony stallion. A servant Arielle had never seen before followed, driving a small wagon for their valises with a roan gelding for Hercules tied to the back.

Tired from lack of sleep, Arielle clung to Sultan's back with a weary determination. Since her dinner with Thane Ryder last week, she found sleep elusive. The dark visage of her enemy, her fiancé, haunted her thoughts as she tossed and turned in the four-poster, suffocating in its enveloping mosquito netting. She had to find the evidence that would prove him a British spy. Her revenge would only be complete when he hung from the hangman's noose.

When sleep would finally claim her she would have terrible dreams. It was what had awakened her the previous night, the horrifying nightmare that caused her moans of anguish to fill the hot, dark room. Sitting up, she had thrown out her arms as if to block the terrible vision she saw before her in the tortured depths of her mind.

"*Non!* Not that, never that! Jacques!" The cry of his name hung in the close, humid air as Arielle awoke from the vision of Jacques swaying back and forth from the hangman's rope, as the crowd in the Place d'Armes cheered.

Giving a shudder at the memory of her nightmare, she tried to put it from her mind, but her dream, seeming so real, had left her with an uncomfortable feeling. She had avoided Thane's gaze that morning when he had arrived at the shop, and as they had to proceed in single file down the narrow path out of the city there had been little chance, to her relief, for conversation.

Looking ahead, her eyes fastened on Thane's broad shoulders so visible in the loose linen shirt. He sat a horse well with the careless elegance of the true aristocrat. Arielle could not keep her gaze from the powerful grace of his sinewy muscles as they rippled under the soft linen with every controlled movement. Astride the stallion, his limp was not seen — only the strong, powerful thighs that were outlined through the tight fawn broadcloth of his breeches. The white broad-brimmed hat he wore at a rakish angle caused Arielle to realize for the first time that Thane Ryder might be a handsome man under all that hair. Even the eye patch was not a complete distraction, for it gave him a rather mysterious air.

"Par Dieu!" Arielle exclaimed under her breath, she was losing her mind. The heat, and lack of sleep, must have made her crazy, for she was admiring the man in front of her as if she had formed *à tendre* for him. Straightening in the saddle, she tried to keep her eyes from that tall, masculine figure riding ahead of her.

Turning her attention to the wild land they were trasversing, Arielle decided they were following the twists and turns of the Mississippi. It had been years since she had taken the land route to Belle Rivière. Usually, when she and her family had traveled to New Orleans, they had gone by boat, but Thane had confided he had wanted to travel by horse to accustom himself to the lay of the land. It had not seemed strange to Arielle at first, but now she wondered if there had been another reason for his choice. How could he tell the British of one of the best overland routes into the city from the south if he did not familiarize himself with it first. Startled by her realization of Thane's objective, she felt the weariness vanish as disquieting thoughts began to race through her mind.

Deep in thought, Arielle did not see Thane hold up his hand in a motion to halt. It was not till he turned and regarded her with surprise that she pulled Sultan to a stop beside Thane's stallion.

"Are you all right, my dear?" he questioned, his raspy voice solicitous.

"Oui, I mean yes," Arielle answered, for she knew he did not like her to speak French to him. He did not understand it, and seemed unwilling to learn.

"It is quite hot, and I fear I have a touch of the *mal de tête* . . . I mean headache," she replied, wiping her forehead with a wisp of a lace handkerchief, avoiding his intent gaze. Sometimes she felt he could look right into

253

her mind and read the plans she had for him. Shuddering inwardly at the thought, she tucked the damp cloth back in the pocket of her blue linen riding habit, playing for time to arrange her features in the bland, fretful expression of a spoiled belle.

"Pray forgive my pushing us so, but I am anxious to reach Belle Rivière. Perhaps you will forgive my lapse of manners if we stop now for luncheon?" Thane inquired, gesturing for Hercules. "We will stop under those trees, I think," he told her, pointing to a grove of oaks beside a slow-moving bayou that fed into the Mississippi.

"That would be delightful," Arielle agreed as he dismounted. She inhaled the clean fragrance of sandalwood as his strong hands encircled her waist and swung her down from the saddle. Her fingers dug into his sinewy upper arms for a brief moment, and she experienced an intense rush of physical awareness of this man she was plotting to destroy. Standing so close to him, she felt his warm hands still at her waist, each fingertip seeming to burn through the thin material of her riding habit. His hat shaded his bearded visage, but Arielle could feel the intensity of his gaze as she stood immobilized, unable to pull away. She felt trapped by invisible bonds, hypnotized by some allure this strange, aloof man cast over her. Her mind told her to resist, pull away, not let him have his way again, but something held her captured once more in the circle of his arms.

"You tremble, my dear." His voice was a husky whisper above Arielle as he pulled her to him. Staring down at her, he lifted her small heart-shaped face with one gentle finger. He bent low until his lips touched her quivering mouth.

The soft fur of Thane's beard stroked her cheek as

254

his mouth brushed against hers lightly, teasing the sensitive curve of her lips with a sensual enticement that feather-touched her with a tantalizing persuasion. Desire surged through her veins, a fire out of control. Her lips parted under his insistent yet tender assault as his tongue slowly explored the moist inner surface of her yielding mouth.

Her breasts, pressed against his chest, throbbed with her longing. She felt the heat of his body through the thin material of his shirt. Lost in the sensation of his sensual kiss, Arielle was aware of the feel of her soft thighs molded against the corded muscles of his long legs and the urgency of his manhood, rigid with passionate desire, pressing her soft woman's mound.

As her hunger rose in her traitorous body, all her resolutions melted, seeming to dissolve her very bones. She clung to his tall frame like the jasmine vine around a giant oak. Her body seemed to have a will of its own that obeyed no laws of conscience. She reveled in the feel of him, hard and lean against her feminine softness, the masculine scent of him in her nostrils, the taste of him upon her mouth.

"You haunt my lonely nights," he murmured against the silk of her skin, his lips trailing down to the slender, sensitive hollow of her throat. "Tonight, sweet, tempting Arielle, I shall not sleep alone."

In the dim recess of her conscience she heard a protest that her masquerade might require submission to his passion, but she did not have to enjoy it with such complete wanton surrender. The voice was stilled by the flame that flared within her at his words. Could she refuse him her bed? She did not know, and that knowledge appalled her even as it sent shivers of excitement down her trembling limbs.

It was the sudden movement of Sultan that shattered

their passionate embrace, breaking the spell of their sensual attraction. The thrashing animal tried to break loose from the low-hanging branch that Thane had tethered him to when he had dismounted.

Lifting his head from Arielle, Thane stiffened as he spied what was spooking the gelding. Thrusting her from his arms and behind him, he reached into his boot, pulling out a small short-barreled pistol. Taking careful aim, he blew off the head of the deadly mud-brown water moccasin coiled at the base of the tall cypress tree to which Sultan had been tied.

Arielle shuddered with revulsion. She had always hated the ugly snake that was so prevalent in the swamps. André had enjoyed shooting the reptiles in the bayou near Belle Rivière, but it was one of the few sports she had not joined in with her brother.

"Are you all right?" Thane questioned as Hercules came running from where he was setting out the picnic on a linen cloth spread on the mossy banks of the bayou.

"Oui, it is only an old fear of mine. I hate moccasins," Arielle replied, turning away from the sight of Hercules throwing the head and then the long body of the snake into the water with a thick, gnarled branch.

"Aye, they are ugly customers, and deadly, too," Thane agreed, stroking Sultan's satin neck to quiet him.

It was only later, as they sat beside the slow-moving olive-green water eating the delicious luncheon, that Arielle wondered how an Englishman, who was supposed to be unfamiliar with the land of Louisiana, could recognize the dangerous water moccasin so quickly. They looked like several other harmless water snakes, unless one could see the characteristic inner white surface of the mouth that gave them the nick-

256

name "cottonmouth." This had not been visible in the moccasin he had killed. It was only the planters, and men of the swamp, who could tell the difference so easily without seeing the open white mouth.

"Such a frown, my dear. You should not let it mar your lovely features," Thane commented, filling Arielle's delicate-stemmed glass from the long-necked green bottle of wine resting in its own narrow wicker basket. "Is it still the headache that is bothering you?"

"A little," Arielle responded, removing her riding hat with its graceful gray plume. "It is so warm, even here in the shade of the trees. When we arrive at Belle Rivière I shall soak for hours in a cool bath."

"The picture your words conjure up is quite delightful," Thane answered softly, a smoldering invitation in his hoarse voice. "Perhaps you will allow me to join you?"

Her pale, honey-hued hair glowed in the afternoon light, and he drank in the sight of her. The delicate ivory skin, now touched with a flush of rose at his insinuation, heightened her breathtaking beauty that quickened his desire and intense hunger. How could such perfection in face and form conceal such a mercenary little soul? Thane mused with a sharp pang.

"There are many tubs for bathing at Belle Rivière. It is not necessary to share," Arielle informed him in a voice low and honey-smooth, obviously ignoring his double entendre as she fanned herself slowly with her hat.

"But it would be so much more exciting to share. We shall soon be sharing everything, my dear, as husband and wife. I fear I find the waiting tedious," he informed her, tracing the curve of her cheek with one tapered finger, down to her long, slender neck. "Such skin . . . like velvet. How I shall enjoy the feel of you, Arielle.

257

You are really quite a prize, but then you know that. I so dislike false modesty in a woman. You are aware of your value, and your price is marriage. Am I right?" His voice held a caustic note of amusement as he saw her anger rise at his words and her attempt to quell it.

"Yes," she spat through clenched teeth as his hand caressed her neck, reaching the buttons of her jacket. Arielle stared straight ahead, not looking at him, hating the words he spoke, hating her reaction to his knowing touch. She felt him unbutton the first button, and then the next, till her linen jacket lay open, exposing the thin muslin of her chemise. Hercules had returned back to the wagon, behind a screen of sweet olive bushes, so they were alone.

Gently, but with determined skill, his fingers traced a taut, dusky-rose nipple that strained against the thin material. First one, and then the other, he tantalized the buds till they had swollen to their fullest with a reluctant desire that she realized was useless to fight. Shocked by the hunger he could elicit, she wanted to pull away, but shivers of delight followed each caress, rushing downward to center in her loins with a fierce demand for release.

"How I should like to taste the perfection of these beauties. To feel the sweetness on my tongue. Ah, I cannot resist," he murmured, slipping the jacket from her shoulder, and then the lace straps of her chemise. Her breasts rose up in passionate longing as he bent and licked first the right and then the left rosebud. She moaned a cry of reluctant surrender.

"Please . . . oh, please!" she begged, and even she did not know if it was for him to stop, or give her the complete fulfillment her body so urgently desired.

"How good you are, how delicious," he whispered against her skin. He slid one erect peak into his mouth, swirling its tip with his tongue, then sucking lightly, driving her mad with desire. She clenched her fist against her mouth to stifle her cries as he sucked and caressed each breast with a rhythm calculated to make her wanton with longing. They were not Thane and Arielle now with all the anger that lay between them. They were man and woman, hot with a passion that knew no right or wrong, only the need for fulfillment.

Lifting his head, he cupped her chin, turning her to face his frightening visage and burning black eye. "I should strip the clothes from that honeyed body and take you naked and trembling on the ground. Yes, you would like that, my little wild one. I should not be a gentleman then like your fine Creoles. How you could hate me for it. You could lie to yourself that I forced you, but you would remember how you wanted me. Yes, you want me, my dear Arielle. I see it in your eyes, taste it on your lips, and feel it in your skin, the hunger you have. Well, my sweet fiancée, you will not get your release this time. Not now, but soon, I shall take you, and you will beg me for it. Oh yes, you will, and how you will enjoy it." His harsh laugh mocked her as she pulled away from his hand, her violet eyes blazing.

"*Batard!*" Arielle hissed in French, raising her hand to slap his face, but he caught her wrist in a viselike grip. "You arrogant bastard!"

"That I am, my dear, that I am," he agreed, rising to his feet, dropping her arm. "How I shall enjoy having you as my wife. You are a woman of spirit. I pray you remain so in the bedchamber. It will make life so entertaining." Laughing at the fierce rage on her heart-shaped face, he handed her the jacket of her riding habit as Hercules came through the bushes at his whistled signal.

Quickly buttoning the blue linen jacket, her fury almost choked her. Whatever she must do, no matter how vile, she would do it. She would bring her revenge on Thane Ryder. Somehow, she would bring him to his knees. Only then would she be free.

Chapter Nineteen

Clang! Clang! The deep, echoing sound of the plantation bell drew Arielle out the French doors of the chamber that once more was hers to stand on the second-floor gallery. It was the sound, the calling of the slaves from the fields each afternoon, that reminded her of her childhood. This had always been her favorite time of day at Belle Rivière, sunset. She stared out across the emerald lawn streaked in the golden light of late afternoon with the shadows of the enormous live oaks. Through the gently waving curtain of Spanish moss she could see the rushing waters of the Mississippi.

How she had missed it all; the house, the land, Belle Rivière's people. They had greeted her with smiles of welcome. The butler Jubal, Tante Marie the cook, Lily and Berthe, the two house maids, had all told her how happy they were to see her again. If they had been surprised to find her returned as their new master's fiancée, their carefully arranged expressions showed no sign. They seemed happy enough with Thane as the new owner of the plantation. Lily had confided, as she unpacked Arielle's valise, that the master was very fair and would not allow the overseer Tureaud to use the whip.

Sighing, Arielle leaned over the railing watching one of the house servants return from the rose garden with a basket full of blooms for the evening's dinner table. Life seemed to have gone on at Belle Rivière in the same routine. Nothing had been allowed to deteriorate. The house gleamed with only a few additions here and there of paintings and furniture. It had changed very little from that day almost two years before when she had left it all behind.

"Mam'zelle, excuse me, but the master wishes to know if you are ready to join him in the salon before dinner?" Lily inquired, opening the double doors that led out onto the gallery from the wide upstairs halls.

"*Oui*, I am ready," Arielle replied, smoothing the skirt of her simple white muslin gown with its blue ribbon tied high under her breasts. She had chosen a chaste, unadorned gown, and had had Lily dress her hair high on her head, threading another blue ribbon through the curls. Pearl-drop earrings and a blue ribbon choker at her throat with a cameo were her only jewelry, except for Thane's sapphire ring on one hand and Jacques' signet on the other. Her appearance would have to do for the new master of Belle Rivière.

"Come in, my dear. You look lovely, so cool and refreshed," Thane commented as Arielle entered the spacious, high-ceilinged room. "We have company. Father Antoine was making his rounds of the river plantations and chose Belle Rivière for his stop tonight."

"Perè Antoine . . . welcome," Arielle murmured graciously, regarding the New Orleans priest with speculative eyes. It had been rumored that the curate of Saint Louis Cathedral was a spy for Spanish interests in Louisiana. His priestly robes were a good cover, for he traveled in that capacity all over the city, and from plantation to plantation in the summer season. Was his appearance at Belle Rivière on the night Thane returned merely coincidence, or did he carry a message for her fiancé from those who would like a British victory.

"My child, I was so happy to hear of your engagement. I can quite understand your wish to be married as soon as possible, and here at your old home," the tall, gaunt priest replied, bowing in her direction. If he noticed her shocked expression at his words, his stern visage remained impassive.

"My dear, I thought how fortuitous that Father Antoine should appear tonight. Such a good omen that our wish to be married at Belle Rivière will now be able to become a reality." Thane crossed to her side, taking her arm with strong fingers that clamped her to him with complete authority.

"It is quite a surprise," Arielle muttered through clenched teeth as his grip tightened. "We will have to send out the invitations on the morrow. How long may you stay with us, Perè Antoine?" Arielle asked, stalling for time.

"Only tonight I fear, my child," he replied, his black eyes glittering as he watched her reaction with a feigned, bored indifference. "I go downriver on the morrow."

"Tonight." Arielle repeated the word, allowing it to hang in the still, hot air of the salon.

"We shall have to do without guests, my dear. It will be more romantic this way, just the two of us and the people of Belle Rivière in the plantation chapel," Thane told her in a voice that allowed no argument. "We can have a reception later in New Orleans when we return to the townhouse. Belle Rivière is the perfect setting for our honeymoon. Here we can really get to know one another." The one obsidian eye drilled into her as she stared up at that closed visage masked in the luxuriant black beard and mustache that gave little hint to the features beneath. He was not going to give her any quarter.

Arielle wavered in her response, trying to comprehend what she was hearing. How neatly he had trapped her into going through with this marriage. If she refused he would be alerted that she had no intention of ever marrying him. Thane Ryder was an intelligent man. He would begin to wonder at her motives since she had told him she was marrying him for his money and position. The only route to her bed was with a wedding ring, she had assured him. *Non,* she decided, it would not be possible to stay at the plantation without either marrying him or convincing him that she only wanted a passionate affair. Arielle did not think she was capable of making him believe the latter. Marriage it would have to be, she thought grimly. Once she gathered her evidence, Claiborne would make her a widow in a short time, and Belle Rivière would once more belong to her.

"Oui, it will indeed be more romantic this way," Arielle agreed after a long pause, during which she imposed an iron control over the disgust she felt.

"Good. Then shall we retire to the chapel? I took the liberty of arranging for your bouquet, my dear," Thane announced, limping over to a table behind the settee. Picking up a sheaf of white roses and baby's breath, he handed them to her.

Arielle realized the maid had been gathering flowers for her bridal bouquet. Thane had planned everything down to the last detail.

The purple shadows of dusk were falling across the gardens as they made their way to the small, thick-walled chapel near the family burial ground, glowing a soft ivory in the twilight. Shuddering as she passed the tombs of André and her father, she whispered, "Forgive me for what I am about to do."

"Did you say something, my dear Arielle?" Thane inquired, tightening his grip on her arm.

"*Non,* nothing."

With Thane's arm holding her tightly, Arielle followed the priest into the chapel. She could see the house servants, grooms, and the gardening staff filled the benches. Tall ivory tapers glowed from brass three-branched candelabrum on the tiny altar and at the end of each row. The scent of roses and night-blooming nicotina was overpowering, for huge bouquets of the flowers stood everywhere in the still, oppressive air of the chapel. Thane had indeed seen to everything, she thought dizzily as he pulled her down the aisle behind the tall, gaunt Father Antoine.

The ceremony passed in a blur as Arielle concentrated on not fainting from the heat and the overpowering scent of the blossoms. Could she ever smell roses and nicotina again without feeling sick?

When Thane's cool lips brushed her own, she realized the dreaded ceremony was over, and she was now his wife. Curiously, she felt nothing but a great weariness and a pounding in her temples that would not stop.

As they faced the servants, she saw smiling dark faces and heard the field hands give a cheer as they walked out of the chapel. Thane's arm was now around her waist as he noticed her pale, trembling face. He was literally holding her upright.

"They are happy to have you back, my dear, and as mistress," he murmured as they acknowledged the cheer with a wave and a smile.

"Please, could we return to the house. I fear I feel a

bit faint," Arielle pleaded.

"Aye, you do look rather pale, dear wife," Thane admitted with sarcastic emphasis on the word wife. Holding her arm in a tight grip, he guided her down the path toward the house, the priest following behind them. "I fear the excitement of our marriage has been a bit taxing for you. A glass of sherry should bring you around. Remember this is our wedding night, and I have rather look forward to the consummation of our bargain," he said softly, mockingly. Arielle flashed him a look of disdain marred by the unwelcome blush that had crept into her cheeks at the thought of the coming night, and what he would expect from her.

"That is not the remark of a gentleman," she managed to stammer as they walked on to the gallery of the house. Her heart fluttered wildly in her chest, for she remembered the feel of his hard, strong arms around her that afternoon by the bayou.

"You will find that I am not always a gentleman, my dear wife, but then gentlemen can be quite boring. They always do what you expect. You will not have to worry about being bored with me, my Arielle, I promise you that," he replied with an edge of steel to his voice and more than a hint of a threat.

An elegant dinner had been laid out on the highly polished mahogany table in the dining salon, and, still holding her arm, Thane guided Arielle into the candlelit room. Seating her at one end of the long table, he waved Father Antoine to the middle chair. He took the master's place, where Faustien Duplántier had once sat.

Her temples throbbing with the headache that would not leave her, Arielle tried to concentrate on the conversation between Thane and their guest. It was as if she saw everything through a red haze of pain, and the sight of the food placed before made her nauseated. What was wrong with her? she questioned silently as she sipped the cool champagne in the crystal flute. Her thirst was great, although she had no appetite.

A single mosquito circled one of the tall tapers on the table, and Arielle seemed hypnotized by its graceful flight. The drone of the insect seemed to echo like a bell in her pain-filled head.

"My dear, you have not touched your food. Is there something wrong with it?" Thane's husky voice interrupted her musings.

Lifting her head, that seemed so heavy it made the slender column of her neck ache to support it, Arielle managed a wan smile. "I fear I have no appetite," she answered, staring down that long expanse of gleaming wood at this man who was now her husband. Her *second* husband, she corrected herself silently. Then, finding the thought that Thane knew nothing of her previous marriage funny, she gave a small giggle.

His ebony eye glared at her across the table at the sound as he regarded her intently, the black patch adding to his malevolent appearance. Although he was dressed in impeccable black evening dress, his hair, black as night with streaks of silver, still hung unfashionably about his shoulders, blending in with the beard and mustache till he seemed some great hairy beast.

Arielle gave a slight shudder as she lifted her glass once more to her parched lips. She now belonged to this dark enigma of a man, and, according to the law of Louisiana, he had the right to do with her as he might choose. Tonight it would begin, this strange marriage, and she wondered with pulse pounding how

267

it would be. What would his lovemaking be like? Her hand trembled as she placed the empty glass back on the table.

"You have imbibed too much on an empty stomach," Thane stated with a tinge of exasperation in his raspy tone. Even his voice seemed inhuman, Arielle decided, returning his stare through a daze of headache and too much champagne.

"Au contraire, m'sieur, I have just begun," Arielle spat back, meeting his accusing gaze. She gestured for Jubal to fill her glass again.

"Enough! The mistress has had enough," Thane told the old butler as he hesitated from where he stood by the sideboard. Rising to his feet, her husband limped in his curious gait over to where she sat glaring at him with stormy gray-violet eyes that looked enormous in the pale oval of her face. "Come, my dear, I will escort you to your chamber. I fear the day has been too much for you."

Arielle sat for a moment in stubborn silence as he stood behind her chair. Once she got rid of this terrible pounding in her head, she would show him that although they were married, he could not order her around like a half-witted child. But for now, she decided as she rose unsteadily to her feet, having to clutch the edge of the table for support, she would retire gracefully from the field of combat.

Placing her hand on her husband's arm, she allowed him to escort her from the room after bowing in Father Antoine's direction. Staring ahead in icy silence, she refused to look at Thane or acknowledge his presence till they reached the curving staircase. "I can manage the rest of the way, thank you," she muttered through clenched teeth, removing her hand from his sleeve. Without looking at him, she started

268

up the staircase.

"I shall be up shortly," Thane called after her.

Stopping her ascent, she turned and stared down at him. "You will be coming to my chamber?" she asked in a tremulous voice, clutching the polished stair rail for support.

"Perhaps you would prefer to come to mine?" he questioned with a significant lifting of one dark brow. His deep laughter filled the hall as she turned her back on him. Her breath coming in ragged gasps of impotent anger, Arielle stared up the stairs, her head held high against his insolence.

Silver streaks of pale moonlight shone through the lace curtains to fall across the muted shades of the Aubusson carpet and onto the mosquito *barre* of the fourposter. The pale light filtered through the gossamer netting on to Arielle's face and slender form. It was too hot for a cover, and her legs thrashed against the silk nightrail she wore. Sleep had proven elusive. The tall clock on the landing struck twice as she rose from the bed, pulling aside the voluminous mosquito netting that had intensified her sense of suffocation. Standing on the soft carpet, Arielle slipped the nightrail from her feverish body. She could not stand the touch of material on her overheated skin. How she wished she could bath in cool water, but the servants were all asleep in their quarters. The bath would have to wait till morning.

The house was quiet with only the sounds of the night creatures of the swamps coming in through the open windows to break the silence. Everyone must be asleep, she mused, including the man she had just married. He had not come to her chamber, and for this, she told herself, she was grateful, even though it was but a small reprieve. How many hours had she lain in that bed awaiting her husband who never came?

Crossing to the elegant white-and-gold dressing table, Arielle searched in the light of the moonglow for a crystal box. Finding it, she took out a swansdown puff covered in body powder in her own special fragrance. With long strokes she applied the cooling powder to her arms and down the backs of her legs. As she lifted one breast to brush under its weight she heard the creak of the door.

Turning, she saw a dark figure of a man, outlined in the light from the hall, standing in the doorway. Her breath caught in her throat as she choked back a cry. It was Thane, her husband.

"It is a hot night," he said in a husky voice that was thick and unsteady with barely checked passion. He shut the door tightly behind him. "You look so cool, so lovely in the moonlight, like a goddess. Are you Aphrodite, or the chaste Diana?"

Arielle stood frozen, unable to move, the powder puff clutched in her hand. She realized she was standing in a shaft of moonlight. Her unclothed figure would be completely visible to him.

"Here, allow me," Thane demanded, reaching out to take the swansdown puff from her hand by the silver handle.

Sensing his palpable physical presence, for she could hardly see him in the dim, shadowy room, Arielle stood mesmerized like a trapped animal, feeling his gaze on her like a leopard eyeing its prey. Slowly, he began to stroke her lightly across her collarbone with the puff moving ever downward till he flicked the feathery puff over her breasts lightly, slowly, as the rose-pink nipples tightened with each stroke. Warm, knowing, masculine fingers reached out and cupped first her right breast, lifting its weight in the warm palm of his hand as he brushed the swansdown under the firm oval, then the left. Trembling, she stood immobile, hypnotized by his touch as he moved the silver-handled puff down over her rib cage, tracing the indentation of her narrow waist with feathery strokes. She gasped as, with a slow sensuous movement, he moved downward to caress the saucy mounds of her bottom.

"Did you think I would not come?" he questioned, his deep, husky voice caressing her, as did the wand he used with such pleasure-invoking skill on the backs of her thighs.

"I thought you had retired," Arielle stammered, her violet-smoke eyes enormous in the pale flower of her face.

"Alas, there was business to finish before I could allow myself the pleasure of your company, my dear wife," he replied with a faint tremor of emotion in his voice that was more a raspy whisper. "And what pleasure it will be to have you now, like this." Thane threw the puff away and swept her into his arms before Arielle could protest. His lips captured hers with a passionate force that sent rivers of liquid fire through her veins.

Crushed to his broad chest, she felt her will weaken as one firm hand cupped her head, the long fingers entangled in her honey tresses overpowering her. The masculine scent of him, mingled with the fragrance of sandalwood, filled her nostrils as his kiss branded her mouth with his seal of ownership. The compelling strength of his desire flowed into her, and she could not resist.

271

As they stood in the shaft of moonlight, Thane felt her resistance wane, heard her moan of surrender as her slender arms stole up about his back. The exotic perfume that seemed so much a part of her surrounded him. It was a haunting scent that plagued his sleep and beckoned him whenever she was near. She was always there on the edges of his mind no matter what he was doing, thinking. The desire for her, the need to possess—it drove him mad with longing. Tonight he would finally find release, and his heart beat against her soft, sensuous breasts with triumph.

With a low growl deep in his throat, Thane pulled her toward the bed waiting in the shadows. Kicking aside the mosquito netting, he laid her down upon the high mattress stuffed with Spanish moss. He stared down at her as he swiftly pulled off his boots and then his breeches.

She lay staring up at the looming dark figure above her, wishing she could leave him, run from the room, but she knew he would find her. There was nowhere for her to hide. She was his wife, and the law of Louisiana said he might do with her as he wished. He was her enemy, and he was her husband. Suddenly, Jacques' beloved face flashed through her memory, and she felt a pain as swift and deep as a knife stab to her heart.

The moon had vanished under a cloud plunging the room into blackness as Thane pulled the mosquito *barre* into place behind him. "How I have waited for this moment—longer then you can imagine, my Arielle, my wife." His voice was a triumphant rasp as he joined her on the bed.

Unable to see him in the now-darkened room, she could only feel his touch, the heat from his body, his compelling presence as he pulled her violently against him, his mouth smothering hers with a hungry ravishment. It was then she realized he had not completely undressed, only relieved himself of his boots and lower garments. He still wore the long, fine muslin shirt, although the jacket and caveat were discarded.

"Take off your shirt," she whispered as his lips moved down to the hollow of her throat. He would not treat her as if she were a whore he was giving a quick tumble. Somehow it seemed obscene for her to be stark naked, and he only partially unclothed. All the resentment of his high-handed treatment of her welled up inside Arielle, threatening to choke her.

"Nay, sweeting, 'tis best I do not," he murmured against the silk of her skin, his tongue lightly circling her ear sending a warm languor through her body, even though she fought the excitement his practiced lovemaking could so easily arouse.

Suddenly it became important to know why he would not do as she asked. What was he hiding beneath the shirt? Was it a secret such as she sensed he was hiding under the long, shaggy hair and beard. She would win some victory tonight, even though a small one. He would take off the shirt as she had asked.

"I want to know why," she demanded, trying to twist out of his arms, pushing him away, her hands against his shirt-clad chest.

"Nay, I said!" he muttered angrily, taking her arms and pinning them to her sides, pushing her down on her back.

He was a dark shadow above her, holding her down so she could not fight him. Did she want to fight him? she thought in that long, timeless second when only the sound of his breathing broke the silence.

"I can give you pleasure, my Arielle. That is all you

need to know. Do not make this pretense at resistance; it is not needed. I know what you need, let me give it to you," he groaned as his body came down on hers.

Insistent and hungry, his mouth covered hers demanding a response. Lost in a whirl of sensation, Arielle opened trembling lips as his tongue, in a touch of fire, caressed the sweet corners of her mouth, then slowly circled the moist coral cavern she opened to him. Hesitantly, she touched his thrusting tongue with her own tongue. They tasted and dueled gently with an exploring joy.

Wanton, she was acting the wanton, a small voice deep within her tried to protest, but the thrilling rigid thrust of his manhood against the yielding suppleness of her belly, his demanding mouth that set her aflame overpowered her will as his strong hands had her body. Arielle had become a creature of sensation ruled by the fiery needs her new husband was so skilled at igniting.

Yielding to his passion that she sensed he held barely in check, Arielle clung to him, her hands tracing the muscles of his strong, sinewy back. She had wondered if he would be a rough or a gentle lover, but she realized now that he had the capability to be both. He was ruthlessly controlling his emotions in order to be gentle with her, leading her tenderly toward fulfillment.

"Arielle," he murmured, lifting his lips from her mouth. The single word contained both wonder and despair. His warm, searching mouth trailed a fiery trail of kisses down the length of her slender neck, the soft fur of his beard as caressing as the swansdown puff. Arielle gave a light shudder as he sucked at the sweet nectar of her skin in the hollow of her throat before moving lower to the firm, ivory mound of her breast.

"Oh, yes!" she whispered into the night as he took one throbbing peak into his heated mouth. His tongue encircled the rosy nipple lightly, teasingly, as fire burgeoned inside her being, growing and spreading till it reached her loins, setting them ablaze. He sucked the taut peak till she arched up to him her hips twisting, turning, seeking an age-old release.

He pressed against her with his erect manhood thrusting into her soft thigh, his hands cupping her silken buttocks. He left one taut, wet nipple and sought the other with a repeat of his delicious performance.

Lost in her instinctive response to his lovemaking, Arielle moved her body to the rhythm he was setting. Her mind was buried in a fog of sensual sensations that celebrated the ancient magic of man and women together. There was no thought of yesterday, only of this moment in time when they blended so well, two halves of a whole uniting in the mystery of life's sweetest pleasure.

As he lifted his head from her breasts, she cried out, but her cries turned into moans of delight as his long fingers found the small, silken, triangular golden pelt at the apex of her slender legs. A desire so intense, surged through her as those masculine fingers found her woman's petals and stroked the hidden rosebud with slow persistence, letting her passion build till she was moist with love's honey.

"Now, my wife," he whispered, rising above her, a dark shadow in the night.

Arielle reached out for him, her hands finding and clinging to his back as he lifted her into his embrace. His hot mouth came down on hers, his tongue thrusting inside as he entered her. His velvet shaft throbbed

275

within her as he moved slowly at first, as if to teach her his rhythm, then, as she arched up against him taking him more fully, his passion grew and his control lessened.

She wanted him, needed him deeper, and deeper still, as her body reached up to him in a dance of passion. He seemed to sense the wild desperation that drove her to seek the fiery pleasure that allowed no thoughts of guilt or betrayal of everything she had loved in the arms of her enemy.

Thrust and counterthrust, they moved on and on, their bodies like weapons in a supremely erotic duel. Giving and receiving a depth of passion they had not known existed, the sound of their moans of exquisite delight echoed in the hot, dark room.

She twisted and writhed under his thrusting, almost punishing hunger, that made her a wild animal caught in a grip of wanton abandonment that left no room for thought or shame. She did not want him to stop, she reveled in his sensual exploration of her body with his own heated flesh. There was a frantic, flaming urgency to their lovemaking that gave her wave after wave of the most intense physical pleasure she had ever known.

At the end of her endurance, Arielle felt her loins quiver as she reached the crest of her desire. Her body shuddering with the rapturous release, her hands clutched him, nails digging into the taut masculine buttocks as a scream of ecstasy was torn from her throat.

"Arielle!" he cried with despair. In a moment of exploding joy he followed her into that valley of complete release where they were truly joined as one. In his act of trying to conquer her he had found sublime defeat, for she had surrounded him with her honeyed warmth demanding his complete capitulation. He had known he had lost when he reached his pinnacle of pleasure and spilled himself inside her. She controlled his heart in a way no one had ever done before, and he almost hated her for it.

He had rolled away from her silently, leaving her to feel suddenly abandoned. They lay side by side, not touching, as Arielle felt tears roll slowly down her face. She stared out into the darkness hearing the ragged breathing of her husband beside her. Their strange marriage was now consummated, and she shuddered knowing now there could be no annulment.

What kind of woman was she? Arielle could not turn away from the realization that she had enjoyed her husband's lovemaking. In his arms she had forgotten her beloved Jacques. No, she corrected herself, it had been as if she had found him once more. Shaking her head on the pillow at the strangeness of her thought, she felt Thane tense beside her.

"Are you all right?" came his husky whisper.

"*Oui*, yes," she replied softly.

Raising up, he sat for a moment on the edge of the bed. His back to her, he spoke tersely. "I shall not bother you often, only when the need is great. Good night, my dear."

Arielle watched in stunned silence as he pulled back the mosquito netting and rose to his feet. Quickly donning his breeches and boots, he strode from the room without speaking another word.

Biting her lower lip till it throbbed like her pulse, she floundered in an agonizing maelstrom of humiliation and anger. How could he treat her so coldly after the rapturous lovemaking they had shared. Is that all he wanted from her, a few moments of passion in the night like he had had with Maura O'Connell? For a moment in his arms she had thought that she could not destroy this man who made love to her with such ardor, such passion, but now she felt only a sickening rage. If he had held her in his arms afterward, shown that somehow he cared, that it had meant something to him, she would have been lost, unable to carry out her plan of revenge. How he must have laughed at her easy surrender. She had not even been a challenge.

Staring into the darkness of her chamber, Arielle realized Thâne must have discovered that he was not the first, and perhaps that was what had caused his coolness toward her. It was a balm to her hurt pride that he had been unpleasantly surprised at that knowledge. He would never hear about Jacques from her.

On the morrow, when they met, she would be cool, aloof, as if nothing had happened. She could play the game of woman of the world. It would only be for a short time till she found the proof she needed that he was a British spy, then Claiborne would exact her revenge. When Thane Ryder hung in the Place d'Armes she would be free of him forever. Arielle gave a shudder as she felt a chill run up her spine even in the hot, stuffy room. The pounding headache was back in her temples. Why did the thought of her husband's, her enemy's, death bother her? Was she beginning to care for this strange, great beast of a man she had married?

Chapter Twenty

Arielle awoke from a troubled sleep as the first light of the pearl-gray dawn seeped through the lace curtains. After ringing for Lily, she stood at the French doors looking out toward the river, where a fiery sun was rising over the east bank. It was going to be another hot, muggy day, she thought, trying to shake off the lethargy that threatened to sap her will. The memory of her wedding night hung on the edges of her mind like the echo of a bad dream. Clenching her fists at her sides, she tried to banish all thought of her husband and his strange, cold behavior after their lovemaking, but the hurt could not so easily be banished from her heart.

Determined to put the night and its revelations of her husband's character behind her, Arielle searched for something to occupy her mind so completely there would be no room for sad regrets and self-pity. Staring out the window, she saw one of the young boys who worked with the old gardener begin to trim the boxwood hedge. Suddenly she knew where she would find both solace and purpose. Today she would establish herself as the mistress of the plantation, and take on all the responsibility the position entailed.

Arielle's mood lightened as her mind whirled with

plans for her beloved Belle Rivière. The day now had a purpose, and she hummed a French song as Lily helped her dress in a simple gown of lilac-and-white dimity.

"Will you wish a tray madame?"

"*Non,* I shall breakfast downstairs with the master from now on. Do you know if he has risen?" she asked coolly, averting her gaze from the knowing expression in Lily's dark eyes.

"*Oui, madame,* Jubal is seeing to his toilette at this very móment."

"Tell Tante Marie I shall wish to speak with her after I have partaken of my *petit déjeuner.* I wish to know if she or Jubal has the keys to the storehouse."

"I believe Jubal does, madame."

"I shall want to see him in the dining room," Arielle told the young maid. It was time she asserted her authority as mistress, and the tangible evidence of her power would be the keys to the storehouse worn on a chatelaine at her waist. With these keys she, and she alone, would parcel out the rations for the quarters and for the kitchen. A mistress of a great plantation like Belle Rivière worked hard, for it was her responsibility to see to the daily housekeeping and seasonal household activities, as well as nurse the sick, both family and servants. Perhaps in the work of the day she could forget the passion and humiliation of the night before.

With an air of calm self-confidence, Arielle ran lightly down the curving staircase and into the dining room. The chamber was not empty, for Father Antoine and Thane sat eating Tante Marie's hot, fresh croissants with strawberry preserves and drinking her rich coffee with the touch of cinnamon that gave it a special flavor.

Both men rose as she entered the room, and Thane limped to her chair to seat her. He was dressed for riding in soft leather boots to his knee, fawn breeches, and a wide-sleeved lawn shirt open at the neck. Arielle quickly looked away from the sight of the sinewy muscles of his thighs and buttocks clearly visible in the tight breeches. She remembered their sensuous, hard feel all too well.

"You look refreshed this morning, my dear," Thane said in a composed, raspy voice, pushing in her chair. "I trust you slept well.

"Like a babe, husband. Thank you for your concern," she retorted in cool, tart tones. She could play this game. Last night she had learned the rules.

"Good. Father Antoine is leaving us this morning for downriver. I will be accompanying him as far as the La Branche place. I should be back by luncheon. Have you plans for the morning, my dear?" Thane asked, passing her the crystal butter dish.

"Oui, I mean yes." To her dismay, Arielle stammered her answer. Why could he not speak French like everyone else? she thought, her ire raised by his bland, polite attitude. He sat smiling at her from the other end of the table like a great black bear. Perhaps she could at least convince him to cut that shaggy mane and trim that wild beard. "As mistress of Belle Rivière I have many duties, and this morning I shall begin to carry them out," she added with a slight smile of defiance.

"You do relish the role, do you not, my dear wife? But then, you have earned the title. At luncheon you must tell me how we are faring. How lucky I am to have a wife who takes her duties so seriously. Do you not think so, Father?" Thane inquired smoothly. Arielle sat stung by the underlying sarcasm she heard in those complimentary words.

"Most assuredly," the tall, gaunt priest agreed, seemingly unaware of the undertones to the conversation.

"How far downriver will you be going this trip, Perè Antoine?" Arielle inquired, deciding it was time she changed the subject. If Thane was trying to make her angry, she would not give him the satisfaction of knowing he was succeeding. Her curiosity had been raised by the priest, for she could not forget the rumors that had circulated around New Orleans that he was a Spanish spy. Could he be a British spy as well? "Pray tell, will you be visiting Grand Terre?"

The silence in the room was palpable after her question. She saw the surprise on her husband's face, and the glances he exchanged with Father Antoine. There was more to the priest's presence than a simple visit. That was obvious, Arielle thought with satisfaction.

"What do you know of Lafitte, my dear wife?" Thane asked with a significant lifting of one raven brow, his mouth spreading into a thin-lipped smile.

"He is supplier of merchandise for my shop, as he is for half of the shopkeepers in New Orleans," Arielle replied in bland tones, signaling Jubal for more coffee. "I thought if Perè Antoine were going to visit Grand Terre, he could convey a message that I will be needing more supplies when we return to the city."

"I fear I must disappoint you, Madame Ryder, but I am not going near the isle," the priest interjected smoothly.

"Such a pity," Arielle retorted, wondering if he was lying. They were up to something devious, she would place a wager on it.

"If you will excuse us, I believe we must be off before the heat of the day," Thane announced, rising to his feet. "Pray take care, Arielle. There is fever about, and several of the field hands are down with it. It is a virulent strain, for, as you know, the hands usually do not contract illnesses of that sort." His voice had sobered, and she caught an almost imperceptible plea in his words.

Looking up in surprise, his intense gaze caught her startled gray eyes with their violet rims and held her in his powerful spell for a magical moment. Did he care, or were these just concerned words that he thought the priest would expect from a new husband? Was this a new twist to the game, that they play the devoted couple in front of others?

"If there is fever on the plantation, then I should know about it. There are medicines that Seraphine swore by stored in the hospital cupboard. I shall see to it immediately. Jubal, the household keys!" Arielle demanded in a voice of authority.

"Take care of her, Jubal. No heroics, my dear. I have sent for the doctor," Thane admonished Arielle before leaving the room with Father Antoine.

"Come, Jubal, we shall go first to the plantation hospital," Arielle ordered.

Following the garden path behind the big house that led through the herb and kitchen gardens, past the brick kitchen house that sent out waves of heat on this warm, muggy day from its huge fireplace, toward the quarters, Arielle reviewed in her mind everything she knew about the dread yellow fever.

Called malignant fever, or bronze john because of the color the skin of its victims turned, it was persistent and deadly. Some years there were only a few cases, and other years full-scale epidemics where many people died. Once the victim was stricken, the course of the disease was erratic. Some lingered a long time till they vomited the characteristic black vomit that signaled they would die eventually of the fever. Others recovered, but no one knew why. Thane had been right that the Negroes seemed to have an immunity to the disease. It was a bad sign that several of the field hands had come down with it. This happened only in the worst epidemics. The strain this year must indeed be virulent.

Swatting at the irritating mosquitoes that seemed more numerous this summer, Arielle and Jubal continued on past the stables, workshops, blacksmith shop, and warehouses till they reached that long dirt street lined on each side by the cabins of Belle Rivière's slaves. These were the quarters, and in a long, low building at the street's end stood the hospital.

The quarters were quiet, almost eerily still. There was fear in the humid air, Arielle could feel it as she neared the hospital building. Yellow fever did that to people, for it was a deadly plague.

"How many are down, Jubal?" Arielle asked as they reached the open door of the building.

"Five hands, ma'am. They took bad, too." Jubal shook his gray head, giving a sigh. They hesitated for a moment before entering the long room that gave out the fetid smell of sickness, steeling themselves for the task ahead.

Arielle spent most of the morning seeing that the thin, dirty pallets were changed, the patients cleaned and dosed with Seraphine's medicine that she found on the shelf. There was pitifully little that could be done once the disease took hold, and she stood by feeling helpless.

"I shall return with the doctor as soon as he arrives," she told one of the elderly women who served as nurses in the small hospital. "Send word if any others are stricken." The woman nodded her understanding as she saw Arielle and Jubal to the door.

The midmorning heat was already oppressive as the two made their way to the kitchen house and Arielle's next meeting of the long day. She had forgotten those months in New Orleans how taxing the running a large plantation could be, but it was hers, and she loved each fertile arpent.

"It is awfully hot, Jubal. Let us sit a spell here in the garden before going in the kitchen house," Arielle suggested, dropping onto a bench in the shade of a giant live oak. Pulling the broad straw sun hat from her head and dangling it by its ribbons, she breathed in the fragrant scent of herbs in the sun. The pounding headache that had really never left, only dulled, was back. She felt so strange, both cold and hot at the same time.

"You want for me to get Tante Marie to come out here?" Jubal inquired, looking down at her with concern on his ebony visage.

"That would be lovely, Jubal," Arielle agreed, fanning herself with her hat.

"You feeling poorly, Miz Arielle?" Tante Marie questioned, ambling over to where Arielle sat exhausted, Jubal hovering behind her.

"I fear so, Tante Marie," Arielle answered, giving the huge black woman a wan smile. "Today I wanted to go over the storerooms with you and see what is needed, but I am not quite up to it." Her temples were buzzing, and she felt weak as a kitten.

She clucked over Arielle like a mother hen. "That is all right, mizzy. Jubal can get my supplies for today. You go up to the big house and rest. We can do this on the morrow."

285

"I think you are right." Stumbling to her feet, Arielle tried to make her way back to the house. What a time, she thought with disgust, to come down with one of the numerous summer fevers that plagued Louisiana in the long hot months. There was a reason they call it the sickly season, she mused with a weak smile.

Reaching the cool shade of the gallery, Arielle slumped for a moment against the cool plaster wall of the house. "Fetch Lily for me, Jubal, I shall be in my room."

As the old butler went in search of the housemaid, Arielle made her way into the long hall of the house. Feeling an overwhelming fatigue, she started to go up the curving staircase when she saw the open door to Thane's study, her father's old office. Looking about the empty hall, she realized she was alone. Now was her chance to search her husband's desk for the list of the members of the Alliance Louisiane.

With unsteady steps she made her way across the hall and into the book-lined room. There was a drawer in her father's old desk that had a secret catch. If one pressed a certain carved rose on the handle, a panel swung open to reveal a hiding place. She was certain Jubal would have told Thane about the hidden compartment. Perhaps it was there that he had placed the important list.

Walking behind the desk, she looked quickly through the few papers that lay on the polished surface. They were only bills of trade for supplies. Slowly, she opened the drawers on the right side and riffled through those in a like manner. With head and heart pounding, she slid her fingers over the carved rose. As it sprung free, she heard a familiar raspy voice and felt as if an icy hand had closed about her

286

throat.

Thane's voice was heavy with sarcasm. "May I help you?" She slowly raised her eyes to meet his sardonic gaze. "Have you lost something, or do you usually invade another's privacy? Or yes, this must be part of your housekeeping duties, but I thought we had servants for the actual work. Is your position not one of overseeing?"

"I . . . I . . ." Arielle stopped. The room suddenly began to move in lazy circles around her. Her mouth was so dry, and her skin seemed to be burning from the inside out. Placing trembling hands on the desk's smooth surface, she tried to remain standing, but she felt her legs bend and sway as if they were willows in a great wind.

"Arielle! Arielle!" Thane cried out, rushing to her side without a limp, to her amazement, as she fell into his arms.

Where has his limp gone? she wondered in bewilderment as she felt his strong arms sweep her up. They were the last thoughts she had as a fiery red haze claimed her, pulling her down, down into oblivion.

Days and nights of intense burning heat and throbbing pain consumed Arielle as she thrashed in fever's delirium. The four-poster became a prison of agony from which she thought in a few lucid moments she would only leave in death.

Nightmares came and went in her fevered brain. She saw Thane standing on the gallows in the Place d'Armes staring down at her as he changed into Jacques before her eyes. It was about Jacques' neck that the hangman slipped his rope as Arielle screamed her protest. Her cries echoed in the huge square, but the crowd around her only laughed as the signal was given to hang the prisoner. As the life slowly drained from her beloved Jacques, Governor Claiborne congratulated her on her achievement.

"No! No!" Arielle screamed aloud, sitting up in the rumpled bed, her hands flaying at the mosquito netting. She was lost in a fog, running, trying to save Jacques from Claiborne and the crowd.

"Hush, it is only a fever dream," the deep male voice reassured as the netting was cast aside and firm, strong arms gathered her against a broad chest. "It will soon pass, poppet. I am here. Nothing can hurt you. I shall protect you from all the dragons the fever can conjure up."

"Jacques? Jacques is it you?" Arielle whimpered against the comforting expanse of a male chest. She sighed, feeling his arms about her, inhaling the fragrance of sandalwood. He was here, safe within her embrace. Tears of relief streamed down her cheeks as she clutched his sinewy back with weak fingers. "So afraid, so afraid that you were gone from me," she whispered into the lawn of his shirt. "Promise never to leave me again," she implored through sobs of thanksgiving.

Her words cut through Thane like a knife. She loved Jacques with a passion he thought her incapable of feeling. Why did she masquerade as a shallow belle interested only in money and position? There was a heart under those perfect breasts that was filled with a love so deep it was tearing her apart. What reason did she have to go through with his farce of a marriage when her loyalty lay with another?

When he had made love to her she had responded with an ardor that had driven him wild, so unexpected was it. He had thought her only to go through the motions to carry out her part of the bargain, but, if feigned, her response had been so passionate to have done credit to a skilled courtesan. Later, he had mulled it over in his mind and come to the conclusion that this is what she was, a woman used to faking the ardor of lovemaking to please a series of wealthy lovers. Had she not lived in Paris where the women had raised such skills to an art. Then the thought had occurred that perhaps she was wanton, like a cat in heat taking her pleasures from the first available male. Now, as he held her delirious with fever, sobbing out her relief that her beloved Jacques was somehow returned to her, another thought surfaced in Thane's mind, and one he realized that was the truth.

The rapturous night of their wedding when he had held her and loved her with all the passion of his body, to her then he had been only a substitute for Jacques. The thrilling response of her loins had been not for him, but for her beloved Jacques. It had been the desperate reaction of a woman hungry for a man she could have only in her imagination. She was not a wanton nor a courtesan, but a lonely woman who had done without the man she loved for too long.

Holding Arielle to his chest, smoothing her tangled honey-gold tresses that he loved so much, his dark brows drew together in a frown. Why had she married him? It still did not make sense that she would consent to marry a man she had considered her enemy. If there was a plan to her madness, what could it be?

"Am I still your *belle blonde?*" Arielle inquired in a dreamlike murmur, stirring restlessly in his embrace. The fever was once more gathering strength.

"Aye . . . , er . . . *oui, ma belle blonde,*" Thane whispered into her hair, pressing her to him more tightly, as if he could protect her from the disease that ravaged her beautiful body. He could, for a few moments, give her back her beloved Jacques if it would bring her peace. Would his embrace ever give her so much joy? Shaking his shaggy head at his own foolishness, he knew that he wanted more than access to her body—he wanted her love, the passion that she gave to Jacques for himself. He wanted to be desired and love as Thane Ryder, her husband.

Sighing with happiness, she yielded to his embrace, snuggling into his chest, but the fever was relentless. As her temperature rose higher, she pulled away from the heat of his body that was adding to her discomfort. Her head turned to and fro as he gently laid her back down on the damp, rumpled sheet and pillow.

"Lily, more cool water. The fever is rising," Thane called over his shoulder to where the maid stood watching, despair in her black eyes.

The master was keeping his wife alive with sheer willpower, Lily thought not for the first time since the yellow jack had struck down her mistress. She had placed a gris-gris bag under the mattress when the master had gone out of the room for a few moments to answer the call of nature. Even voodoo seemed to be losing the battle with the yellow fever in the mistress's worn-out body. The disease had raged for two days and three nights. Most people would be dead now, Lily thought as she hurried over to the canister of cool water the master insisted be kept full.

He would not allow any of the traditional treatments to be used, such as purging with emetics and calomel. When the doctor had advised such a course, and bleeding with leeches as well, the master had thrown him out. After telling Lily he was familiar with the disease, he prescribed his own regime of sponge baths to reduce the fever, covering in the event of chills, and complete rest of mind and body. She was to have cool liquids when she could manage them, and the bed linens were to be changed as often as they became soaked from the fever.

The master was a good man, Lily decided as she poured cool water into a basin and carried it to the bedside, along with fresh linen squares to bathe Arielle's fevered body. He had stayed beside the mistress's bed day and night, barely eating the food Jubal brought up on a tray.

"Bring me a fresh nightrail for your mistress, Lily. She has soaked this one," Thane told the young maid, slipping the silk gown from Arielle's body as she tossed and turned, lost in her nightmare world of fever. "And bring the fan," he called over his shoulder as he began to bathe her slender, heated body. The sound of her moans filled the room.

Lily stood, as she had before, on the other side of the bed waving a huge palmetto fan over her prone mistress as the master bathed the fevered-ridden body as tenderly as if she were a child. The young maid's arms ached from the effort of the fan after a few minutes, but as she saw Arielle finally stop her restless turning and drop off into a calm sleep, she realized it would be over for a while.

"Good, the fever has lessened for a bit. Thank you, Lily. Tomorrow should be the crisis day. When she makes it through that, she will be on her way to recovery," Thane stated with confidence he was far from feeling. He slipped the fresh nightrail over Arielle's limp form. She hardly stirred.

Lily nodded her understanding of Thane's words, for she knew when yellow fever victims reached the third day after onset, the fever would typically subside. This was called the crisis, for fortunate patients began to recover, the less fortunate ones began the

291

black vomit. Once a patient started this stage, death was a slow and painful process as blood began to ooze from the nose and mouth. The skin took on a saffron tinge as they began to vomit a black bile. One never knew who would survive and who would not till the third day. Lily had seen huge, burly men succumb, and young, frail children recover. The only factor that made much difference was good nursing, and her mistress certainly had received that from the master. If strong will and determination counted for anything, she did not doubt that the master would pull his wife through on sheer force of will.

Thane slumped back in the wing chair he had brought from his room two nights before to watch over Arielle. Leaning his shaggy head back against the velvet back, he sighed as he stared at the sleeping figure of his wife. Was this some ironic trick played by fate that he was to lose another he loved to yellow fever at Belle Rivière? Was not a mother and father enough? Was the plantation cursed for him? he wondered, and he was assailed by a terrible sense of bitterness.

"Miche Ryder, a man has brought a note for you. He says it is important you read it now. Waitin' for an answer he is," Jubal said softly as he bent over the chair.

"I will send Lily down with an answer," Thane replied, taking the note and, leaning near the oil lamp burning low, broke the wax seal of Lafitte.

Need to see you most urgently. The British have made contact. There are two alternatives. Claiborne has refused all help. September 16 he attacked and tried to destroy Grand Terre. He captured most of the ships and merchandise in

292

the warehouses. Men have all scattered. Dominique Youx and others taken prisoner and back to New Orleans. I am in hiding, but need safer quarters.

Jean.

"That damn fool Claiborne," Thane swore quietly. Was he so shortsighted he could not see that Lafitte and his men could be a great help to him? Instead of using the men of Grand Terre, he was pursuing old grudges. Giving an impatient shrug of his broad shoulders, Thane rose from his chair and gestured for the maid. "Lily, watch your mistress while I go to my chamber. I will need you in a few moments to take a letter down to Jubal."

Seated at the French writing desk called an *ecritoire,* Thane quickly wrote a short note to Lafitte offering the sanctuary of Belle Rivière. He gave a sardonic smile. Claiborne would not dare come here for he knew about his reputation in New Orleans as a British spy. Frowning, he added a postscript about there being fever on the plantation, but if his memory served him, Jean had had the fever long before and could now consider himself immune.

Returning to Arielle's chamber, Thane gave the letter to Lily and took up his vigil beside the bed. Stretching out his cramped legs, he tried to get comfortable in the wing chair. It would be a long night.

The thin gray light of dawn was seeping into the room when next Thane awoke. His eyes went immediately to the four-poster. Arielle lay curved on her side in a deep sleep, the sleep of the healthy. There was even the shadow of a smile about her mouth.

Reaching inside the mosquito *barre,* he laid gentle fingers on her pearly forehead. Her skin was cool to the touch. For one brief moment there was a moist wetness in that fierce black eye. Quickly, he closed the netting and leaned back in his chair. She had past the crisis. Arielle, his wife, would live. He thanked fate for being, in this instance, kind.

"Jacques," she murmured, remembering how her beloved had come to her and held her. Such a lovely dream, she did not want to wake up. Stretching, she rolled over away from the shaft of light that was calling her back to reality. If she stayed asleep, Jacques would remain with her a while longer.

"My dear, how do you feel?" a raspy masculine voice was calling to her. Arielle did not want to hear it, did not want to awaken to him. She heard the mosquito *barre* open, felt a hand on her forehead, then on her arm. Would he not leave her alone?

"Praise be, is the fever gone?" Lily's voice now joined the clamor to awaken her.

"Aye, it is gone and has not returned. Your mistress will recover, Lily." Thane's deep, rough voice could not conceal the note of relief in every word.

"It was your nursing, Miche Ryder, that did it," Lily assured him to Arielle's chagrin. Had Thane really nursed her through that hell?

Slowly, she rolled over on her back, and, flinging one arm up to shield her eyes from the morning light, gazed up at the shaggy, rough visage of her husband. He looked worse than she remembered, with the one black eye red-rimmed, his hair uncombed and wild about his bearded face. The black patch made him look like pictures she had seen in a book as a child of Blackbeard the Pirate.

"How do you feel, my dear?" he asked softly, and a smile creased his visage.

"Thirsty," she murmured, then added. "You look

294

just like Blackbeard the Pirate."

A deep chuckle greeted her observation as Thane said over his shoulder to Lily, "She will be fine, for already she is criticizing my appearance. Some water for your mistress."

Trying to rise to take the glass Lily handed her, Arielle found, to her surprise, that she was as weak as a kitten and unable to sit up. She looked up at them, disoriented and a little frightened. Swallowing with difficulty, for her throat was so dry, she finally found her voice and croaked, "I am so weak."

"That will pass as you get back your strength," Thane assured her. He sat beside her on the bed, and, reaching down with his strong arms, lifted her up so she could drink.

It felt good, secure in those sinewy arms Arielle thought with embarrassment as he gently lowered her to the bed after she had drunk her fill. He could be surprisingly gentle for such a fierce man. What had Lily babbled, that it was his nursing that had saved her life? That was hard to believe.

"It will take a while to recover, my dear. You were very lucky. Yellow fever is a deadly business," Thane's raspy voice cut through her musings. He smiled down at her as if she were a not-very-bright child, but she sensed he had withdrawn from her again. There was a guardedness about him that she knew only too well.

"It seems I have you to thank," Arielle replied, gazing up at him, her clear gray-violet eyes seeming to probe for answers. Had those long-fingered, strong hands cared for her?

"I have dealt with the fever before." His words were matter-of-fact, but an inexplicable mask of withdrawal came over his dark features. "So I shall take the liberty of prescribing a regime of rest and nourishment

295

till you are fit as a fiddle again." A wry smile accompanied this pronouncement.

"As fit as what?" Arielle grinned back at this most unusual man who continued to surprise her.

"As a fiddle. 'Tis a English expression, my dear French-American wife." His voice was a husky whisper. He reached out and brushed a tendril of hair from her cheek. Then, to her amazement, he caressed down the side of her face with the tip of his finger. "Sleep, little one, and perhaps dream of me instead of Jacques."

A soft gasp escaped her at his words, and the heavy lashes that shadowed her cheeks flew up in shock. Before she could utter a sound, his finger lay across her lips in a gesture to be silent.

"We shall speak no more of him, for I am a jealous man. See if you can put him from your heart." Swiftly, he rose from the bed and pulled the mosquito *barre* closed behind him. His back rigid, he limped heavily to the door.

Alone in the chamber, Arielle lay thinking of his words, her mind in a turmoil. What had she said in her delirium? Then as fatigue stole over her, she knew that she would have to think of this latest development when she was stronger. There was, however, one thing of which she was certain. She would never forget Jacques, nor replace him with Thane in her heart. Never!

Chapter Twenty-one

"Dinner is served, master," Jubal announced in dignified tones. The elderly slave was descended from Ashanti warriors and his breeding showed in his erect carriage. He was one of life's natural aristocrats, thought Arielle as she allowed her husband to escort her into the dining room.

"This is a great occasion," Thane remarked. "My wife's first dinner with me since her illness, and my friend Jean's first night as my guest at Belle Rivière. A night to celebrate."

"*Certainement,*" Lafitte agreed, bowing over her extended hand. "We must offer thanks to the *bon Dieu* that you were spared, madame. Many in New Orleans have not been so lucky, I have heard."

"The fever still rages in the city?" Arielle inquired, allowing Thane to seat her at the end of the long table opposite him.

"Less than before, but it is still dangerous. An early frost should finish bronze John off for good," Lafitte replied, taking his seat halfway down the table.

"It is good to see you again, m'sieur. I was most happy when my husband told me of our good fortune to have you as our guest," Arielle told him with a warm smile. Inside, her heart was beating madly hop-

297

ing that Lafitte would make no mention of her marriage to Jacques. "It has been a long time."

"*Merci*. May I say it is my pleasure to see you once more. You are *ravissante* as always," he sighed with a sparkle in his black eyes.

"You are too kind, m'sieur. I hope we shall have the honor of your company for some time at Belle Rivière," Arielle replied softly, flashing him a flirtatious glance. She avoided her husband's intent gaze as he listened to their exchange. With a graceful gesture to Jubal, she gave the signal for dinner to be served.

"I am glad to see how happy you are to see our guest, my dear wife," Thane observed with a tinge of sarcasm in his deep, harsh voice, observing her as intently as a hawk his prey. "I, too, hope you can prolong your stay, Jean. There is much I would like to discuss with you."

Arielle's smoke-violet eyes narrowed with speculation as she returned her husband's stare. If she did not know better she would think him jealous of her light flirtation with Lafitte. Was he forgetting his insistence that this marriage was a convenience for them both? Love had never been mentioned, and remembering his cold dismissal of her after their consummation of that marriage, she could not believe he loved her, no matter how well he had cared for her during her illness.

"It is possible I shall have to intrude on your hospitality for a few more weeks. I fear Claiborne would not take kindly to my appearance in New Orleans," Lafitte said ruefully, lifting his wineglass to his lips.

"The man's an idiot," Thane muttered in disgust. "With the British on his doorstep, Washington burned and occupied, he turns down an offer of hundreds of men to join him in the defense of the city."

"You have offered help to the governor, m'sieur?" Arielle interjected, stunned by her husband's comment.

"Aye, when Captain McWilliams of the British Army and Commander Lockyer of His Majesty's sloop *Sophia* paid me a call a few weeks ago, they handed me a most interesting packet with my name on it." Lafitte leaned back in his chair, his dark eyes thoughtful as he sipped the golden wine in the crystal flute he held in his tapered fingers. "There were two letters in the packet. The first was a proclamation signed by Captain Edward Nicholls of the Royal Marines, promising the citizens of Louisiana that if they joined the British in overthrowing the United States government, they would be given land and moneys that belonged to the Americans. The second letter was even more interesting," Lafitte mused, stroking his thick, glossy mustache. "The document was written by a William H. Percy who stated he was the captain and senior officer for the British in the Gulf of Mexico. He promised full pardons for all men of Barataria, and, in a addition, American land if we joined forces with the British Marines. I would be commissioned a captain in the Royal Navy and be given thirty thousand dollars in gold, as well as Pierre's freedom. You see, Claiborne's men caught him one night when he was visiting his wife Françoise. If we refused to join the British they would completely destroy Grand Terre."

"A most tempting offer," Arielle commented, her face clouding with unease. Suddenly her appetite had disappeared. She felt the trickle of perspiration between her breasts and knew it was caused not by the hot, oppressive night, but by Lafitte's story.

"Indeed, the British thought so," Lafitte chuckled,

flashing a brief smile. "They, however, did not know of my deep dislike of them and their kind. I asked for a few days to consider their offer, and when they left Grand Terre I sent word to Claiborne by several of my men. They were successful in breaking Pierre out of the Cabildo, but not so successful with the governor. He answered me by invading Grand Terre and leveling it to the ground. As you know, Dominique Youx, Reyne Beluche, and eighty other men were captured, many killed. Pierre and I escaped through the swamps," Lafitte finished with a Gallic shrug, his voice weary with disillusionment. It would seem Claiborne's need to revenge his hatred of me is stronger than his intellect. He leaves New Orleans open and vulnerable to attack."

"Tiens! The man is a fool," Arielle breathed in dismay. Her stomach churned with anxiety and frustration at his story. The dessert placed in front of her made her queasy. If only she were in New Orleans, she would go to Claiborne and speak on Lafitte's behalf. Perhaps if she tried hard enough, she could convince the governor of his mistake in not accepting the men of Barataria's offer.

"I did not know you were so interested in politics, my dear," Thane told her with a tone of mocking surprise. "You continue to surprise, and lead me to wonder what other facets to your temperament I have not yet discovered. Pray tell, how long have you supported the American cause? You Creoles seem so unconcerned with the war, considering yourselves not really American citizens. I find your solicitude most surprising." He gave Arielle a penetrating look that seemed to probe deep within her.

Clasping the delicate stem of the crystal flute with trembling fingers, Arielle nervously bit her lower lip as she tried to regain her composure. Thane knew nothing of her plans, for he could not read her mind, she thought with assurance. He was just very observant, and she had almost given herself away. *Careful, careful,* she chanted silently. *Play the part of the shallow, selfish belle.*

"I care not for politics, or the American cause, only that I lose none of my property to the British," Arielle replied, but to her dismay, her voice broke slightly. Forcing her gaze to meet Thayne's, she affected an innocent expression. Creole ladies were supposed to know nothing of politics. They were expected to be fragile creatures easily frightened and dependent on their men for protection.

"Aye, you have worked hard to return as Belle Rivière's mistress," Thane agreed, and there was no mistaking the sarcasm in his raspy voice. "Pray let me reassure you there is no cause for alarm. You are married to the heir of an old and titled British family."

"You support the British side in the war?" Arielle inquired, quickly lowering her eyes from that intent dark gaze watching her from across the long table. There was a sudden silence in the room as her husband seemed to consider her question thoughtfully. His glance turned from her to stare at the flickering light of the tall tapers in their ornate silver holders. Her heart beat so loudly she thought both men must hear it as she awaited his answer. Would he now admit to supporting the British?

"I take no sides, my dear. Your husband, I fear, is no hero. I prefer to be an observer of some of the more disagreeable facets of life, not a participant. Jean is the only adventurer at this table," Thane replied smoothly, his visage a cool, remote mask. He signaled Jubal to clear the table and bring the brandy

301

decanter and slim cigars he enjoyed.

"Gentlemen, I fear that the day has caught up with me. If you will excuse me, I shall retire and leave you to your brandy," Arielle said with a graceful nod to each man.

"It was a joy to see you again, madame," Lafitte replied, rising with a slight bow in her direction as she stood up.

"*Merci*, good night," Arielle answered softly. She turned without looking at Thane and swept from the room. As Jubal closed the double doors behind her, Arielle walked out the wide hallway onto the gallery instead of to her room. She needed air and space to think on this hot, humid night. Her room had been her prison for too long during her illness. Tonight, she sought the cool sanctuary in the shadows of the giant oaks.

The full moon cast an alabaster glow across the verdant lawn as she walked under the spreading branches of the huge, venerable trees. The Spanish moss was turned into banners of silver lace by the unearthly light. Breathing deeply, she inhaled the fragrance of pungent sweet olive and spicy rose. It was a glorious night, a night that awakened unconscious needs and desires.

Ahead lay the Mississippi, gleaming cool and remote high up on the levee. How she would like to dive into those fast-rushing waters and swim till exhausted, finally able to sleep no matter the heat. Slowly, she climbed the grassy embankment to come to stand level with the river. A slight breeze blew her dress and fanned her heated body. Turning, she looked back at the house, its windows reflecting the candlelight within. How elegant and welcoming it appeared from the levee. It was her home, and she had given everything to have it back, but now it seemed a prison where her husband was the jailer. How long could she endure this mockery of a marriage? She turned back to stare pensively out across the water sparkling in the moonglow. How long she stood there brooding over her situation she knew not. It was only the sound of a stick cracking that brought her back from her black musings.

"Who is there?" Arielle called out sharply, the fine hairs on her bare arms rising in awareness that she was not alone. Whirling around, she stared down the path that led from the levee.

"Do you usually take these night strolls?" The deep, familiar rasp of her husband carried to her on the soft night air. He made his way slowly to the top of the levee, his stiff leg making the going difficult.

Suddenly an image flashed across Arielle's brain, something she had been trying to remember. She had been in the library going through Thane's desk looking for the list of the Alliance Louisiane when he had surprised her. Already ill with the fever, she had fainted, but not before he had reached her side. He had moved quickly, so quickly for a man with a bad leg. Strangely, it had not bothered him then, for he had strode as gracefully as a panther. She remembered it all. He had walked without the limp!

"Your limp is feigned," Arielle stated in puzzled tones as he joined her on the bank of the levee. "Why?" she asked bluntly.

Arielle heard his quick intake of breath at her words. Thane halted for a moment, and she sensed his hesitation. "Pray tell, why do you think that?" he inquired tersely.

"I remembered when I was in the library that you rushed to my side as I fainted. You walked perfectly, with no sign of a limp," she stated with triumph, meeting his icy gaze with a smile of defiance. Let him deny it. She knew what she had seen.

"Some days my leg pains me more than others. If I moved more easily it was because I was having one of my better days," he replied smoothly, but his gaze was watchful, as alert as a hawk. "There is no mystery, my dear. Why should I pretend a limp I do not have? This gait of mine is hardly an elegant walk."

Taking a small step back from him, Arielle slowly shook her head, lowering her gaze in confusion. Her mind still swirled with doubts. While on the surface his explanation could be valid, some sixth sense told her he was lying.

"I know not why you would choose to have such an infirmity, unless perhaps for a disguise . . . as is the beard and mustache," Arielle said softly, staring up at him with a dawning comprehension. "What are you hiding?" Her voice was a tremulous whisper. She stared up at him warily, her eyes deep-purple bruises against her pale visage in the wavering light of the moon.

His hoarse, bitter laugh floated on the soft night air as he regarded her with cynical amusement. "Really, my dear, your isolation during your fever has given you strange fancies. I am hiding only scars from several duels, nothing more exciting than that. Come, it is late, and you are still weak from the effects of the fever. A good night's sleep and you will see how foolish is this fantasy," Thane chided her, cupping her chin as he turned her face up to his opaque, bemused gaze.

Arielle shuddered as his firm, warm fingers touched her skin, and she breathed in the scent of sandalwood mingled with his own masculine aura. The sandal-

304

wood fragrance would always remind her of Jacques Temeraire, her only love. "Jacques, oh, Jacques . . ." She moaned his name unconsciously as her husband's face came closer to her trembling lips.

"Not Jacques! Thane!" he growled harshly, his demanding mouth coming down on hers.

Struggling, Arielle tried to pull away from those hard, searching lips. Tiny hands came up against broad shoulders, but she was a kitten battling a tiger. Releasing her soft chin, one strong, unrelenting arm pressed her to his heated body as long, tapered, masculine fingers entwined in her honey-gold tresses. Quickly he pulled the pins loose from her chignon, allowing her silken hair to flow through his hand. His fingers clutched the satin strands, holding her still so his fierce kiss could continue its assault on her trembling mouth. Slowly, as her traitorous body caught aflame, Arielle's lips parted to the velvet thrust of his tongue. Soft, protesting hands surrendered and stole around the proud column of his sinewy neck.

"You are part of me, you are mine, you belong to me like the earth of Belle Rivière beneath our feet," he murmured huskily against her mouth. "You shall always be part of me, even when we are old with our children grown. I shall want to feel the silken touch of you, the honey taste of you when I am eighty. I am Thane, your husband." His lips moved down over her throat as he bent her back over his arm like a willow before a determined wind.

Arielle shuddered at his words, at his complete mastery over her body, her will. All protest had turned to liquid fire, ignited by his passionate declaration and his knowing mouth that lightly licked the hollow of her slender neck. Arching against him, she felt the strong, hard thrust of his manhood erect with his need. She wanted to feel that ecstasy within her. Her hunger was too great for caution. Here by the rushing river, in the splendor of the night, they would celebrate nature's precious gift of passionate joining into one.

"The summerhouse," she pleaded as he freed one ivory mound from her low neckline and circled the erect, throbbing peak with his tongue. The moisture from his mouth cooled deliciously on her skin as the breeze from the river wafted gently across her bared breast.

"Aye, the summerhouse," he agreed, sweeping her up into his arms and carrying her, his limp gone, the few yards to the white latticed gazebo high on the levee overlooking the shimmering Mississippi River.

Placing her gently on her feet, he pulled cushions from the benches along the wall and placed them on the floor. Removing his coat, he placed it over the cushions and then reached for Arielle. Pulling her against him, he slipped the gown from her shoulders, slowly, deliberately peeling the material and then her chemise, from her slender form, till she stood revealed in the moonlight an alabaster goddess. Kneeling before her, he slipped off first one garter and silk stocking, then the other. Her senses quivered as he pressed his warm, moist mouth against each satin thigh in a lingering kiss.

Moaning with pleasure, Arielle looked out over his bent head to the river, twisting, turning as it gleamed in the glow of the moon. All of nature seemed to conspire to urge them in their joining. This elemental force between them could not, would not, be denied.

Thane gently pulled her down to the bed he had made them on the cypress floor of the gazebo. His soft sigh of satisfaction told her of his happiness as he

306

gazed down at the perfection of her slender, naked form beneath him. He drank in the sight of her honey-gold hair atumble about her ivory skin gleaming in a shaft of moonlight that pierced the lattice of the summerhouse. *I will always remember this moment,* he thought as he stared into the wonder he saw in her wood-violet eyes. No matter what had come between them in the past, it could not banish the sensual magnetism that was like an invisible cord binding them one to the other.

Tenderly, he caressed and explored each silken curve of her lovely body that was displayed for his adoring gaze. She was a tiny goddess whose fragile perfection put him in awe that she was his to enjoy. His hands could not get enough of touching, stroking, soft satin breasts, hips, and thighs. This was the woman who had haunted his nights, and bedeviled his days, with the desire to possess her once more. But it was never enough. There must always be more, and he realized dimly he would never tire of her, for each time carried the wonder of the first time.

As he pulled her to his embrace, Arielle protested his clothing; she had been made wanton by the overpowering emotions that had ignited her body with flame. Her fingers pulled at his fine lawn shirt, and then his breeches.

"Nay, sweeting," Thane protested. "The moon is too bright. I am not a pretty sight with this leg."

"You are beautiful to me," she declared with such feeling that it smote his heart. "I want to feel your skin, your heart against mine."

With a groan, Thane knew he was lost. His desire was too great; he would risk her seeing him. Perhaps it was time she faced the truth about him.

Quickly, he shed his boots and then his breeches,

till he stood before her in his long shirt. As he slipped it from his shoulders, the moonlight fell across his chest and he heard her startled gasp.

"Who are you? *Mon Dieu!* What is this?" Arielle cried out in a suffocated whisper, rising to her knees, her hands pressed to her mouth in shock, her smoke-violet eyes wide with disbelief.

Chapter Twenty-two

"Ma belle blonde, who do you want it to be?" he asked softly in French, his voice no longer the harsh rasp of her husband. The rich deep-timbred tone was a haunting echo from the past.

"Non! It can't be!" Arielle moaned, trying to comprehend what could not be denied. The voice, the lean, muscular body, with the familiar curving scar slashing from one shoulder across the bronzed chest, darkly furred, to the waist on the opposite side, could belong to only one man. Her mind whirled with confusion, for it seemed impossible. Jacques was dead. Lafitte had told her that day two years before, and he addressed this man before her as Thane. Could he, too, have been part of this deception, or was she losing her mind?

Looking up at the man she knew as Thane Ryder with burning, reproachful eyes, her face a mask of pain, Arielle whispered, "Jacques?"

"Oui, pauvre petite, it is Jacques," he answered with a sigh. Then he reached down and pulled her up against his chest.

Arielle stood staring up at him frozen, unable to move, her mind and body benumbed. Wrapping strong arms around her trembling form, Jacques

309

crushed her to him. Feeling the heat of his skin against her breasts as his mouth claimed hers, something deep within Arielle broke free. Scalding tears slid down her cheeks as the quivering petals of her lips opened like a morning glory in the first warmth of the sun. When his velvet tongue swept inside to ravage the sweetness of her mouth, she clung to him, her pearl nails cutting into the beloved flesh of his back that she thought to never feel again.

All questions were submerged in her desire to know the ecstasy of complete union with the man she had loved and thought she had lost. By some miracle he had returned to her, and for this breathtaking moment she wanted only to melt her body against his beloved, remembered flesh.

His hands caressed a burning path down her slender back, molding every soft, feminine curve against the hard planes of his sinewy form. She felt the heat of his bare skin on every inch of her body as his hands slid down to her rounded buttocks and lifted her up. Standing as stalwart as a giant oak, he thrust into her honeyed sweetness as she leaned against the latticed wall of the summerhouse. The unearthly silver glow of the moon shone across the rushing water of the river into the gazebo, which was covered with entwined honeysuckle vines that bathed them in its light. He took her with slow and measured thrusts, impaling her with his passion. The heavy scent of the white blossoms on the vine filled the small structure, overpowering their senses already aroused to a fevered pitch of sensitivity.

Desire rose and flared within Arielle as she arched her hips to meet Jacque's every driving thrust. She gloried in his uncontrolled hunger, matching it with her own. He was starving, and she was subsistence. Her thirst for love was great, and he quenched her need with the flood of his passion. Her body understood his rhythm. Moving with him, she pressed her breasts, firm and full, into the soft black fur of his heated chest. Wrapping her legs around his, she followed his lead, hips moving in an ancient dance of rapture.

He was beyond thought, wild with the need to possess her completely, to conquer her once and for all. She had driven him mad, forcing him into this insane masquerade. Tonight, now, she would pay for two years of unending hunger. She would be his body and soul.

Her senses throbbing with the strength, the feel, the scent of him, Arielle abandoned herself to his deepening thrusts of possession with a wild parry of her slender hips. The giving and receiving of their desire whirled faster and faster till, in a dizzying, uncontrollable burst of joy, they were completely consumed. A single united cry of ecstasy rent the still, hot night and floated out across the river as they found complete fulfillment.

Within the summerhouse all was silent as Arielle and Jacques slowly drew apart, their rapid breathing the only sound in the small enclosure. They sank to the cushions on the floor, exhausted by the intensity of their union.

As Jacques reached out to brush a tangled strand of honey-gold hair from Arielle's cheek, she stopped his hand. Looking at him with enormous, solemn eyes, she gestured toward the eye patch. A slight smile creased his bearded face. Slowly, he reached up and removed another part of his disguise.

There before her were the beloved liquid black eyes with their ridiculously long lashes. The eyes she remembered that glowed like black coals in the moonglow. Lightly, she traced with one finger the small scar that curved up from one heavy raven-black brow, hidden from view by the patch.

"Why?" she asked, sitting back on the cushions, unashamed of her nudity as she pondered his amazing revelation. "Why the masquerade? Where is the real Thane Ryder?"

Taking her hand, he lifted it briefly to his lips as a tinge of sadness flickered in his ebony eyes, then disappeared. "I am Thane Ryder your husband, and Jacques Temeraire your husband," he said quietly. "To have you, *ma belle blonde* I had to marry you twice." White teeth flashed against the sable beard and mustache as he gave a slight smile, but those impenetrable eyes contained a watchful wariness.

Arielle listened with bewilderment to his words. How could this be? Her beloved Jacques was also the real Thane Ryder, the man who had killed her twin brother and ruined her father. She could not look in those all-seeing eyes any longer. Turning away, she stared out at the river continuing its rush to the gulf. Her mouth felt dry, and there was a sickening feeling in the pit of her stomach.

"Aye, I am the man who hurt you so terribly, but that was before I knew you, *ma belle*," he explained softly, as if he were reading each awful thought that was racing through her tortured mind. "When I found you that day in the swamp, I knew only that you were beautiful, and that I was strangely drawn to you. Later, when I found out who you were, I was determined to forget you, but that was impossible. I took the name of Jacques Temeraire when I first joined with Lafitte, it is the custom on Grand Terre, as you know. There are reasons I did not want my association with Jean known in New Orleans; thus Jacques Temeraire was invented."

"And why was I only allowed to meet Jacques? Was I a danger to you?" Arielle lashed out, flashing him a look of disdain. "Perhaps, you thought it quite a jest to fool me into loving my brother's killer?"

312

"Nay, *ma chère*. I admit I planned my revenge on the Duplantier family—your father in particular—but I did not plan on you. If there was any jest, it was on me by fate. You were placed in my path to find and, once found, I could not get you out of my blood. God knows how I tried," he murmured with exasperation, continuing to hold her hand although she had turned away from him. Her rigid profile and stiff posture told him of her hurt and anger.

"Why the farce of the marriage of Grand Terre?" she asked in cold, clipped words, never taking her eyes from the river.

"Another foolish mistake, I fear. They say love and hate are but two sides of the same coin, and, make no mistake, I hated Faustien Duplantier. He destroyed my family. When we reached Grand Terre thoughts of revenge were still with me, and what more perfect revenge than to marry the daughter of the man who treated me less than a slave. I knew you would never marry Thane Ryder willingly, but you did seem to care for Captain Jacques Temeraire. Once married, there would be nothing you could do about it when you found out the truth."

"And what went wrong with your little plan?" Arielle ground out through clenched teeth, trying to pull her hand from his grasp.

"I found I could not continue the lie." He gave a rueful smile and a slight shrug. "Strangely, I would not be satisfied unless you willingly married Thane Ryder . . . so Jacques Temeraire had to disappear."

"Lafitte, Dominique Youx, they were all in on this scheme?" Arielle spat out the question bitterly.

"Do not blame them for betrayal, for even though they thought me mad, they honored the wishes of an old friend. There was a skirmish with a Spanish ship in which I sustained injuries. It was a perfect time for me

313

to disappear and send word to you on Grand Terre that I had died. I needed time to figure out how I was to convince you to marry Thane Ryder, your enemy. It was as I recovered on the isle of Jamaica that this masquerade came to me . . ." He gestured toward the beard, mustache, and long hair, his wry smile half hidden under the black bush of his disguise.

"When you left the isle the next morning after our marriage, what plan did you have in mind?" Arielle inquired coolly, determined to understand everything before she told him exactly what she thought of his deceit.

"Nothing really. I just had to get away and think. It was not clear in my mind what I was to do with you. All my life I have been alone because I prefer it that way. You aroused feelings I was not prepared to deal with, *ma belle*. After we wed, I felt trapped by these emotions you ignited, and sought the freedom and solace I always have found at sea. The battle with the Spanish ship was not expected, but it provided me with a way to get rid of Captain Jacques Temeraire."

"So, you left me to think you dead, and I a widow for two years, while you sorted out how you felt," Arielle replied in a low voice taut with controlled rage. "I mourned you till I thought I should die of the pain. What, pray tell, if I had remarried — or were you so sure of my devotion that you did not fear such an occurrence?" She turned to face him, her smoke-violet eyes darkened like angry thunderclouds in the light from the full moon.

"Lafitte's men kept me abreast of your life. If you would have shown any inclination to wed, I would have made a timely appearance," he replied quietly, but with a steely edge to his voice that told her of his intention that no other man should have her. "There were matters I had to attend to in England before I could be free to pursue you as Thane Ryder."

"Mon Dieu, but you think you can control my life like I am a puppet. You pull the strings, and I move in the direction you desire. No more!" Arielle blazed, pulling her hand free and reaching for her clothes. Turning her back to him, she quickly donned the rumpled garments with shaking hands as he watched her silently. Dressed, she moved away from him to stand in the door of the gazebo staring out at the silvery water of the river.

Her emotions were in a turmoil. First overjoyed to find Jacques alive and returned to her, her elation had quickly been replaced with a deep hurt and anger at his deception. The strange, dreamlike lunacy of this night had completely drained her, leaving her unable to comprehend her feelings. Everything had changed, but outwardly everything would remain the same. She was still his wife, and still Claiborne's spy. What other identities had her husband yet to reveal? British agent?

"You captured my heart, *ma belle blonde.* I never wanted to bring you pain, believe that if nothing else," her husband whispered huskily, coming up behind her. He had donned his breeches and boots, though his chest was still bare. His hands reached out to clasp her slender shoulders, eager once more to touch her, feel her feminine softness. He could express so much more with touch than with words, but was she listening?

Always in his life Thane had reached out and taken the woman he had wanted for the moment. He knew the silky words of seduction to gain him the night of passion, but never had he needed anything more. The women were quickly forgotten. The words "I love you" were as difficult for him to say as they were to acknowledge in his own mind. Deep within him, he knew that the bonds that drew him to Arielle were more than physical lust and desire for revenge. But now, Thane felt strangely tongue-tied, unable to explain actions he barely understood himself.

315

"How can I believe anything you tell me?" Arielle answered bitterly, enduring the touch of his hands that ignited, even now, an unwelcome surge of warmth through her veins. "Everything between us has been a lie."

"Has it, my dear? I have some questions of my own. Are you really the heartless little mercenary you appear? If you loved Jacques so deeply, why did you marry your family's enemy without giving it barely a thought? I really did not expect it to be so easy to convince you to be my bride, or perhaps I judged you incorrectly. Is your anger at my deception merely hurt pride that you were tricked, or do you really care?" he murmured, a bitter edge of cynicism in his voice.

Thane had his reservations about Arielle's behavior. Her quick acceptance of his proposal had surprised and strangely hurt him. Had she forgotten her beloved Jacques? Had their marriage on Grand Terre meant so little to her? Knowing he was being a fool to be upset when she had accepted his proposal so quickly, Thane had still brooded. He had not expected his plan to work so well, and it had opened up many doubts in his mind about his wife. She was Faustien Duplantier's daughter, after all. Perhaps the innocent outrage was feigned. He tried not to acknowledge the instinct that told him her joy at finding Jacques alive could not be that of a shallow woman. There had been real emotion in those beautiful violet eyes, but he ruthlessly suppressed that memory.

"That you will never know," Arielle lashed out at him, pulling from his startled grasp to run from the gazebo as if from hell itself.

He let her go, for she was like a wild creature who had to be alone to lick its wounds and recover its pride. She was his, and never would he be without her again. For a time he could be patient. It was unimportant to him why he must have her. He knew only that she was as necessary to him as food to eat and water to drink.

Across the velvet lawn, now heavy with dew, Arielle dashed, her dress held up to her knees. Honey-gold tresses streamed out behind her while she ran as if she were a vixen pursued by a pack of hounds. Between the giant oaks, avoiding the low-hanging branches, she flitted, her breath now in shallow gasps. Dimly, in the deep recesses of her being, however, she knew that she could never flee from the desires of her heart.

Reaching the sanctuary of her room, she barred the door behind her, knowing full well that if Thane wanted to enter, there was no lock that would keep him out. Dropping exhausted to the counterpane of the bed, Arielle tried to think as she caught her breath.

She had to return to New Orleans. No matter how angry she was at her husband, she knew deep in her soul she could not put the hangman's noose around that proud head. Scoundrel, rogue, he might be, but a part of her loved him. She would fight that love, be ashamed that she was capable of loving the man who had killed André, but she would not lie to herself. Claiborne would have to know that she could not, would not, spy against her husband for him.

Sighing, Arielle rolled over on her back and stared up at the gathered silk *ciel du lit*. It would be her burden to bear—this love, this passion she had for Thane, but she would not be an instrument for his revenge on her family. Her body could betray her resolve if she was alone with him. It must not happen. She might be his wife, but she would never live with him. There was still the store. She would live in the rooms above the shop and continue her life as before. A shiver spread over her as she realized that it would never be as before. He was alive, and she would have to fight a battle of personal restraint every day of her life not to want those

317

strong arms around her.

Sitting up, Arielle knew she could not wait a moment longer. She must dress in riding clothes, and at first light saddle Sultan for the ride to New Orleans. There was a faint trail along the levee following the river. She was not afraid to ride alone, for she had been that way many times. It was more dangerous to remain at Belle Rivière where she would see Thane every day. Her body had betrayed her tonight, and it would again if he took her in his sensual embrace. Her pride could not allow her to capitulate once more till she was his to command whenever he wanted her.

"Non," she vowed in a whisper, stripping the clothes from her slender form. "I shall fight you Thane Ryder . . . and my heart." The words were a strangled sob as she flung open the door of the armoire.

Chapter Twenty-three

The golden sun of late October slanted down on the city, bringing blessed relief from the drenching rains that had turned New Orleans into a sea of mud. Depressed citizens, weary from the season of fever sickness and death, took to the streets trying to find relief from the melancholy pall that had been hanging over their lives.

If the threatened British invasion loomed and supplies were short since Claiborne's rout of Lafitte from Grand Terre, still the populace was thankful. The dreaded yellow jack was on the wane. On this golden day they tried to make merry and forget.

Arielle stood in the shadowed arcade of the Cabildo fastening high clogs on over the delicate slides she had worn in Claiborne's office. The streets were still muddy, but slowly drying in the heat. She had been back in New Orleans a week, and this was the first day the sun had shone.

Leaving the Cabildo for the sunshine of the Place d'Armes, Arielle turned her face up to the warmth of the sun for a brief moment before raising her hinged green silk parasol, with its folding wooden handle to protect her complexion. Strolling with the crowd, she tried to erase the feeling of dread the Cabildo always aroused in her. Somewhere in the damp bowels of the building were Lafitte's men. She shuddered to think of how damp and fetid their cells must be in the humid weather.

Arielle was anxious to return to the sanctuary of the shop. She had finally gotten up her courage to inform Governor Claiborne of her decision that she could not spy on her husband. The meeting had left her shaken.

The marriage at Belle Rivière had long been known in the city. She had written Jules and Lala right after the ceremony. It had not taken her tante Lala long to spread the news throughout Creole society. Thane Ryder's wealth was well known, and he was considered quite a catch. If anyone questioned why a sister would marry a man who had killed her brother, there were a few shrugs. After all, it had been a duel. Affairs of honor occurred frequently among the Creoles, and one often had to turn a blind eye when the matter of a good marriage was concerned. It was not as if Arielle Duplantier had a dowry to draw a suitor. She was considered to have done well, and there were several Creole mamas who gave a sigh of regret that M'sieur Ryder was no longer a marriageable item.

The governor had not only been surprised by the marriage but by the fact the bride had returned to New Orleans alone. He had regarded her with disbelief when she said she no longer wished to work for him.

"I was under the impression this was not a union of love. Indeed, knowing of your hatred for the man, I was considerably surprised you consented to be his wife, but then I thought you must have your reasons," the governor mused, watching her intently from behind the polished mahogany desk.

"While our marriage may be one of convenience, m'sieur, I find it most difficult to send my husband to the gallows. It might prove impossible to gather evidence anyway, since . . . we will be living apart." Arielle stumbled over her words, for she had trouble understanding

320

her own feelings concerning Thane, let alone explaining them to someone else.

"I see," Claiborne replied, leaning back in his chair, his stare never wavering from her pale face. "We seem to misunderstand one another, my dear. My intention was not to send anyone to the gallows, only to be made aware of certain activities of those who feel they had something to gain by a British invasion. I understand the sensibilities of a lady like yourself, but ask only that if you discover the members of the Alliance Louisiane you enlighten me with your information. It would be a great help if we could keep an eye on these poor fools when General Jackson arrives. There have been rumors that an assassination here in New Orleans has been planned. We know not when, or by whom; thus it is important we find out the members of the Alliance, for it could well be one of their members."

Arielle sat back, stung by this revelation. Now in Mobile, General Andrew Jackson was considered the only hope for the city. In charge of the defense of the whole gulf region, he had been fighting with the Indians on the Florida borderlands when Claiborne had sent him a message about the possible invasion of New Orleans. A tough, relentless fighter, affectionately called Old Hickory by his troops, the city had been anxiously awaiting his arrival.

"His assassination would be disastrous," Arielle breathed in shocked tones, her mind floundering. She realized the chaos that would result in all of South Louisiana if such a thing should occur.

"Quite," Claiborne said tersely. "I ask only that you watch and listen to your husband for any indication of the names of the Alliance. It will be difficult if you live apart from him to know of his affairs, but I cannot ask you to live under your husband's roof if that is truly repellent for you."

"All I can promise, m'sieur, is to do what I can. My

321

husband, as far as I know, is still at Belle Rivière. When he returns . . ." Arielle paused, biting her lower lip. She looked away for a moment, then lifting her head, she met his cool, thoughtful gaze. "I shall see what I can learn."

"Excellent, my dear, I can not ask more." Claiborne gave a brief smile, rising to his feet. "I know I can trust your discretion with the information I have just revealed."

Arielle had nodded her understanding as the governor escorted her to the door. Trying to stop the trembling of her limbs, she had made her way out of the forbidding building to the welcome sunshine of the Place d'Armes.

The rich sound of the cathedral bells rang out the hour as Arielle walked with leaden steps toward Royal Street. Her husband could be part of a plot to kill General Jackson. The enormity of that fact shook her to her very bones.

As she crossed the muddy intersection, not yet dry even with the bright sunshine, she was distracted by the sound of a woman's husky laugh coming from the entrance of a cafe a few yards down the street. Recognizing the brilliant red hair of Maura O'Connell, she was stunned to see the woman was not alone. Her mouth dry with a bitter taste, she saw her husband Thane, her Jacques, escort Maura to a waiting carriage.

With shaking limbs and a sick feeling spreading through her stomach, Arielle pressed into a doorway, turning her back to the street so they would not see her. A flash of wild grief tore through her at the knowledge that Jacques—no, Thane—had gone first to see Maura and not her.

The way back to the shop seemed long. The sun was setting as she made her way down Rue Royal like a wounded animal seeking the solace and sanctuary of its lair.

Bébé greeted her with joyful barks as she entered the patio from the porte cochere tunnel. The dog had missed her greatly while she had been at Belle Rivière, and had been disappointed when she had left earlier in the day. Stroking the animal's soft fur, Arielle thought she would give way to the tears that again threatened.

"What is wrong with me Bébé?" she muttered, staring into the dog's liquid brown eyes, annoyed by her lack of control over her emotions. Clenching her jaw to kill the sob in her throat, she fought hard against the tears she refused to let fall.

"*Ma petite,* you are home," Seraphine exclaimed, entering the patio from the door of the shop. "I heard Bébé's barking and came to investigate."

"I am tired, I did not want to meet my customers today," Arielle replied, avoiding the concerned look in the woman's eyes. Seraphine knew her all too well and sensed that something was wrong.

"Of course, *ma chère.* Go upstairs and lie down. I shall fetch a tisane for you. You are still weak from the effects of the fever. Did I not caution you about venturing out," the older woman fussed as she led Arielle up to her chamber.

She was not surprised when Arielle confessed that Thane was actually her Jacques. The only time she had met Thane Ryder she had found something familiar about him. Overjoyed that her mistress would finally know happiness, she had been shocked when Arielle had told her they would not be living together and had refused to elaborate.

As the older woman slipped the clothes from her mistress's tense body, she observed the sadness in the pale, tired visage. What had happened, she wondered, in the few hours Arielle had been gone? Somehow she knew it had something to do with M'sieur Thane Ryder. What a rogue that one was. She smiled as she thought of his elaborate masquerade—all for the love of one woman.

She knew of his love for Arielle, as she knew of many things that were not easily explained. She just felt it in her bones. From that first day at Belle Rivière she had known they were meant for each other. Whatever was keeping them apart must be mended so her *chère* Arielle would smile again.

"Rest, *petite,*" Seraphine told the exhausted young woman. Crossing to the long windows, she pulled the curtains closed. "I shall return with a nice hot tisane and dinner on a tray."

The soft mattress did feel comforting, Arielle thought with a yawn as she lay in a silk wrapper, her hair down about her shoulders. Bébé gave a sigh as she, too, sought rest in her usual place on the floor at the foot of her mistress's bed.

Determined to put the vision of Thane and Maura from her mind, Arielle lay in the warmth of her bed in the quiet, darkened room remembering the confidences Claiborne had shared with her. How could she help him, now? The mere thought of living with him was distasteful. It would be too painful knowing that Thane had only used her body, as he was accustomed to using Maura's, as a convenience when the need arose. The masquerade had all been part of a plan to revenge himself on her family. He had admitted to hating her father, and had not been content till he had made her love him so he could administer the final hurt to the last Duplantier. Thane, or Jacques, had played with her emotions, pulling her this way and that. How he must have relished the power it had given him over the last of his enemies. No more, she vowed. She would not allow him to hurt her ever again.

Bébé's low growl was her first alert that there was someone coming up the outside staircase. Someone with a step much heavier than Seraphine's.

Suddenly the door was thrown open, allowing a shaft of the setting sun into the darkened room. As Arielle struggled to a sitting position, she was blinded by the light, unable to see who had entered her bedchamber.

"I am here, *ma belle blonde*, to take you home where you belong—in your husband's bed," a deep familiar voice rang out, allowing no quarter from the beautiful woman who glared at him from the shadows.

"*Non!* Never!" Arielle spat out the words with contempt. The memory of Maura's hand on his arm when they came out of the cafe flashed across her mind. "I shall not live with you ever again. It is over between us." Violet eyes flashed as she sat up, tossing back the tangled honey-gold mane of hair in a gesture of defiance.

The tall, lean figure of her husband crossed the room to the bed with the sure predatory grace of a magnificent swamp panther intent on his quarry. Gone was the awkward gait, the eye patch, and even the beard; only the luxuriant ebony mustache remained. His hair had been trimmed, she had noticed that on the street, but with his tall hat on, she had not realized that the streaks of gray at his temples were real. It was all that had changed in the two years since she had set eyes on Captain Jacques Temeraire.

With one swift gesture, Thane tore back the mosquito netting, letting it hang in two shreds as he towered over her, his black eyes impaling her as they flashed with imperious fury. "It will never be over between us! Never!" he told her, his voice hard, the words said with savage intensity. "Are you such a little fool you have not realized it yet?"

Arielle shrank back from the sheer animal magnetism that emanated from Thane in the darkened, warm room. This is what she had feared if they were alone—her own uncontrollable compelling desire for him. She was unable to speak, for her tongue seemed frozen by the conflicting, turbulent emotions that coursed wildly through her trembling body. The anger, the hurt—those she had expected to feel, but not the fierce joy, the over-

325

whelming hunger for his touch that vibrated in her blood.

Thane waited for her reply, staring down at her, their eyes locked hypnotically. When seconds passed and she did not answer, he said, "You are stubborn, *ma belle blonde*. I see I shall have to show you."

Arielle's lips parted to protest as she sensed what was in his mind, but Thane gave her no chance. With one quick motion she was lifted up into his arms. The feel of his strong hands about her legs and back sent fire coursing through her limbs as his mouth claimed hers in savage conquest.

She wanted to resist him, but the potent magic flared up once more, engulfing her senses, stifling the guilt, the anger, till, with a moan of surrender, her arms closed around his hard body. Her trembling lips opened to his assault as she let him possess the coral cavern of her mouth. There was passionate need in his kiss, but also anger as he moved his tongue over hers with rough thrusts.

Thane was barely able to control the fierce onslaught of desire that shook his body. He had waited, giving her time to nurse her wounds, till he could wait no more. His patience had evaporated as his hunger had grown. The memory of her silken body and passionate response that night in the gazebo had driven him mad with longing. He had come to claim what was his.

Tightening his hold on her, Thane trailed burning kisses down her slender throat as he murmured against the ivory skin, "You are coming home with me now, where you belong."

Stunned by his drugging kisses, Arielle at first did not comprehend that he was carrying her from the safety of her room. As he crossed the portal of her bedchamber, she stiffened, lifting her head from his broad shoulder.

"Where are you taking me?" she questioned, trying to pull shut the silk wrapper that had slipped low exposing

326

her thin chemise and one alabaster breast.

"To our home, dear wife, on the Rue Esplanade," Thane answered, his tone velvet yet edged with steel as his arms tightened about her.

"I . . . I am not dressed," Arielle stammered as they descended the cast-iron staircase that led to the patio. She prayed there were no customers in the shop to witness this farce. Her name would be ripe gossip in every house in New Orleans if anyone saw them.

" 'Tis not important," Thane assured her, carrying her through the porte cochere. "Seraphine will send you your clothes. Once we return home you will not be needing them for a while anyway," he drawled in smug tones.

"You cannot do this," Arielle protested through clenched teeth, her ire peaked by his arrogant assurance that they would make love once they reached his townhouse on the Rue Esplanade. He was making a spectacle of her as if she were one of Maura's girls. Remembering Maura O'Connell, she felt a fury rise in her till she thought she would choke. Seething with anger and humiliation as they reached the street, she glared up at him, her smoke-violet eyes clawing at him like talons. "This is kidnapping! I will see you in chains in the Cabildo," she sputtered, bristling with indignation as Thane's man Hercules opened the door of the carriage and she was thrust inside none too gently.

"I beg to differ, my dear wife. I am your husband and, according to Louisiana law, that gives me certain rights," he replied softly with a mockingly edge to his voice as he entered the coach, shutting the door behind him.

"I hate you," she hissed, leaning back against the cushions and trying to hide from the interested glances of those passing by on Royal Street. What he said was true. She was his wife. He could do with her as he wished, no one would raise a finger to help her.

"It makes no difference," he sighed, signaling Hercules with a tap on the roof that they were to depart.

"You are a bastard!"

"So you have said before, but I am still your husband. We have been married twice, remember. I believe that makes it quite legal."

Assailed by the memories of all that had passed between them, Arielle looked away from him out the window of the carriage. Did she love his man or hate him? Biting her lower lip, she stared out at the late-afternoon traffic on Royal Street as they made their way to Thane's townhouse. She had loved the man called Jacques with all her heart, but that had been before she knew the extent of his treachery. Had he been real, or only what she had wanted him to be from the start? Perhaps she had allowed herself to be tricked because she had needed someone so desperately at that time, alone after her father and brother's death.

"As my wife, I shall expect you to live with me from now on at the house on Rue Esplanade or at Belle Rivière. You will preside over my table, be a charming hostess to my guests, and accompany me to various social functions," Thane told her, his voice dangerously quiet, the expression on his dark, lean visage remote.

"Do I have any choice?" Arielle gave a bitter laugh, flashing him a look of disdain.

Thane leaned back against the velvet cushions, regarding her silently for several unnerving seconds from dark, insolent eyes that glowed with a savage inner fire. Folding his arms across his chest, he said harshly, "Did either of us have any choice when we met? We belong together. You know it, and I know it. You are mine. You will always be mine. If you run away again I shall follow, even if it means to the ends of the earth." Giving a cynical smile he added, "Stop this hysterical protestation. Your body tells you the truth of what you want, what you need. Listen to it. Enjoy what we can give each other."

"Like you and Maura O'Connell?" Arielle countered

328

icily, pulling the wrapper tighter about her throat, determined he should not see how his words had attacked her composure. It would be so easy to forget everything and crawl into those strong arms. In the ecstasy of his lovemaking, perhaps she could, for a time, submerge the hurt, the fury, at his betrayal. She must harden her heart by erecting barriers of anger, for she knew after the passion, the hurt would return. He was not what he seemed. He was not to be trusted. How many lies had he told her, and how many more would he tell her to bend her to his will?

Thane stiffened at her words, then, giving a slight shrug, said, "Maura is an old friend. I do not know what you may have heard, but that is the truth. Maura is not my *chère amie,* my mistress, but it gives me pleasure to see that you are jealous."

Goaded beyond reason at how close he came to the truth, her embarrassment turned to raw fury. "I am hardly jealous of a whore," she spat out. "You can sleep in the gutter if you so choose, but you do not come from there to my bed."

Thane's ebony eyes blazed with sudden anger as in a tautly controlled voice he said, "Never again refer to Maura as a whore. She is a friend, and I do not allow anyone to speak ill of a friend of mine."

Arielle shrank from the fierce expression she saw in those expressive eyes. Her pale face flushed with humiliation and anger at herself. How could she have said such a thing? She liked Maura O'Connell and knew that only jealousy could have provoked her to say such things. Silent, and defeated by the thought that he would defend the woman who must be his mistress, she turned away from him. Curling into the corner of the carriage, she stared out the window determined to not utter another word.

Thane bit off a curse under his breath. This woman, with the face of an angel, would drive him mad someday.

Bleakly, he looked away from her, wanting her even now with an intolerable ache, and yet wondering how he could be such a fool to do so.

As the carriage pulled into the porte cochere, they were greeted by a graceful young black woman dressed in the gingham dress and *tignon* of a housemaid. Arielle shuddered as she thought of the last time she had visited this house. How stupid she had been not to have guessed that under the hideous disguise lay the man she knew as Jacques. How he must have laughed at the ease with which he fooled her.

"Come, we are home," Thane stated. He alighted, holding out his hand to help her from the carriage.

Stiffly, with as much dignity as she could muster dressed in the silk wrapper and with her feet bare, Arielle ignored his outstretched hand and stepped to the ground. Staring at the maidservant, she saw the surprise in the girl's eyes before she quickly lowered her gaze.

"Miche, Señor de Galvez is waiting for you in the salon," the maid murmured to Thane, never looking in Arielle's direction.

Giving a sigh of exasperation, he nodded. Dropping his hand, he told Arielle coolly, "This is Claire. She will show you to your chamber. If you want anything, just ask her. Hercules will return to the shop for your clothes. I shall be up shortly and we will dine *à deux* in my chambers." Turning to Claire, he said tersely, "Madame Ryder may want a bath. Please see to it and anything else she may desire."

"Oui, Miche," Claire murmured, then, giving a slight bow in Arielle's direction said, "This way, madame."

Padding across the courtyard in her bare feet, Arielle felt the eyes of the other servants upon her from the shadows of the stables and kitchen house. With her head held high, she followed Claire to the curving iron staircase that led to the second-story gallery.

The bedchamber, like the rest of the townhouse, was elegantly furnished with a high ceiling and long French doors that opened onto the gallery. Gleaming Queen Anne chairs, upholstered in evening-blue satin, stood on either side of the white marble fireplace. An enormous armoire of rich mahogany was against one light-blue wall, while opposite stood a high chest of drawers with graceful curved Queen Anne legs next to a long pier glass that tilted for the viewer's pleasure. The focal point of the chamber, however, was the huge four-poster bed with each post carved in the rice design. The soaring canopy was draped in sky-blue silk with a voluminous mosquito netting, also in light blue, giving the bed the appearance that it floated in a mist. The counterpane was a deeper blue with a coat of arms in old gold emblazoned across it. Arielle recognized the shield, for she wore its duplicate on her finger in Jacques' ring. It was the Ryder crest, she now realized.

"I shall have a bath brought up at once, madame," Claire told her. "You will find clothes that the master has provided for you in the armoire," the girl said respectfully as Arielle whirled to stare at her with blazing eyes.

"It seems the master has seen to everything. Tell me, is this his chamber?"

"Non, it is one of the guest chambers. Miche Ryder's rooms are right next door. If there is nothing else you desire, madame, I shall return with your bath," Claire said, leaving through one of the French doors.

Staring after the maid, Arielle quickly crossed to the open door. She would not stay in this gilded cage a moment longer. Feeling the soft Aubusson carpet under her bare feet, she cursed softly — using those few words she had learned from André. She could go nowhere dressed as she was in only a silk wrapper and no shoes. Leaning against the open door staring out onto the lush patio below, she was suddenly aware of someone on the gallery. Turning to her left, she saw an enormous black man dressed in Thane's livery. He was standing with crossed arms looking impassively out at the scene below.

"Who are you?" Arielle demanded.

"Daniel, madame," he replied, continuing to stare straight ahead.

"Why are you here," she inquired with a dawning suspicion that raised her ire to the boiling point.

"To protect you, madame."

"To guard me, you mean," Arielle muttered, flinging the door shut behind her as she stormed back into the bedchamber.

He meant to keep her prisoner. Her every move would be watched. His spies would follow her everywhere. How dare he? she thought furiously, seething with impotent anger. She was his wife, he could do just what he pleased, she realized, and that knowledge made her numb with increasing despair. A suffocating sensation seemed to close about her throat as she huddled on the huge bed not caring if she creased the elegant counterpane.

Biting her lower lip in frustration, she stared about the lovely room that to her could have been the meanest cell in the Cabildo. The freedom was what had attracted her to Jacques. Marriage to a man beyond the law, a privateer who made his own rules, gave her independence as well. They would both come and go as they pleased, asking nothing of the other but the ecstasy of the moment. The secret liaison gave her the liberty to live as she wished, answering to no one but her own heart.

Sighing, she rose to her feet and began to pace the delicate carpet like a caged lioness. What a fool she had been to believe in the myth of Jacques Temeraire. How well he had planned it all from the start. She did not lend credence to his confession that he had staged Jacques' demise because of second thoughts. It had all been planned to give her the maximum of pain and humiliation. How could she have feelings for such a man? For she had to admit, deep within her, she still loved the part of Thane Ryder that was Jacques Temeraire. Did she have the strength to fight her love so she could be free and not allow her husband's revenge to be complete? Somehow she must find the will to fight her own emotions and hunger or she would, indeed, be Thane Ryder's prisoner for the rest of her life.

Chapter Twenty-four

Arielle rose from the soothing bath, fragrant with the scent of lavender. As she stood, Claire dried her with soft towels of the finest linen. The warm water had relaxed some of the tension within her, and she felt more able to cope with the coming confrontation with her husband.

"Madame, the master has requested you wear a particular gown this evening," Claire said softly, taking a delicate heliotrope lace wrapper from a drawer and slipping it about Arielle's shoulders.

"Really," Arielle stated coolly. "Do I have any say in the matter or is he always going to pick out my ensemble?" She looked down at the garment and thought with disgust that it was transparent. She wondered if the gown was, too.

"Just this evening, madame. The master said tonight is a special occasion and asked you indulge him."

"Show me this garment, Claire, and I shall make the decision," Arielle answered tersely.

"It is lovely, is it not, madame?" the young woman commented, taking the gown from the armoire and holding it out on its padded satin hanger.

A stab of pain smote Arielle's heart as she experienced a bitter rush of remembrance, for the gown was the gold silk one she had worn on her wedding night on Grand

Terre. She had left it behind when she departed the island, so deep was her grief at Jacques' death. Touching it gently with the fingers of her right hand, she realized Thane had kept it all this time. Did it mean as much to him as it did to her?

"*Oui*, Claire, I shall wear the gown," Arielle told her in a voice thick with bittersweet tears.

"These gloves and stockings are to be worn with it, madame," the maid said hesitantly, taking the gold lace stocking and fingerless gloves she had also worn that night from a box. "These shoes also," she continued, holding out a familiar pair of gold leather slides.

Not trusting herself to speak, Arielle nodded, staring down at the complete ensemble she had worn that night over two years before. Thane had remembered every detail.

Staring at her reflection in the pier glass after Claire had left her, Arielle could almost believe it was that long-ago night. Thane had given Claire instructions to dress her hair in the same style. The young maid had been embarrassed when she told Arielle that her husband had specified she was to wear no chemise or undergarments, but she had only nodded. He had remembered everything.

The gown clung to her curves as it had on Grand Terre, and Arielle felt her pulse race as she reminisced on how it had excited the man she had known as Jacques. In their chamber at Lafitte's, he had slowly stripped the gown from her body till she stood clad only in her gold lace stockings and gloves. He had made their removal an erotic ritual of love. A wild yearning surged through her. She closed her eyes remembering the feel of his touch, his mouth on her newly awakened body.

Suddenly it was as if her fantasy had become real, for she felt warm, firm lips on the hollow of her throat. She heard her moan of desire as her eyes flew open, and she saw reflected in the mirror the dark, masculine figure of her husband standing close behind her. She watched as his long, tapered fingers, bronzed by the sun, clasp her breasts, pulling the low neckline of her gown lower still till the rose-coral tips were revealed. Hypnotized, she saw those knowing fingers caress the peaks till they throbbed with delight.

Black fathomless eyes met her gaze in the mirror as he lifted his mouth from her throat. Continuing his caress, he murmured huskily, "Remember, *ma belle blonde,* how it was between us."

"Oui." Arielle's lips formed the word, but the sound was inaudible. Transfixed, she could not move, only stare at that image in the silvered glass, the image of a man making love to a woman.

He smiled an intense erotic smile before bending his ebony satin head to kiss the hollow where her throat met her fragile collarbone. She felt his tongue taste her skin in delicious slow circles that sent fire racing through her veins till she was weak with desire.

The magnetic pull of his potent masculine sensuality was overwhelming Arielle, and she felt herself flow into him. He stood pressed against her, the firm sinewy limbs, the rigid shaft of his manhood thrust against her soft buttocks. He courted her senses with gentle, heated persuasiveness, molding every inch of her feminine form to his powerful body.

She watched in the glass as his head moved lower to suck the taut rosy nipple that he cupped in his hand. Swept away by waves of new sensations from the sensual experience of both feeling and seeing him make love to her, Arielle cried out, "Please, please." She did not know if she meant for him to stop or to never stop. The clamorous flame of arousal had destroyed her resolve, leaving her with a wanton hunger that demanded to be appeased.

As he had that long ago night on Grand Terre, Thane slipped the gown from her body till she stood revealed once more in only her gloves and stockings. Her eyes enormous in her flushed visage, she watched as his bronzed, masculine hands stroked and caressed her soft ivory breasts, her narrow waist, and down to the roundness of her hips. She saw his burning ebony eyes in the glass, devouring the erotic image of his sinewy man's touch on her silken, feminine nudity.

"You are so beautiful, *ma chère*," Thane breathed, a sense of awe in his voice, husky now with desire. "How long I have wanted you. You have been a fire in my blood since the first time I saw you riding into the fury of the storm that day by the river. I had no choice then, as I have none now. I must have you."

Arielle's heart skipped a beat at his passionate declaration. If the thought crossed her mind that he spoke only of want, and not of love, it was quickly overwhelmed as Thane swept her up into his arms and carried her from the pier glass to the waiting bed.

Lying on the royal-blue satin counterpane, Arielle realized a storm had risen. She could hear the rain driving against the glass of the French doors that Claire must have closed when she left. A flash of lightning lit up the chamber as Thane pulled the last of his clothes from his powerful, lithe body.

She stared unabashed at him as he joined her on the massive bed. The slashing scar across his muscular chest was visible through the silky midnight hair that led in a V down the bronzed torso, over the slim hips, to his manhood, erect and proud with his demand for her. She thought with a shudder of excitement how magnificent he was with his intense masculine hunger that allowed no refusal.

As Thane drew her to him, all thought vanished, and she was aware only of his entire sinewy length pressed against her as his mouth came down on hers. A wild surge of pleasure swept through Arielle. Her lips opened to him, and she tasted him with a new hunger that came from deep within her being.

Slowly, as he had that night on Grand Terre, he slipped the gloves from first one arm, trailing hot kisses down the bared skin to suck lightly in the soft curve of her elbow, then the other. The removal of her lace stockings was a sheer delight as he pressed warm, moist kisses down each sensitive thigh till she sighed with rapture. He was seducing her with every erotic art and appeal to her sentiment for the first night they had spent together as man and wife, she realized dimly as if through a haze of sensation.

A mutual tremor ran along their length as he pulled her unclothed form on top of him. His strong yet sensitive hands caressed the hollow of her back, the tingling nerves of her spine, and the soft fullness of her bottom. Seeking her woman's petals, he gently, knowingly, stroked her hidden rosebud of passion till she was moist and wanting. Her hips moved in wanton circles against his. He slipped his finger inside her honeyed cavern, teasing her, showing her what he would soon do with his own body. He was making her a wild creature of sensation, but she was unable to pull away from the ecstasy only he could give her.

She moaned as he lifted up her hips to plunge his sword of passion into her waiting velvet scabbard. Giving herself to him with passionate abandon, Arielle was lost, the ache in her loins driving every thought from her mind. She was consumed by her need to feel the magnificent pulsating size of him within her again, and again.

"Look at me, *ma belle blonde*," Thane commanded, his deep voice thick with desire.

Slowly, shyly, she opened smoke-violet eyes, liquid with emotion, to stare down into dark, smoldering ebony pools that held her with the force of his ardor. Yet another barrier was broken as he forced her to acknowledge and revel in their passion. He would not let her hide from him with her eyes closed. As his body moved

338

deeply, embedded inside her with powerful thrusts, he made exquisite love to her with his magnetic eyes till she felt possessed body and soul.

"This is where we belong, my wife, together," he cried out. In a dizzying spiral of uncontrollable joy, the earth fell away, and Arielle joined Thane in that unequaled place of rapture, utterly consumed, utterly fulfilled.

Afterward, as the rain beat against the windowpane, they lay in silence, her head upon his chest, both still shaken by the depths of their passion. Neither wished to speak, for they did not want to break the spell that still lingered between them. Eyelids and limbs were heavy, lethargic from their joining.

"Sleep, little one," Thane whispered into Arielle's honey-gold hair, tenderly kissing the silken strands. With a sigh of contentment, she obeyed.

It was as she slept the deep sleep of exhaustion that the dream came once more, the dream that was a nightmare. Thane was standing on the gallows in the middle of the Place d'Armes. The crowd surged around her as she tried to reach him. Opening her mouth to scream out, she found she had no voice. Tears streaming down her cheeks, she fought the crowd, pulling at strangers' arms, clawing at their broad backs with her fingernails, but it was to no avail. They would not let her through to save his life. He stood above her tall and proud as the hangman's noose was placed around his neck.

"No! No!" she screamed, finally finding her voice. As she pushed out her arms, she opened her eyes to find she was in the four-poster at her husband's house. Shaking, she sat up, the salty taste of tears in her mouth. It had been only a dream, the nightmare she had experienced once before. Thane was here beside her, she thought with relief, only to turn and realize she was alone. The room was dark. It was only as the lightning flashed that she saw the indentation beside her on the pillow to indicate that she had not dreamt their splendid lovemaking.

The dream had left her uneasy, and finding herself alone in the huge bed, she felt a wave of apprehension course through her. Where was Thane?

Suddenly a gust of wind blew open the French doors sending a torrent of rain into the room. Sighing in frustration, Arielle knew she would have to leave the warmth of the bed to close the doors. She made her way to the armoire by the light of the storm and, searching inside, her fingers found the lace wrapper Claire had placed on a padded satin hanger. Tying the sash of the garment under her breasts, she fought the storm to pull shut the French doors banging in the wind.

The cold and wet had fully awakened Arielle. Standing at the closed doors, looking out on the rain-lashed patio, she knew she could not return to sleep. Pangs of hunger tore at her as she pondered the storm and her husband's disappearance.

Remembering their passion, she felt a flush of embarrassment. She had let herself be carried away with his seduction, offering no resistance. Their lovemaking had been wild, touching new depths of ecstasy within her she had not known she was capable of experiencing. She loved him, of that she was sure, but did he love her? He wanted her body. He had shown her the depths of that hunger tonight. Men could want without loving, she knew. Had Thane taken her only to assuage his body hunger and need for revenge? Not once, even in the midst of their deepest rapture, had he professed his love.

What did it matter? she thought with irritation. She was his wife, nothing could change that fact, but she knew it did matter to her. She could not live with a man who did not love her, a man she cared for deeply, no matter how much she might try to hide the fact from herself. The pain would be too much to bear, knowing he only came to her to use her body, to satisfy his masculine needs and warped need for revenge on her family. She would not be just an instrument for his satisfaction.

Tears once more filled her eyes, not from the tortured images of a dream, but from the realities of the empty life she was facing. Staring out into the rainy night, she stood so lost in her painful musings that at first she did not notice the figure of a man illuminated by one of the swinging lanterns hung on posts in the courtyard. The man, dressed in a long cloak and wide-brimmed hat, was making his way toward the doors that led to Thane's study. Arielle remembered those doors well, for it was where she had eavesdropped that first night she had come to this house months before. It had been the first time she had heard of the Alliance Louisiane.

As she stood watching, the study doors were opened by Thane, and the stranger was let inside. She saw her husband clearly in the light from a bolt of lightning before he closed the door behind his visitor.

Although she had no idea of the time, Arielle knew it was late, far too late for visitors. Only someone who wanted to keep his visit a secret from the rest of the house would appear at such an hour. Who was Thane's guest, and what was he concealing? She had to know the answer. Perhaps if she knew the stranger's identity, she could fit together another piece of the puzzle that was her husband.

The darkened corridor stretched in front of Arielle as she slipped out of her chamber. Only an oil lamp, on a mahogany table far down the hall, relieved the gloom with its small circle of golden glow.

Deciding that from her previous knowledge of the house the stair was certain to be on her left over the twin parlors, she walked quietly in that direction. The gold dress shimmered in the dim light. She had donned it and the gold leather slides as well, for she had not wished to prowl the house dressed only in the flimsy wrapper.

Elation filled her as she turned a corner and saw the remembered curved staircase on her right. Pausing at the head of the stairs, Arielle stared down into the darkened foyer. Another lamp burned on a narrow table against a far wall, but the dim light did not reach the staircase.

Arielle quietly made her way down to the first floor, clinging to the waxed banister. As she reached the black-and-white marble squares of the floor of the foyer she saw, at the end of the hall leading to the patio, a strip of light gleaming under a door. It must be the room she had seen the visitor enter as she stood at the French doors of her chamber.

With her heart thumping against her rib cage, Arielle started down the long, dark corridor toward the light that shone like a beacon under the solid door. She had to know who was her husband's guest and why they met so furtively.

Reaching her goal, she pressed her ear to the door, but the wood was solid and she could not hear a word. Frustration mounting, she bent down to look through the keyhole, but all she could see was the back of a man's breeches. It must be Thane. The firm buttocks and slim flanks could only be his, she thought with a giggle. A wife could recognize her husband's backside! If only he would move she could, perhaps, see the other man. She leaned against the door, intent on her spying, her eye up to the tiny peephole.

Finally she was rewarded for her patience as the breeches blocking her vision disappeared, and she could look into the room. She saw a fire had been lit in the fireplace against the night's chill. Straining to improve her view, she leaned heavily into the door as she saw a pair of muddy boots cross in front of the flames.

Suddenly she was falling forward as the solid door gave way. With an undignified sprawl, she landed face-down in front of two feet clad in familiar, highly polished boots.

"Really, my dear, you should have simply knocked," Thane murmured, looking down at her with a mocking smile.

Glaring up at him, Arielle was too stunned to speak. Feeling an unwelcome flush stain her cheeks, she was angry that he could so easily embarrass her. She was acting like a gauche child caught with her hand in the cookie jar.

"Allow me," Thane said smoothly, reaching down to help her up. She accepted his hand stiffly, and, trying to recapture her dignity, rose to her feet.

Feeling his eyes on her gown, then observing her tumbled tresses, Arielle knew she must appear a sight. She had not bothered to pin up her hair. Throwing on the gown after awakening, she had taken no pains to disguise the fact she had just gotten out of bed. At least she was dressed, she thought with irritation at having been discovered. She would just have to brazen her way through it.

"My dear wife does so hate to disturb me, but she has a problem with sleepwalking. Now do not fear, my dear, Will understands these things." Thane grinned down at her, taking her hand and pulling her close beside him. "Gets right up in the middle of the night and pulls on the first gown she can find. Usually I am right there and can stop her, but, alas, tonight she was alone. How fortunate you happened down this hall so I could find you before you hurt yourself."

Arielle stood stiffly beside him, his hand holding hers firmly as he told the preposterous story to a young man who stood near the fireplace regarding her as if she were a madwoman. She could have sworn Thane was enjoying her embarrassment and humiliation.

"Now that she is awake . . . You are awake, my dear?" he questioned with mock concern, making her want to slap him.

"Oui," she answered through clenched teeth, flashing him a look of disdain.

"Good," he replied, his mouth twitching with amusement. "I would like to present an old friend, Will Shelby."

"*Enchanté*, m'sieur," Arielle said softly, with as much dignity as possible under the circumstances, to the young man who appeared to be one of the American frontiersmen the Creoles referred to with the unflattering term, as "kintucks."

"My wife, Arielle," her husband continued.

"How'd you do ma'am," Will Shelby mumbled, giving a slight, awkward bow in her direction.

What in the world was Thane doing entertaining one of those rough men? Arielle wondered, nodding her head in recognition. She was discovering her husband had some strange friends.

"Will and I have business interests in common," Thane informed her as if he were able to read her mind.

"It is a strange hour to conduct a meeting pertaining to business," Arielle replied, determined not to let him evade all the questions that were racing through her mind.

"Will just arrived downriver from Tennessee, and being a conscientious chap, had to come right over," Thane continued in a silky voice, but there was a certain wary look in his dark eyes.

"Really, all the way from Tennessee," Arielle commented as she stared at the young man who seemed to be extremely nervous under her scrutiny. "Have you come to join up with General Jackson when he arrives in New Orleans?"

"Don't rightly know, ma'am," Will Shelby gulped, looking furtively in Thane's direction.

"You will do your part if the time comes, I am sure," Jacques said with quiet emphasis, sending Will a private signal with his eyes.

"Yes, sir, I sure intend to," the young man replied, this time with assurance.

Arielle pressed onward. "But it is a certainty that

344

Jackson is coming to defend the city. The story has flown about New Orleans for days."

"I did not know you were so interested in military matters, my dear, or that you listened so intently to gossip." Thane's tone was coolly disapproving. He regarded her with speculation in his onyx eyes. She felt the tenseness in his body, as if he were a wild animal on the prowl, alert to every danger about him.

"Everyone in New Orleans is concerned with the defense against a British attack. I do not think my question under the circumstances is strange. M'sieur Shelby is from Tennessee, as is General Jackson, so I naturally assumed . . ." She allowed her voice to trail off.

"Quite right, my dear, I see you have found us out. Will is indeed here to await the general's arrival so he can join up. He is the son of an old friend, and I insisted he come see me when he arrived. We did not want to worry you with talk of the defense of the city, but since you put it all together I must confess the truth. Is that not correct, Will?"

"Yes, sir. We just didn't want to worry you, ma'am, with war talk," Will agreed with an audible sigh of relief, after meeting the intense look in Thane's eyes.

Arielle regarded the two men with suspicion, for she sensed they were not telling her the truth. But there was little she could do to shake their story. "We citizens of New Orleans thank you, m'sieur," she told Will, inclining her head in a graceful bow.

"Very prettily said, my dear," Thane murmured. "We do not want to keep you from your rest. Will and I have some discussions to continue that I am sure you would find boring. I shall be up later," he said softly, placing his arm on her waist and steering her toward the door.

"It was a pleasure to meet you, m'sieur," Arielle called over her shoulder.

"The pleasure was all mine, ma'am."

"I am anxious to return to your bed, *ma belle blonde,*

345

but I must see to Will first. When I come up I shall bring a cold supper. We can then satisfy all our appetites," Thane murmured, the timbre of his voice low and seductive, reaching out to vibrate deep within her as he closed the door halfway behind him.

Touching her trembling lips, with one slender finger, he traced their outline slowly before brushing her mouth with his own warm lips. His velvet tongue flicked the corners of her coral petals in a promise of the passion yet to come.

Aware of the intense physical pull between them, Arielle tried to still the wild pounding of her heart. How could she desire him with such a hunger when they had made love only a few hours before? She knew only that when they were together it was as if the world did not exist outside the circle of their embrace.

"Go now," he whispered, his voice husky with the passion he was trying to control, "before I take you here." Looking up at him, she saw the fiery hunger in his eyes. The effect of those burning, ebony orbs was total and devastating, reaching into her soul.

With a shuddering sigh, she turned to leave, hearing the door shut behind her. Taking only a few steps in the direction of the foyer, she stopped, for she realized the door had swung back open a crack. Unable to resist, she crept back to stand beside the door. She had to know the real reason for Will Shelby's appearance at this late hour.

After a few moments she wished she had gone straight to her chamber. With a sinking heart, she heard Will ask if Thane had any information about the Alliance Louisiane. Thane admitted he had a list of names of the most important members, the men who were the leaders of the organization.

"My boss will be glad to have that list. It will make everything easier when the invasion comes to know exactly who will help the British," Will stated, as Thane

346

must have handed him the list containing the names. "One of these will be the assassin, I reckon?"

"No, Carlos de Galvez has agreed that the honor should go to the most important member — myself," Thane admitted quietly.

Will gave a low chuckle. "It is you then who will do the deed, now that is right clever."

Arielle stood transfixed as a glazed look of despair spread over her face. A flash of wild grief ripped through her as she realized her husband was a British spy and intended to assassinate General Andrew Jackson when he came to New Orleans. This Will Shelby must be a British spy also, the frontier manner only a disguise. Swallowing the sob that rose in her throat, she stole away from the door and up the stairs to her chamber.

The storm raged on outside the French doors as Arielle pulled the gold gown from her body. Slipping on the lace wrapper lying on the chair where she had left it, she crawled into the huge bed like a wounded animal seeking refuge.

What was she to do? The thoughts ran through her head till her temples throbbed. Thane was a spy, the assassin Claiborne was looking for, Thane was the man she loved, her husband. No matter what else lay between them in the past, she knew, although she wished it was not true, that she loved this strange man with all her heart. He had been right when he said there had been no choice for them since the first day they met. There was a bond so strong between them. Whether it was love or passion, it did not matter. It was there and would not, could not, be denied.

A sensation of intense despair swept over her as tears slowly found their way down her pale cheeks. Turning over, she buried her head in the feather pillow as deep sobs wracked her slender form.

When finally there were no tears left, she lay exhausted, staring out into the dark room watching the shafts of lightning dart across the night sky. As she lay assailed by the bitterness of fate that would allow her to love a man so wrong for her in every way, an idea formed that seemed to show her some way out of this terrible situation.

It was so simple she wondered why she had not thought of it earlier. She would prevent Thane from carrying out the assassination. Living here as his wife she would be aware of his plans and movements. When Jackson arrived, she would be Thane's shadow. She could prevent the deed without telling Claiborne it was her husband who was the planned assassin. British spy he might be, but unless he actually committed a crime, he would not hang.

The memory of her recurring dream sent a chill through her slender form. It had been a premonition, warning her of the danger to Thane. Seraphine had often experienced such dreams that foretold the future. It seemed she, too, had the gift.

Listening to the rain driving against the window, Arielle stared out into the darkened room. What would the future hold for her after the war ended? Would Thane return to England once he was no longer needed as an informant in New Orleans? Their marriage might end with the war. She might only be a diversion to while away the days till he no longer needed to stay in Louisiana. He had accomplished his revenge on her family. When he no longer needed her as the perfect wife to gain access to Creole society, he could vanish again, as he had as her husband Jacques Temeraire. Arielle shuddered inwardly at the thought of the anguish she would feel if she lost him this time forever.

Struggling with her thoughts, she was startled when the door opened and the object of her melancholy musings stood before her. Smiling, he entered the room carrying a tray containing an oil lamp and several dishes covered by silver lids.

"You are still awake. I am so glad." His deep voice was a velvet murmur as he spoke to her in French. He had told her earlier, as they lay entwined on the bed, that French was their language of lovemaking. They would always speak it when they desired each other. It would be their special signal to each other.

Determined he would not see the tumult in her heart, she managed a nod. "Is that food you bring? I am famished," Arielle replied, with no sign in her voice of the anguish she felt.

"I always keep my promises, *ma petite chère*. We shall feast in bed — first on food, then on each other." He gave a low, husky laugh as he observed her blush, having put the lamp on the table next to the bed.

The golden circle of the light shone on her tangled mane of honey-gold hair and ivory-peach skin just glimpsed through the revealing wrapper. How much he wanted her again. He had hated to leave her side earlier, but the meeting with Will had been arranged for eleven. The rest of the night stretched ahead of them. He would not leave her bed again till morning.

After the cold chicken, crusty French bread, ripe cheese, and sweet oranges had been eaten, and several glasses of cool, dry wine had been drunk, Thane cleared the tray from the bed. Lowering the wick of the lamp till only a subtle glow lit the room, he quickly shed his shirt and breeches.

Arielle watched, trembling with desire, as he approached the bed, his lean, muscular body already in a state of arousal. They had talked only of superficial matters over their late supper, such as how he wanted her to take over the running of the house, a dinner party he wanted her to attend with him, and tickets he had for the opera the following week when they would make their official appearance as man and wife before New Orleans society. Throughout the meal, she had been continuously aware of him and the pleasure they would give each other when they had finished.

"I have often dreamed these last days of having you here waiting for me," Thane murmured, slipping into the bed. "But the reality is far more delightful than the dream. Do you want me, *ma belle blonde*, as I want you?"

Violet eyes, hazy with a melancholy sadness, looked up at him as she opened her arms. Her husband came into them, crushing her frail body against him with a fierce possession. Ragged whimpers of sheer need escaped her lips as she surrendered to the overwhelming rush of passion that drew them together.

Arielle knew deep in her being their nights of rapture were doomed never to last. Once his mission was defeated, and the war over, he would leave her. She would save his life, but lose him forever. She would taste the sweet wine of his lovemaking while she was able and count the cost later.

As his mouth came down on hers, warm and demanding, she moved against him in a wild, wanton invitation that sent a mutual trembling along the length of their entwined bodies. This was all that mattered — the feel of his touch, the scent and taste of him. The morrow would come soon enough, the morrow when she must face the truth that there was not much time left for them.

Chapter Twenty-five

Arielle shivered with the damp cold that penetrated her heavy fur-trimmed cloak as Thane took her arm to guide her over the slippery flagstones of the courtyard. The winter mist, which had brooded over the river during the night, had, with the dawn, swirled over the city to hang like a dismal shroud.

The day she had feared had come. Today General Jackson was to arrive in New Orleans. With an ironic twist of fate, she and Thane were to be part of the welcoming committee. The first event of the long tension-filled day was to be a breakfast at the home of Bernard de Marigny, a member of one of the old Creole families and a pillar of the community.

"Watch your step," her husband cautioned, as they left the familiar covered passageway that opened onto the wooden banquette of Esplanade Street. "With this fog you can barely see your hand in front of your face. 'Tis good that Bernard's house is just a few doors away."

"*Oui*, the cold is most fierce," Arielle agreed with a shiver. She clutched his sinewy forearm, trying not to fall as they made their way down the ghostly avenue. Houses, carriages, other people passing by, were all obscured by the gray-white cloud that cloaked New Orleans. They would appear out of the fog like apparitions

351

for a brief moment, only to disappear as quickly. The weather was a bad omen, she thought, wishing she could make the sign of the cross to ward off the danger that was sure to come. It was a bad portent for General Jackson's arrival.

Her nerves were stretched to the breaking point, for today she must never leave her husband's side. Today was the perfect day for an assassination.

Bernard de Marigny's elegant mansion was a haven from the gloom. At this early hour of the morning it was brightly lit with hearthstone fires and shining candelabra. The host, with his lovely wife, Anne Mathilde, by his side, welcomed the Ryders.

After handing their cloaks to the butler, Arielle and Thane followed their hosts into the dining room where a long mahogany table was set with damask cloth and heavy family silver. Arielle felt her nerves tense as she spotted Carlos de Galvez helping himself to the sumptuous buffet laid out for the guests. She had not known he had received an invitation and was surprised to find out it had been issued. It was no secret in New Orleans that Carlos detested the Americans.

"Help yourself, *mes amis*. It could be quite sometime till the general arrives," their host urged, seating his lovely dark-haired wife at the end of the table. "I myself cannot face the day without several cups of good hot *café au lait*."

Arielle gestured for the maid to pour her a cup of the fragrant brew and give her one of the delicious-looking *calas* cakes made with rice. There had not been time upon awakening for even so much as a cup of coffee, for they had overslept, she remembered with a trace of embarrassment.

"I find I have quite an appetite after such a night," Thane murmured in her ear. He, too, helped himself to an ample helping of the breakfast spread out before them on the sideboard.

352

Arielle felt the color stain her cheeks as she sat down at the long table beside her husband. The rapture of the night they had spent seemed like a beautiful dream on this strange, cold, damp morning when they sat down to a breakfast as elaborate as a dinner party. She wished they were still back in their bed, safe and warm in each other's arms. The events of this long day could very well bring an end to such happiness.

"I did not know General Jackson was a good friend of your family, Bernard." The deep, harsh voice of Carlos de Galvez startled Arielle as he seated himself across the table from them beside another Creole couple, the Valmonts.

"My name is not unknown to him, this is true. The general has very recently been the guest of my father-in-law, Jean Ventura Morles, in Pensacola. It was made known to me of the desire of General Jackson to stay with us," Bernard informed his guests. "I confess to surprise at your request, Carlos, to meet the man. We all know of your feeling toward Americans."

"Ah, Bernard, you know how curious I am," Carlos answered smoothly. "If we must deal with these Americanos, 'tis best to know your enemy."

"You consider Americans your enemy, m'sieur?" Arielle could hardly believe it was her voice that was speaking. She had said the first thing that had come into her mind, and she regretted her outburst as those cold, piercing black eyes turned to stare at her.

"I preferred Spanish rule of New Orleans, madame, even French, to these loutish kintucks. If this makes us enemies, so be it."

"Then you must hope for a British victory, m'sieur," Arielle continued, meeting those cold eyes squarely, not flinching from the cruelty she saw reflected there.

"Do *you*, madame, married to an Englishman as you are?"

"An Irishman, if we are being accurate, for I was born

353

on Ireland's fair isle," Thane interjected before Arielle could answer. "I agree Andrew Jackson is an interesting man to meet no matter what your allegiance. When is he expected, Bernard?"

Their host gave a Gallic shrug as he wiped the crumbs from the corners of his fleshy mouth. "Instead of coming from Mobile, he has chosen to travel somewhat circuitously through the wilderness, overland to see the various points where the British might make a landing. Word was sent yesterday that he is expected in the city midmorning."

Arielle sat silent the rest of the long morning as the guests tried to prolong the meal till the general's arrival. The hours began to drag; the men's talk swirled around her like the smoke from the cigars the women had given them permission to smoke.

As the noon hour approached, and still no sign of the honored guest, the butler came to Bernard de Marigny's side and spoke softly into his master's ear. They watched as their host turned first pale, then flushed red as he listened to his servant. Waving the man aside, he rose to his feet.

"It seems there has been some mistake. General Jackson has breakfasted at the residence of John Kilty Smith on Bayou St. John. He is now on his way to the welcoming ceremonies at the Place d'Armes. They will be commencing within the hour . . ." The strained voice of their host dwindled off into silence. He stood lost in thought at what seemed like a calculated snub.

Arielle caught the look that Carlos de Galvez flashed Thane. From the corner of her eye she saw the slight shrug with which he returned that questioning glance. Strangely, she sensed her husband was not surprised, only relieved, by the change in plans.

"May I offer the services of my carriage to take you and your charming wife to the ceremony?" Carlos inquired of Thane as he and Arielle donned their cloaks.

"I noticed your man was not outside."

"We would be delighted," Thane replied, to Arielle's dismay. She didn't relish spending any more time with Carlos de Galvez than was necessary, and now it seemed they would be in his company for the afternoon.

The fog had lifted slightly, but a light, cold rain was falling as they rode down Rue Chartes to Jackson's welcome celebration to the city. Crowds were starting to form as the carriage pulled to a stop near Saint Louis Cathedral. The cannon from Fort St. Charles could be heard thundering a greeting as it summoned the citizens to the ceremony.

As members of the welcoming committee, Thane and Arielle quickly joined the lawyer Edward Livingston, Governor Claiborne, Mayor Nicholas Girod, and Commodore Patterson of the American fleet. It was suddenly clear to Arielle why Carlos had insisted they accompany him, for as their guest, he was allowed to stand with the other dignitaries. The thought of why he wanted to stand close to Jackson sent a chill through her, and she felt panic well up in her throat.

"Are you all right?" Thane leaned down to murmur in her ear, for he had noticed her pale visage and the look of panic in her violet eyes.

"Fine. It is only the crowd. I fear crowds have always made me giddy," Arielle managed to reply. She realized her husband was the last one she could confide in, for he and Carlos de Galvez were partners in the same plot.

Governor Claiborne stood only inches away as Thane guided her up the stairs to the reviewing stand where the general would say a few words to the crowd. The firm, masculine hand of her husband on her waist was a reminder of how careful she must be in the furtive game she played with life and death. She might love this man beside her with all her heart and soul, but she could never trust him.

Taking their places on the platform, Arielle could look

over the vast crowd that thronged the Place d'Armes. The weather might be miserable, but the city had turned out a large crowd to view for themselves this backwoods curiosity who had come to save them from the British. Turning her eyes back to the tall, gaunt man who was mounting the platform behind Edward Livingston, she wondered what they would make of this man whose appearance at the moment hardly inspired confidence.

General Jackson's dress was simple, almost threadbare. A small leather cap protected his iron-gray hair, and a short blue Spanish cloak his body, while his high dragoon boots were dull from lack of polish. Although holding himself very erect, Arielle couldn't help noticing his complexion was shallow and unhealthy and that his body was thin, emaciated, like that of one who had just recovered from a lingering sickness.

Looking away, Arielle noticed the silence of the crowd and wondered if they, too, were disappointed in his appearance. He looked like nothing more than an old kaintuck flat-boatman. Glancing back in his direction, suddenly all her misgivings vanished as she met those bright blue, hawklike eyes and felt the fierce glare of a strong commanding personality. General Andrew Jackson was a fighter with a rock-hewn will. New Orleans was in competent hands.

When it came time for Jackson to speak to the crowd gathered below, Edward Livingston translated the general's words into French. A vibrant and eloquent speaker, the lawyer captured the people's attention, but it was not his fine voice, rather the words that were distinctly Andrew Jackson's that struck a cord with the citizens of New Orleans.

The effect of the message, that he had come with one single purpose to "drive their enemies into the sea or perish in the effort" was electric. Countenances shone with bright and hopeful eyes as they looked up at the

356

heroic stare of the hawk-eyed Andrew Jackson.

Arielle heard her own voice join those of her fellow citizens as they responded with the cry of, "Vive Jackson!" Caught up in the enthusiasm, she turned and was immediately chilled by the sight of Carlos de Galvez standing with arms folded, his visage filled with an unyielding hatred and contempt.

With the short welcoming ceremonies over, the rain began in earnest, allowing no time for the Ryders to be introduced to the general. He quickly left with his aides for the three-story building, at 106 Royal street, which had been reserved for his headquarters.

Carlos's man brought the carriage around, and fighting their way through the crowd, they sought the dry sanctuary with relief. As Arielle sank back against the cushioned seat, she saw the figure of Bernard de Marigny standing in the shadow of the arcade of the Cabildo. His coat collar was turned up, and his hat pulled low. Thane and Carlos saw the look of pain on his face.

"It was a calculated insult on Claiborne's part to divert Jackson from the breakfast at Bernard's. Never before has a de Marigny invitation been ignored, but then, what do these ignorant, savage *Americanos* know about manners," Carlos snorted with contempt. "It will be good to see them brought low."

Thane made no comment, taking a flat, thin silver case from his breast pocket and offering Carlos a cheroot before taking one himself. Before striking a Lucifer stick, he raised a heavy black brow in Arielle's direction, as if asking her permission. At her nod in the affirmative, he first lit Carlos' thin black cheroot and then his own.

"Jackson is a wily old fox; he might have smelled a trap," Thane mused, blowing a gray ring of smoke.

"Or someone alerted him of the possibility," Carlos replied bitterly. As Thane sent a glance in Arielle's direction, Carlos seemed to think twice about what he was about to say and clamped his teeth down on the cheroot.

"It is true Bernard will take this as a calculated snub, for he has long been a supporter of Jackson," Thane continued. "But then, Claiborne seems a master at angering the Creoles."

"What can one say, *amigo*, the man is an *Americano*," Carlos sighed as the carriage pulled up in front of the Ryder townhouse. "I shall see you both tonight at the Livingston ball."

Hercules met Arielle and Thane in the foyer with a tray containing glasses of brandy. They shed their sodden cloaks and quickly sought the warmth of the fire in the rose salon, glasses in hand.

Taking a long drink of the warm, smoky liquid, Arielle stood in front of the fire letting the warmth soothe her trembling nerves, but the memory of Carlos's expression and words wouldn't allow her to relax. The attempt to murder Jackson was imminent, she could sense it in her bones. Would it be tonight at the ball? There would be crowds of people and the opportunity ripe in the confusion.

"There is a note for you, m'sieur," Hercules announced, putting another log on the fire. Taking the envelope from where it lay on a small silver tray on the table, he handed it to Thane, then left the room.

As she placed her glass on the mantel, Arielle saw with a pang that the paper was lavender and the handwriting that of a woman. She watched as Thane's face darkened with an unreadable emotion as he quickly scanned the letter.

"I fear I shall have to go out for a brief time, my dear. You can rest up for the night's festivities whilst I am gone," he told her with a taut smile that didn't reach his eyes.

"You must leave right now?" Arielle questioned. "We have just returned home."

His voice was a husky, seductive caress. "Ah, *ma chère*,

I hate to leave you, but we shall make up for this wretched day tonight in our bed. He cupped her chin with one warm, firm hand, tilting her mouth up where he could brush his lips against hers as he spoke.

Unable to control the fear that struck through her like a knife, Arielle clung to him, wrapping her arms about his broad back. "Pray do not go," she begged, knowing with some deep premonition that if he left her now, he went to certain danger.

"Ma belle blonde, you make it hard," he breathed against the hollow of her slender neck. His warm lips caressed her ivory, pulsing skin with a series of butterfly kisses.

Instinctively, she arched against him, tempting him with the promise of her body, using every lure she knew to keep him with her a few moments longer. She heard with joy the sound of his groan of pleasure as his hands caressed the planes of her back, his mouth seeking hers with a fiery hunger.

Crushing her to him, he smothered her lips with a demanding mastery that burned into her soul. They stood for a moment, melted into one, before he pushed her away almost violently, holding her at arm's length.

"I must go," he muttered, his breath coming in harsh gasps. His black eyes were burning coals devouring the sight of her heart-shaped visage revealing an emotion that was halfway between pleasure and pain.

"No!" she cried out as he turned and left the room.

With tears blinding her vision, she dropped to the soft carpet in front of the fire. Wiping the wet from her cheeks with the back of her hand, she stared into the flames and saw that the letter Thane had thrown into the fire had not burned completely. She could make out a few words as the flames licked closer and closer.

" 'Lafitte needs your help in speaking with Jackson. Pray do not fail me, Maura,' " Arielle whispered, reading the letter aloud just before the fire reduced these words also to ashes. Maura had not known she could be giving a British agent the perfect scapegoat for Jackson's murder in Jean Lafitte.

Rising to her feet, Arielle saw with perfect clarity what she must do. She must go to Maura's brothel and warn Lafitte. Thane had to be stopped. The looks exchanged between her husband and Carlos today had only confirmed her worst fears. They still planned to carry out their assassination of Jackson.

Perhaps Lafitte could help her convince Thane to leave New Orleans once he understood they would not let him carry out his plan and seek safety with the British fleet at the mouth of the Mississippi. There was nothing she would not do to keep the man she loved from the hangman's noose, but there was so little time. She had to arrive at Maura's before Thane left with Lafitte or all would be lost, and she would be responsible for General Jackson's murder.

Chapter Twenty-six

Dressed in André's old breeches, scuffed riding boots, and a jacket he had discarded while still a young boy, Arielle braided her hair in a single plait, stuffing it under a wide-brimmed hat she found in Thane's armoire. Her husband's wardrobe had also yielded a sword cane, a twist of the head revealing a slim rapier. Slipping gray suede gloves over her slim fingers, she stood in front of the pier glass observing her reflection.

In the dying light of the winter afternoon, she could, if one did not look too closely, pass for a rather effete young man. Pulling the hat down lower, she decided her disguise would have to do. Time was flying. She must be off.

Slipping out of her chamber, she sped across the courtyard and out to the street. Pausing for a moment to catch her breath, Arielle was glad to see the fog had thickened once more with the early-winter darkness. It would make it easier for her to succeed in her masquerade in masculine attire.

Walking in the direction of the river, she kept a rapid pace, her head low as if in deep thought. Maura's establishment was many blocks away and the neighborhood was not the best.

The brothel, considered one of the finest in the city,

was quite near the disreputable area near the docks called the Swamp. Arielle could never have walked these streets at night dressed as a woman, for she would have been taken for a street whore playing her trade; thus the need for the masculine disguise.

Passing the French market, the stalls in the arcade, closed for the night, Arielle quickened her pace as she skirted the open doors of grog shops beginning to stir with the rowdy laughter of sailors and flatboat men. She was almost there, for she could see the walled garden of the brothel.

A few more steps and she was before the lacquered black door with its distinctive brass door knocker in the shape of the head of Bacchus, god of wine and frivolity. Taking a deep breath for courage, she lifted the head and gave a brisk rap.

The door opened immediately to reveal an enormous black man dressed in servant's livery of scarlet and gold. Trying to peer under Arielle's wide-brimmed hat, he asked, "What you want?"

"I wish to see Madame O'Connell," Arielle whispered in as husky a voice as she could manage.

The man stood back to allow her to enter the foyer. As soon as she was inside, he slammed and locked the door behind her. The sound made her flinch, causing the sword cane to bang against the wall.

"Clumsy one, ain't you," the black man sniffed, trying once more to see under the hat in the dim light from an oil lamp burning on an ornate hall table. "First time here?" He gave a lewd chuckle.

"Aye," Arielle muttered, hoping the man would take her for one of the Americans who had come with Jackson, for some had appeared mere rough frontier boys. Her clothes were old and too casual for a Creole residing in New Orleans.

"Maura's real good with boys," the black man laughed, starting down the hall toward a closed door. Flinging it open, he the man gestured for her to go inside.

Hesitating a moment, for she had not thought what she would say to Maura, she squared her shoulders and forced herself to walk inside. The room was a small salon decorated in garish reds, gold, and pink. The furniture was ornate with carved legs and much gilt trim. Red velvet curtains at the long French doors shut out any view, and the walls were papered in a pink watered silk.

"She be with you in a while. You best sit," the servant stated before shutting the door behind him, leaving Arielle alone.

It is like being in a huge candy box, she thought as she stared in disbelief at the decor. Gold cherubs on the wall held up paintings of nude, fleshy women in provocative poses. So this was a brothel, she thought, both repelled and intensely curious.

Her musings were brought to an abrupt close as the door slowly opened and Maura, dressed as Arielle had never seen her, came into the salon. A gown of black lace over flesh-colored silk floated about her figure from an extremely low-cut neckline that showed her heavy breasts, including the tops of her rouged nipples. Her hair fell in ringlets down her back to her bottom, and her face was heavily made up.

"How good of you to come. I am sure we will enjoy ourselves. Shall we sit on the settee and get to know one another," Maura suggested, smiling sweetly as Arielle turned around, taking the hat from her head. Her smile turned to an expression of horror as Arielle's heavy plait fell down her back and the light from an oil lamp shone on her face.

"I had to come, Maura. There was no other way. I know my husband is here."

"It is not what you think," Maura gasped. "Lafitte had to speak with Thane. There is much you do not understand."

"I understand what is between you and my husband

363

all too well," Arielle said with a bitter sigh. "But you are right there is something about Thane even you and Lafitte do not know. *Tiens!* I do not have time to discuss it with you. Please take me to Lafitte, it is a matter of life and death."

"That, I am afraid, I cannot do."

"Maura, what can I say to convince you how serious this is?"

"Even if I believe you, I could not help you. They are not here."

"Where have they gone?" Arielle pleaded.

"That I will not say," Maura stated firmly, having recovered from the shock of Arielle's appearance at her brothel dressed as a man. "I suggest you leave and we both forget this unfortunate episode."

"Maura, what I am going to tell you must go no further than this room. If you care anything for Thane, you must swear your secrecy."

"Aye, you have my promise on my sainted mother's grave."

"I have reason to believe that Thane is a British agent and, as such, is planning on assassinating General Jackson. If Jean is hoping Thane will arrange a meeting with the general, he must be made to understand why that would be impossible. Thane would be able to use such a meeting as the perfect opportunity to make Lafitte a scapegoat. Although, and I hate to say this about my own husband, he could kill the general and denounce Jean as the assassin."

Maura stared at Arielle in disbelief, awkwardly clearing her throat before asking, "Who else knows of this idea of yours?"

"No one. I hope to stop the murder before it takes place and convince Thane to leave New Orleans. He could seek refuge with the British fleet at the mouth of the Mississippi. I . . . I cannot let him hang, nor can I allow him to do this terrible deed. I thought Lafitte could help me reason with Thane. Once he knew we were aware of who he was working for, and what he had planned to do, he would have to give up," Arielle explained, a look of tired sadness passing over her features.

"You love him that much?" Maura questioned softly, understanding on her weary features.

"*Oui*, yes, God help me but I do."

"Dearie, sit down. We could both use a drink," Maura replied, giving a slight smile at her visitor. She walked to an ornate cabinet that, once opened, displayed several bottles of fine brandy and whiskey as well as crystal glasses. "We best have a talk, as you said there are some things about Thane that are secret. First, he is not a British agent, but an American one, working for old Andy Jackson. Jean knows it now, but even he was kept in the dark till Claiborne, the fool, ran him off Grand Terre. When he came to Belle Rivière, Thane told him the truth. He convinced Jean that when Jackson came to New Orleans he would arrange a meeting."

"But I heard Thane talking to Will Shelby about killing Jackson. He admitted he was a British agent," Arielle argued, taking the glass of brandy from Maura. Her hostess nodded as she turned and poured herself a liberal amount of whiskey.

"That was all part of the plan," Maura explained after a long sip of the amber whiskey. "Thane had his orders from President Madison to come to New Orleans and seek out any group that was against the American cause. The city was known to be a hotbed of dissenters who were still angry that Napoleon had sold the territory to the United States. They wanted either French or Spanish rule. The British knew this also, and the President was afraid such people would be ripe to listen to the English promises of New Orlean's return to the Spanish if they won the war. Thane was to pose as a British agent making contact with such a group. It was all to be a secret; not even Claiborne knew the truth. When Thane did manage to join the Alliance Louisiane, he found out they were planning on assassinating Jackson to prove their loyalty to the British. Thane offered to be the assassin when Carlos, whose plan it was, first told him about it. He knew that was the best way to prevent such a tragedy from happening."

"That is why he came to New Orleans?" Arielle asked, stunned. "I thought it was to seek his revenge on my family for some old imagined wrong."

"That I am afraid occurred once he returned and old memories surfaced. You see, he never forgave your father for his parents' death when *his* father worked for your father clearing that swampy land. They came down with yellow fever. My folks, too, and then your pa put me in his brothel," Maura said with great bitterness, staring across the room as if she were reliving the sad memories.

"My father put you in this brothel," Arielle repeated, her face gone white as she tried to comprehend what Maura had just told her.

"Aye, your father had many sources of income that I am sure he did not want his daughter to know about. Now André knew . . . He was a regular customer, he could be real mean, too, when he wanted. He was here one night when Thane first came back to New Orleans. Perhaps, I should not tell tales about a brother to his sister, but I think you are stronger than these milksop Creole ladies. André could be real disagreeable to women when he had been drinking. I think he got that from your father. That night, he had been drinking a lot, and when I refused him, he hit me not once, but several times, just as Thane came through that door. I thought Thane would kill him that night, especially when he found out who he was, but Thane bided his time making his plans."

"André hit you," Arielle whispered, stunned by Maura's revelations. Suddenly her whole world seemed to be turning upside down.

"Aye, and it unleashed something wild in Thane, as if

366

all the old memories came flooding back. I will not hide the facts from you. He cold-bloodedly planned to ruin your father, but then your father was a nasty customer, Madame Ryder, as low down as they come. You must have taken after your ma . . . heard she was a real nice lady. I saw her once when I was just a little thing. She was arguing with your pa over how terrible the Irish workers' quarters were, but he just ordered her away. She didn't have much happiness with that old devil, I reckon. Heard she died not too long after that in child-birth. He got even worse when she was gone, treating the Irish meaner than his slaves. Had more money in-vested in the slaves, that was why he hired the Irish fresh off the boat to build his levee. They died like flies, not being use to the climate and having to live in those shacks in the swamps. They got worn down by working on the slim rations they were allotted. Their food was worse than that given the slaves, and Lord knows they were fed none too good. Aye, your pa was a nasty cus-tomer." Maura sighed, taking another long drink of whiskey.

Arielle was in shock, unable to move, tormented by what Maura had revealed. She had known her father was a cold, hard man who had never had much time for her, but to hear of his brutality was overwhelming. No wonder Thane had hated him so. Suddenly she felt a ray of joy pierce the darkness that had filled her with Maura's story. Thane was not a British agent, but an American one. Could there be a life for them together after all, or was their marriage only another twist in his game of revenge against the Duplantier family?

"I do not understand. Thane was never a privateer?" Arielle asked, in confusion, trying to sort out all that Maura had revealed.

"Nay, he was a privateer all right. After he returned to England, upon his parent's death, he lived with his grandfather who made him his heir. Your husband is a real lord of the realm. But sadly, upon his grandfather's death, he discovered the woman the old man had married after his mother had left had been, along with her brothers, swindling the old lord for years. There was nothing left but the estate, and it had to be sold to meet the old man's debts. They tried to even take his title from him, dragging his name through the mud and the courts, saying because he was a bastard he couldn't inherit the title or the estate. They called his mother all sorts of names when they found his father had been married to some poor women in Ireland and that his parents had never married. The whole thing made Thane hate the British, so after his grandfather's death, he took what little money he had and went to Jamaica. He fell in with a rough lot, but finally had his own ship. A real terror of the Spanish Main he was, that was where he met Lafitte. He also had acquired a plantation by that time in Virginia, decided he wanted to be an American after all."

"You must have been overjoyed when he returned to New Orleans," Arielle said softly, realizing with a stab of jealousy how close their relationship must be for Maura to know the truth about him.

"Aye, that I was, for I had not seen him since the day he fought your father when they came to get me after my ma and pa died. He was only a young boy, but he fought your father like a tiger. That is how he got that scar above his eyebrow. Your father hit him with the end of his whip, cutting a real gash." Maura shook her head in disgust at the memory, then finished the last of the whiskey.

"He must trust you to tell you the truth about his . . . activities," Arielle prodded, determined to know just how close they really were no matter how much it might hurt.

"Aye, but then you see I was to be his contact. Whores make good spies and, being Irish I never did like the English. We hear a lot. Men tell us things they would never tell their wives," Maura chuckled. "I will never forget his

368

face when he found out Madame Maura was his own little Maureen. He is a good man, your husband, one of the best."

"Yes, I see," Arielle said stiffly. She realized just how close they were, for Maura, his childhood love, was now obviously his mistress.

"No, you do not see at all," Maura said with a sad smile, hearing Arielle's tone. "I am not your husband's mistress. Oh, I would like to be, for he is quite a man. To him I will always be little Maureen. Wanted to set me up in some respectable business after the war, but, no, like I told him, a whore is what I am. I guess I am too old to change. Take care of him, for if you do not, I know a lot of other ladies who would give their eye teeth for the chance."

"Thank you, Maura, you did not have to tell me all that."

"He loves you, you know. He doesn't want to, but he does. Treat him right, or you will hear from me." Maura gave Arielle a brief grin before staggering to her feet and going to the cabinet for more whiskey. "You best be off before your husband returns home and finds you gone. And not to mention what we discussed. New Orleans is still dangerous for Thane, and will be till this wretched war is over. At least old Andy Jackson is here, that is something in our favor."

As Arielle rose to leave, the door opened slowly. As Maura turned to bid her good-bye, they both stared in shock at the sight of Yolanda Torres holding a pistol aimed in their direction. Shutting the door behind her with her foot, she motioned for them to move back.

"What is the meaning of this, Yolanda? Have you been drinking again? I thought you were with a customer," Maura stated wearily.

"He is gone, the stinking *Americano*." Yolanda spat out the words with contempt. "I come to see you after and hear much interesting talk. Now Yolanda thinks, and thinks, how she can use such information, and then she decides. She remembers Señor de Galvez has dropped by and is upstairs with Monique. So a little voice within says tell him. It will pay back the man who hurt you by taking up with this yellow-haired one." Yolanda gave a mad laugh as she gestured in Arielle's direction.

"*Mon Dieu!* How could you?" Arielle exclaimed as Maura slowly put down the bottle of whiskey. "Carlos will kill Thane to shut him up if he thinks he is a American agent."

"You are so right," Yolanda agreed, giving an evil smile. Señor de Galvez was very angry, and left immediately when I told him they had gone to this Jackson's headquarters. Soon your husband will be a dead man, Madame Ryder, and I will make sure you stay right here till it is done."

Arielle glanced wildly in Maura's direction, looking for some way out of this situation. She had to warn Thane that Carlos knew his disguise as a British agent was false, but they were trapped here in this room with a madwoman. The striking of the hour by a clock on the mantel seemed to echo the pounding of her heart as her brain worked furiously seeking some solution. Every minute that sped by brought Thane closer to death. She had to do something; she could not lose him now. Fate could not be that cruel, or could it?

Chapter Twenty-seven

"Yolanda, put down that gun," Maura admonished, in a strong, firm voice, seeming to have recovered her wits. "Lafitte could be killed as well. You would not want that."

A frown creased the woman's visage as she turned in Maura's direction, her firm grip on the gun wavering slightly. "Señor de Galvez has no quarrel with Jean," she said hesitantly, as she thought over Maura's statement.

Arielle was standing to Yolanda's left, and when she turned toward Maura, Arielle acted on instinct. Grasping the head of the sword cane she had placed on the table beside her, she lunged forward to strike Yolanda's hand, knocking the gun to the floor as the woman screamed out in pain.

Maura quickly reached down and grabbed the weapon. "Go now!" she cried to Arielle. "I will take care of Yolanda. There is no time to lose!"

Arielle ran for the door, cane still in hand, as Maura aimed the gun at the furious Yolanda. Racing down the hall, she tried to yank open the front door, but it held tight. The memory of the servant locking it behind her tore through her mind in a flash of frustration. Glancing about wildly, she gave a cry of relief as

371

she realized only a bolt held the door locked, not a key. Giving a mighty pull, she shot back the bolt and was out on the street.

The light from a lantern beside the door fell across a horse tied to the hitching post. It probably belonged to one of Maura's customers, Arielle thought as she untied the reins and quickly mounted the man's saddle. Thank the *bon Dieu*, the good God, she knew how to ride astride. Urging the animal on with the toe of her boot, they were off with little thought that the owner could accuse her of horse stealing. They hung horse thieves.

She rode like all the furies of hell were chasing her as she headed toward Jackson's headquarters in the three-story building at 106 Royal Street. It was awkward for her riding the strange animal with the sword cane still clutched in one hand, but she was afraid to discard the weapon, for she feared she might have need of it.

All was quiet when she pulled the horse to a stop in front of General Jackson's quarters, too quiet, she thought with alarm as she dismounted. Running to the massive front door, she beat upon it with all the might of her small fists. It seemed forever before the door finally opened.

"Yes, what is it?" the cool, stern voice of a man in an American uniform inquired. He stared down at Arielle dressed in her boy's breeches as if she were some strange apparition that had materialized out of the fog.

"I must see General Jackson. It is a matter of life and death," Arielle gasped.

"He is not here."

"Where has he gone? Please, it is most important."

"Where most of New Orleans is on this hellish night, at the Livingston ball."

Without another word, Arielle whirled and quickly untied the reins. She was back astride the horse as the officer watched in disbelief. Urging the animal on, she

372

rode toward the mansion of Edward Livingston.

The house was ablaze with light, a welcome sight in the murky, damp, cold night. There were several late arrivals who looked aghast as Arielle jumped from the stallion, handing the reins to a startled groom who was seeing to the guests' horses.

Brushing past the butler who tried to stop her, she walked through the crowd staring in shock at her attire. From the corner of her eye, she saw her Tante Lala hurry toward her.

"Ma chère, whatever has possessed you to appear in such . . . such a costume?" Lala moaned, clutching her fleshy hands to her round, visage.

"I have no time to explain. Have you seen my husband?" Arielle asked in impatient tones.

"Why, yes, now that you mention it, he, too, was acting most odd," Lala replied, her small features puzzled. "He came through here, not even in evening dress, demanding to speak to General Jackson. Governor Claiborne was most upset but finally agreed to take him to the study where the general was conferring with leaders of several of the local militia companies. It was quite embarrassing the fuss your husband was making, *ma petite."*

"He is in the study, then?"

"Well, I really couldn't say. You see, Carlos de Galvez arrived a few minutes later, and he was most concerned about Thane. The man was quite rude, demanding I tell him where your husband had gotten to," Lala Boudreaux huffed, fanning herself rapidly with her black lace fan. "I declare I don't know what this city is coming to when a fine upstanding Creole gentleman acts in that manner. It's the influence of those Americans . . ." Her voice trailed off as Arielle left her before she finished. Really, she thought, that young woman was wild, just like all the Duplantiers.

The object of her dismay had quickly found a French

door that led out into the fog-shrouded courtyard. Shutting the door behind her, the sound of the ball was muffled as Arielle stood on the slippery flagstones peering into the darkness. Where would the study be located? She had been to the Livingston home before, but always for parties. There had never been a reason to enter the study, for that had been the master's retreat.

Arielle could barely see her hand in front of her face, so thick was the fog. Keeping close to the side of the house, she slowly made her way past each set of French doors that led into the various rooms of the mansion. The study must open out onto the courtyard, for the house was built like the others in the city. She prayed she was not too late, and that Carlos de Galvez had not managed to find Thane alone.

It was as she walked cautiously around an enormous potted sweet olive that she saw him: the outline of a man, just visible in the light from the long French doors, standing outside looking in. Her breath catching in her throat, she watched as he lifted a long pistol from beneath his cloak and pointed it at the glass of the door.

"Non!" she cried, her voice muffled in the fog, but he heard her.

"Who's there?" the harsh whisper of Carlos de Galvez inquired. He turned, pointing the gun in her direction.

Arielle stood transfixed, staring down the barrel of his gun. Every instinct told her to run, but she could not move a muscle. He was going to shoot her. Her body went numb with terror as the shadowy figure came closer.

"Don't move, boy, or I promise I will shoot."

A bubble of hysterical laughter grew in her throat as she realized he took her for a boy in the dim light from the house. His words somehow broke the spell, for as he came closer, she inched slowly toward the French doors.

"I told you to stop," Carlos rasped, grabbing her arm with his free hand, pulling her against his chest.

"Let me go," Arielle screamed, having found her voice at last. She struggled against the arm held under her chin that pinned her to him.

"Shut up you, little bitch!" he hissed, placing the cold metal of the gun to her temple as he recognized a feminine voice.

Breathing in quick shallow gasps, she bit her lower lip to stifle the cry that begged to be let out of her trembling lips. If she moved, or spoke, she feared he would pull the trigger.

His voice was a harsh whisper in her ear. "Come with me. The bottom of the river is the place for a curious young woman like you, Madame Ryder." He half dragged her back from the door into the depths of the courtyard. He had recognized her in the dim light.

She had to escape him here on the patio, for once they left the house she was lost. Pulling her on, into the fog-shrouded garden, she felt her boot catch on an uneven flagstone. Letting herself go limp, as if in a faint, the weight of her body caught Carlos off balance long enough for her to sink to the wet stones.

"Puta!" he swore, reaching down to pull her back to her feet by the braid that hung down her back.

As she cried out in pain, she heard Thane's voice, as well as the clatter of the pistol hitting the ground. Carlos's grip loosened till she fell back against the flagstones.

"Let her go, *amigo,* or this blade goes through your back and into your heart," Thane ordered, appearing out of the fog.

For long seconds there was only silence — then she heard it, the swish of a rapier, and the return clash, as Carlos whirled around to pull his sword from the scabbard on his hip. Looking up from where she lay, she

375

saw the two shadows engaged in their deadly dance.

Rising to her feet, she picked up her own sword cane that she had dropped when she had fallen to the ground. She stood mesmerized as she watched the two duelists thrust and counterthrust. They moved back and forth in graceful movements as stylized as some morbid ballet. As they lunged near the house, the light from the French doors threw a ghostly pallor across the intent features of the two men as they moved in and out of the fog. It was an unreal scene, as if they represented all those duelists who had gone before them fighting to the death in the infamous Code Duello.

It was as Carlos lunged forward, and Thane parried in quinte and drove into a riposte, that her husband's foot slipped on the wet stones. Arielle heard the clang of his rapier fall to the ground with him as a death knell.

"Non!" she cried out, rushing forward and causing Carlos to turn in startled amazement. The split second of lost concentration was all the advantage Thane needed. Springing to his feet with the lithe grace of a panther, he caught Arielle's thin yet deadly rapier as she flung it to him from her cane.

Carlos whirled, his rhythm gone, and lunged with clumsy fury toward his opponent. Thane once more parried again, and again, until, with a swift riposte, he circled Carlos's blade and plunged through his guard, piercing his heart.

"Traitor!" he hissed as he fell to the ground breathing his last. Then there was nothing but the silence of the fog swirling about them.

Arielle stood for a moment, transfixed by the horror of it all as Carlos's blood seeped out onto the wet of the flagstones. Then, as Thane swept her into his arms, she sobbed in relief against his chest. It could have been him dead at her feet, and she clutched him to her as if to never let him go.

"Hush, *chérie*, it is over. Nothing will ever hurt you again, I swear it. What a team we make, you and I, *ma belle blonde*," he laughed huskily, tilting her chin up so he could kiss her damp cheeks and then her waiting lips.

"Where did you come from, and how did you know?" she gasped, after a most thorough kiss.

"I was waiting for the general. He was in the foyer talking to one of his scouts returned from the gulf, when I heard a noise outside the door. Not wanting to walk into a trap, I quietly left the room and circled through the house till I could come out on the other side of the patio. What should I see, but my wife dressed in her breeches struggling with Carlos de Galvez. What were you doing, *ma chère?*"

"That is rather a long story," Arielle sighed. "You see, I thought you were a British agent sent to kill General Jackson, so I went to Maura's to try to stop you. She told me the truth, but while we were talking, Yolanda came in and told us she had heard every word. She had informed Carlos you were an American agent. He . . . he was with one of the girls. I came after him, for he had come to kill you to shut you up."

He had no time for a reply, only an amused shake of his handsome head as the French doors to the courtyard were suddenly flung open and an a distinctive American voice boomed, "Ryder, are you out there?"

"Yes sir," Thane answered, walking toward Andrew Jackson his arm around his wife. "There was a bit of trouble, but it is taken care of."

"I can always depend upon you, Ryder. Gads, let us get out of this damp air."

"May I present my wife, Arielle, sir," Thane said formally as they came into the light streaming out from the ballroom.

"*Enchanté*, General," Arielle answered softly, giving a slight bow of her head. Looking up, she stared into the most piercing blue eyes she had ever seen. They swept

377

down across her man's shirt and breeches, then back up to her pale visage.

"How do you do, Mistress Ryder. I will have to introduce you to my Rachel when she arrives in New Orleans. She will certainly like you, for she prefers the unconventional in dress herself." There was the merest trace of a smile on those frosty, weary features, gone before Arielle was sure she had seen it.

The next few hours were a blur in her mind, and it was with relief that she sank gratefully down before a roaring fire in her own bedchamber to think of everything that had happened. It seemed Lafitte had returned to Maura's when he and Thane discovered Jackson had already left for the Livingston ball. He had arrived back at the brothel, shortly after she had departed, to help subdue Yolanda.

Thane had stayed to talk with Edward Livingston and Jackson after the ball, arranging a meeting at Maspero's café with Lafitte and the general, having sent Arielle home with Hercules. He would return as soon as possible, he had promised, giving her a fierce, passionate look that had told her of what he would do when they were alone.

Drowsy now from a long bath and supper on a tray, she lay in a sheer, lacy nightrail awaiting the man she could now love without reservation. Even the need for revenge was gone as she thought with a deep sorrow of what Maura had related. She would always love André, for he had been her twin and had treated her with love, but she was reconciled to what he had been with others. Their father's cruelty had surfaced in his son, and she was glad she had never been a witness to it. What her father had been, she preferred not to think. He was gone, and she would mourn him no more. There was only the future and Thane to think about, and that was a happy thought.

He awakened her with a light kiss on her forehead

378

where honey-gold tendrils curled in adorable profusion. As her lashes fluttered open to reveal the smoke-violet eyes he loved, he was reminded of that first time she had awakened in the cottage in the swamp so long ago. From that first meeting of the eyes he had been lost, for she was what he had sought all his life, and he had not even been aware of it. She completed him, softened his anger, and brought light into the darkness of his moods. *If this be love, then I, too, can love,* he thought with sudden clarity. To love was not to show weakness, but was the ultimate strength. Without love one could not be whole, he now knew, and smiled down at his center, his salvation.

"I love you, *ma belle blonde,*" he whispered, his dark eyes gleaming with the intensity of his emotion, "and I shall love you for all eternity."

Arielle smiled up at him, meeting his gaze and allowing it to flow into her, touching every fiber of her being. His beloved eyes showed the entire man, for they were luminous with the gentleness that he had hidden deep within him for so long. There was nothing so strong as real gentleness in a man.

Holding out her arms to him, she sighed, "And I will love you, my Jacques, my Thane, my husband, throughout time and beyond."

Epilogue

Belle Rivière
June 1815

The golden sun of June shone down on the spreading live oaks, making patterns through the gnarled branches onto the long verdant grass. Bees droned in the honeysuckle entwined on the solid columns of Belle Rivière, and all seemed peaceful and right with the world.

Thane stood on the second-story gallery staring out to the gazebo on the riverbank. It shimmered in the sunlight that reflected off the river, and his thoughts drifted back to that night the autumn before when he had stood revealed to his beloved. From that splendid night of love, and reunion, had come the child, the child he now awaited with frantic anticipation.

His fists clenched in frustration and fear as a cry rent the hot, still air from the direction of the master bedchamber. Bébé lifted her shaggy head from where she lay outside the chamber door and growled.

"Hush, girl, she will be all right," Thane reassured the animal, but there was no one to reassure *him*.

Clenching his jaw, he turned, determined to go back into the room Seraphine had just insisted he leave. Arielle, his beloved, his reason for living, was struggling in pain and anguish to bring the life they had created from their love into the world. Each moan was a knife-sharp pain through his heart.

Their life had been so good since old Andy Jackson, with Lafitte and the help of his men, had led them victorious against the British in what was now called the battle of New Orleans. The memory of Arielle, dressed in her man's breeches, coming to his side in his duel with Carlos de Galvez had warmed him through that long, cold battle at Chalmette. Upon his return from battle, flushed with his man's sense of victory and conquest, she had told him that she carried his child. He knew in that moment that there was nothing that would ever separate them again.

Suddenly he knew his instinct was right, he was not going to pace outside while his wife labored alone. Arielle needed him. He would not allow her to face this ordeal without him.

"No. Save your breath, Seraphine, I am here to stay," Thane announced, as he flung open the door to the bedchamber. "That husband of yours, Lucien, will feel the same when your time comes due."

"I certainly hope not," Seraphine sniffed as she turned back to Arielle, now in the last stages of her labor. She was embarrassed M'sieur Ryder even would mention such things. Then she gave a small smile. To think at her age she and her new husband were expecting a baby! Life was full of miracles.

Arielle tried to smile at her husband as he took hold of her hands, but the pain was too great. She tried to push with it as Seraphine had instructed, but it had been so long, and she was so very tired.

"Ma belle blonde, look at me, take my strength and use it," Thane commanded, holding her hands tightly in his as she pushed with all her waning strength. "Good, good. Just once more, we are almost there," he crooned, willing his stamina and energy into her.

Then Arielle felt it, his life force, like an infusion of power, flowing into her from him. She gathered his strength making it her own, and with a force she thought long since exhausted, gave birth to their child. The sound of its healthy cry brought tears of joy to her eyes, and as she looked up at Thane, she saw the strange sight of tears of happiness on that stern visage.

"We have a beautiful daughter," he breathed with a sense of awe as Seraphine placed her in his sinewy arms. He held her like a piece of priceless porcelain, then placed a tender, reverent kiss on the soft reddish hair that covered her little head like feathers. Turning, he bent down and placed her in the curve of Arielle's arm. "I give you your beautiful daughter, my dearest love, and I thank you from the bottom of my heart."

"We shall call her Jacqueline . . . little Jacques," Arielle told him, her eyes shining like stars. She stared up at him with all the love and rapture he had given her reflected in her radiant smile.

The sound of his rich, delighted laughter filled the room as he lifted her hand to his lips and said with a husky catch in his deep voice, *"Ma belle blonde,* how I love you."

Author's Note

The Alliance Louisiane exists only in the author's imagination, but there are many historical references to the fact that some of the old Creole families would have preferred a British victory, such was their dislike of being sold by the French to the United States. There were also many valiant Creole men who fought courageously with General Jackson's army, believing it was their duty.

Jean Lafitte is a legend in New Orleans, and the stories about him vary from book to book. There are certain facts about the famous privateer that are recorded history. He did help General Andrew Jackson at the Battle of New Orleans and received a pardon from the Americans for his efforts. The legends revolve around the question of who arranged the meeting between the crusty old general and Lafitte. Perhaps it was a handsome American agent like Thane Ryder. Who knows? The author would like to think such is a possibility. One only has to walk the streets of the old French Quarter to sense in the shadows the shades of the brave, dashing men of history who contributed to the city's fabled romantic past.